Millennial Hospitality III

The Road Home

By

Charles James Hall

This book is based on my true personal experiences. However, names, characters, places, and incidents, are used fictitiously. Any resemblance to actual events, locales, or persons, living or dead, is entirely coincidental.

ISBN: 1-4107-3397-1 (E-book)
ISBN: 1-4107-3395-5 (Paperback)
ISBN: 1-4107-3396-3 (Dustjacket)

Library of Congress Control Number: 2003091885

This book is printed on acid free paper.

Printed in the United States of America
Bloomington, IN

1stBooks – rev. 04/04/03

This book is dedicated to the greater honor and glory of
God
Who created us all, aliens included.

Acknowledgements

Millennial Hospitality III is in print only because of my wife's support and encouragement. She is also responsible for the books title and the design for the cover. I am also grateful to the young men whom it was my privilege to serve with during the Vietnam War years.

Other Books by Charles James Hall

Millennial Hospitality

Millennial Hospitality II The World We Knew.

Table of Contents

Forward

I have enjoyed telling family, friends, and the wonderful people whom I have met at book signings the story of how the Millennial Hospitality series came into being. I thought other readers might like to hear it as well.

Over the last 18 years, from time to time when I entered the room where my husband sat at the computer, I noticed that he would quickly shut the screen that he was working on. When I asked him what he was doing, sometimes he would answer, "Nothing" or "Just relaxing".

Other times, he would say that he was working on a book. In May of 2002, he became unemployed. After he was a month into unemployment, this scenario repeated itself. He said he was working on his book. I said, "Well, you know, if you die tomorrow, there is no way I am going to go hunting through the many files you have, to look for any book. I suggest that you print some of that out right now; I would like to see it."

Charles said, "Which book did you want to see?"

"What do you mean, which book? How many books do you have in there," I asked?

He said, "Oh, a couple, three."

Naturally, when I saw some of the chapters, I was determined that we should publish it. I felt it was excellent material and it should be picked up by one of the major houses, but I knew that would take time and since no income was coming into our house, we decided to self publish.

The manuscript needed editing badly, partially because he had started the books on an old Tandy 2000 and there were technical difficulties in retrieving it. The major problem I had with the book was the macho language he thought he needed to use. My daughter and I were up to the task of editing the material and Charles was much in agreement when we told him that the story was so good, the swear words added nothing and furthermore, deleting them would make the book appropriate for mid-schoolers.

Well, Charles worked hard implementing all of our corrections, but then, inadvertently used older unedited files to compile the CD to send to the publisher. I will leave out some of the drama that followed. It slowed thingsdown considerably, and because we were so anxious to start marketing our books, I ordered 500 copies of *Millennial Hospitality* before I saw one bound copy. We decided to re edit immediately and Charles sat for days and hand edited some of the worst mistakes from the 500 copies we already had in our house. If you have one of those copies, they have already become collector's items.

That was then and this is today, the day it is that you are beginning to read *Millennial Hospitality III, The Road Home*. We both hope that you will enjoy reading it and if you have not already read *Millennial Hospitality* and *Millennial Hospitality II The World We Knew*, we know that you will want to read them as well.

14 February 2003
Valentine's Day
Marie Therese Hall

Prologue

As is written in the book
    of the words of Isaiah the prophet:

"A voice of one calling in the desert,
    'Prepare the way for the Lord…'…"

Luke 3:4

This is the third book in the Millennial Hospitality series. If you just finished reading Millennial Hospitality and MH II, The World We Knew, you can just skip this part. In book one, we meet Charles Baker, a twenty-year old Airman from the Midwest who has been stationed as a weather observer out in the desert southwest. Now this was in the mid-sixties before satellite imagery. The job of weather observer was pretty hands on. Charles has not been briefed on what he might find out in the desert. What he discovers turns out to be aliens. Much of the book is devoted not just to his experiences with the aliens, but the denial involved in coping with things he didn't really believe could be happening.

The second book, Millennial Hospitality II, The World We Knew, is a continuation of Charlie Baker's adventures with the aliens. It starts out dramatically with the death of Charlie's friend Bridges, who was not lucky enough to use denial or some other coping mechanism in order to deal with his introduction to the aliens. Eventually, Charles develops a working relationship with the few aliens who can speak English. They ask him to call them by their various assumed names, The Teacher, Range Four Harry, The Tour Guide, and the School Bus Driver. One young female alien even assumes the name of Charlie's girlfriend, Pamela.

Winter Roads

Lord, let me know my end,
    the number of my days,
        that I may learn how frail I am.

       ...

Mere phantoms, we go our way;
    Mere vapor, our restless pursuits;

We heap up stores
    without knowing for whom.
                Psalm 39:5,7

    Winter had come to the gunnery ranges. I had just celebrated my twenty-second birthday. Day by day the desolate desert valleys surrounding Mojave Wells became colder as the Christmas holidays drew nearer. The snow draping the mountains became thicker and exceedingly beautiful as the season progressed. Through my theodolite, the views of the distant mountains and peaks were more breathtaking with each passing day. On some days, the view of the sparkling sunlit snowfields in the distance with their soaring black-green pine trees swaying in the mountain winds, held me paralyzed at my theodolite. I frequently wished that I were a better painter so I could capture it all with a paintbrush. Unfortunately my "paint by number" sets with their mountain scenes that had so captivated me during the previous summer now seemed pale in comparison.

To the joy of the local inhabitants, the ski area near the top of the mountains in the distance to the southeast opened early. The lodge, parking lot and nearby bunny slope weren't large, but they could be easily located. Against the backdrop of the natural pine forest and the overlapping snowdrifts, they could be seen almost immediately in any kind of weather, using just the naked eye. The mountain was part of a national forest. Except for the privately owned ski area with its beautifully peaked lodge, restaurant, a handful of associated cabins, garages, warehouses, and ski lifts, the mountain was used only for hiking, picnicking, and camping. The parking lot and bunny slope formed almost the only open level areas.

With the onset of cold weather, most activity on the gunnery ranges went into hibernation, including the US. Air Force training flights. Most of the few men who were stationed at Mojave Wells returned south to the Desert Center Air base for the duration of the winter. On weekends, it was an easy matter to take the bus from the base into nearby Palm Meadows and then catch the bus up to Las Vegas. The casinos in Las Vegas, of course, considered winter to be just another time to dress up and party.

As the duty weather observer for the gunnery ranges, I continued my daily ritual of taking the wind measurements five times a day. Every Monday through Friday, I would wake up at 3:00 a.m. hoping I was alone in my barracks, and get dressed. Then I would make the long cold drive out into the nighttime desert to Range Three for the 4:30 a.m. run. There, after starting the diesel generator so my weather shack would have both heat and electricity, I would fill a balloon with the required amount of helium, attach a light,

2

take it outdoors to my theodolite stand and release the balloon into the wind. I would track the balloon for several minutes, usually twelve, as it rose into the nighttime sky. Finally, I would return to my weather shack, perform the wind computations and phone my home weather station at the faraway Desert Center airbase. Usually I would repeat the ritual four more times during the day, taking breaks to drive back into Mojave Wells for breakfast and lunch as necessary. It was lonely duty for a young enlisted man like myself, especially now that winter had set in, but I had gotten used to it. By now I had performed the runs so many times that I could do everything, including drive my pickup truck out onto the ranges and back to base, totally by touch and feel.

The U.S. Air Force didn't use the ranges in the wintertime. For that reason, taking the daily wind reports now that winter had set in, didn't seem to me to be as necessary as it had seemed during the heat of the previous summer. Most of these wintertime wind and weather reports that I was ordered to take, were never used. I took them anyway as best I could, and phoned them in to desert Center as ordered, even if most of them served only to grace the wastepaper basket that sat next to the Desert Center forecaster's desk.

For some reason, the Desert Center base commander considered the continued measurement of the Mojave Wells winds to be of the highest priority, even though the command post itself wasn't using them. Two days after the October full moon I submitted my request to take Christmas leave. My request was approved by my immediate chain of command. However, the Desert Center base commander himself unexpectedly denied it. According to my immediate commander at the time my request was denied, the base commander had stated that it was "…frightfully important that Airman Charlie Baker personally remain on station for the next few months." It didn't make sense to me, but the military was the military.

As the days marched on towards Thanksgiving and Christmas, it seemed as if the Desert Center base commander kept getting more and more edgy about my leaving the Mojave Wells area and coming in to Palm Meadows, even on weekends. He ordered that the supplies I needed at the end of November be delivered to me, even though the ranges weren't in use. Of course, since I was the only person allowed out onto the ranges, closed as they were, I had to drive in to the Mojave Wells motor pool to exchange trucks in order to actually receive my supplies. When I inspected the new supply shipment I discovered that a double shipment had been sent on the General's orders. Yes, something about those early winter days in the mid 1960's certainly seemed out of place.

A brutally cold blustery Friday came in early December. I had just returned to my Range Three weather shack after driving to the Mojave Wells chow hall for my noon lunch. A huge winter storm was moving in from the west and the valley was already overcast. An advancing wall of snow clouds already hid the mountains that formed the valley's western wall and was relentlessly pursuing the mountains to the north. Some of the clouds to the west and north were producing bolts of lightning and peals of thunder, as well as large white snowflakes. The valley itself was slowly filling with scattered thick, low clouds, and the wind was mounting. All in all, the day was rapidly becoming gloomier and gloomier. The temperature outside had fallen to 15 degrees Fahrenheit and the winds had picked up to more than 25 miles per hour. Sitting warm and snug inside my weather shack, I now appreciated the fact that I had carefully winterized it months before. I had worked long and hard on this shack and on all three of my other weather shacks so that I could easily survive for a week in any one of them if I ever got snowed in when out on the ranges alone. I had even stored spare crackers, candy bars, vitamin pills, cans of peanuts, and other sealed dry snacks. I had made certain that the shacks would remain warm and secure places of refuge in the worst of storms, even if the outside temperature were to fall to 30 degrees below zero, which sometimes happened during winter storms. I had also very carefully inspected the supporting diesel engines on all four of the ranges and made certain that their fuel tanks were filled. The desert was a merciless environment both winter and summer. Being out there alone day after day, I felt that it behooved me to leave nothing to chance.

I was preparing for the 1:30 p.m. balloon release. I was sitting at my desk next to the kerosene heater listening to its humming fan, the music playing on my radio, the whistling of the wind, and the sound of the diesel generator running smoothly in the nearby generator building. The inside of my shack was pleasant enough. I was filling out my 1:30 p.m. weather reporting form and as usual, I noted on the form that sundown tonight was expected at 5:28 p.m. local time. I also noted on the form that this was the evening of the full moon.

Just then my telephone rang. I answered, "Range Three weather shack. Airman First Class Charlie Baker here."

The voice on the other end sounded like my good friend Dwight, working days down at the Desert Center weather station. Desert Center was located perhaps 90 miles away, down between the mountains and across the desert valleys to the southeast. "Hi Charlie," he began. "I am sorry I had to interrupt you. I suppose you are busy getting ready for the 1:30 p.m. balloon release."

"That's OK, Dwight," I laughed. "On a day like today, it's nice to hear the voice of another human." He laughed too. He seemed to find my statement to be very amusing. I was taken a little off-guard. Dwight was from the south, and we were the very best of friends. Yet, here on the telephone, he seemed to be speaking in an unusually stiff and formal manner. Also, he seemed to be speaking perfect English, unusual for Dwight. I thought about it for a moment. Then I shrugged off the questions forming in my mind. I could hear several deeply worried voices in the background, so I decided that there were probably just some high-ranking officers in the Desert Center weather station with Dwight, and he was therefore, just being extra military. Situations like that had happened in the past. I took a deep breath and continued, "What can I do for you before I take the last run of the afternoon?"

"Well, the Desert Center base commander wanted me to make certain that I spoke with you before you left the ranges for the day," responded Dwight. "Something about this winter storm that is coming has him unusually worried. This huge snowstorm has been knocking down power lines and telephone lines and closing highways all over the west. It has even been playing havoc with the navigational beacons that the airplanes use.

"The base commander is hoping that you will remain on duty out at Range Three until at least 6:30 p.m. this evening. He says that it is absolutely necessary for you to make two additional balloon releases this afternoon. Besides the scheduled 1:30 p.m. release, he is asking for a 3:30 p.m. release and a 5:30 p.m. release. He specifically asked that you include the tracking lights on the 3:30 p.m. and the 5:30 p.m. releases."

"Yes," I answered. "Whatever you guys want, I'm happy to do it. You know, of course, that this entire valley is soon going to be nothing but falling snow and wall-to-wall clouds. I wouldn't expect much for wind numbers from the 3:30 p.m. or the 5:30 p.m. releases."

"He knows that, but he does not care. He said that you should just release the balloon and do the best you can." Then Dwight made an unusual request. "The base commander wants to be certain that you carry the balloon to the actual base of the theodolite stand before releasing it. Be certain to record the direction that the balloon takes even if you are not able to actually measure the winds themselves."

He paused for a moment to let his words sink in. Then he continued, "No matter what the roads are like out there, the base commander is asking that you remain out at your weather shack until at least 6:30 p.m. tonight. They will keep the chow hall open for you."

"Roger," I answered, wondering why the balloon release instructions had been so explicit. "I'll do it just like the base commander wants."

"You be very careful out there," cautioned Dwight. "The forecasters expect this to be one terrible storm. The snow and high winds have already closed all of the main highways leading in and out of Palm Meadows. The power lines are down because of ice and the aircraft navigational beacons will not turn on. We are only running on reduced emergency power here at the station. Things are expected to be even worse where you are, but I know you were born in Wisconsin. I know you can handle being outdoors in the winter."

"Thanks for the warning but don't worry about me," I laughed. "I have a full tank of gas, a nice set of chains, a good snow shovel in my truck, and jars of peanuts hidden all over the place. If I'm not careful, Range Four Harry will think I'm half squirrel."

For some reason, Dwight seemed to find my joke to be immensely funny. For a minute, it sounded as if he was almost barking with laughter.

I wondered about that for a few seconds. Then we both said "Good bye," and I hung up the phone.

I adjusted the volume on my radio and continued with my 1:30 p.m. preparations. The heavy steel helium cylinder that I was currently using was nearly empty, so I began moving a new full one from the storage area in the back southwest corner of my weather shack. I moved it forward into a waiting position next to the existing cylinder that sat next to the side door on the east side of my shack. Walking the cylinder past the warm kerosene heater that sat in the center of the shack required considerable care. Then, using my carefully positioned wrenches and tools, I attached the spare mechanical helium gauges, weights, and filling hose. The heavy steel cylinder was plenty cold. The new set of winter work gloves I was wearing served me well. I was somewhat confused at the time. During the course of my tour of duty as a USAF weather observer, I had worked during many power outages at the weather station down at Desert Center. I wasn't aware that the Desert Center station had access to an emergency power supply. It didn't seem like Dwight was phoning from the same station that I remembered.

I finished the 1:30 p.m. preparations and filled the balloon. The 1:30 p.m. run was very difficult. The cold winter winds caught hold of the balloon as soon as I stepped outside. It required all of my skill to keep the fragile balloon from breaking as I carried it out to the theodolite stand. Once I released it, the turbulent wind almost crashed it onto the hard gravel covered ground and then into the cable fence that marked the boundary to the skip bomb area. Then the wind lifted the balloon and immediately carried it bouncing at high speed down towards the mountains and the ski area to the distant southeast. Using my cold brass theodolite I was able to take only a few readings before the balloon had been blown out of sight, disappearing into the distant haze and gloom. "Oh well," I sighed, "if that's the run, that's the run. That was an awful lot of work in this cold weather just to take a few sets of numbers that no one is ever going to use."

More out of curiosity than anything, before I closed up my theodolite to protect it from the winter storm, I turned it towards the mountain base located high up in the trees on the large granite mountain to the distant north-northeast. The mountain was beautifully sculptured in snow and captivating to look at in its own right. The base of the advancing winter storm clouds lay just above the top of the entrance to the large concrete hanger that was dug into the mountain's southern face. The hanger's entrance was set into the granite just below the mountain's upper tree line. The distant blowing snow showed that the high winds up there were from the north, so the hanger entrance was currently on the sheltered side of the mountain. I hadn't seen any activity in the hanger area for more than two months. I found this total lack of activity to be somewhat curious. Month after month during the previous summer, I had regularly observed the deep-space craft of the tall white aliens arriving at the hanger entrance precisely at sundown on the evening of the full moon. The large sleek black craft would park on the landing pad out front and wait, sometimes for a full hour, for the hanger doors to finish opening. Once cold weather had set in, I supposed that they had broken off the schedule. As far as I knew, the last arrival had been on the night of the full moon during the month of September. Yet, while I was watching on this stormy winter afternoon, to my immense surprise, the concrete hanger doors, section by section, began opening. The lights inside the hanger had already been turned on.

The cold winter wind reminded me that winter is harsh on squirrels that don't hibernate in warm places. Quickly I closed and covered my theodolite and hurried back to the warmth of my weather shack.

I quickly completed my calculations and phoned Desert Center. The phone wouldn't actually give me a dial tone, but when I dialed the number anyway, Dwight answered. I read him the wind results such as they were, along with the azimuth readings for the initial direction the balloon had traveled when it was first released. Then Dwight made another unusual request. "The base commander was wondering, Charlie," he asked, what direction is the ski area from where you are?"

"It's down to the southeast," I answered. "According to the map on my wall, it's approximately in the compass direction of 162 degrees from north, from where I am."

"What I mean, Charlie," he continued, "Is what are the actual azimuth and elevation readings of the ski area from your theodolite? Would you please do me a favor and go out and record them now before this storm becomes any worse. Then would you include them in the report when you take the 3:30 p.m. run?"

"Yes," I answered. "That's no problem whatsoever."

"Thank you," he said. "The base commander would also like to know the distance from your theodolite stand to the ski lodge as accurately as you can determine it from the maps in your weather shack."

"Sure," I answered. "I'll do my very best with that."

He thanked me and we both hung up the phone. I warmed myself for a few minutes over the stove, munched some peanuts, took a drink of water, and returned outside to my theodolite to take the readings as requested. Once back in my weather shack, I did my best on the distance measurements and recorded the information in my logbook and on my weather reporting forms. Then I settled back down by my warm stove and returned to one of my history books.

This book was on the history of the discovery and exploration of Australia. In this cold northern winter weather it was nice to know that it was now summer in the southern hemisphere, since the seasons below the equator are reversed from those above the equator. "At least it's warm somewhere," I mused.

After reading for a while, I took a short break to recheck my inventory of batteries, tracking lights, and cord. The batteries were specially constructed for military use. Each battery was made from cardboard and pasty chemicals, and had a socket for a small light bulb on one end. It was rectangular and about the size of an ordinary flashlight. The final assembled battery with its small light bulb was first soaked in water for several minutes until the electricity began flowing and the light was shining brightly. Because the battery's paste was full of acids and chemicals, along with a large sheet of zinc metal inside, the battery worked even if the temperature was 50 degrees below zero Fahrenheit. Of course, each battery could be used only once. Once activated the entire electrified wet assembly was attached to the balloon. One end of a piece of cord was tied through a grommet on one end of the battery and the other end of the cord was tied around the neck of the filled balloon. Usually I used two or three pieces of cord to insure that the battery and its light were securely attached to the balloon. I made the cords equal length and long enough so that the battery hung down for several inches below the balloon as it ascended into the air. As I was measuring out the lengths of cord and tying them to the battery that I planned to use, my mind wandered for a few minutes. The batteries were manufactured in Madison, Wisconsin, just up the road from my hometown of Cambridge. Working with the batteries always made me feel homesick, and frequently filled me with a desire to re-travel the road home.

The time for the 3:30 p.m. balloon release arrived. The weather outside had become much worse. As requested, I prepared the balloon and attached a battery powered tracking light. I attached a long piece of rope to the outside handle of the side door to my weather shack. The door opened towards the inside and was hinged on the north. The rope allowed me to close the door after stepping outside with the balloon. That way, my shack would remain a warm haven of refuge while I was outside taking my wind report.

Taking the fragile balloon outside and carrying it over to the theodolite required all of my concentration. Big snowflakes were falling and the fragile red balloon was very hard to control in the wind. As soon as I had arrived at my theodolite I brought the balloon into launch position and released it. The wind immediately jerked the balloon from my hand and tossed it, well, like a balloon, back and forth as it sent the balloon on a line towards the southeast and the ski area. I took what few readings I could get as accurately as I could, before giving up on the run only three minutes into the flight. Trying to make the best of the situation in the cold afternoon gloom, I focused in on the ski area to recheck my previous azimuth and elevation readings. The ski area and the ski lodge sat with all of the lights on, both the outdoor lights and the indoor lights, as the storm slowly advanced towards it. The ski lodge had been designed to provide a warm safe haven during the worst of winter storms. It was well equipped with its own emergency diesel electric power supply.

The lodge, the parking area, and the bunny slope all set down somewhat in a wide canyon on the slope of the mountain. The canyon wasn't straight, but rather, it wound back and forth to a certain extent on its path down the mountain. The ski lodge and its parking lot were sitting in an area that had been chosen because it naturally offered a great deal of shelter from winter storms. As I studied it through the theodolite I couldn't help but notice how the snow covered ski area looked remarkably similar to the mountain base to the north.

While I was studying the ski lodge, I was surprised to see a state trooper with his lights flashing, pull up into the ski lodge parking lot. The trooper then proceeded to help evacuate the few members of the family that ran the lodge. In a very hurried fashion, he helped them to their cars and sent them hurrying along the paved road that led down from the mountain. Surprisingly, he appeared to insist that all of the cars be taken, leaving the parking lot empty. The trooper completed his task by closing, but not locking, the front doors of the lodge. To my further surprise, he left all of the lights on. From the mist on the lodge windows, it seemed apparent to me that the heaters inside of the lodge were also still on.

The entire episode seemed odd to me. The ski lodge was privately owned. Within its supply sheds there were enough provisions for the owners to survive being snowed in for two or three months. They even had their own snowplow. It didn't make sense to me that the state police would want even the lodge owners to evacuate in front of the advancing storm. Down at the base of the mountain, other state troopers had blocked off the road up to the ski lodge, and sat in their cars with the red lights flashing.

To the north, the concrete hanger still sat with its doors open and its lights on, still waiting.

By now the cold wind was making me shiver too intensely to see much of anything else through the cold brass theodolite. I closed it up and hurried back to the protection of my weather shack. Running late, I hurried through my wind calculations and picked up the phone to dial Desert Center. As before, there was no dial tone, but Dwight answered as soon as I finished dialing the numbers. He was his usual friendly self, although he seemed to be very worried about something. When I asked him about it, he just said simply that he was worried about his sister who I understood to be out traveling in this storm. He implied that she and her traveling companions were new to the area and not used to storms of this type and magnitude. I responded with the usual sympathy and comfort, which he seemed to deeply appreciate. He also seemed to be unusually appreciative of the azimuth readings and the distance measurements. He told me at least twice how helpful I had been and how useful the information was, even though he didn't say why.

After completing the phone call, I sat down and warmed up by the heater again. Darkness was falling and the storm was becoming steadily worse. After resting a while, I decided that it would be a good idea for me to put the chains on my truck now, while there was still some daylight left. I would certainly need them for the long drive back to base in the evening. After getting nice and warm, I bundled up and went back out into the cold. I walked over to my pickup truck. It had been parked over by the generator shack. I started it up, turned on the headlights, and drove the truck around to the front door of my weather shack. Out of force of habit, I parked it facing southeast. I left the engine idling and the headlights on bright. Then working quickly in the cold wind, I put the chains on the rear tires, making certain that the chains were both tight and secure. Doing it properly in the winter weather took me a great deal of time. When I had finally finished, I carefully turned off the headlights, as well as the engine. Now, ready for anything, I went back into my weather shack to warm up again.

By the time for the 5:30 p.m. run arrived, the storm had become simply brutal, and the winds were increasing dramatically. I was worried that the fragile balloon would break and my run would come late, so using my spare helium tank, I partially filled a second balloon. Then, five minutes early, I very carefully opened my side door and carried my primary balloon out to the theodolite stand. I stood there with my back to the wind, holding my fragile balloon and its battery powered light for the final five minutes before releasing it at 5:30 p.m. sharp. Just holding the balloon for that long was a considerable accomplishment, and I was quite proud of my skill. The inflated balloon was more than four feet across and quite slippery to hold. I had to hold it high above my head, battery powered light and all, with my arms outstretched in front of me in order to keep the turbulent wind gusts from smashing the balloon into the theodolite stand or onto the gravel covered ground around me. Holding the balloon in that wind for five minutes seemed like an eternity but 5:30 p.m. finally arrived, and I was able to release the balloon on schedule. The wind continued to increase and as before, I wasn't able to get much for readings. The second reading was already questionable and the third reading was little more than a guess, but it was the best I could do. More out of frustration with my failure than anything, I turned the theodolite towards the ski area to the southeast. Once again the wind had blown the balloon down the valley in that direction and I was sort of hoping that I would be able to relocate the balloon in the storm. The ski area looked so beautiful in the distance and the snow filled nighttime as the storm slowly approached it. The lights of the lodge and the nearby ski slopes sparkled in the nighttime darkness and through the falling snow. Occasionally the passing low clouds would drift into my line of sight and temporarily obscure some of the tantalizing and distant lights. While I watched, an unusually large dark object appeared to descend out of the clouds near the top of that distant mountain peak and float slowly down one of the ski runs, temporarily obscuring the lights as it did so. It continued its descent, passing in front of the lights of the ski lodge, and appeared to slowly and finally come to rest in the lodge parking lot. Based on the lights that remained obscured, I estimated the object was perhaps 70 feet high and 500 feet wide. The dark object had just finished floating to a secure resting place in the parking lot when the low clouds of the oncoming storm finally reached the mountain and the ski area, covering everything with a captivating nighttime snowy blackness. Since the winter snowstorm now covered the mountain completely, I supposed that what I had witnessed was an ordinary avalanche of snow. At the base of the mountain, the state troopers continued to keep the road blocked.

To the north, the concrete hanger was almost completely covered over by the storm. Through the occasional gaps in the clouds I could get glimpses of the concrete hanger still sitting with its doors open and its lights on, waiting.

The next cold gust of wind reminded me that I was still outdoors. I closed up my theodolite, prayed that Desert Center would understand my failure to take a complete set of readings, and hurried back to my weather shack and to its warm, cozy interior. Having only three readings, the wind calculations were little more than child's play. After writing down the results, I reluctantly picked up the phone to dial Desert Center, embarrassed by the few readings that I had available. Like the two previous reports, the wind reporting form in front of me was almost completely blank. Thanks to the storm, the falling snow, and the low clouds, I had spent an entire afternoon on Range Three, released three balloons, and had measured next to nothing about the winds that were blowing the clouds around above me.

As before, the telephone wouldn't give me a dial tone, but Dwight apparently answered as soon as I had finished dialing the numbers. He was jubilant and elated about something. He began by nearly shouting, "Charlie, you did it! Your ski lodge readings were correct! You got this balloon off exactly on time and everything turned out perfectly!" In the background I could hear happy shouting and laughter and someone saying, "He's done it, General! Only God knows how, but he's done it!"

I was almost too confused to respond. Weather stations on cold stormy wintry evenings are usually pretty lonely places. I had expected the Desert Center station to be one as well. Hearing a General in the background also caught me totally off guard. I nervously caught my breath and responded defensively, "I was only able to get the first three readings, Dwight. It was so windy and the clouds are so low that it was the best I could do. I'll be happy to give them to you as soon as you're ready to copy. I'll try again if you want."

Dwight, himself, was laughing happily in a manner so intense that he was almost unable to answer me. Finally he calmed down somewhat and said, "No, that is not necessary, Charlie. This evening has already been too perfect for me to waste your time like that. The last run was perfect! I am almost afraid to ask for another one, but the base commander was wondering, Charlie, if you could stay out there until 9:00 p.m. this evening, and give us another run at 7:30 p.m.? Do just as you did for the 5:30 p.m. run, only this time it will not matter if you are a few minutes late releasing the balloon."

"Yes," I responded, still confused, defensive, and believing that another run was being requested because I had failed on the 5:30 p.m. run. "I'll be happy to stay out here and try again at 7:30 p.m. It won't be the slightest problem."

Laughing and happy, Dwight said, "Last time was perfect, Charlie. The General will be giving you a big award for that one. Do it just as you did last time." Then he quietly hung up the phone.

After I too, hung up the phone, I sat for a few minutes in front of my warm stove trying to decompress emotionally. Since I had never seen a General actually visit the Desert Center weather station, hearing the General in the background had shaken my nerves when I was talking to Dwight. It didn't surprise me that Dwight would still be working even though the time was rushing on towards 6:00 p.m. and his day shift would have normally ended at 4:00 p.m. Dwight was like that. Between the storm and the General, it seemed only natural that he would have stayed on after the end of his day shift to help out the evening observer.

It was only after a long time had passed that I realized Dwight had complimented me for having taken a perfect run without ever having been told the results. I wondered about it for a minute or so. Then I shrugged it off. Dwight and I were such good friends perhaps he had just made up a reasonable set of winds by studying the wind charts down at Desert Center, and was covering for me with the General. He always said he would cover for me if I ever needed him to.

The storm outside kept getting worse and worse. The thick low clouds were now scraping along the exposed valley floor, leaving a covering of snow and ice on everything outside. Inside my weather shack, warm and snug, I turned up the music on my radio, munched some peanuts, drank some soda pop, and spent my time resting for the next wind measurement.

The time for the 7:30 p.m. run arrived. Outside the storm still raged. My first balloon broke in the icy cold wind almost as soon as I was outside. It was only through luck that I was able to get the second balloon released on time. As it was, I didn't arrive out at the theodolite stand until 7:29 p.m. As soon as I released the balloon it was blown down to the southeast and out of sight before I could locate it with the theodolite. The clouds were so low and so thick that nothing whatsoever could be seen in any direction. In frustration, I vented my anger at the wind and closed up my theodolite. The wind was so strong and the snow began falling so heavy that I almost became disoriented in the storm. I began by walking towards the east, keeping my back to the wind, instead of heading directly southeast back towards the security of my weather shack. When I bumped into the cable fence, I cautiously worked my way south until I was in the shelter of my shack. Then I reentered the safety of my shack by way of the side door. Through the entire brutally frustrating experience, I hadn't been able to record a single balloon reading.

With the empty reporting form in from of me, once again I dialed Desert Center. As before, Dwight answered. As before, he could hardly have sounded happier. "Hi Charlie," he said. "That was perfect. That was just what we wanted. Your Generals are more impressed with you than I have ever seen them."

"I did my best," I responded. "I'm sorry but I wasn't able to get any readings off the balloon. The storm is so bad the balloon was out of sight before I could locate it."

"It turned out just great," said Dwight. "You did it exactly the way we needed. When you drive back in to base tonight at 9:00 p.m., the Base Commander was hoping that you would leave the diesel generator running. He would also like you to leave the light on in your weather shack. This storm is so intense that he is thinking it might be a good safety measure. That way, if anyone is lost out on the ranges tonight, they might be able to find their way to the safety of your weather shack."

"Yes," I answered. "I'll be happy to do that. It sounds like a good idea plus if my truck can't make it back in to base, I'll just turn around and spend the night sleeping in my shack here."

"Thanks, Charlie," said Dwight. "None of us here can thank you enough. You be very careful driving back in to base." Then he quietly hung up the phone.

As I hung up the phone, it seemed like my friend Dwight was just thinking of me. Leaving the diesel running in this storm seemed like a reasonable safety precaution. It had enough fuel to run continuously for several months. If I shut the diesel down in this cold, restarting it again might be a problem. If I couldn't make it back into base, the lost traveler who might need the lights in my weather shack to guide him back to safety would, most likely, be me. I was, after all, totally alone on the ranges. "Yes," I remarked to myself, "I sure am lucky to have such dedicated friends."

I rested by my warm stove, filled myself with peanuts, some dried apples, warm coffee, and a vitamin pill. Finally 9:00 p.m. arrived. I dressed myself for the winter, turned off my kerosene stove, and its fan. Then I walked out into the storm. I closed the door behind me, but I did not lock it. Naturally, before I left, I checked the position of everything. I wanted to make certain that nothing flammable was touching my stove or any electrical outlet. For that reason, I moved my swivel chair back to its normal position in front of my desk. In that position, it more or less blocked the space just inside of the front door. That was hardly a problem for me as I closed up and stepped outside into the wind and silently falling snow.

The snow covered world outside was a wonderland of wintry enchantment. The storm had covered everything with a thick uniform blanket of ice and snow. The ditches and valleys had all been drifted in and smoothed over. Large snowdrifts had formed behind my weather shack, in between the mesquite trees, the sagebrush and other bushes, and next to the other buildings on Range Three. I stood protected in the shelter of my weather shack for a few minutes, enchanted by the snowflakes as they silently fell onto my face, my nose, and my lips. Then I finally trudged to my truck and turned myself to the task of brushing several inches of the fluffy white stuff off from the windshield and hood. The bed of my truck was filled with snow, covering the four large bags of sand that I kept back there in the wintertime. I climbed in at last, started it up, and began searching for the snow covered road back in to base. It was easy to become disoriented because of the storm, and I missed the road back to town on the first try. After driving for about ten minutes I discovered that I was driving in the frozen open desert way out to the west of the Range Three buildings. I followed my truck tracks back to the graveled area, very carefully located the generator shack, and started again on the paved road back towards base. Staying on the road and out of the ditch was quite an accomplishment. The snow was falling so thickly in many places that all I could see was white in every direction. With my chains on, I was driving only 15 miles per hour, and several times I found myself driving in one or the other of the ditches that lined the road.

Locating the Range Three gate and its connecting snow filled antitank ditch was quite a problem. I checked my odometer carefully as I drove. I had long since memorized every aspect of the road by heart. When my odometer calculations showed that I was getting close to the gate, I stopped my truck, set the brake and left the engine running with the headlights on. I got out into the snowy wonderland outside, and carefully walked a short distance on ahead. I repeated this process several times until I had located the gate with its deep antitank ditch hidden underneath the snowdrifts nearby. Then I marked a safe path through the gate area using my footprints. Once I was back in my truck, I now had a safe path to follow through the gate as I continued on my way back to base.

After driving for perhaps another hour, I found myself plowing through four-foot thick snowdrifts that had formed in the sunken area of the road. I had to speed up in order to plow through several five-foot deep drifts that had formed in the curves next to the ends of the base runways. For the biggest one I had to stop and use my snow shovel to clear the way.

The time was going on 11:00 p.m. when I finally arrived at the main Range gate. Opening it was easy enough, after I shoveled the snow out of the way, and broke off the ice that was encrusting the latch. After driving through, stopping, and closing the gate behind me, I plowed through the smaller snowdrifts until I arrived finally at the parking lot in front of my barracks. In the distance, I could see that all of the lights in the chow hall were dark, so I decided that no one was waiting up for me. Relieved that I had made it in from the Ranges safely, I shut down my truck, thanked God for His help, got out and carefully climbed the icy wooden stairs up to the warmth of my barracks. Once inside I was happily surprised to find a nice box lunch sitting on my bunk waiting for me. My friend Smokey, who was the cook in the chow hall, had a way of always looking out for me.

I had just sat down on my bunk and opened my lunch when I heard my Air Policeman friend Bryan pull up with his squad car out front. He turned on his flashing lights and siren, and then announced loudly with his bullhorn, "This is the police. Come out with your hands up." His job could be pretty boring, and on many cold winter nights he loved to pretend that he was protecting the base from bank robbers.

I got up from my bunk, walked over to the front door and waved for him to come in. In a few minutes he came in laughing, "I'll bet I had you scared, didn't I Charlie?"

"You sure did Bryan," I answered. "I was afraid that I was going to have to get used to jail food instead of eating these nice sandwiches from Smokey."

After we both finished laughing, Bryan continued, "This storm has been so bad that early this afternoon the Pentagon Generals ordered nearly everyone to return back down the valley to Desert Center until the weather improves. That's everyone except you, Smokey, one of the electricians, and me. The four of us are the only airmen still here. Of course, you're the only one who is allowed out on the Ranges."

"That's not enough men to play poker, so I guess the four of us will have to spend our time baking vanilla cookies and telling stories up in the chow hall," I laughed. "You know that good vanilla extract is nineteen percent alcohol by volume. This storm is so bad that our bodies may need the antifreeze."

Bryan laughed for a time, and then continued, "The three of us may try that, but you're going to be too busy to join in, I'm afraid."

"How so?" I asked.

"About an hour ago on my car radio, I received some orders for you from the Desert Center base commander," said Bryan seriously. "They're expecting the storm front to pass over us about midnight or so. The base commander wants another balloon run. This time he wants it from Range One at 4:30 a.m. tomorrow morning."

"But tomorrow morning is Saturday," I responded. "The U.S. Air Force never needs Range wind reports on Saturday. Besides, Range One is more than twenty-two miles out in the desert along unpaved roads. In this weather I'll have to spend a good two hours fighting the wind and snow just to get there. Then, once I am there, I won't be able to get anything for readings. Are you sure he meant tomorrow?"

"Yes, Charlie," Bryan said. "I'm an Air Policeman. Keeping the General's orders straight is my job. Believe me! He means tomorrow! You can use any vehicle in the motor pool to get there, but he means 4:30 a.m. and he means tomorrow! Naturally, you'll have to drive out there alone. The General doesn't want any of the rest of us to get even close to the main Range gate, let alone to go past it.

"The General may want another run at 5:30 a.m. as well, so you're to take breakfast with you and hang around until 6:00 a.m. once you get there. He also wants to make certain that you attach a tracking light to the balloons, the way you have been doing."

"Order are orders, I guess," I responded. "They're probably in the middle of some military winter war games and the General is probably just upset because I wasn't able to get any useable wind readings from my last three balloon releases. I'll bet he just wants me to be better trained for winter warfare.

"I'll use my pickup truck with chains and gas up at the motor pool before I leave for Range One. I'll set my alarm clock and sleep in the barracks for a couple hours. Then I'll leave early so I can get out there on time. Stop by my barracks at 1:45 a.m. and check up on me, would you please? Make sure I'm up and moving?"

"Sure, no problem," said Bryan. "I'll keep you posted if anything changes. My car radio is our only line of communication with Desert Center because the phone lines have been down since noon."

"Since noon," I asked surprised? "But my lines were still working. I was talking to Dwight just three hours ago."

"Yes, since noon," answered Bryan. "I don't know who you were talking to or what you were doing out at Range Three this evening and of course, I'm not supposed to know, but I don't think your reading of the Desert Center base commander is quite on the mark. He came on my car radio along about 6:00 p.m. this evening. He was happy as the devil. He was so full of praise for something you had done that at first I thought you were going to marry his

26

daughter. I can't believe that he's just doing this to train you for winter warfare."

"Well, Generals are Generals," I said, "And orders are orders. Call him up on your car radio and tell him I'll make the balloon release as ordered." With that we said good-bye and Bryan went back out into the cold to his squad car.

I finished my meal, hurried through my evening shower, set my alarm, and went to sleep. When 1:15 a.m. arrived and my alarm clock sounded, I arose, got dressed, and set about my duties. I was quite tired, but during the short walk to my truck, the cold air woke me right up. I stopped by the motor pool and struggled with the snow covered gas pump. For safety, I picked up two five gallon gasoline "jerry" cans from the motor pool, filled them with the high octane, and placed them securely in the back of my truck. I also tossed in a long stemmed gasoline funnel. Then, after filling my truck's tank with gasoline as well, I headed for the main Range gate.

The drive out to Range One was hauntingly beautiful. The storm front had just passed an hour or so earlier, the winds had let up, and only a light snow was now falling. The previously fallen snow lay like a soft, velvet carpet, beautifying the mountainsides and flowing smoothly down over the desert floor, filling in the depressions, crevices, ditches and gullies.

I followed the main Range road for three miles or so until I reached the intersection with the Range One road. Several huge snowdrifts blocked the turn onto the Range One road. However, I was able to detour around them by driving out into a smooth section of desert nearby that had been blown clear of snow by the night's high winds. After a detour of a mile or so, I was able to return to the snow covered Range One road and proceed on my nighttime journey.

My truck continued plowing through medium sized snowdrifts for several miles as the road headed uphill towards the low pass that was several miles up ahead in the darkness. The snowdrifts became deeper as the road continued uphill. I knew that up ahead the road would pass between a series of unusually large rocks. I expected that snowdrifts would be blocking that section of road, so as soon as I reached another smooth open section I took a detour out into the desert. My detour was several miles long. It arced in jagged fashion to the north and continued uphill, passing between several large boulders, bushes, and arroyos. It finally sliced through some medium sized snowdrifts and rejoined the Range One road just below the cloud filled pass. The pass itself was blocked by a huge snowdrift and was choked with low clouds. The winds were gentle and light snow was still falling. There was no way to detour around the pass. I parked my truck, left it idling with the headlights on, and attacked the huge snowdrift with my snow shovel. After working for fifteen or twenty minutes, I was finally able to cut through the top of the drift to the other side. Then, with a great deal of difficulty, I struggled through the waist-deep snow back to my truck. I checked my chains, re-stowed my shovel in the back of the truck, placed it in gear, and carefully plowed through the huge drift to the downgrade on the other side.

The road on the other side of the pass was much easier going. The snowdrifts weren't as large and the truck easily plowed through them as it traveled downhill towards the dry lakebed that lay several miles in the distance. The artistry of the winter winds had formed the falling snowflakes into long powdery drifts that lay across the road, one on another, row on row, connecting the tops of the tall sagebrush on one side with the frozen dirt and rocks that lined the ditch on the other.

After traveling for about two miles, the road finally descended below the cloud layer and the visibility greatly improved. To the northwest, through the lightly falling snow, I could now see the lights of my Range Three weather shack still shining in the distance. The base of the low cloud layer could be seen drifting slowly across its roof. The light shining out from the square window on the eastern side of my Range Three weather shack reminded me of the light of a distant lighthouse overlooking a rocky shore.

Down to the southeast, I could see the lights of the ski area as they twinkled in the distance. The base of the cloud layer was higher in that direction. The bottom of the low clouds could be seen drifting slowly across the lights of the ski runs, obscuring the top of the mountain starting perhaps 500 feet above the lights of the ski lodge. At the base of the mountain the flashing lights of the state police patrol cars showed that the road up to the ski area was still closed.

I had to pay careful attention to the frozen snow-covered dirt road and to my driving, so several minutes passed before I realized that the lower lights of the ski lodge, the lights on the stairway leading up the side of the mountain to it, and the lights of the ski area parking lot were still obscured by a large dark object. It didn't surprise me because I supposed that piles of snow were obscuring the lights.

I continued my steady progress downhill towards the frozen snow covered dry lakebed. I paid careful attention to my driving and several miles passed behind me. Driving through the light falling snow had been quite tiring on my eyes, so I stopped for a minute or so to rest them. While I was temporarily stopped, I rechecked the lights of the ski area that were twinkling in the distance. The lights seemed to be twinkling in an odd manner for some reason. I thought about it for a minute. Suddenly I realized why. The dark object sitting in the parking lot of the distant ski area was moving. I remained stopped in my truck for a few minutes more, resting and studying the moving object. Slowly it rose up perhaps fifty feet or so. It drifted to the south. Then it began following the paved road that led from the ski area parking lot down the canyon to the north. The object appeared to have some dim lights shining from a few small windows, along with a number of small running lights similar to those on the trailer of a semi-truck. As the object disappeared into the darkness downhill to the north, one by one, all of the lights of the ski area now became visible. I had no idea what to make of it all. After giving the matter some thought, I decided that I was probably just seeing snowdrifts and another avalanche.

After resting for a few more minutes, I put my truck back in gear and continued heading downhill. After traveling several more miles I reached the edge of the frozen snow covered dry lakebed and continued on across it. Soon, the buildings of the Range One area loomed out of the darkness as my truck finally reached the safety of the snow covered graveled area. I flicked my headlights two or three times, making certain that they were now on bright. Then I pulled my truck up next to the Range One weather shack and stopped several feet from the cable fence that marked the boundary to the skip bomb area. My truck sat facing southeast with the engine idling and its headlights shining out over the sagebrush and the snow covered desert. Some seventy feet off to my left and next to the cable fence stood the Range One control tower with its snow covered wooden steps. The drive out had been long and tiring. While I rested, enjoying the warmth of my well-heated truck, I said a prayer, thanking God that I had arrived safely. It was now going on 4:00 a.m. While I sat watching the lights of the ski area, the dark object in the distance appeared to pass in front of the state police cars that sat parked on the road at the base of the far away mountain. It continued on its path downhill towards the north, reaching at last the distant extension of the valley in which I sat parked.

After resting for a few minutes more, I carefully got out from my warm truck into the cold night air, opened my weather shack, and brought Range One to life. Fifteen minutes or so later, with the lights, heat, and the radio going in my weather shack, I turned off my truck's engine and headlights, and went inside to begin the morning's balloon release. All the while my truck had been sitting idling, facing down the valley towards the southeast with its headlights on bright.

The reception on the radio was unusually clear so I tuned in some Christmas music and turned the radio up loud. As my weather shack began to warm up, I opened a jar of peanuts and munched a couple of handfuls. I washed them down with a newly opened can of soda pop. I concluded that the life of a squirrel wasn't all that bad.

I began filling my weather balloon with helium and making entries on the morning weather report. I noted that the temperature outside was only seven degrees. "There are

31

so few degrees outside, why bother counting them," I
laughed to myself. "Why not just say, 'here's a degree,
there's a degree; or better yet, maybe I should just start
naming them. Degree number five, I named 'The Blue Cold
degree'. Degree number four, of course, was 'The
Government's degree'. That's the degree you can trust!" I
laughed. Soon the loud Christmas music, mixed with my
happy off-key singing and laughter was flooding outside
into the cold winter night, floating out across the icy
sagebrush on the gentle frozen winter winds.

My balloon finished filling, so I attached the tracking
light and went outside to unlock my theodolite. Light flakes
of snow were still slowly falling and it was an absolutely
enchanting winter evening in the desert. I considered myself
to be quite lucky, just being able to see and experience it.
While I was adjusting my theodolite and turning on its
battery powered scale lights, I could hear just a faint
amount of static begin to mix in with the otherwise clear
Christmas music on my radio. I shrugged it off and
completed my set up. "Perhaps the radio is just warming
up," I said to myself. Then I walked quickly back to the side
door on my weather shack to get my balloon and clipboard.
Just before I rounded the corner of my weather shack, some
more light static could be heard on my radio, and something
out in the darkness down the valley to the southeast caught
my eye. There seemed to be a small yellow light next to an
unusually large black area just beyond some large bushes
out in the valley, perhaps two or three miles down to the
southeast. A light snow was falling at the time.

Since it was nighttime and the valley was completely
covered with low clouds, naturally, the entire valley was
filled with a certain snowy darkness. Just the same, I

32

couldn't help but spend several minutes studying the unusual large dark area in the distance that appeared to be sitting motionless on the valley floor. Finally my eyes became tired from staring out through the cold darkness and the snow, and I began to feel noticeably foolish. I wondered, "How can one snowy black area look any different from any other snowy black area? It must just be that my eyes are tired."

Laughing at myself, I entered my weather shack. I picked up my balloon and clipboard. I stepped back outside, closing the side door behind me. Carrying the balloon, I walked quickly to my theodolite stand and stood waiting for 4:30 a.m. sharp, checking the time on my watch as I did so. I had perhaps two minutes to wait. While I stood waiting in the lightly falling snow, holding the balloon high above my head, down to the southeast, it seemed as if the large dark area began slowly moving up the valley towards me.

When 4:30 a.m. sharp arrived, I released the balloon and began the process of tracking it using my theodolite. Although the winds were gentle, the clouds were so low that I was able to get only two adequate readings before I lost the balloon into the snowy dark clouds above me. Giving up on the balloon, I tried to focus my theodolite on the dark object down to the southeast. However, nothing in particular could be seen.

Having taken as much of a balloon run as the weather permitted, I carefully closed up my theodolite and locked it, in order to protect it from the elements. Then, clipboard in hand, I walked back to my weather shack, listening to the increasing static on the radio as I did so. However, before I opened the side door and went back inside, I stood in the shadows of my weather shack for a few minutes and again carefully studied the darkness down to the southeast. Alone as I was in this frozen, nearly impassable, snow covered desert, the dark object's presence was starting to make me feel uneasy. While I stood watching, it continued its slow silent advance up the valley. Now it sat motionless on the snowy desert floor perhaps as little as a half mile down to the southeast. I noted that the object had a certain black titanium metallic luster to it, whereas the regular nighttime just appeared to be dark, snowy, and cold.

Still not certain that something solid and real was resting out in the darkness, I opened the side door to my weather shack and went back inside. I closed the door behind me, warmed myself at the stove, quickly performed the two wind calculations, and munched a few peanuts before phoning Desert Center. The music on my radio was now as much static as anything else.

The phone here at Range One, just like the phone on the previous night at Range Three, would not give me a dial tone. Having nothing better to do, even though the line was dead, I dialed it anyway and my friend Dwight answered as soon as I had finished dialing the numbers. As before, he could hardly have sounded happier or more wide-awake. "Dwight," I exclaimed, "I'm surprised you're up this early."

He was laughing like it was already Christmas and, apparently caught off guard. He responded, "I do not sleep as often as you do Charlie, and with an event like this going on, I would not miss it for anything. You certainly have given us plenty to celebrate." In the background it sounded as if a large detachment party was already in full swing. For a minute it sounded as if some General was happily teaching everyone how to sing songs about Santa Claus.

Totally off balance and confused, I continued in a happy tone of voice, "I have the 4:30 a.m. winds, as the base commander has requested. I can report them to you as soon as you are ready to copy."

"Sure," he laughed, obviously trying to calm down. "Go ahead, read the report to me."

I proceeded to carefully read him the morning wind and weather report. About halfway through it seemed obvious that he really didn't care what any of the numbers were and obviously wasn't writing anything down. However, I continued smoothly anyway. I had gone through so much trouble just to get out to Range One that I was determined to report the weather to somebody.

After I had completed reading the regular wind and weather report, I waited for a break in Dwight's laughter. Then I continued pleasantly and carefully, "There's something else, Dwight. I know it sounds ridiculous because of this winter storm and everything, but I don't seem to be alone out here at Range One."

Dwight's laughter noticeably increased and the static on the radio also noticeably increased. I continued, "There is a large shiny black metallic object sitting behind some bushes out in the desert just southeast of here. It appears to be much larger than a three-story house and it is sitting no more than a half-mile down the valley from me. It's not threatening me, or anything, and it seems to be friendly. I'm just a little nervous because it is so large and it moved in there so silently while I was releasing my balloon. For a minute there, I felt like it was watching me."

Dwight could no longer contain his laughter. After a bit, he collected himself and responded, "Charlie, you are such a card! You are so much fun to talk to. Every time you talk

35

to any of us, we all come away laughing hysterically. The stories that you tell! They are so entertaining! How do you ever think them up? Here tonight, I thought you were going to tell me about how difficult it was for you to drive your truck out to Range One. I expected to hear about how you had to heroically struggle in the cold and scrape off ice and worry about frostbite and detour around snowdrifts and shovel snow in the pass. Yet, here you are trying to get me to believe that on a night like tonight, after all that you have been through, your problem is that something friendly is watching you from out in the darkness." Then, Dwight and the people in the background could be heard laughing hysterically. Someone was shouting happily, "He's too brave a man to get me to believe that one, General."

Embarrassed with myself, I chuckled and said, "I guess you're right, Dwight. I just need to eat some more peanuts, warm up, and get my courage back. Don't worry about me. The men of my family have never had any fear of darkness."

Finally Dwight said, "The only thing you have to be afraid of, Charlie, is that the award you will be receiving from the base commander for this perfect evening, may be too heavy for you to carry.

"There is one more thing the base commander would like you to do, Charlie, before you return to Mojave Wells this morning." Dwight paused for a few seconds before continuing.

"Yes. Anything he wants," I answered, as though I could say "No" to a General's request.

"After you have warmed up and rested a few minutes, the General would like you to take a special type of snowfall measurement as part of a climate study," Dwight said. "You know where the switch is to the outdoor lights for the control tower there at Range One?"

"Yes," I answered. "It is in that large weather proof metal box located at the bottom of the tower, just next to the wooden steps."

"Right," said Dwight. "As soon as you're ready, the General would like you to go outside and turn on the outdoor lights to the control tower. Then he would like you to climb up the stairs to the wooden balcony on top and go around to the south side. Take your wooden ruler, your clipboard, and a weather reporting form with you. The General would like you to stand by the railing on the south side for exactly a half hour, right there under one of the lights. Using the ruler, he would like you to measure the rate at which the snow is accumulating on the corner of the wooden railing. He would like the measurements recorded every ten minutes. When you are finished, you do not have to phone them in. Just record them on the form, and include them on the month-end report. OK?"

"Yes," I answered slowly. "If that's what the General wants, that's what I'll do. I'll be ready to start in ten minutes."

"Yes," Dwight answered, "The General is so proud of you. He would just love to see you do that. When the half hour is up, you can return to the inside of your weather shack and warm up. Stay out at Range One until 7:00 a.m. Then you can shut everything down and head back in to Mojave Wells. Your morning run has been so perfect that we will not need any more reports for today. There is no way that any of us can thank you, Charlie." With that, Dwight hung up the phone.

I hung up the phone and sat musing about things for a minute. The General's request for me to go out and stand in the snow for a half hour actually didn't seem particularly unusual. A good military tour of duty frequently contained many similar experiences. One time in the fall, a year or so before, when I was still stationed at Weather Training School at Chanute AFB, Illinois, the thirty men in my class and I were ordered to spend every day for a week raking leaves in an open twenty acre field. Since there weren't any trees in the field, there weren't any leaves in the field to begin with. I raked one piece of open ground four times before the Captain was happy with it. By comparison, for the General to order me, an experienced weather observer, to stand for a half hour watching the snowflakes fall seemed pretty ordinary.

I opened a can of soda pop and spent several minutes munching peanuts, dried apples, and other snacks. I popped a vitamin pill, washed it down with water, and adjusted my winter clothing. Then, with my clipboard and wooden ruler in hand, I stepped outside, closing the door behind me. In the distance, down to the southeast, I noticed that the police cars had turned off their flashing red lights, and reopened the road up to the ski area. It seemed odd since a light snow was still falling.

As ordered, I walked to the base of the control tower and, after struggling with the cold metal box, turned on the outdoor tower lights. The tower's balcony wasn't very high up, perhaps fifteen feet. Still, I had to be very careful climbing the snowy ice covered wooden stairs. Once up on top, I walked around to the southern side, took a snow depth measurement and began my vigil.

It was immediately obvious to me that the large dark object was quite real. It now sat behind some tall bushes, down to the southeast. It was sitting facing due west, exposing the angled length of its right side to me. While I had been in my weather shack, it had silently closed the distance to less than a quarter mile. With the tower lights on, my night vision wasn't particularly good, so I had a hard time making out any details on its black metallic surface. However, after careful study I could make out four rows of portholes that were very dimly lit. It also appeared to have a number of very dimly lit running lights, similar to those on a semi-trailer. The light on the top, front, right of the vehicle was light yellow and was noticeably brighter than the others. I estimated the vehicle's size to be more or less seventy feet tall, at least 300 feet wide, and probably 500 feet long. It was smoothly molded all around. Two large cockpit windows, apparently for the pilot and co-pilot, were positioned in the front and center, about one third of the distance up from the ground. As it sat silently out there in the darkness, it reminded me, for all the world, of a Caribbean cruise ship resting in port.

When my watch showed that ten minutes had passed, I looked down at the tower railing to check on the depth of the fallen snow. A cold gentle breeze passed by, blowing some snowflakes onto the back of my jacket, and also onto the back of my neck. I shivered for a minute or so and then brushed them off. Suddenly I realized that the dark object was one of the deep-space craft built by the tall white aliens. I guessed that it was probably the craft that had been scheduled to arrive during the full moon of last October, but was now arriving late.

After another fifteen minutes or so had passed, the static on my radio suddenly became very intense. Then the craft silently raised up several feet, just enough to clear the tops of the sagebrush. It slowly came towards my weather shack, rotating to my left as it did so. This maneuver left it not more than an eighth of a mile from me, and I could see its entire left hand side. Now, facing northwest, and sideways to me, it began slowly and silently passing by. Up on top of the vehicle in the front, where the left hand front running light should have been, was a gaping hole, perhaps ten feet across. A large rectangular sheet of the thin outer metal surface next to the hole was draped down over the side, perhaps concealing additional damage. At the time, I guessed that the large craft had experienced some type of meteor damage while traveling out in the deep space that exists between the stars. There wasn't much to be seen when I looked through the windows into its darkened interior. A few of the rooms underneath the gaping hole appeared to have been storage rooms and were now filled with wreckage. Other rooms further down and along the angled path of the meteor, were heavily damaged. Those rooms appeared to have been closed off. However, through one darkened window towards the middle of the second row, I could see the faces of two chalk white creatures on board looking back at me. They seemed to be very happy.

The craft floated by me so slowly that it took almost twenty minutes for it to reach the snow filled arroyo to the northeast of the Range One area. For my part, I was so startled to see such a large vehicle so close up, I did little more than stand under the tower lights staring at it, and studying it intensely. It was only after the back of the vehicle had reached the arroyo that I finally collected myself again. Still curious, especially about the meteor damage, I picked up my ruler and clipboard, and carefully negotiated my way back down the snow-covered stairs. I hurried north towards the Range One road, trying to follow after the craft as it silently headed away from me. By the time I reached the sagebrush that lined the Range One road, I realized how pointless it was for me to be chasing after it, especially in this wintry weather. I stopped on the gravel road and watched the craft as it slowly and silently floated off towards the northwest and the distant buildings of Range Two and Range Three. The sight of the large craft with its gaping hole, on that cold wintry night, silently retreating from me, is one of the images that has been indelibly fixed in my memory.

I watched for another twenty minutes or so as the craft silently disappeared into the darkness to the northwest. Then, I returned to the base of the control tower, turned off its lights, and returned to the warmth of my weather shack. The Christmas music on my radio was now static free and crystal clear. I munched some more peanuts and recorded my snowfall reading. Then, short on sleep, I positioned my chairs to form a bed and rested. In the warm cozy interior of my weather shack, I quickly fell asleep.

It was well past 8:30 a.m. when I finally woke up. The sun was up and the snow had stopped falling, but the day remained cold and gloomy. The valley was still overcast with low clouds. I got up, stretched, and had a quick snack. Then I put on my winter coat and gloves, and went outside to warm up my pickup truck. Once it was warm, I shut down Range One, locked everything up, checked my tire chains, and began the long drive back to Mojave Wells.

The drive back to base was much easier than the drive out had been. It was a simple matter for me to follow the path through the snowdrifts that I had made coming out. As I was on the upgrade heading towards the pass, I got a good view of the snow-covered valley that lay to the northwest. It was overcast with low clouds and blocked by a wall of storm clouds that lay just a couple miles or so north of the Range Three buildings. Out there in the distance, many miles away, I could see the large black craft sitting on the desert perhaps a quarter mile due east of my Range Three weather shack. I temporarily stopped my truck and watched it for a few minutes. Seeing that nothing was happening, I put my truck back in gear and continued the long drive back to Mojave Wells.

Of course, once I had re-plowed through the snowdrifts in the pass, my return route, just like my trip out, included the long detour out into the desert and around the huge impassable snowdrifts. It also included a quick stop to refill my truck's gas tank using the extra gasoline in my "jerry" cans.

I finally arrived back at the main Range gate, and completed my journey by parking my white topped, deep blue pickup truck in front of my barracks. By now it was past 11:30 a.m. and time for the noon meal. My Air Policeman friend, Bryan, was waiting for me, standing by his parked squad car when I arrived. He greeted me once I had gotten out of my truck, "Hi Charlie. I'm glad to see that you made it safely back to base. We were all pretty worried about you in this snow."

"Thanks," I said. "Some of the snowdrifts out there on the Range One road are quite high, but I took my time and my truck made it OK. Naturally I'm very tired so I thought that as soon as I finished lunch, I would spend the afternoon sleeping in my barracks and getting rested up."

"Sounds like a good idea," he responded. "First, though, I need to relay the new orders that I received for you on my radio from the Desert Center base commander this morning."

"New orders," I asked in surprise? "Lucky me, I enjoy being remembered."

Bryan laughed some and said, "Oh, the Desert Center base commander remembers you, alright. I understand that whatever you did last night and this morning averted quite a disaster. He sure is mighty happy. He was singing Christmas songs and everything when I was talking to him. He said there were an awful lot of people who would never forget you."

"What does he want me to do now," I asked?

"The General has requested one more balloon run for tomorrow, just after noon at 12:30 p.m. in the afternoon from Range Three," said Bryan. "The weather is expected to be much better tomorrow, so he's expecting it to be an easy run. He said that you would have to go back out to Range Three to shut down the generator and lock up everything for the winter anyway, so for a man like you to take another balloon run on a nice afternoon won't be any more work than entertaining a group of children for a few minutes.

"You don't have to phone the run in to Desert Center. Just record the results and turn in the form as usual at the end of the month. Then shut everything down and lock everything up and come back to Mojave Wells."

"Yes," I answered. "I suppose the General knows that tomorrow is Sunday. I hope that the Catholic priest can make it down here from San Bernardino early enough tomorrow so I can attend mass before heading back out onto the Ranges."

"Yes, I'm sure he knows that," said Bryan matter-of-factly. "He said this coming Monday morning, you're supposed to pack up all of your belongings and load them into the back of my squad car. I'm supposed to take you back down to Desert Center so you can begin the Christmas leave that you requested last October. I understood the General to say that he was giving you an extra month's free leave because you saved so many lives last evening."

"That's nice of him," I said. "Now let's locate the chow hall and have lunch. It's been a long morning and I'm hungry as the devil." Bryan and I proceeded to laugh our way up to the chow hall. Together, with Smokey, we enjoyed the lunch that Smokey had prepared.

I rested a great deal and took life easy for the rest of the day. The next morning, the storm was over and the weather had greatly improved. The sun was shining, most of the clouds were gone, and the temperature had risen to twenty degrees Fahrenheit. The priest made it in to Mojave Wells for the Sunday morning mass on time. I took my lunch early, filled my truck with gasoline, and began the long drive out to Range Three.

It was an easy drive. I plowed through the snowdrifts following the same path that I had used coming in late the previous Friday night. On a couple of the drifts I had to stop and use my shovel.

It was almost noon when I arrived out at Range Three. I parked my truck in front of my weather shack and took stock of the situation. Perhaps a mile out in the desert to the northeast, sitting just beyond a ridge was the large sleek black craft. It was sitting facing north, with its damaged left side towards me. It appeared that some temporary repairs had been performed on the gaping hole up on top in the front of the vehicle. Not much could be seen through the windows because of the glare of the sunlight, the viewing angle, and the distance, but it was obvious that a good deal of repair activity was taking place inside the craft. On the side of the mountain to the far north, the distant concrete hanger could be seen sitting with its doors still open, still waiting.

"Well, there's no point in waiting," I said to myself. "This is after all Sunday."

I turned off my truck, got out, and opened up my weather shack. One look inside and it was obvious that I'd had company. In addition to my chair being moved, some of my tools and several of my jars of peanuts had been moved as well. What surprised me most was that my radio had been unplugged and carefully moved to one side, thereby providing someone with access to its electrical socket.

I shrugged the entire episode off, quickly tidied up my weather shack, and began taking the 12:30 p.m. balloon run. It went smoothly enough. With the skies nearly clear, I chose a white balloon and tracked it to 25,000 feet. Naturally that took a few minutes longer than normal. After finishing my balloon run, I took a few additional minutes and used my theodolite to visually inspect the large black craft. There appeared to be a large number of small white faces looking out through the rear windows of the second and third rows.

As I was closing up my theodolite, I saw two of the alien's ordinary white scout craft flying side-by-side coming slowly down the valley from the north. They were separated by perhaps 500 feet of airspace. While I watched, the alien's large black craft silently rose up perhaps fifty feet off the desert and began heading north towards them. The two white craft stopped in mid air just north of Range Four and waited a few minutes until the much larger black craft had closed the distance. Then with the two white scout craft leading, the formation of all three craft headed silently and slowly up the valley, apparently towards home.

Burnt Curtains

The Lord's fire came down
and consumed the holocaust,
wood, stones, and dust,
and it lapped up
the water in the trench.

1 Kings 18:38

It was a mild winter Sunday morning at the Desert Center air base. I was scheduled to work the day shift. I set my alarm clock for 5:15 a.m. and was standing in line at the entrance to the chow hall when it opened for breakfast at 6:00 a.m. During the many months of duty that I had spent out in the desert at Mojave Wells, I had gotten into the habit of waking up precisely at 3:00 a.m. Consequently, laying in my bunk with my eyes wide open until my alarm clock rang at 5:15 a.m., made me feel as if I had already wasted the best part of the day.

After finishing breakfast, I headed directly over towards the base weather station. It was a lovely morning and the clock now showed 6:40 a.m. The Desert Center airbase was generally quite level and I enjoyed the walk. I was still perhaps a quarter mile down the road from the weather station, when I happened to notice my friend Small Jimmy Payne up ahead in the distance. He had just finished emptying the contents of one of the large tall metal wastepaper baskets into the "White Elephant" dumpster that

47

sat in the parking lot across from the weather station. He stood at least 6' 4" tall in his stocking feet and weighed at least 240 lbs of solid muscle and bone. He was tossing the large metal basket around using only one hand, as easily as most men would toss around a coffee cup. It was such a comical sight that I had to laugh about it to myself. Of course, I was still a safe distance away. Up ahead, without ever noticing that I was watching from down the road, Payne carried the basket back into the weather station and closed the front door behind him.

As I continued my journey toward the station, I became curious about what I had just witnessed. Emptying the wastepaper baskets wasn't normally one of the weather observer's duties. The station had a civilian janitor that came around every day, including both Saturday and Sunday afternoons. The civilian janitor normally mopped and waxed the floors, performed all of the necessary cleaning, and emptied all of the wastebaskets. I had worked the Saturday night mid shift, 12:00 a.m. to 8:00 a.m., many times, as Payne was now doing. Except for perhaps a few candy bar wrappers, the large baskets were usually perfectly empty on Sunday morning. As for Payne's natural tendency to keep his surroundings clean, well, I had chosen to have my tetanus shot updated before I entered his barracks room a few days before.

Finishing my journey, I arrived at the door to the weather station and went inside. It was 6:58 a.m. Payne was in the teletype room. He was preparing his 7:00 a.m. weather report for transmission to Tinker AFB in Oklahoma.

The Desert Center weather station was electronically connected to the section of the Air Force weather network that had been named SAUS 5. The name was a military acronym for "Standard Air [Force] United States [area] 5". Desert Center was the second station polled on SAUS 5 when the network was scanned.

Regulations required that every hour on the hour, both day and night, every day of the year, each station on the network prepare a weather report and place it on their transmission equipment. Air Force regulations required that this activity take place precisely during the two-minute time span immediately before the beginning of each hour. Weather information was always summarized for transmission using codes, numbers, and special symbols. There were more than 105 different sets of encoding conventions. Each observer had to learn these different encoding conventions and have them committed to memory before they were allowed to graduate from the USAF weather training school. Small Jimmy Payne was quite intelligent and an excellent observer, when he wanted to be. He had summarized the current hourly report, for example, to a sequence of only 102 characters and symbols. The resulting piece of paper tape, therefore, wasn't very long. Consequently, an evening's worth of such paper tapes would hardly have covered the bottom of the wastebasket that I had seen him emptying into the large dumpster earlier.

"Hi Jim," I said loudly as I came in. "I'm here early to relieve you for the day shift. That way you can still catch the 8:00 a.m. Mass at the chapel if you want." Like me, Jim Payne was Roman Catholic.

"Good morning, Charlie," Payne bellowed back. "It's good to see you. I'll take you up on that. I'll be finished here in a minute."

The teletype room was a very noisy place, and it was normal for observers to shout at one another so they could be heard. Of course, Payne was so large and muscular that he could easily shout loud enough to make an ordinary man's ears hurt.

Payne was typing up the paper tape that would be placed on, and then locked into position on the teletype tape reader. Once the tape was locked into position, the observer would press a small red transmit button, notifying Tinker AFB that the hourly weather report was ready for transmission. When the electronic equipment on the other end at Tinker was ready to receive the report, it would activate the transmission sequence. The local hardware would respond by first transmitting the three letter airbase ID. Then the hardware would mechanically read the sequence of punched holes on the paper tape, and the resulting weather report would be electronically transmitted across the network to Tinker. After collecting all of the hourly reports for weather stations on a given network, Tinker would assemble them into appropriate lists, and distribute the lists by transmitting them back to each of the weather stations on the network. The Desert Center weather station received hourly and special weather reports from all over the world. The reports would automatically print out on the various teletype printers that were also located in the teletype room. The room contained seven teletype printers, along with a fax machine that received electronically transmitted weather charts. The machines ran constantly and printed out huge quantities of weather reports. In addition to preparing weather observations, the duty observer also had to perform a wide variety of clerical duties. These included tearing the printed reports off the machines, cutting them into useable sections, and posting them in their designated places in the forecaster's room, which was connected to the observer's area. The walls in the forecaster's room were covered with current weather maps, charts, and paper reports, all posted for display. The weather information was constantly updated. Keeping the weather displays current required a large percentage of the observer's time and attention.

Every morning at 1:00 a.m., the old reports and charts were taken down from their display cases, and archived to one of the storage closets at the station. The weather officers periodically reviewed the archived reports and disposed of them as appropriate. Enlisted men like Payne and myself, never threw much of anything away. Consequently, as I stood outside of the doorway to the teletype room waiting for Payne to finish, I couldn't help but wonder what it was that he had thrown into the large dumpster outside.

While I waited, the nearest teletype machine started printing the first of the hourly reports received from SAUS 4. The loud noise made by the printer attracted my attention. Out of force of habit, I visually checked the printer's paper supply. Suddenly, my mind took note of the cleanliness of the teletype room and of the weather station in general. The entire place was clean, neat, and orderly. There wasn't a single printer or a single weather report that hadn't been properly tended to.

I found that to be very surprising. I always conscientiously performed my weather observing duties, even when I was working alone on night shifts. My good friend Dwight did also. Most weather observers did not. Once in a while, late at night, I sometimes allowed a complete hour to pass before I made another round of the teletype machines. Usually I would be reading an interesting book, day dreaming. or something. Then I would hurry and catch up again. Most observers, however, would go to sleep on night shift, even though that was a court martial offense. Jim Payne was no exception. On many past occasions when he had worked the mid shift, I had come in early at 5:45 a.m. to wake him up and help him clean up the piles of teletype paper that lay untended in the teletype room. On one comical and rainy morning, the piles of untended printed reports were so deep and convoluted they were tangled around the fluorescent light fixtures that hung from the ceiling. While I was cutting the continuous rolls of paper down from the lights, Payne was exclaiming to me in satisfied tones, "I tell you, Charlie, that was some nap I had."

Payne finished typing up the report. He locked the resulting paper tape in the tape reader and punched the red 'ready to transmit' button. Everything after that would happen automatically. Usually several minutes passed before transmission actually occurred. He turned towards me, smiling and happy. "See how clean everything is, Charlie," he said proudly. "I'm getting to be just like you. I stayed up all night, wide awake, just as I'm supposed to. I spent the entire evening just cutting paper."

Good friends that we were, we both laughed together. I responded, "I'm really impressed, Jim. That new girl friend you met in Phoenix when you were on Christmas leave must be a good influence on you. When will you see her again?"

"Not until Easter," he said. "I can hardly wait. My parents are going to drive over to Arizona and get her. They'll bring her with them when they come to visit me."

We both laughed some more and I said, "If you're not careful Jim, your mother and father will have you married off by the Fourth of July."

"No, no," Payne responded in a comical manner. "I'm too young to die."

Yes, Small Jimmy Payne could sure be a fun person to be around. As we both walked back towards the large observer's desk located in the northwest corner of the room, Payne said, "This has been a good week for me, Charlie. A few days ago, I won $200 playing seven-card stud poker up in the casinos in Las Vegas. Then on Thursday, Dwight and I both had a good laugh at Master Sergeant Walters expense."

"Really," I answered. "How did that happen?"

"Well, you know that story about Range Four Harry, you were telling Walters, Dwight, and I, last fall," said Payne.

"You mean about the time last summer that I was down on Range One and I was closing up for the afternoon and I happened to see a white woman and three children playing out in the sagebrush," I said.

"Yes," responded Payne. "Remember how you were saying that she and the children were playfully chasing around a quail hen with her string of baby chicks while Range Four Harry stood guard. You said that for twenty minutes he blocked the driveway that connects the Range One graveled area with the Range One road?"

"Yes," I answered. "I remember that day quite well."

"Well, after you left here, that day," Payne said, "Sergeant Walters stated he didn't believe the story. Well Dwight and I just laughed at him. Dwight and I reminded Walters that both of us had personally seen Range Four Harry from a distance out there on the Ranges, so we knew you were telling the truth. Well, Walters told Dwight and I that he would buy us both a cup of coffee if we could ever demonstrate that your quail story was believable."

"And last week, you did," I exclaimed?

"Yes," Payne laughed, "and Sergeant Walters was so shocked he was speechless."

"How did you do it," I asked?

"Well," said Payne, "Captain Grant was reading through the archived weather reports last week. It is part of a climate study that he is doing. He came across a group of Mojave Wells wind reports from nine years ago. They were taken in the summertime down on Range One by an observer named Davis."

"I remember seeing a few of his entries in the old Range One log books," I responded.

Payne continued, "Well, on one of the afternoon reports, in that bottom section of the reporting form that's used for comments, he made an entry. He wrote that he believed he saw a white woman with several children playfully chasing a quail hen with baby chicks. He wrote that because of the intense heat waves coming off the dry lakebed, he couldn't see them very well. However, he believed they were out in the sagebrush just beyond the skip bomb area east of the Range One weather shack. They were more than half a mile away at the time. I tell you Charlie, as soon as Dwight and I saw that report we took it to Walters. We told him that we both took our coffee black." Payne stood laughing for a bit, obviously proud of his accomplishments.

I laughed too. Then I said, "Thanks, Jim. I really appreciate what you did. Master Sergeant Walters has been treating me with more respect these past few months. That must have had made a big impression on him.

"You know according to Davis' entries in the old Range One logs, he started having missing blocks of time a few days after that incident. One afternoon he couldn't remember anything that had happened for more than two and a half hours. When he finally came to his senses, he wrote that he had become absolutely terrified of the sagebrush down there. The next log entry states that Davis just couldn't take being alone out on the Ranges, and he was transferred to someplace in Europe."

"It doesn't surprise me," said Payne. "Nobody can take the Ranges except you, Charlie. None of us who have seen Range Four Harry walking around out there in the sunshine, can ever figure out where you get the courage to go out on the Ranges alone, day after day, the way you always do. Man, after that white alien woman scared me off from Range One that time, there's no way in the world that I would ever go back out to any of those Ranges alone. Even when Dwight is with me, we only take the 8:00 a.m. run. We make up all of the rest of the reports and phone them in from the chow hall.

"But you, you're so brave you still drive way out there even at night without giving things a second thought. I will just never know where you get the courage. If you ever got in trouble when you are out there, you would be totally on your own."

"Well, I'm not smart enough to make up a decent looking set of wind measurements like you, Jim," I chuckled, "So I have to drive out onto the Ranges and actually measure the winds."

Payne laughed and slapped me on my left shoulder, "You're something else, Charlie," he said, "I better hurry if

I'm going to make it to church on time. Thanks for relieving me early.

"By the way, don't let the Major surprise you today. Last week I saw him typing up a big award for you. It was something about you holding a balloon with a light attached for five minutes before releasing it during a snowstorm up at Mojave Wells. Some General kept bugging him on the phone to make sure the wording was correct. It's supposed to be a secret award so I suppose he intends to come in unannounced today and surprise you."

With that, Jim Payne quickly picked up his things and hurried out through the front door of the weather station. "Thanks, Jim," I shouted after him as he left.

Since it was a pleasant morning and the weather was nice, there really wasn't much for me to do for a while. The place was already tidy, so I sat down at the observer's station and took out a blank weather chart. Preparing the local area weather charts, maps, and diagrams was one of the observer's routine clerical duties. Just to pass the time, I thought I would get an early start on the set that I was responsible for.

The duty forecaster for the day was the Irish American sergeant named O'Keefe. He arrived on schedule at 10:00 a.m. sharp. I held a deep respect for O'Keefe. He was dedicated, hard working, and intelligent. He was also quite proudly Irish. Ordinarily on Sundays he was quite light hearted and fun to work with. However, today, he was unusually serious. He spent the first twenty minutes of his shift studying the charts in the forecaster's section. Then he came into the observer's section where I was working. He carefully checked everywhere including the teletype room. Then he asked very seriously, "Charlie, where are the

56

SAUS 4, 5, and 6 weather reports from last night? We seem to be missing all of the reports from 8:00 p.m. last night until 5:00 a.m. this morning. Was there a power outage or something?"

"I don't think so, Sergeant," I answered. "Small Jimmy Payne didn't mention any problems. I suppose the reports have been filed on the clipboards out front where they're supposed to be."

The two of us proceeded to walk out front to the forecaster's area. Sergeant O'Keefe picked up the clipboard labeled "SAUS 5". It appeared to contain the proper number of pieces of teletype paper and therefore, appeared at first glance to contain all of the weather reports transmitted by Tinker AFB for at least the last eighteen hours. However, Sergeant O'Keefe flipped through the reports with a practiced hand and said, "Look at those date-time stamps, Charlie. All of the reports from last night are missing. It's like that for all of the reports from SAUS 4 and 6 as well. All of the weather reports for the entire western United States are missing."

I was shocked. Quickly I checked the clipboards holding the reports from SAUS 1, 2, and 3. Their reports were missing also. "I don't know what could have happened, Sergeant," I exclaimed. "Everything looked fine when I came in this morning."

"I'll bet I know, Charlie," he smiled. "Last night was Saturday night. I'll bet that last night the airmen down in the base operations section of this building got into a big poker game. Sure as the devil, Small Jimmy Payne and the weather observer who was working last night's swing shift joined in the game. Like as not, they took turns sending the hourly weather reports, so those are accurate. However, the weather was good all over the southwest so the two of them let the teletype machines run unattended. When the game finished up at 5:00 a.m., the swing shift observer was too tired to help clean up the huge mess of paper in the teletype room so he just went home. Payne knew it would take him hours to clean up the mess, so I'll bet he just carried all of the missing reports outside to the white elephant in the parking lot.

"I wonder if you wouldn't do me a favor, Charlie, and go out to the dumpster and bring in all of the missing weather reports that you can find. I know cutting, sorting, and posting all eight hour's worth of those reports is going to be a big job, but I really need to see them in order to make up a reliable forecast for tomorrow."

"Yes, Sergeant," I answered carefully and slowly. "The extra work is no trouble."

Seeing the surprised look on my face, Sergeant O'Keefe began laughing. "See, Charlie. Payne can't fool me because I'm all Irish. He can fool you because you're only half Irish. Your other half is English. When you're around Small Jimmy Payne, you need to get in touch with your Irish half or he'll pull the wool over your eyes every time." Then the good Sergeant walked happily back into the forecaster's section, laughing every step of the way.

I spent the next four hours working at a feverish pace, cutting, sorting, and posting all of the missing reports from the previous night. At one point, I had to actually climb into the large rectangular dumpster to retrieve some reports from the midnight printout. Sergeant O'Keefe spent those same four hours laughing and teasing me. He said the experience qualified me to march in the next Saint Patrick's Day parade.

A week passed. Sunday morning arrived. Once again I was scheduled to work the day shift. As before I would be relieving Jim Payne. The Major had given Payne a good chewing out for the previous episode so I was expecting the station to be fairly ship-shape when I arrived early at 6:45 a.m. I wasn't disappointed. Payne met me at the door when I arrived. He was happy and smiling. He showed me all around the station. It was shiny and spotless. He even offered to show me the dumpster. "It is so empty that you can even climb inside," he laughed. We parted, still the closest of friends. He made it to church for the 8:00 a.m. Mass.

An hour passed. I checked the dumpster. It was quite empty, the way it should have been. At first glance, all of the displays in the Forecaster's section appeared to be in order. I took the 9:00 a.m. hourly report and transmitted it as required. Alone in building, I walked down to the break area and got a cup of coffee with lots of cream and sugar, just the way I liked it. As I was walking back into the observer's section, I suddenly noticed that the wind recorder had been moved slightly. It sat on a table that was positioned in front of the window on the east side of the observer's section. That window was nicely framed and decorated with two cotton curtains. The curtains had a crisp blue and white checkered design, and the wind recorder now sat in front of one of them. I didn't think much about it. Jim Payne was so muscular he could move heavy equipment like that as easily as ordinary children play with their toys.

As I walked across the room towards the chair on the north side, I noticed that the waist tall wastebasket had also been moved by a small amount. It now sat in front of the other curtain. It didn't seem important at the time, either. Payne had, after all, swept the floor before I had come in this morning.

I shrugged everything off and went back to reading the history book that I had brought with me this morning. The book was on the history of the Black Hawk war of 1832. According to historians, one rainy afternoon during the war, the Sauk Indian leader named Black Sparrow Hawk, led his followers in retreat directly across the piece of land that now formed the front yard of the house where I grew up in London, Wisconsin. I became quite engrossed in the book. Consequently, I was quite startled when Sergeant O'Keefe walked in at 9:40 a.m. He was carrying the clipboard that held the SAUS 5 reports in his hand. He was laughing quite heavily as he said, "I see Small Jimmy Payne has pulled one over on you again, Charlie."

"Good morning, Sergeant," I said in surprise. "You are here early, as usual. Why do you say that I've been tricked again?"

O'Keefe could hardly contain his amusement. "All of last night's weather reports are missing again. Only this time Payne has tried to conceal it by placing some of last year's reports on the display boards in their places. I sure hope for his sake that he's been winning at the Saturday night poker game."

"How can that be, Sergeant," I asked.

O'Keefe handed me the clipboard, and said, "Here, Charlie. Look at this date-time stamp the way an Irishman would. What year is that 1:00 a.m. report for?"

Shocked, I saw immediately that it was last year's report for the same day and month as today was. It couldn't possibly have come off the teletype machine the night before.

O'Keefe continued chuckling, "I'm afraid that if you can't locate the missing rolls of teletype paper, Charlie, you're going to have to send a procedural message to Tinker and ask them to retransmit the missing reports for SAUS 4, 5, and 6. I'm sorry, Charlie, but it's going to be another busy Sunday for you."

He was quite right, another busy Sunday it was. While I was waiting for the retransmission from Tinker to begin, I checked everywhere for the missing reports. I checked the dumpster in the parking lot. I checked the White Elephant dumpster that sat outside of our building on the flight line. I even checked the two similar dumpsters that sat on the flight line down by the nearby hangers and the fire station. The missing reports simply weren't anywhere to be found. They had simply vanished into thin air.

As I was returning to the weather station, I got to thinking. The easiest way for paper to vanish into thin air is to go up in flames. When I got back inside the weather station, it seemed reasonable, therefore, for me to carefully check the tall waste paper basket that sat next to the curtains. The morning light on a section of the curtain immediately revealed a problem to me. The lower edges had been singed in a fire. Further inspection showed that both curtains contained burn marks. The heat had also pealed off the paint on the inside of the tall metal wastebasket.

Wednesday arrived. Jim Payne and I were seated alone at a table in the chow hall enjoying the evening meal. Close friends that we were, I began by pleasantly teasing him. I was no dummy. He was too big to fight with. "You know, Jim," I said, "The men in my family have a saying."

"Yes, Charlie," he replied.

"We always say that 'two moves is a fire'. You see, whenever we see that two things have moved around in the world we live in, such as a table or a wastebasket or a wind recorder, we figure it means that there's been a fire."

He began laughing immediately. "I notice that you didn't tell the Major about the curtains, Charlie. Thanks. I owe you a favor for that one. You should have seen me as I stood next to the burning paper, holding the fire extinguisher. I was in perfect military form and everything. I started by burning the high altitude wind reports. They were simply reports about the thin air going up into the thin air. I just hadn't expected the curtains would be so flimsy."

After he finished laughing, I said, "If the Major sees those burn marks, we can tell him it's just the curtains showing their age, but Jim, please be more careful in the future. That fire extinguisher isn't very large, and the weather station is built like a tinderbox. Those spare bottles of ink for the wind recorder that are sitting on the table are highly flammable, and those bottles of cleaning fluid have alcohol in them. That fire could have easily gotten out of control and trapped you inside the building. When you started the fire, the wastebasket was positioned between you and all of your safe exits. A big man like you might never have gotten out of there alive."

"You're right, Charlie," answered Payne thoughtfully. "I'll be more careful in the future."

The following Sunday morning arrived. Weather observer's worked rotating shifts, and I had been scheduled to work the mid shift from 12:00 a.m. to 8:00 a.m. Sunday morning, with Payne relieving me. However, it was common for observers to trade shifts. Payne asked if he could once again work the mid shift, and I would work the day shift instead. I readily agreed, so once again, I was working the Sunday day shift. As usual, I woke up at 3:00 a.m. By the time that 4:00 a.m. arrived, I found myself dying of curiosity over how things were going for Payne on his shift. I decided that I might as well get up and go down to the weather station and help out. It was easier to clean the printed weather reports out of the teletype room then to clean them out of the dumpster. I put on my duty uniform and began the mile long walk to the weather station. I was still several blocks away when I suddenly saw large red and yellow flames coming from the white elephant dumpster out in back of the weather station. The building blocked part of my viewing angle, so at first I wasn't sure that I could believe my eyes. Once I realized that the dumpster was actually on fire, I began running down the street towards the weather station. While I was running, a large red fire engine with its light flashing came out from the fire station located down on the flight line. It went rushing up along the parking ramp and stopped next to the burning dumpster. In a few minutes, the fire had been put out. Seeing that the fire had been extinguished, I stopped running. I was still two or three blocks from the weather station. I could see that the building had not been damaged, and Jim Payne was talking to the firemen standing out in back of it. I stopped and thought things over. No one had seen me yet, or knew that I was up and about. Payne obviously had all of his bases covered. The military being what it is, I decided that my life would be better off if I quietly returned to my barracks and went back to bed for a while.

Along about 6:30 a.m., I decided it was safe to get out of bed again. I walked to the chow hall and ate breakfast in a leisurely fashion. I arrived at the weather station at the respectable time of 7:45 a.m., and nonchalantly walked inside. Jim Payne had been sweeping the floor, as well as the concrete tarmac outside. He was just finishing up. "Hi Jim," I greeted him. "I'm here to relieve you. I'll take the 8:00 a.m. hourly report, and you can still catch the morning Mass if you hurry."

Payne was all smiling and happy. "Thanks, Charlie. I'll take you up on that offer."

"How did the evening go, Jim," I asked innocently.

"Not bad, Charlie," Payne responded with a good natured smile. "We had a short network outage, so I have already sent a procedural message to Tinker Air Base requesting that they retransmit last night's SAUS 4, 5, and 6 reports. They responded saying they will begin the retransmission at 8:30 a.m. this morning. Thanks for switching shifts with me, Charlie."

"Anytime, Jim," I responded, "Say, Jim, before you leave, I was just wondering how you came out at the poker game down in Base Operations last night?"

"Really great," smiled Payne. "I made almost seventy five dollars."

"Well I figured that things must have been pretty hot last night for you," I teased.

Payne chuckled and looked straight at me. "You know perfectly well what happened last night, don't you Charlie," he asked.

"Officially, I don't know a thing," I said laughing. "My lips are sealed. However, Jim, while I was walking to the station this morning, I happened to notice that the fire station has a large incinerator right behind it. According to Air Force Regulations, they have to test it everyday by starting a large fire in it. It looks like it might be able to hold as much as two large wastebaskets of paper. Those guys are always scrounging around for things to burn. Of course, in good weather, a big muscular man like you could probably trot down there to get a better view of the sky, and be back here inside of five minutes, even if you were to, say, be carrying one of these tall wastebaskets in each hand. I wouldn't think much of anything would slow you down. On Saturday nights, they're all young enlisted men down there. It's not likely they would be asking much in the way of questions, especially if you happened to buy them a cup of coffee from time to time."

Payne's eyes lit up and he exclaimed, "You're a genius, Charlie. That's one place Sergeant O'Keefe would never think of looking." Then he slapped me on the back of my left shoulder in a friendly manner and exclaimed, "Thanks. I better hurry so I can get to church on time." The front door of the weather station slammed shut behind him as he left.

I put my things down on the observer's desk and hurriedly took and transmitted the 8:00 a.m. weather report. Doing so took a great deal of skill since I had to do so one handed. My left shoulder ached for half an hour. Small Jimmy Payne was, after all, at least 240 pounds of solid muscle.

A week passed. During that next week Payne went on leave. I was working mid shift from 12:00 a.m. to 8:00 a.m. Sunday morning. It was a very cold and very rainy evening. The rain had started up at about 9:00 p.m. on Saturday night. It was obviously raining heavily all over the Palm Meadows valley. As usual, the forecaster left at 5: 00 p.m.

in the afternoon, leaving the duty observer alone in the station, as well as alone in the building.

Having nothing better to do, I reported for duty at 9:50 p.m., two hours early. As I entered the weather station, I could see that the weather observer before me was already sleeping soundly at his desk, even though the airbase was still open. I signed in. I quietly took and transmitted the 10:00 p.m. report before I awakened the sleeping observer. He was one of the married observers with children, so I helped him wake up over a cup of coffee before I walked him to his car and waved him goodbye. Of course, before I took the 10:00 p.m. report, I removed the junk weather report from the transmitter that he had placed there two hours before. In my hourly report, I intentionally closed the Desert Center airbase for the entire evening because of the rainy weather. Part of being an effective weather observer was knowing when to shut things down and take things easy. I phoned the control tower and informed them that if some airplane were out flying tonight and had an actual emergency, they should phone me and I would help them land at Desert Center if it was at all possible. The tower operator, alone in the tower, thanked me profusely for letting him know that I was there to help him.

A short time later, I was reading over the 10:00 p.m. weather reports from SAUS 5. I was surprised to see that every other weather station, except my station at Desert Center, was reporting that they had clear skies, warm temperatures, and dry air. This included the weather report from Palm Meadows, located only twenty miles down the valley from my station at Desert Center. According to their reports, the weather all over the Desert Southwest was perfect for flying. Of course, all of the other airbases remained open as well.

I got a fresh cup of coffee, finished posting the printed reports, and turned to reading some more pages from my history book. As the evening progressed, hour after hour, this simple sequence began repeating itself. I would take and transmit the hourly report for Desert Center. It would say that the base was closed, the clouds were laying on the runway, the visibility was zero, the temperature was cold enough to form ice on the wings of airplanes, and the winds were light and gentle. Every other station for more or less 200 miles around was reporting perfect weather, clear skies with warm dry winds. Palm Meadows also continued to report perfect evening weather.

This went on, hour after hour, until after 5:00 a.m. At 5:15 a.m., after I had received the Palm Meadows report, I picked up the telephone, and phoned the Palm Meadows weather station. I let the phone ring. After ringing for a very long time, perhaps as long as four minutes, a sleepy voice answered on the other end. Speaking pleasantly and distinctly, I said, "Hi. This is Airman Charlie Baker. I'm the duty observer up here at Desert Center. I was just wondering if it was still clear and warm down at Palm Meadows because it is cold and raining where I am."

There was a short pause on the other end. Then the observer on the other end shouted in a shocked manner, "That's rain out there!" and slammed down the phone. Hardly one minute later, the teletype machine began printing out emergency weather change notices as first Desert Center, then every other station in SAUS 5 in tern, reported that their bases were rained in and closed due to weather.

When Sergeant O'Keefe came in later that morning, he spent his first hour of duty phoning many of the other weather stations just to laugh. When he phoned George AFB, he was laughing, "Some nights it just takes an Irishman."

The Present Time

He said to the crowd:
　　"When you see a cloud rising in the west,
　　　immediately you say,
　　　　'It's going to rain,'
　　　　　and it does.

And when the south wind blows,
　　you say,
　　　　'It's going to be hot,'
　　　　　and it is.

You know how to interpret
　　the appearance
　　　of the earth and the sky.

How is it that you don't know
　　how to interpret this present time?

　　　　　　　　…Luke 12:54,56

It was a warm Friday afternoon at Mojave Wells. Early spring was well underway and the desert was just beginning to warm up after the long cold winter. The valley had been filled with the quiet nighttime beauty of the full moon only two evenings before. As far as I knew, I was alone on base.

I intended to catch the afternoon bus into Palm Meadows and then make the long bus ride up to Las Vegas for a weekend of gambling. I was taking a shower. Of course, military showers seem designed to be sung in, and this one was no exception. Its extra sturdy tile covered walls added interesting acoustical overtones to the songs that I enjoyed singing, usually off-key. On this afternoon, I was dusting off my new spring repertoire, so I guess that every seagull within three miles would have been able to tell that I was in the shower.

I heard a noise coming from my barracks area. Of course, it had to be a fairly loud noise for me to hear it above my singing. Dripping wet, I left the shower, grabbed my towel, and casually wandered over to the door of the bathroom. I was drying myself off as I looked out into the main part of the barracks. My bunk area was at the far end of the barracks, off to my right and across the aisle next to the outer door. The barracks wasn't particularly large, having room for perhaps sixteen or twenty men, so the distance from the bathroom door to my bunk wasn't long. Practically all of the bunk areas were unused. This barracks had a reasonable number of windows. I had previously opened the window next to my bunk, although I had left the screen on.

Looking out through the open bathroom doorway, I could see the same, chubbier than usual, little white boy I'd last seen the previous October. He was wearing his protective suit and floating several feet off the floor. He was happily inspecting my metal locker. I had left both of its doors open while I showered. I could see that the guard had removed the screen to my open window. The guard was standing outside watching everything. It was the guard who had told me to call him "The Tour Guide". Several feet behind the little chubby boy floated another boy, this one quite thin. He, too, was wearing a protective suit. I had never seen the second little boy before. He seemed quite nervous and noticeably afraid of me. The noise had been created when he had accidentally knocked one of my canteens onto the floor. The little chubby boy had apparently been showing him the contents of my metal locker, so I guessed that the other must have been a new arrival.

I stood silently at the doorway to the bathroom watching them. I thought it would be nice to live to an old age, so I had no intention of scaring them. Even so, as soon as the newcomer saw me, he reacted in a frightened manner. He headed towards the open window and made good his escape. Both the guard and the chubby boy were laughing. They apparently found the entire situation to be quite humorous. The chubby boy, who knew me, was totally unafraid of me. He took his sweet time checking out the inside of my metal locker before he too, exited out through the open window. After they had left, I said to myself, "I see that springtime has returned to the Ranges."

I noted that the familiar boy appeared to be quite healthy and he was still the same size as he had been during the previous summer. From this I concluded that the tall white children must grow much more slowly than human children. I decided that perhaps the tall white beings might live to be much older than humans.

I finished drying myself off and wandered casually back to my bunk area. As I got dressed for my trip to Las Vegas, I wondered why the guard had been willing to bring the new boy in so close to town. Surely he must have known in advance that my locker contained very little that would be of interest to children. My metal locker was of the usual design. It was six feet tall or so and locked with a key. It had two metal doors, some drawers, some metal shelves, and a place to hang my uniforms. I kept it clean and uncluttered. At the time, for example, the open shelf in the middle held only a couple of decks of cards, a half written letter home, a book I had purchased on the game of Blackjack, and two books on western history that I had checked out from the Desert Center base library.

I put on my underwear and tee shirt and wandered back to the bathroom to brush my teeth and shave. Out through the open bathroom window, I could see in the distance the group of white beings as they retreated out into the desert, and to the safety of the distant sagebrush covered ranges. Surprisingly, the group appeared to include only one guard and the two children. The group was traveling quickly and was more than a mile away at the time, so I wasn't able to make out many details. However, the guard did not appear to be wearing his protective suit. He was walking quickly through the lanes in the sagebrush and across the various open areas covered with soft dirt and desert sand. I went back to shaving and getting ready for the weekend, wondering why he was willing to bring the two boys so close in, with so little in the way of military protection.

Ten days or so passed. I was taking the 4:30 a.m. run at Range Three. The Ranges had appeared to be deserted and everything seemed quite normal. It was a warm morning with very little wind. I was carrying my balloon out to the theodolite stand before releasing it when I saw that same guard, The Tour Guide, step out from behind the Range Three lounge building. Without greeting me, he walked smoothly over to the base of the control tower. He was the guard whose life I was credited with saving the previous autumn. Of course, he and I trusted each other.

He took up a position twenty feet east of the base of the tower, and stood sideways, looking back towards the hidden area behind the lounge building. Then three young white females walked out from behind the lounge building. They looked as much alike as any three sisters. In a very formal fashion, they lined up side by side at the base of the control tower and stood watching me, all in near total silence. They were all the same height, standing perhaps an inch shorter than I. They were wearing their ordinary chalk white aluminum canvas clothing. This meant that neither the guard nor any of the three white females were wearing the protective suits that were commonly worn by the tall whites. I checked my thoughts to see if they were trying to communicate with me, but drew a blank there as well. I wasn't afraid, but I was somewhat mystified. It was unusual for the white beings to be willing to meet me so completely on my terms. I was further perplexed because I supposed that the three white females were new arrivals and yet, they appeared to be totally unafraid of me.

I released the balloon and continued with my morning wind measurements. I didn't say anything to the white beings, or make any attempt to walk over by them. They were standing probably seventy-five feet away from me at the time, too far to carry on a conversation. "Anyway, why risk upsetting them," I thought to myself. "They are certain to be well armed. They have their business and I have mine." Experience had taught me that my business was staying alive. Interfering with their business wouldn't help that any.

When I had finished taking my readings, I left my theodolite open in case they were interested in looking through it. I picked up my clipboard and returned to my weather shack. The tall whites, however, remained on station watching me. After I completed my calculations, I phoned Desert Center, tidied up the inside of my weather shack, and locked up. Still the tall whites remained on station, watching my every move. Hungry for breakfast, I locked up my theodolite, shut down the diesel, started my truck, and headed in to base, wondering what could possibly be going on. All the while, the tall whites remained on station, watching my every move.

When I returned from breakfast, the Ranges were deserted and everything was back to normal. However, a careful inspection of my weather shack convinced me that the tall whites had opened it up and checked out the interior during my absence. What I found surprising was that only my personal items showed any evidence of having been moved or looked at. All of my tools and supplies appeared to have been untouched.

Another ten days or so passed. Since it was now past the evening of the new moon, I supposed that the three white females and the new little boy may have left on the deep space craft which I had observed departing on a fairly regular schedule. It seemed logical since they had all presumably arrived on that same craft two weeks before during the night of the full moon. Still wishing to live to an old age, I went about my business and didn't bother looking for them. I completed the morning run, shut down the diesel, and headed in for breakfast.

When I returned after breakfast, once again the Ranges were deserted and everything seemed normal. I brought out one of my two western history books and spent an enjoyable day reading. Over the noon break I stopped by my barracks. Everything inside was quite normal. At the end of the day when I returned to my barracks, I found that my metal locker had been unlocked. The door on the right stood part way open, and someone had been paging through the other one of my two library books on western history. I had previously left the book closed, sitting on the shelf of my locker. The hardbound book now sat half open on that same shelf. Whoever had opened up my locker, appeared to have read at least the first 200 pages. "Somebody around here enjoys reading," I said to myself as I closed the book and tidied up my locker. I checked my watch. Whoever had been in my locker would have had no more than two hours to read the first 200 pages of my history book. That, of course, is a reading rate of approximately 100 pages per hour. Since I typically read those same books at the rate of less than forty pages per hour, sometimes only twenty pages per hour, I noted that whoever was reading my books was a much faster reader than I was. I concluded that the books in my locker must have attracted someone who was interested in history. I did find the entire incident somewhat mystifying, however, since none of the tall whites in the past had ever shown any particular interest in reading my history books.

Another week or so passed, not without some moderate excitement. One afternoon out at Range Three, two fighter planes flying side by side on a training run, collided. Both pilots parachuted out safely. I had used my theodolite to record the place out in the desert where one of the pilots had landed. He had a broken leg at the time, and had fallen into one of the numerous depressions. My help had allowed the ground maintenance crew, the Range Rats, to drive directly to him, without having to search the surrounding desert to find him. The other pilot had landed in the skip bomb area, so I was able to walk out with some water and help him with his parachute. I was happy to help and I received a commendation for pointing out the location of the downed pilot to the Range Rats.

Shortly after that, I was again driving out to Range Three for the morning run. I could see that the same group of three tall white females and the guard were already waiting for me at the base of the control tower. As usual, I ignored them and went on about my business. As I was filling the balloon in my weather shack, the group changed station. This time, in a very formal manner, the three females formed up side by side in a line facing me. Then, in unison they advanced towards my theodolite stand, all in near total silence. They stopped about twenty feet north of the stand. The guard remained at the base of the control tower. When I brought my balloon out from the side door of my weather shack, I could see that I had no choice but to walk directly over towards them in order to reach my theodolite stand. This caused me a great deal of apprehension. Except for the Teacher, the Tour Guide, and a handful of other white beings I was familiar with, I ordinarily didn't feel safe approaching them. They panicked easily and they were always well armed. I greatly preferred to stand in one place and let them approach me.

Having no alternative, I began singing one of my favorite songs, and with my balloon and clipboard in hand I walked slowly over to my theodolite. I released the balloon and proceeded with the morning wind measurements. The three females were a little too far away to carry on an ordinary conversation. However, I felt that just for my own safety, I should greet them in some manner. So, after recording the second reading, I spoke to them politely. Looking at them, I said, "Hello. I'm Airman Charlie Baker. I hope this evening air is warm enough for you."

There was no response. They simply remained standing silently, observing my every move. "Well, if they're happy, I'm happy," I thought to myself as I continued with my morning balloon run.

When I had completed the last measurement, I stood up carefully, took my clipboard in hand, and said to them politely, "Please don't be surprised. I'm going to go back to the weather shack now. I need to complete these calculations and phone Desert Center. If you want to look through my theodolite, you should feel free to do so."

Once again, there was no response. Once again, they remained standing silently, observing my every move. This time, however, the two females on the right appeared to smile a little, in a very formal manner. The third female appeared to show a slight twinge of nervousness and fear. Instinctively I responded, "Don't be afraid. I'm leaving now. I won't come any closer." I carefully backed away from the three of them. As soon as I had noticed the third female's apprehension, the guard appeared to respond by giving me a look of tremendous respect. He appeared to have been impressed by my ability to observe small details in the behavior of the three females.

I turned slowly and walked back to the safety of my weather shack. As before, the tall whites remained on station, watching my every move. As before, I completed the morning run, shut down the diesel, and headed to base for breakfast.

Another two weeks passed. Reading my western history library books was taking longer than I had expected, so it was necessary for me to drive in to Desert Center and renew them. It was a beautiful drive. The desert was covered with spring flowers, although the tops of the mountains remained covered with snow.

I scheduled a routine trip to the Desert Center base dentist for the same afternoon. Of course, I informed Desert Center that I would be skipping all of the afternoon runs so that I would be able to make it to the dentist on time. My weather commanders and the base commander all readily agreed.

I felt that my teeth could use a routine cleaning. Of course, all dental work in the U.S. military is free to soldiers, so having my teeth cleaned was sort of like taking the afternoon off. It was, after all, spring and dental offices frequently have beautiful young female assistants.

The dental offices were in another wing of the Desert Center base hospital, and the medical personnel tended to exchange stories over lunch. All of the medical personnel seemed to know me, although none of them would say why. I was sitting in the waiting room reading a sports magazine when a lady probably in her late thirties, wearing dentist's attire came out through the double doors. She cheerfully approached me. "So you're Airman Charlie Baker," she exclaimed, offering to shake my hand as she did so.

I took note of the bird Colonel insignias she was wearing and decided that she must be the dentist who would clean my teeth. Since I was only an enlisted man, it seemed odd that she was so eager to meet me, and so willing to shake my hand, but I obliged her. I responded, "Yes, ma-am. It's nice to meet you. I'm here to have my teeth checked and cleaned."

"Yes, of course you are," she responded. Then she showed me the way to one of the dentist's offices in the back. Along the way I noted that I was the only patient that she had scheduled for the entire afternoon. "Well, she is a bird Colonel," I said to myself. "I don't suppose that any of them work very hard."

Once I was in the examining room, I climbed into the dentist's chair and made ready for my routine exam. The exam started with a routine set of x-rays of all of my teeth, both top and bottom. When the x-rays were ready, she took a stool next to me, positioned the x-ray photos so we could both see them, and began talking to me in a friendly manner.

"Airman Baker, it's so nice to finally meet you. I'm new here. I've heard so much about you. You're not anything like what I was expecting," she began.

I really wasn't prepared to receive so much attention from an officer. "Perhaps you were expecting someone taller than me," I awkwardly responded. "If you'd like, I can begin eating more sweets and try to grow six inches."

She had to laugh for a moment before responding, "You sure have that sense of humor I've heard about. I'm a dentist, you know. Eating more sugar never makes me happy." Then she pointed to the x-rays of my back molars, especially those in my lower left jaw. "Is that why you have such big fillings in those teeth?" she asked.

"Perhaps," I responded.

"You know, the base commander was impressed with you when he was in here yesterday," she said.

"The base commander was in here yesterday talking about me?" I asked in surprise. "You know I'm only an Airman First Class."

"Yes," she responded. "Since I'm new here, and you had a visit scheduled, he wanted to personally make certain that I had properly memorized the rules."

"The rules," I asked. "You mean the rules for dentistry, filling teeth, and things?"

"No, airman," she responded laughing. "The rules about you. He wanted to make sure that I knew how special you are. He said that you were not restricted in any way regarding the Ranges. He said that if you ever needed emergency dental assistance, that I would be the one who would be sent. He wanted to make sure I knew that even though there was nothing about your assignment that was classified, I was never to ask you any questions or keep any records of our conversation. He further said that you were never to be debriefed, criticized or reproached for any reason."

After that, she stood up and said, "Will you excuse me please? I need to show that gold and ceramic crown on your right front incisor to the other members of the staff."

She walked back to the medical offices down the hall. In a few minutes she returned with four more doctors and dentists following her. "Airman Baker," she said, "Please open wide."

"Yes, ma-am," I answered. Lady officers are always addressed using "ma-am", not "sir". Then I opened my mouth wide for the dentist.

Holding a dentist's type oral mirror, she proceeded to show my gold and ceramic crown to the other members of the group. She was saying things such as, "Have any of you ever seen a gold crown made that perfectly? See how the ceramic is molded in with the gold so the entire crown is just one piece. It appears to be brand new and what's more, the nerves to that tooth are still live. I've never seen anything remotely like it."

After several minutes of inspecting and studying, the Chief Medical Officer asked seriously, "Airman baker, was that crown put on by a human?"

"Why, yes, sir," I answered, thinking he was only trying to make a point of humor. "It was put on by an excellent dentist in Madison, Wisconsin just three years ago."

"Are you sure?" he asked. "I've never seen anything like it."

"Of course I'm sure," I said respectfully. "For all of the pain I went through getting it, I could hardly be mistaken."

"How'd you get it?" he asked.

"Well, when I was only eight years old and those two front teeth had just barely finished coming in, I was playing baseball at grade school. I was pitching and a baseball straight off the bat hit me directly in my upper jaw. It shattered a front tooth, but did not knock it out or expose the nerve. Since I come from a poor family, nothing was done about it for all the years that I was in grade school and high school. The September when I was a freshman at the University of Wisconsin in Madison, the tooth finally started aching and showing signs of some decay. Since I was a poor college student with very little extra cash, I picked out a brand new dentist and went to him for an exam. The dentist that I chose had only five other patients at the time. He did not even have a dental assistant, so during most of the sessions I had to hold some of the tools myself. He did all of the work. He personally went down to the dental lab and hand made the gold and ceramic crown. He mixed the glue and everything. If you look in the medical journals, you'll see that now he is world famous for showing the world how to make more perfect dental crowns and bridges. You'll also see pictures of this crown that he took when he was putting it on.

"I had to sit through several sessions so he could complete the work. I could only afford one shot of Novocain on one of the sessions. All of the rest of the work had to be done with the nerves in the tooth live. I had to just brace myself and ignore the pain. One session started at 4:00 p.m. and lasted all evening until almost 1:00 a.m. The entire job took almost three months. We had to wait for my jaw to heal up between some of the sessions.

"Believe me, when he put on the final crown and the work was completed, I was happy beyond words. I'm quite certain that it was put on by human hands, both his and mine."

The doctors appeared to be unconvinced. The Chief Medical Officer continued, cautiously, "Does that ever give you any trouble? For example, does it ever give a tingling sensation when you're around high power lines or radio station transmitters like it's transmitting or reflecting microwaves or anything?"

"No, of course not," I laughed. "Although it is a little sensitive to very cold weather. In Wisconsin, in the wintertime when the temperature goes down to thirty degrees below zero, I have to be very careful to keep it warm."

"To say nothing about your whole body," exclaimed the lady dentist. "One thing I don't understand, Airman Baker, is where did that dentist ever get the courage to begin drilling on that tooth when it was broken, without first desensitizing the nerve? Every patient that I have ever worked on, I have begun by first deadening the nerve. I would be scared to death to begin a job like that if the patient's nerves were still live. That sort of procedure isn't taught in dental college, even in Wisconsin. I mean, who in the world did the dentist practice on before he began working on you?"

"At the time, he said that he had practiced on the patient before me," I answered.

"The patient before you?" exclaimed the lady dentist. "Was he an alcoholic or something?"

"No," I answered. "He was a Norwegian patient, a little bit taller than I, who looked like he was in his early thirties. He had only twenty-four teeth, not thirty-two like the rest of us. I met him one winter evening when he was leaving the dentist's office. I used to see him around from time to time on the streets of Madison. Once I saw him with a lady, who also looked Norwegian. He spoke good English, although with a European accent. He had a calm and relaxed appearance."

The dentists and doctors stood stunned, just staring at me. Since they were all high ranking officers, their stares made me feel quite ill at ease. Nervous, I stammered on. "One night while the dentist was working, I jerked my head some in pain, the drill slipped, and the drill bit cut my nearby gums. Of course, I had no choice but to shrug it off and put some cotton on the wound. While the dentist and I were waiting for the bleeding to stop, I asked him about the Norwegian patient. The dentist showed me the guy's x-rays. He had only twenty-four teeth. The roots of his teeth were only half as long as the roots on my teeth. In addition, his teeth had far fewer nerves than my teeth do, so, according to the dentist, he never felt pain or toothaches like we do.

"The x-rays clearly showed that he could re-grow any tooth that he lost. As you know, ordinary people have only two sets of teeth, baby teeth and second teeth. This Norwegian, though, had a complete third set of teeth always ready to begin growing whenever the current tooth was lost.

"According to the dentist, the Norwegian first came to him with a broken front incisor just a day or so after I came to him. He had broken it while swimming in one of the nearby lakes. He also had a back molar that had worn down a great deal and he wanted it pulled out.

"The dentist claimed that the patient didn't need to have the nerves in his teeth desensitized, and just sat there while the dentist pulled out the back molar. The dentist showed it to me, by the way. It looked normal enough, but it was about twice as large as my molars, and it had real short roots.

"I guess the guy wasn't at all upset, and stated that a new molar, just like the new incisor, would grow back in within three months.

"The dentist was really shocked, and asked him if he could practice for a few minutes drilling on his front incisor before pulling it out too. The guy agreed, so the dentist took out his drill and practiced away. The guy just sat there. Then, after practicing for twenty minutes or so, the dentist put away the drill and pulled his broken incisor.

"Anyway, that's how the dentist claimed that he had practiced so he could drill on my tooth without desensitizing it."

The doctors and the dentists just stood there, speechless. Finally, the Chief Medical Officer asked cautiously, "Where did you say this guy came from, Norway?"

"I don't really know," I said. "He never actually claimed to have come from Norway. He only claimed to be Norwegian. Wisconsin was certainly the place for him. One afternoon in November of that year I saw him down by lake Mendota. It was only twenty degrees out and he was walking around in his shirtsleeves, without a sweater or overcoat or anything. He looked Norwegian enough. He sure was at home in the cold. He wasn't shivering or anything. He had quite a sense of humor. He told the dentist that he had slightly webbed feet and that he expected to live to be 140 years old. He said he didn't remember much about where he came from. He insisted that it was pretty close by. Of course, in Wisconsin there are lots of towns that were settled by Norwegians, so he could have come from anywhere.

"He further claimed that he and his parents had left their home when he was only four and it took them twenty years to get here. He told how one of his sets of grandparents had come here before him. He believed the Nazis in World War II had put the grandparents to death, claiming that twenty-four teeth made them less than perfect humans. I used to laugh about that, but the dentist was sure the guy had not meant it to be funny.

"Wherever he came from, I guess that the sun there wasn't very warm or very bright. He claimed that his sun was small, even though it was close up, and lots of days you couldn't see it through the clouds. He seemed to know a lot about glaciers, frozen lakes, artic mountains, and fiords. He seemed to abhor jungles, deserts, and tropical islands. He said there weren't any jungles where he came from. Anyway, at the time, neither the dentist nor I, questioned him when he said he was Norwegian."

The doctors and the dentists all looked at each other. Then the Chief Medical Officer said quietly, "We need to discuss this out back."

They filed out and continued down the hallway to a back office. As they were walking down the hallway, I could hear the lady dentist saying, "I knew you needed to see that crown. You know, of course, that every mammal and every human that have ever lived here on this earth have had only two sets of exactly thirty-two teeth."

The Chief Medical Officer responded by saying, "Now you see why they picked him. Where does he get the guts?"

A long time passed. After a half hour passed, I became afraid that the dentist had forgotten about me. Very carefully I got out of the dentist's chair and walked slowly out into the hallway. I could see that the doctors and dentists were cloistered in an office way at the back, so I slowly walked back up front to the young lady receptionist and asked her if everything was OK. She smiled and said, "Yes, Airman Baker. Everyone is well aware that you are waiting in the dentist chair." Through the front windows, I could see the Desert Center base commander's car parked out front.

Totally confused, I slowly walked back to the dentist's office and got back into the chair. After another fifteen or twenty minutes, the lady dentist came back in, smiling and distantly friendly. This time she was extremely formal and acted as though the entire previous discussion had never taken place. Since she was a bird Colonel, I certainly had no intention of pushing the issue. She cleaned my teeth in a quick and efficient manner, and sent me on my way, hardly speaking another word to me. Just before I left her office, I turned to her and asked defensively, "I didn't do anything wrong, did I, ma-am? I mean, I was happy to answer your questions as best I could."

She smiled and responded, "No, of course not, Airman Baker. Your answers to the questions were absolutely perfect. We are always happy to listen to anything that you feel like sharing with us. You may come back anytime. You are the bravest man that any of us have ever seen, and you certainly have some excellent dentists in Wisconsin."

Then she turned and walked slowly back to the office in the back where the other doctors and dentists remained cloistered.

For my part, it was a beautiful drive back to Mojave Wells, although I was far too confused at the time to enjoy it. A few years earlier, events in my life seemed simple and reasonable. Now on any given day, more questions were raised than answered.

A few afternoons later, I ran late coming off the ranges after taking the last run of the day. I had to stop by the motor pool and refuel my truck. Then I passed some time talking with my mechanic friends there. When I finally returned to my barracks, once again I found the doors to my locker standing open. Someone had apparently finished reading my western history book, and had started reading my book on blackjack. I always made my bunk before leaving for the morning run. Someone had used my bunk and one of my decks of cards to practice playing blackjack. The cards remained laying on the top blanket of my bunk where they had been left. There had been a dealer and two players. Although I was surprised, I did have to chuckle.

The dealer had blackjack using the ace and queen of diamonds.

As I was picking up my cards and tidying up my locker, a very unusual thought crossed my mind. I wondered if I would have been able to join in the game as the dealer if I hadn't been late getting back from the ranges. I noticed that the cards and my bunk were arranged such that if I had returned on time, I would have been able to enter from the barracks door on the north, walk over to the chair that sat in the corner next to my bed and sit down. I would have been able to pick up my deck of cards that had been pre-positioned there on my side of the bunk. Then the three tall white females would have been able to approach my bunk from the south, using the south door and the north-south aisle. They could have taken up the usual positions that players assumed by arranging themselves on the south and east side of my bed. Then, with me dealing, the game of blackjack could have proceeded, continuing for as long as they felt comfortable.

I stood there for a few minutes, stunned by the simplicity of it all. The point of such an exercise obviously would not be for them to practice the game of blackjack. Rather, it would give them an opportunity to practice handing me cards and receiving the cards that I dealt to them. Yes, as I tidied up my bunk area, I was intrigued by the thoughts that suggested themselves to me.

The following Friday, the Desert Center command post requested only one balloon run for the afternoon, and they asked that it be taken early. They said that as soon as I had finished the 1:00 p.m. run, I could head in to base. It seemed ordinary enough. However, according to my good friend Dwight, the Desert Center base commander specifically suggested that I hurry back to my barracks, shower, and make the long bus ride up to Las Vegas for a fun weekend. It seemed unusual. Why would a two star General care about my weekend plans?

I was singing one of my favorite songs as I arrived back at my barracks that afternoon. I parked my truck out front on the north side and skipped up the steps to my barracks. As soon as I opened the door, I saw the tall white guard known as the Tour Guide standing in a relaxed manner behind the metal locker in the empty bunk area opposite the doorway to the bathroom. He was tall enough to observe me by looking over the top of the metal locker. He was standing next to the north-south aisle in near total silence. He had obviously been waiting for me to arrive. Since we trusted each other, I wasn't afraid, although I was noticeably surprised. It was quite rare for him to actually come inside any of the barracks. Usually he greatly preferred to stand guard outside, content to observe events through the windows. I greeted him. "Oh, hi," I said, showing some surprise.

He only smiled in response. I stood there with the door open for a minute or so. Then I cautiously entered my barracks, took off my canteen belt and laid it on my side table. I turned slowly towards him and asked politely, "Is there anything I can do to help you?" I noticed that the right door to my metal locker was open, and that one of my history books was missing.

The three white females very carefully stepped out from the bathroom and formed up into a line, crossways in the aisle facing me. They did so in a very formal manner. The aisle wasn't particularly wide and the line was positioned on a slight diagonal towards me. The three white females were noticeably cramped as they stood there. The last of the three appeared to be quite reluctant to take up her position.

The female in the middle stood holding my missing history book, so I supposed that she was the one interested in history. She was holding it with her hands slightly extended from her body. Although it was an ordinary book of only 200 or 300 pages, she obviously found it to be quite heavy and was on the verge of dropping it.

I stood quietly thinking for a minute. The tall white beings obviously intended that I should come get my book. I saw immediately that for them, this was a training meeting. They had to train themselves to overcome their fears. I decided that for some reason they wanted to practice handing me objects, just as I, myself, if I were out hiking in the African jungle, might wish to train myself to hand objects to the local gorillas. Of course, knowing that the tall white females were always well armed and capable of instant panic didn't make the training lesson any easier for me. Therefore, in order to calm both my nerves and theirs, I began by gently speaking to them, "Hello. Did you enjoy reading my history book?" There was no response. I continued, "The book is quite heavy. Would you like me to walk over to where you are so you can hand me the book?" There was still no response. Very slowly, I walked about halfway the distance to where they stood waiting. I stopped for a moment and visually checked the guard. I felt that if I were getting myself into trouble, he would give me some kind of sign. Since he remained standing with a pleasant expression on his face, I decided to proceed. Very slowly I approached the middle white female, and stopped perhaps ten feet away with my right hand slightly outstretched. As I did so, I was saying, "Don't be frightened. I won't come close enough to touch you. I only intend to come close enough so you can hand me the book if you want to."

I was going to take another few steps closer when the middle female, speaking near perfect English said in a feminine voice, "Do not come any closer. You will frighten my sister. I will bring the book to you."

While I remained standing still, she took two steps forward in a very formal manner and placed the book in my outstretched right hand. Then she stepped back to her former position. I took the book and said, "Thank you. I hope you enjoyed reading it". Then I stepped backwards several steps before I turned and walked slowly back to the corner of my barracks, placing the book on my side table as I did so. I turned again to face the three white females. The guard seemed to be quite pleased. Without further ado, the three white females turned and walked single file down the aisle away from me, and exited using the door on the southern end of the barracks. Still without saying a word, the guard turned and followed them.

I suddenly realized that these were the same three white females that I had seen the previous summer when I had walked my friend Bridges from his bunk area over to my barracks. Now I understood why they weren't afraid of me. I hadn't panicked on that occasion when I had walked in among them. They weren't expecting me to panic now, either.

Through the windows of my barracks I could see them outside in the distance, as they circled to the west and then to the north and headed back out into the desert at a fast pace. They all seemed to be very happy.

Later, as I was taking my shower and preparing to catch the bus up to Las Vegas, I thought further about these events. I wondered if they had been on a similar training mission the previous summer when they had approached Bridges in his barracks. I wondered about that. Why Bridges? The tall whites would surely never have come in so close without a very good reason. Bridges had been a world-class expert at the game of pool; a game that the tall whites might well enjoy playing. He was also famous for having self-control. His opponents had always wondered if he had ice water in his veins. There was a certain logic to it. The tall whites would not have expected Bridges, of all people, to become hysterical. He had, after all, played pool up in Las Vegas with unusual looking humans from all over the world. Playing pool is an enjoyable way of meeting people and making friends, and the tall whites could almost certainly have shown him a few new pool shots while overcoming their own fear of being around humans.

I recalled something else. There was a pool table as well as a television set in the airman's day room, here on base at Mojave Wells. I had enjoyed many relaxing evenings there. I remembered several times the previous summer when I was the last person to leave the day room at night and the first person to open it up the next morning. I had left the pool balls scattered around the table when I had left at night, only to find all of the pool balls neatly placed in the pockets the next morning. At the time I hadn't thought much about it. Now I wondered.

Then there was the question of why the tall whites were so intent on coming in this close to humans in the first place. None of the tall whites ever wanted to be actually touched by a human. Usually a group of new arrivals very meticulously kept their distance, no matter how curious they were. Scientific information could always be exchanged visually and verbally. It seemed to me that only books and government documents would ever need to be physically handed from one person to another. I wondered. Government supply requisitions needed to be filled out in writing and signed by both parties. In order to supply even an ordinary sized base up on the mountains, someone on the base would have to sign and hand back to humans a very large number of supply requisitions. Yes, there seemed to be a precedent for the strange events I was witnessing.

"Well," I said to myself later, as I quickly said a prayer for Bridges' soul and hurried across base to catch the bus, "They must be very good at pool since they have to play it with their space craft in order to travel from one planet to another. Out in deep space, the nearby stars must look like one giant pool table. If Bridges hadn't panicked, they might have played him quite a game."

Three weeks or so passed. They were pleasant weeks and not much happened. The deserts began heating up again as the days got longer. There were a few spring rains and the snow line on the mountains was receding. Friday came. I notified Desert Center that I was canceling the last run of the day and coming down for the weekend. I collected my library books and caught the afternoon bus into Palm Meadows and Desert Center. I had finished the evening meal at the Desert Center chow hall and dropped off my library books at the library. It was about 6:00 p.m. in the evening when I strolled in through the front door with my two books in hand. I returned the books as I entered. I expected to read a few newspapers and magazines, and then walk next door to the theater to catch the evening movie.

I didn't pay much attention when a young man wearing a nice suit with a narrow tie got out of a nearby car and entered the library a minute or so after I did. He was carrying a fine quality brief case. While I was reading the newspapers he walked quietly up to the librarian's desk, took out a current issue of one of the major news magazines and handed it to her. Then he left the library and went back to his parked car and sat waiting. After a little while, I finished my newspaper and went to read the news magazines. To my surprise, none of the current issues were on their racks. Instead they were stacked on the librarian's desk. I naturally walked over to the librarian and asked if I could read the current issue of one of the news magazines. She was an older lady. She looked up at me, smiled, and asked, "You are Airman Charlie Baker, aren't you?"

"Yes," I answered. It was nice to feel remembered, military life is often quite lonely.

"Here is your copy," she said. "It just came in. Please return it to me personally when you are finished." Then she very carefully picked up the new copy of the magazine that she had just received from the young man and handed it to me.

I took the magazine over to one of the tables, sat down, and began paging through it. The magazine seemed ordinary enough. However, the corner of one of the pages had been very carefully folded over so that the magazine opened naturally to a specific page. Curious, I began by reading that page. It contained a one-page article describing an apparently ordinary reception party that had just been given for Senators and Congressman in Washington, D.C. The party was given so that new lobbyists and representatives of special interest groups could be introduced to the various Senators, Congressmen, and their staffs. Even the U.S. President was in attendance, along with some cabinet members, some foreign ambassadors, and some high-ranking members of the U.S. military.

According to the article, the party was given in the ballroom of a large hotel in downtown Washington, D.C. The ballroom adjoined several rooms, one of which was a poolroom, since pool is a favorite evening pastime of Senators and Congressman. The article stated that betting on games of pool was quite common and the poolroom was a place where a great deal of money changed hands. Lobbyists were invited to play pool with their favorite Senator, and to bet on the game if they so chose. Naturally, the lobbyist also had to hand the senator a great deal of money if he 'lost' the game.

At the top of the page was a black and white picture of three young, thin, very light complexioned sisters wearing pretty, non-revealing formal dresses, gloves, and simple stylish hairdos. They were standing in a reception line just inside one of the doors, with a tall male guard in a nice three-piece suit standing next to them. The three of them were standing in a diagonal line facing the camera, while the guard was standing sideways to the camera watching the three young women, and anyone else who might choose to approach the line. In one section of the article the correspondent had written about a group of three very special young lady lobbyists who attended the party. They were introduced as representing a new trade mission designed to increase trade between America and Northern Spain. He said that one of the ranking staff members at the Spanish Embassy told him later that he was unaware of the existence of any such mission. The three sisters came in a half hour late to the party and entered quietly with their bodyguard by way of the swinging double doors on the northern side of the room. They formed a line and began politely receiving selected Senators and Congressmen, although this is backwards from the way things are usually done in Washington. After another half hour had passed, one of the ranking Senators on the Senate Appropriations Committee very forcefully came over to introduce himself. He had been drinking heavily. When he reached out to shake their hands, one of the ladies panicked. All three of them and their bodyguard quickly retreated back through the swinging north doors and didn't return for more than an hour. The Senator was very embarrassed but didn't know who to apologize to. When the ladies and the guard did return, they entered quietly through the double doors on the west side of the room. They remained standing nervously in a receiving line for almost two more hours. Finally they formed up into a tight little group and very carefully walked over to the poolroom to observe the party from that vantage point. After passing another quiet and nervous half hour, they left the party early.

That was about it for the article. What was interesting was that the correspondent had written an additional folksy note as if to explain why he'd written the article as he did. Apparently, it was not the kind of coverage he had originally intended. He said that while they were standing in line, one of his best friends came over to him to make sure that he got a picture of the women. He is a high-ranking officer in the Pentagon, and they had been friends for years. The correspondent said that they had both been drinking quite a few martinis at the time. The Pentagon officer asked the correspondent to write an article about the sisters attending this party and submit it to him for approval. Once the article was approved, he wished to present them with a copy of it, along with a marble plaque commemorating this day in history. The correspondent said he was surprised and asked why he would want to do anything that special, since the three sisters appeared to be quite ordinary. The officer said that according to rumors he had heard, the three sisters were extremely special. He'd heard that they had trained for almost a year on a military base out in the desert southwest just so they would be ready to attend this party. He said it was his understanding that the young man who had been their trainer was held in very high regard over at the Pentagon. The correspondent said he found his friend's statements to be quite comical and laughed a good deal because of them. Being a military officer, he didn't seem to mind. I told him that he made it sound as if the three young women grew up on some other planet. He just stood smiling at me and said, "Yes, I guess I did make it sound that way."

"Surely that can't be right," the correspondent said "That entire rumor would have to be nonsense. How would a young man ever get started on such a training program? When I was a young man, I couldn't find the courage to walk across a dance floor and ask a young classmate of mine to dance. I almost fainted half way across. Where in the world would you ever find a young man so brave that he could walk up to three young females out in the desert, who aren't even from this planet, and ask them anything? After all, for such a training program to be accurate, the man has got to make the first move."

According to the correspondent, the Pentagon officer said, "Now you see why a man that brave would have to be told 'Thanks'. I'm hoping you can have that article on my desk by next Monday." Then the officer walked away from the correspondent and rejoined the party. Out of respect for him and their many years of friendship, the correspondent hoped that the article was what he was expecting.

I finished reading the magazine and returned it to the librarian, handing it directly to her before leaving the library. Interestingly, when I returned to the library the following weekend, a different magazine was hanging on the rack. The replacement copy of the magazine had, instead, a nice one-page article on new car interiors. I didn't mind. I only needed to be told 'Thanks' once.

Star Dust

When one finds a worthy wife,
her value is far beyond pearls.

...

Like merchant ships,
she secures her provisions from afar.

...Proverbs 31:10,14

It was just after dark on this particular Saturday night in Las Vegas. I was alone as I walked the sidewalks in downtown Casino Center. I felt drawn for some reason, towards a certain large new hotel and casino. It was one of my favorite casinos, even though it was the casino where I first caught a blackjack dealer stacking the deck and dealing me seconds.

As it was on many other nights, it felt as though there was a party inside just for me. As soon as I entered, I felt encouraged to play certain specific slot machines, a feeling not unusual to an experienced and superstitious gambler like myself. Tonight, however, I had hardly gotten past the first two rows of slot machines when I was sure that some young lady had followed me into the casino. I felt as if she wanted to practice communicating with me while I was walking around, playing the games, experiencing distractions, and otherwise enjoying myself. First I felt as if she wanted me to place two nickels in a slot machine here, then a quarter in one over on the wall, then one hand of blackjack at this table and two rolls of the dice on my way to the restaurant. A good meal and several free soft drinks later, I found myself leaving and laughing, thirty dollars richer. "Whoever this lady luck is," I laughed to myself. "She can talk to me anytime."

On several occasions in the days and weeks that followed, it happened again, always at night, and almost always in the same casino. On the other nights, it happened when I was in one of the casinos across the street. On each occasion, I felt as if I was communicating with the same young lady, who always stayed hidden in the crowds and in the maze of slot machines, never wanting me to actually see her. After a while I wasn't sure if I was sane, superstitious, or just lucky. One thing stuck in my mind and returned to me over and over. It was that she seemed to ask questions about every young, beautiful woman who approached me, and she seemed to pay very careful attention to whatever my thoughts were in return. They were questions such as, "What store did that woman buy her dress in? Are her shoes in fashion? Does her dress match her shoes and purse?" and so on. Of course, when a single young man wins money in Las Vegas, he finds himself being approached by a lot of beautiful, young, single women, all of whom have suddenly fallen in love with him. On one night, I won $100 and soon had two women flirting with me.

Nights of this type had been occurring, off and on, for several weeks when I found myself again in Las Vegas on an ordinary summer Saturday night. Once again I entered my favorite casino, took a chair at the nearest table, and began playing blackjack. I was sitting with my back to the main doorway into the casino. I was counting my $10 in winnings. From out of the blue, the dealer said to me, "That wife of yours is so beautiful, I can understand why you become insanely jealous and never let anyone touch her."

"What wife?" I responded laughing. "I'm as single as a man can get."

The dealer responded, "That woman standing over by the door. The way she studies you, I thought for sure that she was your wife."

Without hurrying too much, I turned towards the door. It was a busy summer night. The casino crowd had herded itself around until it blocked the view. Dazed, a little, I picked up my chips and wandered slowly through the crowd, over towards the huge open doors, wondering which woman the dealer was referring to. By the time I got over to the doors, the crowd had milled around some more, and I was down to guessing. I felt a little foolish. After all, what would I say if I saw her, "Excuse me young lady, but do you think we're married?"

I stepped outside into the warm night air, laughing at myself a little. The street was crowded with tourists. I stood in one place for a few minutes studying the crowd. I couldn't help but notice two attractive young women who were walking away from me. One was about my height. The other was perhaps an inch shorter. The taller one was crossing the street at the lights to my left. The other was retreating quickly down the street towards a dark alley and a construction site for a new hotel on my right. They caught my attention because they both had an unusually smooth manner of walking, and both of them were wearing long sleeve blouses, heavy winter skirts, winter gloves, and thick stockings, unusual attire for such a warm desert evening.

When the shorter one arrived at the construction site, I noticed that she immediately hurried into the partly constructed building, even though it was as dark as night inside. She disappeared from sight into the darkness between some wooden beams and half completed concrete walls. The entire episode confused me. "Why would such an attractive woman, dressed in nice clothes, be so willing to walk around a dusty unlit construction site on such a dark night," I wondered? "She must feel awfully comfortable walking alone out under the starlight." I couldn't think of any answers to my questions, so I called it an evening, and spent the next few minutes laughing to myself over the unusual occurrence.

A few weeks passed. Once again I was alone in Las Vegas on a hot Saturday evening. It was another one of those unusual nights and I had won almost twenty-five dollars playing blackjack. I decided to celebrate by having a nice late dinner before calling it a night. I was in a casino restaurant down on the strip, when the waitress brought me the wrong order. I teased her about it, saying, "I didn't know there was anyone else like me here in the restaurant."

To my surprise, she replied, "Why yes, that man sitting right over there reminds me of you. He looks different than you, but I can hardly tell you two apart. He has the same name, and his mannerisms are identical to yours. He came in right behind you. When you first came in, I thought you might be related."

I didn't get to see much of him. He was about my height. He wore a black suit with a white shirt. He was wearing sunglasses even though it was the evening, not unusual for Las Vegas at the time. When I looked over in his direction, he seemed to anticipate my every move. He immediately arose, turned his back towards me, put money on the table for the meal, and exited back into the casino. His behavior seemed a little unusual because he hadn't eaten any of the food that he had ordered. It was sitting on the table as he left the restaurant. After he'd gone, I felt for a moment as if he had been following me around, just learning how to imitate me.

I sat there laughing at myself, "Right, Charlie. Everyone just wants to be you." Yes, I decided, a man who wins money in Las Vegas can sure find his mind filled with a lot of weird notions.

The End of the Innocence

...Jesus looked directly at them
and asked,

"Then what is the meaning
of that which is written:

"'The stone the builders rejected
has become the capstone'?..."

...Luke 20:17

On this warm summer morning, I drove happily out towards Range Three to make the 4:30 a.m. balloon run. I had long since gotten used to the idea that the white beings came when they wanted to, and left when they wanted to. I was in a party mood this morning as I headed out towards Range Three and I almost didn't notice the two tall white fluorescent suited older men floating a short distance out in the sagebrush as I drove past the intersection with the Range One road. Then I noticed two additional tall white fluorescent suited older men floating several miles down on the Range One road. They appeared to be guarding its intersection with the Range Two road. It took a while for the details to penetrate through the festive atmosphere within my truck. Finally, when the facts sunk into my brain, I didn't know what to make of it. All four white men were unusually tall, standing maybe eight to ten feet tall. It meant that all of them had to be older well-armed guards.

There was little point in turning back now, I thought to myself. After all, if they meant to do me harm, they could just come and kill me anytime they felt like it. "I wonder what they've got planned now," I thought to myself.

I had little choice but to drive on. I was, after all, in the USAF. My orders were to drive out to the Range Three weather shack every weekday morning and measure the winds. Being in the military, I wasn't free to just say "No" to my orders.

I drove on and sang partly out of fear. Off to the northeast, at the base of the mountains in the distance, I could see perhaps as many as thirty-five or forty white beings of different sizes, floating in groups in their fluorescent suits. Many were obviously children. Others were obviously tall, older adults. The largest group appeared to be equivalent to teenagers and young adults. They were formed up into a long thin patchy line on the valley floor. The line started at the end of the paved road that ran by the billboards of Range Three. "Well, I hope they brought lots of casino chips with them," I laughed nervously to myself, "because lately I've been feeling awfully lucky."

As my truck arrived at the Range Three compound, the motor quit abruptly just short of the diesel shack. I guessed it was as far as they wanted me to bring it. After looking around, I carefully got out of my truck and slowly walked the last quarter mile to the buildings. In the distance, several miles up the valley on the Range Four road floated two more pair of tall fluorescent white patches. "They sure have taken total military control of this valley," I thought to myself.

Arriving outside my weather shack, I saw there was no point in trying to start the diesels. Since the white beings had turned off the electrical power in my truck, I decided that they must have also turned off the flow of electricity to the diesel generators. Usually they didn't want any stray electricity interfering with their communication system. I visually searched the buildings and the billboards until I finally located the School Bus Driver. He was standing calmly on the railing of the control tower watching me. The instrument that he carried in his hands was obviously a weapon of some power. Standing on the balcony of the tower, he was probably twenty feet above me. He stood there in the open for a long time before floating around to the opposite side of the tower. He obviously wanted me to know that he was there.

I tried to communicate with him both by thinking and by speaking directly to him, but there was simply no answer. I concluded that the best thing to do was to just go on about the business of taking the morning weather report. I sang nervously as I did so. With all of the white fluorescent beings floating over along the mountains, and out in the desert northeast of me, I decided that something big must be afoot.

As I was unlocking my weather shack, I noticed the Teacher with the three children floating perhaps a quarter mile out on the paved road northeast of me. The desert formed a slight north-south ridge there. This ridge was free from sagebrush, and in effect, formed a second viewing gallery. This was in addition to the viewing gallery just across the cable fence next to my weather shack. She was floating there, with the children behind her, obviously watching everything I was doing.

Seeing the Teacher calmed me down a great deal. Tonight, however, two additional tall white creatures were floating next to her. Since one of the children, the little girl, was her child, I concluded that the additional two white creatures must be the mothers of the other two children. It was all beginning to make sense to me. Tonight must be 'show and tell night' for the children. Tonight must be Parent's Night, I supposed.

I unlocked the front, northern, door of my weather shack and entered the darkness inside. I opened the side door and began the process of inflating the balloon. Enough moonlight came in through the open doors so the work progressed smoothly. As I was kneeling on the floor by the open side door and holding the balloon steady, my mind began to be filled with fragmented thoughts. They appeared to be coming from the Teacher's electronics. Their communications were 'Line-of-Sight'. The transmissions were entering through the open side door. The little chubby boy appeared to be telling his mother how much he enjoyed looking through my theodolite. Then the Teacher was telling the mother about the time the boy had been hiding behind my truck, and how I'd waited for him to leave before putting the truck in reverse. His mother seemed to find it all very amusing, but insisted that her son obey the Teacher in the future.

Then the thin young Einstein began telling his mother about the things he'd discovered. It sounded as if he'd measured every conceivable dimension relating to my theodolite and the stand that held it. His mother appeared to be extremely pleased.

The thing I found so surprising about the young Einstein was that his measurements were given in English units of feet and inches. I wondered if he'd really taken the measurements in feet and inches, or if the electronics that the Teacher was wearing, included a computer that was doing the necessary conversions. At the time, his measurement of the height of my theodolite stand stuck in my head. He stated that it was 5' 2" above the ground. I remembered specifically writing a letter home in which I'd estimated the height to be only 4' 8". I mentally made a note to check his measurements after the sun came up.

The two mothers asked the Teacher to tell them about her little girl. It was now time for me to take the balloon outside and release it. So I turned on my flashlight momentarily and took hold of the now filled balloon. The balloon was more than four and a half feet across when full. I carefully carried it outside, through the wide side door. Once outside, I carried it to the open area in front of my weather shack. I checked my watch and released it. Then I got my clipboard and pencil, and walked directly over to my theodolite. After quickly removing the cover, I began taking the position readings. As I did so, the Teacher was telling the other two mothers, "My little girl has always loved to play around him. When he first came out here, she would hide out in the sagebrush by the fence over there, and follow him around. He never knew she was there. He would be singing. My little girl had so much fun."

"But what if he had seen her?" asked one of the mothers. "He would not have known what she was. Were you not afraid that he might hurt her?"

"No," answered the Teacher. "We have never seen him hurt anything. Whenever he comes up against something new, he does not lose control of himself like the others do. He just pauses and thinks about it. He used to stay in that white barracks that is near where the other buildings are. The children and I used to go in the barracks when he was sleeping and read his thoughts. The electronics that the children and I wear, let us tell what some of his thoughts are, even if he is sleeping.

"One night we had so much fun. The children almost started laughing out loud. It would have awakened him. He was dreaming that he was in the big city several hundred miles northeast of here, the one they call Las Vegas. He was dreaming that he was playing cards at one of the tables and that he was winning lots of money. In his dream, some beautiful young earth woman was sitting next to him, helping him count all of his winnings. Of course, in his dream, the earth woman was only wearing a few clothes. The children found it most amusing.

"Another time I gave the children the assignment of painting a picture of how he looks when he shaves the hair off his face. He does it every morning and it looks very comical. First, he puts white soap on his face. Then he tightens his face muscles in a way that makes him look really funny. Next, he takes this sharp piece of metal in a holder, I think it is called a razor blade, and he uses it to cut off his facial hair. The razor also cuts his face a little in the process, so when he is finished he puts alcohol lotion on all of the places where he has shaved. When he does so, the children are almost unable to control themselves with laughter. He pours some in his hand. Then he slaps it up against his cheeks and rubs it all over the skin on his face. Sometimes he even jumps around and says funny things like, 'Thanks, I needed that.'

"One night, I am certain that he saw us by accident. I thought he was going to panic like the others did, but instead, he just went back to his bed and went back to sleep.

"Another morning, he noticed one of the doors to his barracks was propped open with a chair. I always propped it open for the children when we came at night. The aisles inside are narrow and I did it for their safety. I wanted the children to be able to run away if we ever frightened him. But he has so much self control that he did not panic. He just asked his friend, the policeman, to patrol past his barracks at night while he was sleeping. One night when we were all going into the barracks, the policeman saw us. He got a very good look at us. He walked up to the windows outside of the barracks and was looking in on us. My brother, the one on the tower now, was guarding us. He planned to stun the policeman if he came inside. But the policeman thought we were ghosts because we were all wearing our white suits. He went back to his car and called for help from the policeman who patrols the highways. This gave us time to get the children back out into the desert."

By now I was almost finished taking the wind measurements. One of the mothers asked the Teacher, "Teacher, your Pet Project is progressing so perfectly. We are all so impressed with the progress that you have made. Do the electronics that you always wear, allow you to communicate with him, as well as allowing you to tell what he is thinking?"

"Yes," responded the Teacher. "Right now, he is thinking about his work."

"Is he not afraid of us? Does he not know we are out here," the mother asked?

"Yes," answered the Teacher. "He knows we are here. He is still a little afraid of some of us. He knows the men will kill him if he ever hurts one of the children, but my brother and I do not think he would ever do that. We are certain that he knows he is helpless against us. He has such control over his emotions that he just goes about his business whenever any of us come around him."

"But you have your electronics on now," said one of the mothers. "Why can he not tell what you are saying while he works?"

"He can," answered the Teacher. "He is just used to us communicating with him, and sometimes interfering with his thoughts. It does not bother him anymore."

"But if he is used to being around us, is he able to go back and be with the other earth people?" asked the mother. "Will they let him back into their living areas? Will he ever be able to go home again?"

"Yes," answered the Teacher. "He is very intelligent and the other earth people love having him around. I have also noticed that he does not tell them everything he knows."

The Teacher paused for a minute, and then continued, "He has finished taking his readings now. He is going to turn around and start walking back to his building. See how he left his telescope open. He does that so the children can go over and look through it if they want to. The children just love to look through his telescope. If you approve, I will let the children go there now and play. We should stay back here, or else the power of our suits will prevent him from thinking clearly."

The other two mothers appeared to think about this. Then they gave their approval. As I was walking back to my weather shack, I could see the Teacher's little girl and the chubby little boy floating slowly through the sagebrush towards my unlocked theodolite. I entered my weather shack. Using my flashlight for light, I completed the wind computations. I took my time and I wasn't paying much attention to what was going on outside. When I had finished the computations, I phoned them in to Desert Center. The phone line had only a little static on it, and Dwight had answered on the other end. Since we were good friends, we talked for a long time about his family and other things. I found the conversation quite entertaining and also quite humorous. At one point, Dwight was saying, "I still can't understand why they're only willing to send you up there, Charlie. I don't understand why Range Four Harry never bothers you the way he used to terrorize the other observers we sent up there. You do see him every now and then, don't you?"

At the time, I answered Dwight calmly and casually, "Yes, Dwight. I do see Range Four Harry out here from time to time but he never bothers me. He feels bored or lonesome every now and then. He just wants to walk around in the moonlight for the fun of it, I guess. I don't know why they are only willing to send me up here either, but I'm glad that's the case. I just love being up here with the extra pay, and having the weather truck all to myself. Whatever their reasons are, it's OK by me."

Dwight and I finished our conversation laughing, and I hung up the phone. I left the weather shack and locked the door. Then I looked around to check the status of the white creatures. All of them had left, just as silently as they had come. Off in the distance along the mountains to the northeast, I could see the last of the white beings, apparently the Teacher, the two mothers, and the three children, floating silently and slowly north over the last ridge before the hidden valley. They may have felt some sadness because they appeared to turn towards me and wait for a little while. As I started my truck and headed down the road back towards base, I could see them in my mirror, still standing and watching me as I left. It seemed as if they wanted to come with me. It seemed as if they wanted just to play where I was. As my truck bounced past the road junction, I could see that even the tall white guards had retreated back towards the mountains to the northeast.

As I drove back to base for breakfast, I couldn't help but wonder. At least forty white creatures had been watching me from up along the slopes of the mountains to the northeast. Yet except for the guards, only the Teacher, the three children and the two mothers had come forward. I wondered why so many creatures had come, with so many guards, just to stand watching me from so far away.

When I returned from breakfast, the ranges were deserted. They remained deserted for the rest of the day. I took advantage of the peace and quiet to measure the height of my theodolite stand. After measuring it four different times, I accepted the inevitable conclusion. It stood exactly 5' 2" above the graveled desert below. Young Einstein was a boy a mother could be proud of.

I arose at 3:00 a.m. the next morning. It was a Tuesday. I left the barracks by way of the door on the north. I studied the base of the mountains that lay so many miles away towards the northeast. I could see that this was going to be another busy morning. Along the base of the mountains in the distance, was a patchy line of chalky white fluorescent suited beings. I estimated that there had to be more than seventy-five white creatures out there waiting for me, all in total silence. "Looks like they are planning quite a party," I muttered grimly to myself, as I headed out towards my waiting weather truck.

I started the engine and brought the truck slowly onto the Range Three road. Once again, I eased my truck past the two guards, positioned as they had been before, along the road at the Range One intersection. I wondered why so many creatures would care what I was doing with my weather balloons. "I couldn't get seventy-five of my father's relatives to come watch me release one of these balloons," I said to myself.

As before, my truck engine died as I was approaching the Range Three buildings. Walking the last quarter mile allowed me to locate the School Bus Driver, positioned on the tower railing, and the Teacher, watching from the second gallery out on the bunker road. This morning, she informed me that I could start the diesels, if I wanted to. I felt I needed the light and I wanted to listen to my radio, so I did.

As I came out from the diesel shack, I could see that the Teacher's daughter, two new children, and two new mothers had joined the Teacher. I opened my shack, filled my balloon, and played my radio loud. It helped me calm my fears. Soon, I was deeply engaged in recording numbers from my theodolite. Whenever I visually studied the two new mothers and their children, who floated a few inches off the ground in the distance, they appeared to become highly agitated. I went back to watching my balloon and ignoring the white beings. I felt it was safer for my health.

As I took my measurements, the Teacher was conversing with the new mothers and children. "He will not hurt you," she was saying. "Just stay back, and do not get in his way. I am going to take you up closer, so you will see more."

After a couple of minutes had passed, I glanced quickly over my right shoulder, to see what was happening. The Teacher, her daughter, and the new arrivals had floated up into the first viewing gallery, directly behind the cable fence that defined the skip bomb area. The Teacher continued, "When I bring your children with me on the next field trip, I will keep them over there on the paved road by the billboards. That way, if your children become too frightened of him or if he gets too close to them, they can just run back to the protection of the others. Do not worry. He never follows. When he finishes his measurements, he just phones Desert Center and goes back to those buildings down there in the valley to eat breakfast."

One of the new mothers spoke, "He is very close right now. I am afraid to be this close to him. He will not come any closer, will he?"

"Yes," answered the Teacher. "He will walk over to this building right beside us, so he can communicate his results to Desert Center. Do not worry. The cable is between us. He will not cross the cable."

"But what if he does?" asked the mother nervously.

"I will ask him not to," answered the Teacher. "He will understand."

"But what if he does not understand?" continued the mother nervously. "What if he crossed the cable anyway and attacked us?"

"He would never do that," answered the Teacher. "He is very intelligent. He knows that if he did that, the guards would kill him."

Upon hearing this, the mothers seemed to calm down. I calmed down too. Knowing where the cable was and the line where they'd kill me if I crossed it, made me feel more secure.

Since I'd finished my last reading, I stood upright and slowly turned around. I realized that the Teacher could monitor my thoughts, so I thought, slowly and clearly, "I won't cross the cable. I need to walk to my weather shack now." Then I stood there, waiting for an answer.

The Teacher communicated my message to the two new mothers. They appeared to be shocked. One said to the Teacher, "I have never seen a human like him. He has so much self-control. How did the committee ever find him?"

In an unusually pleasant manner, the Teacher replied proudly, "My little girl and I picked him. The committee only agreed to my request.

"We can come whenever we want to. He just does not want us to scare him or sneak up on him. We agreed that as long as my cousin, my brother, or I come along, we may bring anyone with us when we come. He has trained himself to settle down whenever he sees either one of the three of us."

Still waiting, I asked again by thinking slowly and clearly, "I am going to walk to my weather shack now. I do not want to frighten you."

Without actually responding, first the two mothers, then their children, then the Teacher and her daughter began floating slowly backwards, back out into the desert towards the second gallery. When they had retreated ten or fifteen feet or so, I walked to my weather shack and finished my calculations. Through the open front door, I could see the Teacher's little girl, showing the other two children the view through my theodolite. By the time I'd finished the morning weather report and phoned it to Desert Center, the range was deserted. Leaving my shack and locking my theodolite, I could hardly have been more alone. The Teacher, the children, the mothers, and the other seventy-five creatures along the mountains had all left. Once again, as I drove into base for my morning breakfast, I was left wondering, "Why had so many come from so far, and stood at so great a distance, just to watch me release a balloon?"

The next morning, Wednesday, the ranges were deserted. I wasn't surprised. I had learned that the white beings always had two days of activity, followed by two days of rest. At Range Three I was greeted by little more than blowing sagebrush in the morning, and blowing dust in the afternoon. Then came Thursday morning. It was an instant replay of Wednesday. Same dust, same sagebrush, same desert, same loneliness.

Friday morning came. Once again I arose at 3:00 a.m. Once again, I left the barracks by way of the door on the north. One glance towards the mountains that lay so many miles away towards the northeast, convinced me that reporting the weather at Mojave Wells wasn't a job for the faint hearted. The base of the mountains, for a distance of more than five miles, was one solid line of soft, glowing, white fluorescent light. I estimated that there had to be more than 200 or 300 white beings out there waiting for me, all in total silence. Even if they had all been humans, I would have still found the situation intimidating. For some time I seriously considered staying in the barracks and faking the morning winds. Finally I collected myself and decided that I would take the morning winds as ordered, even if it killed me.

As before, the drive out to Range Three was uneventful. The tall white guards were posted in their normal places. The entire base of the mountains off to the northeast appeared to be one solid line of liquid soft white fluorescent light. Creatures of every size and age could be seen floating excitedly between the valley ridges and the ammunition bunker. The line continued for several miles up along the mountains and out into the nearby desert valley. I estimated that between thirty-five and fifty brightly lit scout craft were parked some forty-five miles up the valley, out on the valley floor. Around these vehicles was posted a picket line of some two dozen tall white guards. "It looks like a summer church revival meeting." I grimly muttered to myself. Still, I wondered, "Why? All I'm doing is releasing a weather balloon."

As before, my truck engine died while I was still a quarter of a mile from the Range Three buildings. I didn't mind. I felt I needed the hike to settle my nerves. Between their electronics and my fears, it was a gingerly hike. As I walked into the open square of buildings that held my weather shack, I located the School Bus driver in his customary position on the railing of the tower. As usual, he chose not to respond to my greeting. I located the Teacher. She was floating in front of a large group of new arrivals over by the ammunition bunker at the end of the paved road. I was unable to pick up any of her thought fragments, so I decided that she had her electronics turned down. Floating next to her appeared to be another young female. The second young female appeared to be an inch or so shorter than the Teacher. I realized that I had seen her with the Teacher several times before during the previous summer. On all of those occasions, she had appeared to be terrified of me. Having nothing better to do, I went on about my business of starting the diesel, turning on the lights, and collecting the morning weather. With so many white beings watching my every move from over by the mountains, I decided I needed my radio and my electric lights to keep my fears from overtaking me.

As I was measuring the temperature and the dew point, the Teacher, with the second young woman somewhat behind her, began slowly floating towards me. They began coming down the paved road from the ammunition bunker. The young woman's father was clearly identifiable in the crowd behind her. He appeared to be wishing her well and helping her get started. Whatever they had planned, it was making me noticeably apprehensive. If my truck had started, I probably would have driven back to base and faked the morning winds for my own protection. Under the circumstances, I decided the best thing for me was to continue with the wind measurements as usual. I thought about what was transpiring. I decided that the young woman's father must be another individual of considerable importance within their community. Why else would so many of them come to witness this event?

The Teacher referred to the young woman using the name "Pamela", and to the young woman's father using the name "The Captain". On several occasions during the previous summer, it had appeared to me that the second female white creature was intentionally practicing her imitation of the moves, mannerisms, and speaking habits of my friend Michael's sister, my girlfriend Pamela. For that reason, I had decided that the female white creature, who was now coming down the bunker road towards me, had intentionally chosen the same name, Pamela, for use when she was talking to humans.

When the Teacher had closed the distance between us to half a mile, her electronics finally came within range. It was immediately obvious that the young woman was also wearing similar electronics. The two different sets of thoughts began to electronically invade my consciousness. By now the little procession had reached the turnoff to the barren desert ridge that I had dubbed the second gallery, and the Captain's daughter was becoming panicky.

"He is terrifying to be around," Pamela was saying. "Do we have to do this? He will certainly attack us."

The Teacher responded, "We are perfectly safe. See, my brother is guarding us from the tower. He knows my brother will kill him if he attacks us. He is a very gentle creature. He has never attacked any of us before. Why are you so afraid now? You have already communicated with him many times down in the casinos. It will be just like it was then. All we are going to do now, is travel up to where the posts are and speak to him in English."

"No, I can not. It is not like before. This time he knows we are here. This time he can recognize us. It is just too dangerous. He can defeat our weapons. He will certainly attack us," responded Pamela in terror.

"Oh, he will not," responded the Teacher pleasantly. "You saw me and my little girl travel right up to him and nothing bad happened. You, yourself spoke English to humans in Virginia, just a year ago. Now the American Generals have decided that he has to be told what we are planning and the Committee has decided that you have to do it as part of your training. Do not worry, now. Talking to him is very easy."

"But this is different," answered Pamela, trembling in fear. "In Virginia, they were just two little children playing in the woods. Look at him. He can see us. He is strong enough to tear us into pieces. This is his planet. His body is built for it. He feels comfortable when he is breathing this thin air. He does not get cold as we do. Look, he is not armed. He is not even afraid of the animals out here. Remember when we were watching him from the mountain last week. He was down there near those dogs. They were barking at him and he was not even afraid of them. He walked over to them and fed them. Then he just spoke to them. Now they are his friends. Now he controls them. He makes them lie down. They roll over whenever he orders them to. They are all his slaves. They will attack anything he tells them to attack. I read his thoughts. He was not even afraid. He will do the same to us. He will certainly attack us."

"There is nothing to be afraid of," answered the Teacher. "The children and I have been around him many times. He knows we are not dogs. He does not try to control us. Here, use your communicator. You will enjoy talking to him. It will be excellent education."

"How do the guards know what he is thinking?" asked Pamela, nearly breaking down in terror. "This is his planet. He can outwit the guards. He is not afraid to hide out there in the sagebrush the whole day and sneak up on us at night. He is not afraid of the desert. He enjoys it. He is not afraid of the darkness, or the moonlight. He is not afraid of coyotes, or bees, or horses. He even knows how to milk cows and feed calves. His very thought processes are made to control all of the animals. He enjoys it. He is not afraid of anything out here. I tell you, the guards can not handle him."

Then Pamela, her fears finally overcoming her, broke and ran, floating quickly back to the safety of the crowd of white beings waiting for her by the ammunition bunker.

The Teacher seemed bewildered and confused by Pamela's behavior. After waiting by the second gallery for a few minutes, the Teacher slowly returned back down the road to the ammunition bunker. As she was moving out of range of her electronics, she seemed to be saying to the Captain, "This is the third night she has refused to talk to him. He has to be told and she has to tell him. He will be back from breakfast at 8:00 a.m. We will try again then, in the daylight."

The remainder of the balloon run was uneventful. The two or three hundred white beings continued to play over by the mountains, many of them watching as I locked up my theodolite and shut down the diesels. The Teacher spent most of the time standing noticeably out in front of the crowd, on the end of the paved road down by the ammunition bunker. Eight or ten children who were perhaps the equivalent of second graders surrounded her. The distance was too great to receive any of her thoughts with her electronics turned down as they were, but she appeared to be instructing the children. At one point she was pointing up at my balloon that was now several thousand feet in the sky. Because of the darkness I couldn't be certain, but standing in the crowd behind her appeared to be two American USAF Generals, one wearing four stars, and one wearing three stars.

As I drove back into base for breakfast, I was surprised that all of the white beings were still watching me from up along the mountains, and the tall white guards were still in place, posted at the road junctions. It wasn't until the sun was coming up that they finally fell back towards the mountains to the northeast.

At 7:30 a.m., with the sun now well above the horizon and the temperatures rising all over the Mojave Wells valley floor, I started my weather truck and headed back out towards Range Three. Now that daylight had arrived, I was expecting a fairly uneventful day. When I arrived at Range Three, I parked my truck next to the diesel shack. However, I did not restart either one of the diesels. The events of the morning had left me feeling nervous and jittery. I felt that I needed the quiet silence of the desert morning to calm down.

I had already unlocked my weather shack and my theodolite when I noticed something moving over by the ammunition bunker. I adjusted the magnification on my theodolite to seventy-five, and began studying the situation more carefully. I could see a large scout craft parked behind the ammunition bunker. It was so large that its ends stuck out beyond both sides of the bunker. I noticed that the door to the bunker was slightly ajar and the alien School Bus Driver was just entering the unused bunker. I was surprised to see that he wasn't wearing his usual fluorescent white travel suit that allowed him to float. He was just walking on the ground. His clear blue eyes, chalky white skin, aluminized clothing, and short blonde hair were clearly visible. As usual, he was carrying a weapon of some type in his left hand.

I continued scanning the area with my theodolite. I could see the white being that I had nicknamed the Copilot, who also functioned as the flight mechanic, standing next to the bunker on the left. For some reason, Copilot never liked being referred to as "Copilot". Instead, he seemed to be immensely proud of his abilities as the flight mechanic, and of his ability to repair the scout craft. In any event, Copilot was obviously heavily armed, as were the others. Still, I couldn't see any sign of the Teacher or the Captain. Scanning up above the white object, up on a rocky ledge on the mountain, I could see the communications officer. He was the white being who identified himself as Range Four Harry. I had learned over the months that when the Teacher and the children were out hiking in the desert, they usually stayed well hidden. It appeared to be the duty of the communications officer to maintain the communications link between the Teacher and their home base. Consequently, it frequently happened that the communications officer had to expose himself in order to maintain the communications links. Although I knew the men were always heavily armed, I was surprised to notice that Range Four Harry didn't appear to be carrying any weapons, although he did have several packages of communications equipment sitting on the ledge next to him. This left me with a bit of a mystery. The School Bus Driver, now resting inside the bunker, usually accompanied the Teacher and functioned as the traveling guard. If he was in the bunker, I wondered, where are the Teacher and the Captain?

I studied the communications officer for a few more minutes. Based on the direction he had his packages pointed, I decided that the Teacher and the Captain must be close by, probably hiding behind the Range Three lounge. I saw no reason to go looking for them. I had come to believe that I would live longer if I never surprised them.

I glanced at my watch and saw that it was time to begin the balloon run. I left my theodolite and walked back to the weather shack. A few minutes later, with my clipboard under one arm and holding the now filled helium balloon, I emerged from my weather shack and walked slowly back to the theodolite. I released the balloon, looked at my watch and recorded the time on my data sheet, 8:00 a.m. In a routine manner, I began taking the balloon ascension readings. I had just finished taking the last reading when I heard someone calling my name. Looking around, I noticed the Teacher standing beside the corner of the Range Three lounge. She was wearing her favorite earth woman disguise, that of a nurse. "Charlie. Come here please," she called to me.

Having no reason to refuse, I replied, "Yes", and calmly walked towards her. As I approached her, she retreated slowly before me until she was standing perhaps ten feet back from the corner of the lounge building. As I reached the corner of the building, I could see the Captain standing motionless by the other corner, facing me. He was holding a thin tube weapon probably eighteen inches long, in his hands. It wasn't actually pointed towards me, but just the same, it made me a little nervous. Although he, like all of the white creatures, had only four fingers on each hand, and no visible thumbs, he had the weapon under complete control. I realized that the Captain was the one who had burned Washington two summers before and would have killed him, had not the Teacher ordered him otherwise. I felt safe enough because the Teacher, being the Ambassador's only daughter, greatly out-ranked the Captain, and the white creatures never attacked without first being provoked. The Captain was quiet, taciturn, authoritative, and exceptionally well armed, even for him. I stopped immediately and came to attention. Standing some distance off to my right, between the Captain and the Teacher, was the young white female being who used the name Pamela when talking to humans. Her tendency to panic made me quite apprehensive.

Pamela was disguised as an earth woman and was attired in a beautifully designed blue and white-checkered dress. The dress was not the least bit revealing. It was designed with a high collar and came down below her knees. Along with her make-up and her obvious wig, she also wore white stockings and a stylish cap. The wig, I supposed, must conceal an electronic package similar to the one the Teacher and the Captain always wore. In her hands, she also held a thin, tube weapon. Her weapon was only about six or seven inches long.

I turned slightly towards the Teacher and greeted her. I knew the Teacher was always well armed, but the Teacher was holding a small, different shaped rectangular object. The fact that the three of them stood deployed around me in military fashion did not alarm me. I had become used to their ways. I knew that they always deployed in a manner that gave each of them a clear field of fire, just in case they should ever need one. The Teacher and all of the white females appeared to immensely enjoy dressing up like earth women. I saw immediately that the point of this meeting was for me to critique Pamela's disguise. Their women were like intelligent playful children who never seemed to grow up. The Teacher spoke first.

"Charlie, this is Pamela. Does she not look nice?" asked the Teacher playfully.

"Yes", I answered, continuing to stand without moving my feet or hands. I felt my life would last longer if I didn't interfere while they monitored my peaceful thoughts. "She certainly is wearing a beautiful outfit."

The Captain continued to stand motionless by the end of the lounge. Knowing that I was helpless against any one of them, I chose my words carefully. "She certainly looks beautiful this morning."

The Teacher pointed her device towards me and another mild shudder passed through my body. My mind seemed to wander and I felt as if I were dreaming for a few seconds. Both the Teacher and Pamela walked slowly up beside me. The Teacher was saying, "See Pamela, there is nothing to be afraid of. He is really quite gentle and we can control him if we have to." Then my mind seemed to blur for a few more minutes before it suddenly cleared again.

When the dizziness left my mind, I found myself still standing by the corner of the lounge with the three white beings still deployed around me as before. The Teacher was returning the rectangular object to its normal storage place located up the sleeve on her right arm. I noticed that the morning shadows had changed substantially. I guessed that perhaps as much as an hour had passed while I had stood there dazed. I glanced down at my watch that had stopped. Their electronics frequently did that. The Teacher spoke to me, "Charlie, the Captain has something important to tell you. The Teacher, still standing off to my right, giggled pleasantly. Something about the confusion I felt over my stopped watch and the block of apparent missing time, amused her greatly and she'd gotten her earth woman impersonation down to near perfection. She was even learning to use English contractions when she spoke.

The Captain, still standing some distance in front of me, began speaking to me in an unusually quiet voice. "Your bravery has greatly helped both your government and ours. Both of our governments are sorry about the injuries that we were forced to inflict on your friend Washington almost two summers ago. I have been instructed by both of our governments to thank you for your heroic contributions to…"

Then, the desert wind picked up somewhat, blowing some fine desert sand around the corner of the lounge, making it impossible for me to hear what the Captain was saying. With my mind still a little dazed from the morning's events, I stood motionless and respectful until he had finished speaking. This caused me a great deal of concern. I knew that I would be risking my life if I were to do anything that offended him. On some days previously, it hadn't seemed as if he understood humans very well. Thus I felt that I didn't dare either approach him or leave his presence without first hearing what he had to say. I gently informed him that because of the wind, I had not been able to hear what he'd said. I asked him to repeat what he'd said, but to speak a little louder. He seemed to take some mild offense at this. He responded by saying that I should have listened more carefully. Then the Teacher pleasantly interceded on my behalf. She pointed out that my hearing was not as good as theirs and that the wind had been blowing into my ears. Smiling pleasantly, the Captain began again, still speaking in his unusually low voice. Once again, I was unable to discern what he was saying. Feeling tremendous anxiety because of this, I carefully requested the he repeat what he was saying a third time. Standing now, in fear of my life, I began by carefully reminding him of my numerous shortcomings as a human, and expressed hope that he would understand.

Still wearing his pleasant smile, the Captain began a third time, still no louder than before. Still unable to make out his words, I inadvertently began to take one step forward, closer to him, so that I could make out what he was saying. My right leg had just come forward, my foot had just touched the ground in front of me when, once again, Pamela panicked. Their nervous system, running two and a half times faster than ours, allowed her to point her white pencil at me and activate it before I could do much more than tighten my throat muscles and blink my eyes. Screaming to her father, she blurted out in a panicky manner, "He is out of control! See I told you, father! He has broken out of the controls! See, I have to readjust them!"

Instead of the usual dizziness, this time I felt a mild tingling in my left arm and a certain numbness in my throat. I immediately stepped back to my original position and wondered what had happened. Then the Teacher grabbed the white pencil from Pamela's hand and forcefully exclaimed, "He meant no harm. He just could not hear your father! There was no reason to kill him!"

I waited patiently for the numbness to leave my throat and for the tingling to leave my left arm. Confusion started to flood my brain. On the one hand, I hadn't felt much, if any, pain. On the other hand, I realized that something very serious must have happened, or else the Teacher wouldn't have grabbed the weapon from Pamela. The tall white creatures never fought with each other.

I stood patiently waiting to regain my ability to speak. The Teacher took out the rectangular white object that she had previously placed up her right sleeve. She quickly adjusted it and pointed it at my exposed right temple. She activated the instrument for a few seconds and then returned it to her sleeve. My thoughts suddenly cleared and a momentary slight dizziness left my mind. I had complete freedom of movement, complete control of my thoughts and of my body.

After a couple more minutes passed, the numbness finally left my throat and I found myself just barely able to speak. Addressing the Captain in a hoarse voice, I asked respectfully, "Am I going to die?"

The Captain, still wearing his pleasant expression and speaking louder now, answered simply, "Yes. It was an accident. My daughter's instrument was not set correctly."

Stunned, I was preparing to ask another question when the Captain continued, "Do not speak. It only makes it worse. You should run to your truck, if you can. That will let you die in a soft place. Your government will come for your body after sundown."

Still in disbelief, I slowly turned around and took a couple of steps back towards my theodolite. After taking only a couple of steps, I noticed that blood was collecting in my throat and a faint numbness started spreading through my upper chest. My stomach became very upset and I began by vomiting onto the gravel. Understanding, now, that I must be on the verge of bleeding to death from my throat, I decided that I had only seconds to live. With my mind racing, searching for answers, I decided my only hope was to lie down and somehow use pressure to stop the bleeding. It was a desperate plan but I realized that, alone as I was, and some twenty-two miles from help out in the desert, it was my only hope.

I remembered that several feet off to my left was a thin place in the sagebrush, covered with soft dirt and small gravel. Realizing my life was at stake, I stepped quickly to the break in the sagebrush and laid face down in the dirt. My knees and legs smashed down into the sharp pieces of gravel, and into the thorns on the sagebrush. It was extremely painful but I knew that I had neither the time nor the strength to do anything different. Using my hat as a pillow for my face, and using my handkerchief to protect my hands, I built a low mound of soft dirt. I pressed my knuckles up under my throat, placing as much pressure as I could on the numb area. Then I laid down on the dirt in such a way that my hands remained up under my throat, and the weight of my body pressed my throat down upon my hands. I had just barely finished this when I started coughing up blood. Soon I had coughed up what appeared to be at least a pint of blood. My fatigues were covered with blood and torn in several places. The bright red blood splashed up into my face and my hair. After several desperate attempts, I was finally able to position myself so that the weight of my body was pushing my throat down onto the mound of rocks and bloody dirt that I had constructed. Finally the flow of blood began to stop. I felt desperately weak, and as the flow of blood was ending, I passed out in the gravel. Because of the position that I had chosen, the weight of my body maintained the pressure on my throat, even as I lay unconscious. All of the time, the three white beings just stood by the corner of the Range Three lounge, watching in silence. As I was passing out, I could hear the phone ringing in my weather shack some 200 feet distant.

I lay passed out in the gravel, for a long time. When I finally regained consciousness, my head was splitting with pain and my body ached in every cell. The three white beings were still standing by the corner of the lounge, watching my every move, but they made no apparent move to help.

As I regained my consciousness, at first I didn't move. My lips, my face, my fatigues were all caked with blood and dirt but the bleeding had stopped. I had blood all over my face. I had been bleeding in my throat and up through my nose. I could have remained there for hours but lying motionless in the thorns and gravel was extremely painful. Anyway, lying out in the hot open sun didn't seem like the best idea. I also worried because I was located more or less in the roadway from Range Three out to Range Four. I feared that it would be night before anyone came looking for me. Since I was in the roadway, I was afraid that if I didn't move, I would get run over by the Range Rats when they came to search for me. I lay motionless for a few more minutes, wondering if I dared to move to a safer position. I began to feel a little stronger. I carefully pulled some of the caked blood from my lips, face, nose, and eyebrows and decided to try to make it back to the cool safety of my weather shack.

At first, I had enough strength to stand up carefully, but the dizziness wouldn't leave my head. I was afraid that I would pass out again without warning, so I remained bent over and started walking slowly towards my theodolite. My theodolite was located about half way to my weather shack. By the time I got to my theodolite, I was feeling weak again, and the dizziness was getting worse. As I dropped to my hands and knees, I now realized that the bleeding had started again. I tried my trick of scrapping together some soft dirt, but the area around my theodolite was nearly as barren as open concrete. Spitting up small globs of blood now, I realized that I had to make it to my weather shack before I passed out again. It stood there with the front door open, some 100 feet away. Inside I had some pillows and once inside, I would be able to use my trick of collapsing onto my hands again. In my weather shack in the distance, I could hear my phone start ringing again. I began crawling towards my weather shack. The sagebrush thorns and large pieces of gravel cut into my hands and knees but I had no other choice. Soon sweat, dirt, and caked blood dripped or had been wiped into my eyes. My vision became blurry and my strength was leaving me. Leaving a trail of blood, sweat, spit, and small pieces of skin, I crawled on. There was nothing to be gained by stopping. Still the phone rang incessantly. I could no longer see where I was going, so I decided to crawl towards the sound of the phone, now off to my right. The three white beings stood silently by the corner of the lounge, watching me as I crawled.

When I was twenty feet from my shack, my legs went numb and I could no longer rise up on my knees. Dragging myself on, using my hands and arms alone, I finally reached the front door of the weather shack. Still the phone rang. The weather shack was raised up on blocks and the floor of the shack was some two feet off the desert. I lay for a few minutes, using the wooden doorway as a headrest, still coughing and spitting up blood through my nose and mouth. After a few minutes, some strength returned to my legs, and I was able to crawl up into the safety of my weather shack. My head felt like someone had been pounding on it with a steel hammer, and every cell in my body was screaming in pain. I had a jar of water sitting on the floor of my weather shack. I always kept the cap loose. Taking a small sip of water, I washed the blood from my mouth and took a small swallow. My throat felt like every nerve was exposed. I was almost over-powered by the pain, but it helped me regain a little strength.

The phone kept ringing. After an immense effort, I was able to position myself so that I was sitting in the doorway, leaning against the door jam for support, coughing and spitting blood onto the ground between my feet. Reaching the cord of the phone, I gently pulled it off the shelf where it sat. The phone fell onto the padded chair next to me and the handset fell onto the floor beside me. I didn't have the strength to remain sitting in the doorway anymore, so I crawled into my weather shack and laid face down, before lifting the hand set to my ear. I jammed the knuckles of my other hand up against my throat, and lay there in the warm sunshine, trying to get hold of my dizziness. My thoughts felt fuzzy and indistinct. I moved my head slowly, back and forth, trying to bring my thoughts into focus but I couldn't. I couldn't seem to remember anything very well. My mind became filled with fragments and isolated glimpses, and what seemed like daydreams. I could remember standing by the corner of the Range Three lounge, and the Teacher speaking perfect, careful English to me, in a pleasant feminine voice. She was saying, "This will not harm you. The effects will wear off by this evening." I struggled and struggled with my dizziness, and the fragments I could remember. I could remember the Captain saying, "This is my daughter. She pleases me greatly," and the Teacher saying, "Do you see that she looks just like a beautiful young earth woman? She enjoys her new disguise as much as I enjoy my nurse's disguise."

I continued lying in the warm sunshine that was coming through the doorway. Both the front door and the large side door were open, and a soft cool desert breeze gently washed through the interior. I wanted to speak into the phone but I couldn't bring my mind or my thoughts into focus. Another fragment crossed into my mind, "She is going to be working with your scientists in Northern California. When she is around earth people she is going to call herself Pamela. Is that not a nice name?"

After a long period of lying in the warm sunshine, my mind finally cleared somewhat. The three white beings still stood by the corner of the Range Three lounge, watching me in silence. I could hear someone shouting at me on the phone. It was Master Sergeant Adams from Desert Center on the other end. He was working the forecaster desk. He was an unusually soft spoken, considerate sergeant. Like the others, he was under orders to never ask me any questions about the Ranges, and I was unprepared for his shouting. He was screaming into the phone, "Charlie, Get out of there, now! I have the Desert Center base commander personally on the other line. He's been shouting at me so loud my ears hurt. I can't make any sense out of anything. The General claims that some woman has phoned the Pentagon from Mojave Wells. The General said that she was using her special "Critical Purple" priority code, 'The Teacher'. That's supposed to mean something to you. She got some four star General out of a National Security meeting. She insisted you were in desperate trouble up there, that something had gone horribly wrong. She said something hadn't been properly adjusted for you. She said you needed rest and help immediately. The General just told me personally, you are ordered to get off the ranges this minute, and back to your barracks. NOW, Airman! You're ordered to spend the rest of the day resting in your barracks, in your bunk. NOW, Airman! Get out of there, Charlie, NOW!"

Groggy, bleeding, close to blacking out, I struggled a slow, thick, answer, "I can't, Sergeant."

"Do you understand me, Charlie? Get off the ranges, NOW! Those are the General's orders! Can't I get through to you? Are you OK? Can you still understand me? I need you alive, Charlie! I need you off the ranges and back resting in your barracks! Get off the ranges! NOW! The danger you're facing is too great! GIVE IT UP! Use your common sense and run. Run to your truck! Get out of there, NOW!"

My mouth was filling slowly with blood. I hesitated to speak again while I coughed and spit and vomited the blood out onto the floor of my weather shack, and out through the front door into the desert outside. When I could speak again, I answered, still thick and slow, "I need the chopper. I need it now." I was holding my sides down by my ribs, in agony at the time.

There was a short pause, while Sergeant Adams spoke with the General. I could hear him screaming at the General on the other line, "He needs the chopper, General! He needs it now!...You promised him the chopper if he ever needed it. He needs it now!...What do you mean he can't have it until sundown? Who is the Teacher that's canceling it?...I can see it sitting right out here on the tarmac. It's gassed and all ready to go! The pilot and medics are sitting in it and everything! They could be airborne in seconds!...You promised him the chopper if he ever needed it. General, he won't need the chopper after sundown. He'll be dead by then! He needs it now!" Then there was another short pause, and the good sergeant came back on my line, screaming in return, "The General says he can't send the rescue chopper for you until sundown. The Teacher, whoever she is, canceled the chopper flight. She says it's too dangerous. Are you still able to drive?"

After a period of coughing and spitting blood from deep inside my guts onto the floor of my shack and out onto the desert gravel in front of my shack, I was finally able to answer, slowly and thickly, "No, Sergeant. I need help now."

There was another short pause while the Sergeant checked with the General on the other line. I was becoming too dizzy to understand most of his words but I could make out his screaming, "All I'm asking for is one power wagon! Steve could just drive out real fast and grab him. Steve wouldn't do anything stupid! He's been out there for years! He's already seen whatever it is that's hiding out there! He wouldn't look around or anything!" There was another short pause, and the Sergeant responded, still screaming, "The General won't let anyone come get you! Charlie, can you hear me? He says the Teacher has canceled everything. The Teacher says the power wagon is just too dangerous. None of us even know who the Teacher is, but she's canceled everything. She's canceled everything. Can you hear me Charlie? Only you know what is going on out there! You're the only one allowed to see it close up! Whatever it is, the base commander said you have to face it alone, even if it kills you. You have to face it totally alone! He swore he'd court martial any man that left the base area! No one can come for you until sundown! The Teacher said it's just too dangerous! Nobody's coming for you, Charlie! Can you hear me? NOBODY'S COMING FOR YOU UNTIL SUNDOWN! We need you alive, Charlie! Get out of there and back to the barracks while you still can!"

I was no longer able to respond. As the phone was slipping from my hand, the Sergeant was screaming, "Remember, if you can't get back into Mojave Wells, the General swears the Pentagon will have that whole valley crawling with a complete Marine division looking for you, just as soon as the sun sets! He swears he's spoken to the Pentagon and they'll send an entire division with tanks, guns, the whole kit and caboodle, and search under every rock in that whole valley looking for you, just as soon as the disk of the sun disappears below the horizon!"

My strength was fading fast. The bleeding had started up again. I crawled into the center of my weather shack where my pillows lay. I formed them into a large soft mound. Then I used my trick again. I formed my hands into fists, pressed my knuckles up under and against the soft part of my throat where the bleeding was coming from. Then I collapsed face down into the pillows, letting the weight of my body maintain the pressure on my wounds. Thought fragments kept circling through my consciousness. Some young woman was saying, "It was not supposed to be this way. It was supposed to be more like a party for you. It was supposed to happen in one of the casinos in Las Vegas. You have been so valuable to both of our governments. Both of our governments have learned so much by watching how you and I and Harry all work together as a team, trusting each other. Harry loves you like a brother, and I have even fallen in love with you the way Pamela has. This test with Pamela is so important. We cannot let you remember what

Pamela looks like in this disguise or it will ruin the test. Now Pamela, both of our governments said that you have to overcome your fear of him and talk directly to him, face to face." As I was drifting away into unconsciousness, I noticed that the blood oozing out of my mouth was beginning to stop.

When I came to again, quite a while had passed. The shadows had shifted and it was getting close to noon. I lay without moving for a long time. The floor of my shack was comfortable and warm. The blood had dried and I was in no hurry to go anywhere. The telephone lay dead on the floor of my shack. I could hear one of the white beings moving in the sagebrush outside my side door. After watching for a while, I was able to catch a glimpse of the tall white being. It was Pamela. She had changed out of her disguise and was wearing her usual aluminized single piece protective jump suit and boots. She was obviously standing guard outside my weather shack, protecting me from any bees, hornets, snakes, and whatever that might be found in the desert outside my weather shack.

A large pool of dried blood lay on the floor by my face, and my pillow was bloody. My head still pounded in agony. The numerous cuts on my hands and knees hurt immensely but otherwise I was feeling much better. My head had cleared and the dizziness had left me, so for the first time since the accident, I was free to think. Carefully, I moved my body and my pillows to a cleaner spot on the floor. This let me look out the front door towards the north and towards the Range Three lounge. I noticed that the tall whites had moved their craft. It now sat on the desert floor fifty yards or so northeast of the Range Three lounge. It was unusual for them to bring their craft in so close to the buildings. I decided they must be in the middle of some kind of emergency.

As I lay there, I wondered what I should do next. At first I thought I would just wait there until sundown and let the range rats come rescue me. After thinking about it for a bit, I began to wonder if anyone would come to rescue me at sundown. As my strength began to come back, I started to worry that the General would send a complete division to rescue me at sundown and that I wouldn't need rescuing any longer. That would mean I'd be court-martialed for sure, wouldn't it? After all, I had been ordered off the ranges, hadn't I?

As I lay there, thought fragments kept invading my consciousness, as though I was recovering from a mild form of hypnosis. I remembered the Teacher laughing, "Is he not intelligent, Pamela. Range Four Harry told us he was so intelligent that it would never work. Harry said we might as well tell him because he would figure it out anyway."

My strength was increasing and the bleeding had stopped, so I moved over to my jar of water and slowly drank the rest of my water. Drinking was still extremely painful but I felt that my body needed the fluids. Anyway, I had another jar of water in my truck.

As I slowly gained strength, I carefully considered my next move. I sat up on the floor and rested my back against the gas stove. Turned off as it was for the summer, it felt comfortably cold against my back. My head still pounded in agony and it took a long while for me to collect my thoughts. My position gave me a nice view towards the north, out my front door. Two of the white beings still stood motionless over by the corner of the Range Three lounge, while the third seemed to be watching me from out in the desert northeast of my weather shack. A second white scout craft could be seen floating a few feet off the desert far up the valley to the north. It was floating slowly towards the Range Three area, so I guessed that it was returning from a trip up to their distant mountain base. Still further up the valley, I could see a third white scout craft floating slowly towards the Range Three area, along the same path as the second.

After giving the matter some thought, I decided that I should close up my weather shack and rest in my truck. I was still unable to speak on the phone, but my strength was returning. I decided that if I rested some more in my truck, I might be able to make it into town. The only problem I faced was that my truck was parked further away than usual. It remained where I had parked it over on the other side of the generator shack.

After resting for a while, I decided that I had enough strength to make the attempt to reach my truck. I closed the side door to my shack. I hung up the telephone and replaced it onto the shelf where I usually stored it. Standing carefully, and holding onto the doorway to my weather shack, I slowly stepped outside into the sunshine. I closed the front door behind me, but did not lock it. Using the side of my weather shack to steady myself, I began walking slowly towards my truck. By the time I got to the corner of the weather shack, I was already becoming shaky, but I crossed the gap between it and the storage shed beside it without too much trouble. Then I began following along the side of the storage shed. I got to its closed front door and tested the lock before dropping to my knees. It was now obvious that the attempt to get to my truck was a mistake, but there was no going back because I was no longer able to stand up. I would have had to stand up in order to open the front door of the weather shack that now stood closed. I could hear the phone in the weather shack start ringing, but I pressed on towards my truck. My strength began leaving me, even faster now than it had before. Falling to my hands and knees, I crawled on.

My vision was becoming blurry as I reached the near corner of the generator shack. Directly in front of me, a thick patch of sagebrush formed an impenetrable barrier. I was forced to detour, so I crawled out onto the hard open surface of the graveled area. My head began pounding worse. My hands and knees were now livid with pain, scratched, and bleeding. As I circled the block of sagebrush, I noticed that the bleeding in my throat had started again, this time much slower than before. My last ounce of strength was beginning to leave my legs as I finally reached the front bumper of my pickup truck. I had left it parked on the west side of the generator shack facing north, less than ten feet from the generator doors. Next to the truck, between the generator shack and the truck wheels, was a small raised mound of soft dirt and small gravel. Realizing that I would never be able to open the truck door and climb in, I decided that I had no choice but to try my trick again. I hardly expected it to work a third time. As I formed the soft dirt into a mound, praying as I did so, I really didn't expect to ever again rise from that spot of earth. Using my now bloody hat to protect my face, and using the soft dirt as a pillow, I pressed my knuckles up under my throat for the last time and let my body press its way into the soft cool dirt. Once again, the bleeding seemed to be stopping. I lay with my eyes facing north towards the Range Three lounge. As my consciousness was slowly fading, I could see the two white scout craft slowly and silently float to a soft landing perhaps a quarter mile out in the desert, north and east of the Range Three lounge. The Teacher was no longer wearing her nurse's disguise. She had changed back into her natural white aluminum canvas jump suit. Thought fragments kept invading my mind. I remembered the Teacher laughing, "Is he not intelligent, Pamela. Range Four Harry told us he would figure it out." As I drifted off, I could see that six or seven of the white creatures had left the two scout craft and were standing around the Range Three buildings. The Teacher was speaking to them, saying, "Stay back. Do not disturb him. Make sure there are no snakes anywhere around this area. Remember, if you speak, even to each other, you must speak in English. He must not be frightened or disturbed." She was the Ambassador's only daughter, and I could see that she wielded tremendous authority.

I lay there unconscious for a long time. When I finally came to, I was so weak that at first I thought I had died. I lay there for many minutes without moving, waiting for my mind to clear and waiting for the angels to come for my soul. After several minutes had passed, I started to wonder what was taking the angels so long to come and free me from my pain-racked body. Then I heard something moving slowly in the dry sagebrush off to my left, hidden behind the southern end of the generator shack. With considerable pain I slowly raised my head and turned it so that I lay looking in that direction, towards the south. Then I lay my head back down on my blood soaked hat and the small mound of dirt. As I watched, a young chalk white girl, probably equivalent in development to a junior in high school, stepped slowly and carefully out from behind the generator shack, facing me, and watching me carefully as she did so. When she was about seven feet or so, out from the southwest edge of the generator shack, she stopped and stood there, studying me intently. She was wearing her aluminized white protective suit. As she stood there some twelve feet from me, she and her suit seemed to have been created entirely out of sunlight. Dizzy and in agony from losing so much blood, it was an easy thing for me to suppose that I was looking at an angel from Heaven. Then a young chalk white male who appeared to be her slightly older brother, also slowly and carefully stepped out from behind the generator shack. The two of them stood there, side-by-side, almost hidden in the bright sunlight, watching me intently for several minutes. For my part, I lay motionless, watching them. I supposed they were angels, and I was waiting for them to come get my soul. When several minutes had passed and nothing had happened, I became concerned. I supposed they, as angels, were waiting for me to pull my own soul up from my body, to stand up, confess my sins before God, and prepare myself for the trip to heaven. With great difficulty then, I slowly and carefully formed the words, "Help me. I am not able to get up." They responded by slowly stepping two or three feet back away from me. Worried and anxious now, with tremendous difficulty I formed the words, "I am going to heaven, aren't I?" The young male responded by quickly stepping back out of sight behind the generator shack. Then the young girl slowly followed suit. As she was doing so, I whispered after her, "No, don't go. Please don't go. Please stay and help me. Please help me."

The young white male and the young white girl continued back out of sight, behind the generator shack. My mind raced in silent confusion. After a few more minutes when no devils from hell showed up to replace them, I decided that the angels must just be waiting for me to finish dying before taking my soul. After a few more minutes of laying in the dirt and gravel, I got a glimpse of the young white girl circling some fifty feet to the south, watching me from the distance as she did so. From this I concluded that the angels were probably still not ready for me, and that I still had more dying to do. The bleeding had slowly started up again, and I was on the verge of passing out. It was with tremendous difficulty that I turned my head back towards the north. I gently pushed the knuckles on my fists back up into my throat, and collapsed back into my bloody hat and into the mound of soft, blood soaked dirt. As I passed out, I could hear the Teacher speaking pleasantly to someone off to the northeast, "You were in way too close…He must not be disturbed…I know he looks dead, but he is much stronger than the others were."

A long time went by before I became conscious again. I was in such great agony and pain that this time I was certain I had died. I was certain the time had come for me to lift my soul up out of my body and go searching for my Guardian Angels, who would certainly take my soul off on the journey to heaven. When my soul wouldn't lift up out of my body, I became confused. I tried just letting my soul float away to heaven, but that didn't work either. Then I tried moving my feet slowly, trying to position my body so that it would be easier for my soul to get out of my body. I couldn't move my left leg at all, but after an immense effort, I was able to slowly move my right one. Then after another immense effort, my left leg finally responded as well. I was shocked and surprised to discover that my body was still responding to my commands. Just the same, the realization that I was still alive was a long time coming. For several minutes I thought I was still dead, and that I was moving my feet for the last time.

After giving the matter due thought, I decided that I would just lay motionless in the dirt, with my knuckles pressed up against my throat, until I finally died or until sundown, whichever came first. Anyway, I was far too weak to do much else. I felt safe enough, protected as I was with my truck on one side of me and the generator shack on the other. There was no danger that I would be run over when the range rats came at sundown. Since I was by my truck, I was certain that whoever came would find me right away, dead or alive. I was no longer worried about being court-martialed. Since I was by my truck, I felt that I could prove I'd tried to follow orders. Lastly, the shade of the generator shack and the truck did offer some protection from the desert sun. The prospect of lying there for six or seven hours until sundown seemed inevitable if not inviting.

Since I hadn't moved my head or my body, I still lay looking towards the north and the Range Three lounge. As my vision cleared, I noticed that the first of the three scout craft remained sitting out in the desert northeast of the lounge. The second one had been brought in by the lounge, closer than I'd ever seen before. The third one was terrain following up the valley towards the distant mountains towards the northeast.

That second scout craft was sitting parked less than 100 feet away from the northwest corner of the lounge. It looked like a giant white oval engine on a passenger train. The door on the near side was open. It opened by rising up, and a short block of steps led from the open door to the ground.

The inside portion that I could see, appeared to be reminiscent of a recreation vehicle. It contained numerous buttons and hieroglyphs. Realizing how much the white creatures liked to keep their craft hidden far away in the mountains, I wondered why they were willing to take the risk of bringing their scout craft in so close, and leave the craft parked out in the open. An American three star USAF General and his aide, a bird Colonel, stood about a hundred feet from me. They were approaching me in a slow, halting manner. Just behind them and to their left, stood the Teacher, still wearing her natural pleasant smile. With her natural white skin, her thin humanoid frame, her sparkling blue eyes, her blonde hair blowing slowly in the wind, she seemed right at home in the hot desert sunshine. Off on the eastern side of the lounge I could see an American USAF one star General wearing a white lab coat. He was obviously a medical doctor. Following him like a puppy dog was his aide, a bird Colonel, acting as medical technician. The medical technician was carrying a tray holding probably eight pints of blood. I was far too weak to move. I decided to continue lying motionless in the dirt and just follow them with my eyes.

The three star General, who was approaching me slowly, turned to his aide and stated matter-of-factly, "So that's the poor airman laying over there now."

The Colonel responded sympathetically, "Yes General. What a way for a man to die. All alone out here in this hellish desert with none of your own kind around to even hear your last prayer."

The General responded, "Yes. Where do they find men of such bravery? He came out here night after night, never

knowing what might be hiding just around the next corner.
We'll never find another man like him."

The Colonel continued, "They say he liked the desert,
General. They say most days he'd be out here in this
wasteland, listening to the radio and reading history books.
On many days he'd even sing and dance."

Then the General said, "I wonder what he looks like.
You know I've never really gotten a good close look at his
face. That time we had him up on the mountain I never got
a good look at him from the front. As I remember Colonel,
you never got to see him close up from the front either."

The Colonel nodded his approval. The General
continued, "You know, those security people would never
show me a picture of him. They won't even allow one to be
placed in his file in my office safe."

"Really General," responded the Colonel.

"Yes. The boys in security didn't want anyone to be able
to recognize him once he left the ranges. They said that for
all he was being put through, he deserved to be left alone
once it was all over. If you'll come with me, Colonel, I
think I'll walk over there and turn him over. I just want to
see what a man that brave looks like close up."

"Yes, of course, General," replied the Colonel. "I was
wondering what a man that brave looked like too."

They had already started walking slowly towards me
when the Teacher spoke, "No, General. Don't go over there.
You should not disturb him."

The General and the Colonel stopped immediately in
their tracks. They were apparently used to the ways of the
tall white beings. The tall whites seldom said "No", but
when they did say "No", they meant exactly "No".

"I heard you say 'No", Teacher. Why?" asked the General.

"Because he is still alive," the Teacher responded.

"Still alive?" asked the General in surprise.

"Yes," answered the Teacher. "He is just lying motionless because he is so intelligent he knows it will stop the bleeding. Do not disturb him. Let him handle his wounds himself."

"What difference does it make?" asked the General. "That poor airman is obviously not long for this world anyway. At least he'll die knowing that some humans were here by him, listening to his dying prayers. He'll die knowing that somebody cared about the sacrifice that he made for all of us."

"No," stated the Teacher. "I picked him because he is so intelligent. He never panics. When something unexpected like this happens, he just calms down and thinks it through. He is so intelligent that he can handle his wounds. He has even figured out where he is bleeding in his throat. If you just let him lay there until he is willing to move, he will live through this. The cells in his throat are healing very fast. He will probably be well enough to move by sundown."

At this the General and the Colonel started to appear noticeably happier. Still showing some disbelief, the General turned and slowly approached the Captain, who was standing by the northwest corner of the lounge with his daughter beside him. The Colonel tagged along behind. Approaching the Captain slowly, the General asked, "Do you agree? Does that poor airman have a chance to live?"

The Captain thought for a few seconds, then replied, "I do not think so. I do not see how he could possibly live through this. I have never seen any earthman take that much

149

damage and survive. The weapon was set thirty percent higher than the level needed to kill the biggest earthmen. Usually when the beam hits them, they panic and start running. All of the others we have killed have bled to death through their mouths. Most died before they had taken even a few steps. But the Teacher has the best electronics and she knows him better than any of us. She thinks he will live and the Teacher is never wrong."

The General turned slowly and pleasantly towards the Teacher, who had retreated from her exposed position. She was now standing next to Pamela. In the meantime, the one star General and his medical aide returned from the far side of the lounge to join the meeting. Finally the three star General spoke, "Why do you think he can survive, Teacher? He hasn't moved a muscle since I've been here. I can see him still lying there in the dirt where your people cut him down at 8:50 a.m. this morning. The poor airman hasn't moved an inch in several hours now. Even if he is still alive, isn't it time we started loading him into the coffin we brought with us? That way, at least he can die in a soft place."

The Teacher stood motionless until the General finished speaking. She seemed to be scanning me with some type of electronics. Then she spoke. "You do not understand, General. The accident did not happen over there by the corner of the generator building. It happened over here by the corner of the lounge building. He is only lying over there because he is so intelligent that he was able to place himself in that position. He has not been willing to lay down just anywhere. The places he has chosen have very special soil conditions. Before he lay down by his truck, he was lying in the sagebrush over behind the lounge. Then he was lying in his weather building. During the last year that he has been coming out here, he has studied every square inch of the ground in this area in great detail. He has used that knowledge to keep himself alive today. Remember, he has already lived longer than anyone expected."

The three-star General stood for a minute or so, thinking while the doctor and the medical aide headed over towards the sagebrush, obviously to check on the Teacher's words. Suddenly the medical aide let out a huge shout, "General, I've found something. The Teacher is right. That poor airman was lying over here in the thorns. Look at all the blood he's lost."

The one star General hurried over to the same place in the sagebrush. Then the two of them began following my trail of blood to the weather shack. Opening the front door, the one star General shouted, "General, you should see the blood in here. That poor airman had one awful time once he got to the weather shack. There's blood all over his floor and his pillows and everything."

The three-star General remained standing with the small group of tall whites by the corner of the lounge. The one star General and the medical aide came hurrying back to the lounge corner, and the one star General exclaimed forcibly, "General, he's lost several pints of blood. He needs a transfusion and he needs one now. We could give it to him right where he lies. We have eight pints of his blood, type O positive, with us here, General. We have another two pints on the craft. It was all they had at Andrews. Maybe we should order Kelly air base in Texas to fly up another ten pints, just in case we need it. We could have them fly it up here in an F104. The pilot could go supersonic so it wouldn't take him long to get here. The plane could land right up here at Mojave Wells Field. One of the scout craft could drop me off in that hollow down at Range One. Then the scout craft could go back to the mountain and leave me alone out in the desert. We could order the range rats to take two power wagons out to Range One to get me. I'd take one of the power wagons myself and get the extra blood and bring it out here. The range rats would go back to Mojave Wells. That way we'd have the extra blood and no one would have seen anything. General, we have to do something. That poor airman can't be more than half alive as he lies there. If he starts bleeding again, he'll die for sure, and we'll never be able to replace him."

The Teacher interrupted pleasantly, "No. It is too dangerous. If you disturb him now, he will start bleeding again. If you put more blood into him, it will raise his blood pressure and his bleeding will become even worse. If that happens, his throat will rupture and he will certainly die. The place where he is bleeding is deep down in his throat. You could never find it and stop it in time. He is so intelligent, he knows where it is and only he can stop it. Just let him lie there and let him handle his wounds the way he wants to. Wounds of that type heal very fast. If he just lies there without bleeding for another three hours, his body will have the damage repaired enough so that he will be out of danger. Then he will live for sure."

"What are his wounds like?" asked the one star General. "I mean, how does the instrument work?"

The Teacher responded, "The way the instrument was set, the beam did not permanently damage any of his tissue or nerves. It did not burn or scar any tissue. It only affected the blood arteries in his throat where they enter the thyroid gland. The microwave beam excited the iodine atoms and caused a chemical change that allows the blood to bleed through the walls of his arteries into his throat. Usually for those instrument settings, the victim bleeds to death in a minute or so. However, the human body has the ability to repair the damage in just a few hours. If the bleeding can be stopped, the victim will recover quickly. If he does not start bleeding again, his throat will be completely healed by this time tomorrow. He will not have much endurance for a few days but he is young and strong. His body will quickly replace the blood he has lost."

At this, the three star General started laughing and looking extremely happy. He exclaimed, "That would really be something if that poor airman could pull through this after all he's been put through. No wonder your people call him Teacher's Pet!!"

Then the three-star general turned to the one star general, and said, "Do as the Teacher said. Just stay away from him, and let him work it through in his own way. You better get that blood back into the cooler on board, just in case we need it later. It'll fry out here in the desert. Have some of it sent down to the medic at Mojave Wells just in case it's needed. Leave the rest at the Desert Center hospital as an extra precaution. Call Desert Center. Tell their base commander that all the ranges are to remain closed up tight as a drum until a week from this coming Monday. Nobody comes out here except the weather observer, and he only comes out here if he feels like it. Make it clear that I don't care if he makes up all the winds in the meantime. Got that General?"

"Yes, Sir," responded the one star General. Then he and his aide hurried over to their waiting scout craft. It was sitting a short distance out in the desert northeast of the lounge.

The three star general turned to the Teacher and stated, "As long as he's going to have to lay there for a while, could your people post a guard by him to protect him from the snakes and spiders and things that invest this hellish wilderness? It'd be a shame for him to get bitten by a snake after all he's lived through."

The Teacher smiled and answered, "Yes." Then turning to Pamela, she continued in English, "Go back to our mountain base with the medical General. Have your cousin, the younger one, put on her travel suit and her electronics. Then have the craft bring both you and her back here. She is not the slightest bit afraid of him. She can watch over him until he recovers. It will be very educational for both you and her. She just loves being around him. She will have a wonderful time playing next to him as he lies out here in the desert." It was just like their women. They were simply children who never grew up.

As I lay there watching, Pamela boarded the first scout craft with the one star General and his aide. Without hesitation, she took a seat alongside them. Then the door to the scout craft closed and it carefully lifted off, rising and floating slowly, silently out over the desert, turning at last towards the north. I watched it for a while as it skirted the Range Four buildings and headed north towards their distant mountain base. The three-star General and his aide remained behind with their Captain, the Teacher, and the crew of the second scout craft.

The three-star General paced anxiously back and forth for a minute or so, obviously choosing his next words carefully. Then the General turned to the white beings and began talking to them as though he were scolding a group of children who had been caught with their fingers in a cookie jar. He began by obviously touching a nerve, "How could an accident like this have happened? I thought your people never made a mistake?"

The white creatures became noticeably agitated. The General waited for a minute or so for his words to sink in. He was obviously capable of dishing out a fine piece of military discipline anywhere on this inhabited planet or on the next one over. He continued slowly, "You know it took us more than ten years to find a man like this. He's so unusual, if you kill him, we may never find another man like him. Because of his bravery, our joint project is generations ahead of schedule. Before him, we'd tried out more than 100 weather observers up here, and good ones too. After just a couple of weeks, not one of those observers would drive out here alone, even in the daytime. None of them would ever drive out here at night, even if another man came with them. Most of them wouldn't even sleep nights in the barracks down at Mojave Wells. Man after man panicked and became hysterical at the first sight of your people, even when they were still miles up the valley. Man after man spent his days and nights making up fake wind reports, and hiding in the chow hall down in Mojave Wells. This is the only man we've ever found who has been willing to come out here day or night, rain or shine, just as we've ordered him to. This is the only man we've ever found that has been willing to stand his ground out here, day or night, and let your people walk in on him. What could he have possibly done that was so wrong? You know he's so gentle that he would never harm any one of you.

155

"Remember last year how he saved your little girl when she was lost in the thick sage down on Range One? How could an earthman be any gentler?

"Remember that night when your guard, the Tour Guide, collapsed from that disease. Your own people would have left without the guard on board and your guard would have died. You remember how Teacher's Pet over there, risked his life for you guys?

"I'm mystified. How could your people possibly have become angry with him? How could your people not trust him? Why were you even using the electronic controls at all? Hasn't he proven himself trust-worthy? Hasn't he earned the right to talk with your people without using any electronic controls, even if now and then he made a few minor, human mistakes? If he was doing something wrong, couldn't he have first been warned? What possible reason could your people have for cutting him down out here in the sagebrush? I'm mystified. Why did your people choose to fire on him?"

The white creatures stood there for a few minutes like small children, looking a little sheepish. Then the Captain spoke, louder and more slowly than usual. He obviously intended to offer up their best defense. He began, "My daughter is terrified of him. She believes he is so intelligent that he can defeat our equipment. For the last several months, we have been trying to convince my daughter to speak with him, the way that both of our governments require so that she gains the experience she needs before meeting with your scientists in northern California. However, each time she has panicked. This morning when he was taking his 8:00 a.m. wind measurements, the Teacher, my daughter, and I were waiting for him behind the lounge building. We called him over so she could talk with him and I could present him with his award for heroism, just as we had planned. At first we set our electronics so he would only remember the presentation of his award for heroism. Unexpectedly, he switched to an entirely different set of thought processes deeper inside his brain, and broke free from the controls. My daughter could no longer tell what he was thinking. She tried to readjust the controls but he had readjusted his way of thinking so that the controls would no longer work. He began stepping closer to me so he could hear what I was saying.

"My daughter has never been close to him when he was not under our control, as the Teacher has. My daughter panicked. Remember, sometimes his ability to conceal his thoughts, used to cause even the Teacher to panic when he first came up here.

"My daughter was only going to give him an electric shock to make him step backward. She was only going to set the weapon to excite the sodium atoms in his nerve cells. That would only have given him a harmless, but still very painful electric shock. The effects of the shock only last for ten minutes or so. However, in her haste, she accidentally moved her weapon to the wrong setting, to the Iodine setting, before she fired it. Her aim was perfect. The weapon was set to its highest power. It hit him directly in the middle of his throat. It should have killed him immediately.

"I expected him to bleed to death where he stood. I am really surprised that he is still alive. My daughter must be correct when she says that he can defeat our weapons once he gets used to them. We are sorry for the accident, and we sincerely hope that he can survive. We have learned so much from him. Like you, we do not believe that we can ever find another earthman like him, either."

The General stood silently thinking for a minute, slowly comprehending what the Captain was saying. Then he responded slowly, "If what you say is true and I believe it is, does that mean he can remember other things too? Does it mean that he can remember the time we thought his knee was broken and we took him up to the medical facility in your mountain base to perform surgery on him?"

"Yes," answered the Captain simply.

Shaken, now for the first time, the General continued, "But I thought you said your electronics had induced a mild state of hypnosis in him and that he wouldn't be able to remember anything about the trip up to your mountain base. As I remember, only Range Four Harry and the Teacher disagreed. As I remember, Range Four Harry had said that Teacher's Pet would eventually be able to remember everything about the trip."

"Yes. That is correct," responded the Teacher. After a short pause, she continued, "Just last week I was monitoring his thoughts from the mountains over by Range Two. It was a nice warm day for him, and he was sitting quietly in the sunshine. I am certain that he can remember everything that happened to him during that trip."

"Really?" asked the General, now showing real concern.

"Yes," answered the Teacher.

The General, now showing shock and concern, asked anxiously, "But what about now? I thought you used your electronics to hypnotize him this morning. I thought it also deadened any pain. I thought that's why he was able to endure the intense pain caused by laying over there in the thorns and sagebrush. How else could he have survived by dragging his body through the thorns and over all those sharp rocks and gravel out here? How else could he have gotten back to his weather shack, and over to where he's laying now? I thought that's why he was able to survive the terror and the awful agony. I thought you used your electronics to focus his thoughts so he could stop the bleeding. I thought you still had him hypnotized while he's been lying over there. I thought the electronic hypnosis was all that was keeping him alive."

"No," answered the Teacher. "After the accident happened, we turned off all of our electronics so he would have the best chance to survive. Once he started bleeding, we could no longer tell what he was thinking anyway. He did all that you described completely on his own. He ignored all of the pain and focused his mind on saving himself, completely on his own. He is very strong willed."

The General now appeared to be completely shaken. In an anxious and raised voice he asked, "But if that desert hardened airman is still alive, and if he's just laying over there motionless so he can control the bleeding, doesn't that mean he has seen and heard everything that we've said and done while we've been out here? Doesn't it mean that tough airman is just lying over there like some big mountain cat, watching and listening to us even now as we speak? Won't he remember every single detail that happened here today after he's recovered?"

"Yes," answered the Teacher. "Remember that was another reason why we chose him. He is one of the few earth men who knows how to handle the knowledge."

"He's still wide awake and alive," exclaimed the General. "We had better step over behind the lounge where he can't see us. He'll have the entire program figured out before any of us know what happened."

"Yes. I told you he was intelligent," stated the Teacher. Then continuing with obvious great satisfaction, "You see, he is so intelligent that it would frighten anyone, General, even you."

The little group moved smoothly out of sight, moving to the north side of the lounge, leaving only the Captain standing by the lounge corner. Occasionally the Captain would peer around the lounge corner to see if I was still lying by the generator shack. I continued to lay motionless in the cool dirt. I was still extremely weak and tired. Since I could no longer hear the conversation between the General and the white beings, I decided to sleep for a while. I needed more rest before I would be able to do anything else. In the distance to the north, out by Range Four, I could see another white scout craft floating slowly down the valley towards Range Three. In a few minutes it finally arrived at its landing place some fifty yards northeast of the lounge, where it settled down. It sat slightly angled towards me. The door on this side opened and a young white female creature floated out. She was perhaps equivalent to an eighth grade girl and was fully outfitted in a white aluminized travel suit. This suit, like the other travel suits, gave her the ability to float. It obviously protected her from everything including gunshots. The Teacher met the craft. The Teacher appeared to be pointing towards me and giving instructions. I was growing stronger but I was still exhausted. I started drifting slowly off to sleep. Through it all, I hadn't moved from the cool dirt where I lay.

When I came to again, the shadows had moved. I had been sleeping probably two hours. The second white scout craft remained sitting by the northwest corner of the lounge, but the first craft was now parked on the desert floor several miles northeast of the lounge. I was feeling better but my head was still pounding. The entire inside of my body still seemed to be alive with liquid pain. I remembered that I had another jar of water in my truck, and I decided that I would feel better if I could get another drink of water. I wasn't sure if I dared make the attempt to rise up and climb into my truck, so I lay there for twenty minutes or so thinking about it. Around the generator shack to my left, I could hear the protecting white creature as she moved through the open lanes in the sagebrush. The other white creatures appeared to be still hiding on the north side of the lounge, but I couldn't see any evidence that the General or his aide were anywhere around. It was a beautiful day in the desert and the afternoon winds started making me feel better. The bleeding did appear to have stopped permanently. I began feeling more optimistic after I was able to clear my throat, painful as it was. I tested my legs and I was still too shaky to stand up and walk around to the driver's side of my truck, so I decided to attempt to get into my truck from the passenger side. Rising slowly, and using the side of the truck to balance myself, I raised up enough to reach the door handle. It took me a couple of tries before I finally got it open. The pain in my head was so great that at first I couldn't remember how to operate the door handle. Then I had to drop back down into the dirt and rest a while before rising up again and attempting to climb into my truck. Finally I was able to crawl into my truck on the passenger side and collapse onto the soft seat. I rested there with the door open, for another twenty minutes or so. Then I started feeling a little better. I located my jar of water that was sitting on the floor on the passenger side, and after a great deal of effort I finally got my hands on it. I rested another ten minutes or so before I finally sat more or less upright, opened the water jar and took a few slow sips. It did my body good, but my throat and my insides were awfully dry. The pain of the first drink was almost unbearable. I stopped drinking, and replaced the cap as soon as I saw that a small amount of bleeding was starting up again. The truck door was still open, so I used it to steady myself as I vomited up some of the water, now bloody, from deep inside. The whole bloody mess fell out of my mouth onto the dry dirt outside that I had so recently used to save my life. My vision blurred, and my mind was spinning with thought fragments.

"Both of our governments wanted me to study the way earth women behave when they are around you. I have picked one of them who is in love with you. I have learned to imitate her. Now, while imitating her, I practice pretending to be your wife."

Hanging onto the open door of my truck, I vomited some more blood onto the dirt and gravel. Only after considerable agony was I able to sit back again into the seat on the passenger side, and get the door to the truck closed. In my mind, some man was saying, "This will make it easier for my daughter to disguise herself as a very pretty earth woman, without looking too attractive to other earthmen. Earthmen can sense that, you know, when a woman is in love with another man. It makes them naturally stand back from her. Pamela's disguise will make it easier for your scientists to talk to her about science. Using her as a translator, our scientists and your scientists will be able to exchange advanced scientific and technical information."

I lay down on the front seat of my truck. I knew at last that I was going to live, but just the same I was in total agony. The thought fragments kept invading my mind. "If you recognized her when she was following you around in Las Vegas, and you had not been told, both you and she might panic. That would ruin everything."

And more thought fragments, me answering, "I understand. You want to share advanced scientific knowledge with our scientists without them knowing where it comes from."

Then the Captain's response, "That is what your government wants. We think they should be told that it comes from us."

And me answering, "The guard who stays alongside her, pretends to be me so they look like a husband and wife team. That way she is perfectly safe while appearing to be playful and very beautiful to earth people. It makes it fun for her and it makes the earth people more willing to accept her advice without becoming hostile."

And the Teacher laughing, "Is he not intelligent, Pamela? Range Four Harry told us he would figure it out."

My thoughts continued, "After she and the guard have done that for a while, and everyone on both sides have worked out all of the details, then she will assemble and train more 'husband and wife' teams of translators to share scientific information. Pamela will become the Director of the joint US / Tall White team of scientific translators. The Americans receive increased scientific knowledge and will be able to build better equipment. The tall white people are able to monitor American scientific development, and receive a desert base that is better furnished than it is now. Right now, there are many supplies that you need that we are not able to provide to you. This new cooperation opens the road for the Americans to travel into deep space and on to the stars. It also allows the white people to better equip their safe haven from which they rescue, repair, and re-supply their space ships that are traveling in the vicinity of the solar system.

"Since white people and humans are naturally terrified of each other, you need a place like Range Three with a person like me to be the 'Hospitality Host'. So everyday the American Air Force has had me come out here, release a balloon, measure winds that nobody cares about, and phone them in to Desert Center to prove that I'm still OK, just so the white people can come around whenever they want and practice talking to me. I'm supposed to be the sample human who shows newcomers, tourists, and other passers-by, both white people and humans, how to overcome their natural fears and enjoy talking to each other. The Teacher and I were chosen by both of our governments because we are the first two individuals who learned to trust each other on an individual level. Now, we're supposed to show everyone else how it's done. Everyone else has had to travel in groups governed by military and diplomatic protocol. They've all had to be accompanied by guards and translators. They could only travel along a few restricted corridors because nobody else ever trusted each other on an individual level."

The Teacher giggled in response, "Perfect. See Pamela, he has reasoned it through perfectly. Of course, Charlie, sometimes the Americans at Desert Center really do need to know what the winds are here in this valley. They do not always throw them away."

It was a hot day, and dizziness was again flooding over me. The windows of my truck were rolled up. Sitting in there, with the doors closed, made the truck exceptionally warm. A certain calm seemed to be overtaking me as I fell off to sleep.

When I came to again, my head was still spinning and my stomach was still full of nausea. At least I had slept peacefully without bleeding. My watch showed that another two hours had passed. I was especially surprised to discover that now both windows were rolled down. The extra ventilation made me feel a great deal better, but I was certain that I hadn't rolled them down. Thought fragments were still passing through my mind. I remembered the Captain and Range Four Harry standing a short distance in front of my truck while Range Four Harry showed the Captain how to adjust one of his instruments. I remembered Pamela opening the truck door and rolling down the window on the driver's side, while the Teacher did the same on the passenger side. The Teacher was saying, "The only thing that will help him is to rest with his friends. You may inform the American Generals that Teacher's Pet is going to live. The effects will wear off. He will be healthy again by tomorrow."

I shook my head slowly until my thoughts cleared a little. I decided that even though I was still in bad shape, I should move my truck and try to get closer in towards base before I passed out again. I was awfully weak and it took me several minutes to slide over into the driver's seat. I moved the gearshift to neutral, and started the truck's engine. Then I had a problem. I couldn't remember how to make the truck go forward, or what to do next with the gearshift lever. After grinding a few gears and experimenting with the clutch, I finally found low gear and put the truck in motion. Once the truck was moving, I started feeling a little better. I noticed that I had a full tank of gas. I made a wide arcing turn to get the truck pointed back towards base. My head was pounding too bad to make a short turn, so my turn took me way out into the desert to the west of the Range Three buildings. As I negotiated the turn, in my rear view mirror I could see the Captain and the Teacher still standing by the northwest corner of the range lounge watching me. I also noticed that the large white scout craft was still parked a half-mile or so, out in the desert northeast of the lounge.

I couldn't figure out how to get the truck out of low gear and into a higher gear, so I decided to just bounce my way back into base in low gear. For the first two miles, I was quite dizzy and the truck was weaving around so badly that for safety, I just drove out in the desert west of the pavement. Finally, my head cleared a little more. Still in low gear, I bounced on over to the pavement and straddled the centerline while I headed in towards base. Thought fragments still floated around my brain. I remembered the Teacher saying, "Both of our governments consider you to be quite a hero. They weren't going to try this experiment until forty or fifty years from now, maybe even longer. Then we located you. At first we were going to have you accompany Pamela on her travels. But her father wanted the guard to pretend to be you and accompany her instead so she would be better protected. The guard was not willing to pretend to be you until we showed him how intelligent you are. Our people are very selective, you know."

I remembered answering, "But, forty or fifty years from now, will you still be here? I mean, won't we all be old and won't you have already left for home?"

My statement seemed to generate a great deal of laughter, which sounded like the quiet yapping of a coyote. Then the Teacher responded, "We live much longer than you do. When my grandfather died from old age, he was more than ten feet tall and almost 700 years old. But we also grow much slower than you do. That's why my bones take so much longer to heal than yours."

The Teacher added, "The Captain's daughter was born right here in this valley when James Madison was your President. She actually has never been back to where we come from. Forty or fifty years is not much time to us."

I remembered responding, in surprise, "But how can you be that old?"

Then the Captain responded, "I don't know why you find it surprising. Right here on earth, you have turtles that live more than 500 years."

I was snapped out of my thought fragment by a sudden surge of nausea. I was coming up on the Range Three gate and it was closed. I couldn't remember how to get the truck out of gear, so I took my foot off the gas, stepped on the brake, and turned off the engine. My truck stopped just short of the gate, although at first I thought I was going to run into it. My nausea was getting the best of me as I slowly got out of my truck. After some vomiting, I sat down on the front bumper and rested. In the distance, down by the base, I could see Steve and the range rats, waiting in three power wagons for me to clear the range. Using binoculars, they appeared to have spotted me, and Doug, in one of the power wagons, appeared to be carrying a message back to the command post. After resting a while, I got up and slowly opened the gate, so they'd know I was going to make it. Then I went back and sat down on the front bumper. I felt a certain consolation in noticing that the last time I vomited, I hadn't vomited up any blood. It meant that, at last, my stomach and my insides had stopped bleeding. I was starting to get pretty thirsty again, so I got up slowly and found my drinking water. I stumbled back to the front of the truck, and I sat down again on the bumper.

More thought fragments began floating through my head, as I sat there slowly sipping the water. After a few minutes, I started feeling much better. I found my dizziness was leaving me, my thoughts were clearing, and I felt well enough to drive again. Climbing back into my truck, I started my engine, and pulled through the gate. Once through, I just kept going, leaving the gate open behind me. I got the truck into second gear and started closing the gap between the range rats and me. As I left the Range Three road and entered the base, I pulled up alongside Steve and the range rats. They had waited patiently for practically the entire day. Looking out my open window, I could hardly find words to thank such loyal friends. Surprisingly, after determining that I was well enough to drive myself back to the barracks and put myself to bed, all Steve would say was, "Charlie, that General down at Desert Center has ordered us not to ask you any questions, but you know that anytime you need someone to talk to, you can tell us men here anything and we'll believe you. We were all worried sick about you, and don't give us any of that nonsense about you having the flu. We men here, we know what is out there. We have seen it plenty of times in the distance, and some of us, Bryan, Doug and I, have seen it close up. We know it came in close today and we know you're lucky to still be alive. We men here, we know that those white things nearly killed you out there today. Knowing them the way Doug, Bryan, and I do, they probably didn't mean to, but they nearly killed you anyway. Anytime you feel like talking about it, you can tell us men here anything, anything at all. We won't ever tell anyone what you said."

I was so exhausted, all I was able to say in response was, "Thanks, Steve. You're such good friends. I really appreciate it." Then, putting my truck into gear, I headed for my barracks. A few minutes later, I finished tucking myself in under the covers of my bunk and was fast asleep.

Later, along about six in the afternoon, the ringing of the barracks phone awakened me. Doug, who had volunteered to stay in the barracks and watch over me, in case I awoke in pain, answered the phone. I lay in my bed still half asleep listening to him.

"Yes, General," said Doug, "I don't want to wake him. He's sleeping here in the barracks now......Yes, Sir, he's feeling much better, and if he can get some more rest, he'll be over it. The Range Rats and I are right here, so if he starts vomiting up blood again, we'll call for the medic immediately...Yes Sir, I know you're willing to send the medical helicopter now that he's gotten off the ranges, but it looks to me like he doesn't need it... No, Sir, none of us have asked him a single question...Yes, Sir, every man has obeyed your orders...Yes, Sir, I'll tell him that whatever he's doing, the Air Force is proud of him... Did I understand you correctly, Sir, all of the ranges are totally closed for the next week. Charlie is the only person allowed out on the ranges until a week from tomorrow...under penalty of court martial. Yes, Sir... All daytime weather reports next week are canceled. Charlie may take the morning report, that's the 4:30 a.m. report, if he feels able to… or he may skip the morning report and remain sleeping in the barracks, if he wants to…Yes, Sir, I'll see that he receives your orders as soon as he wakes up." With that Doug hung up. It was a warm afternoon and I needed my rest. Closing my eyes, I drifted back to sleep.

It was almost midnight when I awakened again. I was feeling much better. The growling in my stomach reminded me that I hadn't eaten for many hours. I got out of bed, put on my civilian clothes, and decided to walk the mile or so over to the hamburger stand in Mojave Wells. I was still shaky and I felt that a little exercise might do me good. I certainly was ready for ice cream or something. It was Friday night. I expected the stand to be open until 1:00 a.m.

The walk over to the hamburger stand was a pleasant one. My sides and my insides hurt terribly but walking slowly made them feel better. It was a beautiful warm summer night. The moon was full and the stars were out. I was more than halfway there before I noticed that the tall white teenager assigned to protect me, had fallen in behind me on my right, all in total silence. She was about five feet tall, obviously young and very active. She appeared to be able to control the floating fluorescent white suit better than any of the other white creatures that I'd seen. I couldn't recognize exactly who she was, and she wouldn't communicate with me. Whenever I turned towards her, she would float out several feet away from me, and wait for me to continue walking. At the time, her appearance actually took me by surprise. As I was walking down the left side of the paved frontage road, a car suddenly exited the divided highway, and came traveling down the road towards us. At the time, the white creature had been following me by floating down the middle of the highway. Seeing the car coming, she slipped to her right and hugged the fence on the far side as the car sped past. As she did so, I noticed that the light from her suit was generated uniformly from a zone of fluorescent sub-atomic particles. The zone appeared to be several inches deep, all around her suit. I found her silence to be kind of annoying but I decided that, considering the day's events, she had probably been told to make certain I was recovering, but not to interfere electronically with my thoughts. At one point, I stumbled on some gravel alongside the road and nearly fell down. I noticed that she immediately closed the gap between us, coming to within six inches of grabbing hold of my arm, apparently eager to come to my aid if I needed it. It appeared to me that her thought processes were operating almost three times faster than mine and I found the entire experience to be quite humbling.

When I finally arrived at the hamburger stand, I was disappointed to find it closed. Since I was tired, I sat down at one of the deserted wooden tables out front. I decided to rest for a few minutes before heading back. I remember how beautiful the evening was. I was sitting quietly on the wooden bench, while the white teenager floated in among the nearby trees, obviously watching me. She apparently found it easy to balance herself when she was wearing her suit because she floated up in between the lower branches of the large oak trees next to the hamburger stand and played in and around the leaves. I estimated that those branches were fifteen to twenty feet above the ground.

After a few minutes, I was feeling better. I decided to walk back to my barracks and go back to sleep. As I arose, I noticed that the white teenager had floated over the fence into the nearby trailer park, and took up a position watching me from behind some trees there. Her position gave her a good view of me as I walked the entire distance back to my barracks. As I arrived back at my barracks, I could hear the dogs barking loudly over in the trailer court. Looking over in that direction, I could see the white teenager and two other white children, apparently the equivalent of sixth and seventh graders floating over behind the trees. I found the situation noticeably humorous. The white children appeared to be trying to get the dogs to roll over, the way I had done several weeks earlier. Poor kids, all the dogs would do for them was bark.

The next morning, Saturday, my growling stomach guaranteed that I would be waiting outside the chow hall as soon as it opened for breakfast. After a man-sized breakfast, I felt tired again, so I spent the rest of the day sleeping. I remember drinking lots of coffee, milk, and water. After having an early supper, I started feeling normal again, noticeably weak, but normal. I put on my party clothes and caught the bus for the long ride up to Las Vegas. I had gotten used to sleeping on the bus. It seemed like a perfect evening for a quiet night on the town.

Several hours later, it was well after midnight, I found myself playing blackjack at a secluded table in one of my favorite major casinos downtown in Casino Center. I was sitting in one of the first seats just off the dealer. It was a busy Saturday evening in the summertime and the casino was packed. There was an open seat across the table from me. A middle-aged man in ordinary clothes walked smoothly up to my table and sat down at the end seat across from me. I took note of his mannerisms immediately. He was obviously the one star Medical General I'd seen out in the desert. I sat quietly, playing my cards, waiting for him to make the first move. After two or three hands of blackjack, he looked across the table at me and addressed me pleasantly, "I see you're drinking soft drinks. The next time the cocktail waitress comes, will you ask her to get me one too?"

"Yes," I responded and returned to playing my cards.

"You're awfully quiet tonight for a young man," he continued. "I've seen you in here before, Charlie. Usually you like to laugh a lot. Does your throat feel OK?"

"I'm fine," I replied. "I'm just being quiet tonight because I'm feeling a little homesick." Nothing sticks out like a sore thumb faster than a General trying to look inconspicuous, I mused to myself.

"How does your throat feel," he continued, looking intently at my throat? He was trying hard not to look like a doctor checking up on his patient. "Do you cough any? Have you been having any dizzy spells?"

"Don't worry," I answered respectfully, remembering that Generals are always Generals, even when they're out of uniform. "I'm perfectly OK. I feel fine. I just need to take things easy for the next few days and get my strength back. That's why I was sitting quietly."

The ease with which I responded seemed to satisfy him. He finished his hand, stood up and stated in friendly, sincere tones, "Well, Charlie, I'm as happy as I can be that you're here tonight playing cards. You're the toughest airman I've ever seen or heard tell of." Then he smiled, turned, and disappeared outside into the crowd in front of the casino.

"He has a fine casino-side manner," I laughed to myself, "If I lose too much money at this table, I may need that transfusion he was waiting to give me, only not in my arm, but in my wallet." Then I went back to playing my cards.

The next Monday morning at Range Three passed uneventfully. I wasn't surprised to find myself alone on a deserted range in an empty desert. "After all, 96 hours is 96 hours," I said to myself. "They have to sleep sometime." I finished my balloon run by 5:00 a.m. and cleared the range before sunrise as ordered. That night I got a good night's sleep. I knew Tuesday morning would be a different story. I agonized over the possibility of not taking the Tuesday morning run. After all, the General had said I could cancel it if I chose to. After mulling things over in the shower, I decided that I had nothing to be afraid of as long as I kept my wits about me. I just hoped they never put me through that throat bleeding routine again.

The drive out to Range Three began easily enough. As I passed the road junction to Range One, I noticed that the desert was empty all the way down the Range One valley. The fluorescent white beings floating in the distance, up along the mountains by the Range Three ammunition bunker came as a mild surprise. I wondered why they hadn't deployed the guards the way they had the week before. On this night, the guards had been pulled way back to a small area around the bunker, and back to the line of communication that ran from the bunker, up along the foothills of the mountains to a valley a few miles to the northeast. When I finally arrived at the Range Three buildings, I was surprised to discover that no guards had been posted in the building area, and no one interfered with my truck. I stopped my truck next to the generator shack, turned off the engine, and the headlights and cautiously got out.

To the northeast, over by the bunker, I could see two guards and no more than ten adult white creatures. The guards seemed to have formed a line, across which the white creatures were obviously unwilling to cross. I stood beside my truck for a few minutes. It was a dark night with very little moonlight. I turned off my flashlight and waited a few minutes to acquire my night vision. Then, in darkness lit only by starlight, I began visually checking the Range Three building area for guards. It was a quiet night and I could hear something move in the sagebrush and shadows over behind the range boards. "Who's there?" I called out several times. There was no answer. I could hear someone walking slowly and heavily on the gravel. I strained my eyes, but I couldn't see anything in the darkness. I knew that with so many tall white creatures watching me from the distance, I couldn't possibly be in any actual danger. The Teacher would never have permitted it. Just the same, I was reluctant to enter the generator shack and start the diesels until I knew what I was going to have to face in the darkness outside. After thinking things through, I decided to walk over to my theodolite and look as if I were proceeding normally. I began singing one of my sunshine and desert songs. I walked to my theodolite and noisily began the process of opening it up. Then a fatherly voice spoke to me in authoritative tones, from the dark shadows beside the Range Three lounge, "Airman Baker, come to attention."

Turning, I could see the dim outline of a middle aged man in a dress blue Air Force uniform standing there in the darkness. The starlight glinted off the three stars the General wore on each shoulder. I came to immediate attention, saluted smartly, and reported my name, rank, and serial number. He returned my salute and approached me slowly until he stood no more than ten feet from me. The darkness prevented me from seeing his face and most of the details of his uniform. As I remained standing at attention, the General turned on the flashlight that he was carrying in his left hand and illuminated me, concentrating on my face. After he was apparently satisfied, he turned off his flashlight. Then he spoke using the same fatherly, yet authoritative tones, "You may stand at ease airman but you're ordered to leave your flashlight off at all times while I am in your presence. You are also ordered to remember at all times that you are in the presence of a commanding General."

"Yes, Sir," I answered. The General's presence could hardly have made me more nervous. Although I always kept my uniform and my weather shacks clean and in military order, being inspected by a three star General was another matter.

"How are you feeling this morning, airman?" he asked.

"Fine, Sir," I answered respectfully. "I am completely capable of performing my military duties as ordered, Sir!" From the shadows behind the range boards, I could see a second Air Force officer. He had left the safety of the deep shadows and began walking slowly over towards the gravel where the General and I stood.

"Yes, airman. I can see you are," the General responded. After a short pause, he continued in that same fatherly manner, "You know, Charlie, you're the bravest airman any of us have ever laid eyes on, coming out here alone every morning as you do, never knowing what is hiding out in the shadows or around the next corner. I don't know where on

God's green earth the Air Force found you, but I wish I had a hundred more men just as brave as you are. Look at you. This morning, after all you've been put through, you've come out here alone. You were challenging me in the shadows and you're not even armed. I never would have believed it if I hadn't seen it for myself. I just want you to know that the very highest levels of your government are proud of your accomplishments. Your bravery, your hard work, and your sacrifices have allowed the American government to accomplish something that I personally never thought could ever have been accomplished. You've taught people who can never possibly meet you personally, how to become friends and trust each other. You've allowed our government to make trusted friends in places I can't even describe. You've even allowed me to make my fourth star. I will be receiving it soon. I stopped by tonight for the privilege of meeting you personally and to personally give you my highest commendation."

Nervous, defensive, and taken totally off balance by both the General's presence and his praise, I stammered a respectful response, "Thank you, Sir, but I'm only following my orders. If I didn't come out here every night as ordered, Sir, you would be forced to court martial me."

The General thought for a few seconds and then began laughing as a father would. "You're right there, Airman, but there isn't that much to being court-martialed. I court martial men all of the time. Usually they do a couple years in some chicken wire brig and they're right over it." The General kept laughing for a while, as though doing a mere two years in the brig was something of a lark. I could see he was in a much better mood now that I had reminded him

177

how much fun he'd been having, court-martialing enlisted men like me.

The General continued, "I see they're right about you, Charlie. You sure do have that sense of humor they say you have. No wonder the Teacher fell in love with you two years ago." He paused momentarily to chuckle some more, before continuing authoritatively, "Well, Airman, the Colonel and I had better get back to our duties. Good night, Charlie. Carry on."

"Yes, Sir," I responded respectively. The General, the Colonel, and I exchanged salutes and parted. I turned and walked slowly to my weather shack. The General and the Colonel turned, walked over to the range boards, and began walking down the road towards the ammunition bunker and the tall white creatures in the distance.

I opened up my weather shack and began preparing for the morning weather report. I had long since gotten used to filling my balloon in near total darkness. I waited until the General and the Colonel had disappeared into the darkness down the bunker road before I turned on my flashlight. Once the balloon was full, I collected my clipboard, took the balloon outside and released it. As I did so, I noticed a large group of tall whites many miles to the northeast. They were positioned in a pass to the northeast that lead out of Mojave Wells valley. The logic of it struck me immediately. They were gathered just over the ridge of the pass, and therefore weren't legally in the Mojave Wells valley. Knowing the careful logic that the white beings lived by, I concluded the General must have insisted that my activities not be interfered with and that only a few white beings could enter the valley at night during this cooling off week.

As I was preparing my theodolite for use, I noticed the Teacher and Pamela, floating in their fluorescent white suits over by the ammunition bunker. With a careful, deliberate motion, they crossed the line and began floating down the paved road towards me. Both had their electronics on, and my mind began to fill with their thoughts. The leader of the guards was saying to Pamela and the Teacher, "Now remember, once you cross this line, you are both on your own. In order for us to protect you, you must get back to this line."

"I understand," Pamela responded.

The leader of the guards continued, "Remember, the American Generals insist that you can not harm him when he is out there. That is his area. He is only doing what they ordered him to. We agreed not to touch him unless he comes over here by us. If he does that, if he should chase you across this line, then we get to kill him. So if you become afraid when you are out there, remember, you are on your own until you get back to this line."

Pamela agreed. I, myself, was glad they'd showed me where the line was. I noted that the line was approximately one mile northeast of me. However, it wasn't as if I had any plans to chase any tall white beings for more than a half of mile in any direction.

The Teacher responded to the guard, "Pamela is not afraid of him any more. She trusts him now."

Pamela responded affirmatively. Properly prepared, she and the Teacher began floating slowly down the paved road towards me. The Teacher stopped and waited by the turnoff to the second gallery while Pamela continued on towards me. What she had to do, she had to do alone.

179

As I took my balloon readings, Pamela continued slowly to the near end of the billboards. Then, between readings, she greeted me. Her electronics placing the thoughts in my mind, "Good evening, Charlie," she said.

I responded speaking out loud, "Hello, Pamela. You mean good morning, don't you?"

Their logic, always flawless, she responded, "No, The disk of your sun has not come up above the horizon, yet. That means it is still evening. Do you enjoy being a weather observer and coming out here alone in the darkness?"

"Yes," I answered, recording my next reading. I felt that if I kept working as I talked, she was less likely to panic, and I was more likely to live to an old age. Then I continued, "Do you enjoy wearing your earth woman disguise and dressing up in women's latest new fashions?"

"Yes, very much," she giggled. Then, she left her position by the west end of the billboards and in a natural fashion, began closing the distance between the two of us. I had finished taking my readings so I stood upright in relaxed fashion beside my theodolite, and stood ready to meet her. I noticed that Pamela wasn't using the electronic hypnosis equipment as the tall whites had been on the day of the accident. Even though the tall whites were always well armed, I was surprised by Pamela's newly found courage. She was walking slowly towards me, knowing that I was in complete control of myself. The prospect of her panicking again, once she realized that she was meeting me on my own terms, made me quite nervous.

I understood the point of this meeting. Pamela had to prove to both her government and mine that she was perfectly capable of disguising herself as my wife. Before she could perform her assigned task of exchanging technical

180

information between her scientists and ours, before she and her guards, accompanied by American guards, could travel to various U.S. government facilities, Pamela had to pass her final exam. She had to come and stand in front of me naturally, and talk to me exactly as my wife would have. Once this realization had finally sunk into my brain, I continued in happy, playful fashion. I called it staying alive, "Does your male cousin enjoy pretending to be me, and do you enjoy pretending to be my wife?"

She giggled for several minutes as though she were an earth woman, closing the distance all of the time as she did so.

"You're getting that imitation down pretty good," I noted. Even the Teacher occasionally broke into her natural barks and whinnies when she was laughing.

Then Pamela turned off her electronics all together and began speaking to me out loud. Using perfect English, she answered, "You were not supposed to know what we are planning." She paused for a few seconds. Then she continued speaking pleasantly to me, closing the distance to less than ten feet as she did so "How did you ever figure everything out? The Teacher and Range Four Harry keep telling me that you are more intelligent than the other earth men they have met."

Forgetting that she was an alien creature, I answered, noticeably flattered, off balance and laughing, "Well, I'm a pretty tough guy to fool, you know. I get around. I've been to L.A. and a lot of other places," as though beings who could make the deep space crossing between the nearby stars would be impressed that I'd been to Los Angeles.

Pamela caught the humor in my statement immediately and found it quite amusing. She was laughing harder now.

After a minute or so, she was finally able to speak again. She had a surprisingly feminine voice. Closing the distance to less than five feet, she continued, "You know, Charlie, if I were an earth woman, I really would dream of being your wife."

"That's really nice of you to say," I responded.

Pamela and I stood laughing together. Then Pamela, as though she were dancing a slow dance, moved smoothly and naturally to my right. Proving she was now totally unafraid and proving that she trusted me. She rotated slowly, completely turning her back to me, before turning slowly again to face me. Now standing at less than arm's length, she continued, as a young wife might have, "I am sorry about the accident, Charlie. The Teacher was right. I should never have been afraid when I was around you. I am glad you survived. I hope you forgive me."

Finally forgetting completely that she really wasn't human, I responded laughing, "Of course I forgive you Pamela. I understand completely. Anyway, I'm a rough, tough, kind of guy, and I need a little pain to add excitement to my life."

As Pamela and I stood facing each other barely three feet apart, she, too, appeared to have completely forgotten that I really was human, that I really wasn't one of the tall white creatures.

Then she said, "I will never forget you, Charlie."

"I'll never forget you either, Pamela," I answered.

After gazing deeply into my eyes for a minute or so, she smiled, turned slowly until her back was turned towards me once again, and walked slowly back towards the billboards. When she arrived at the west end of the billboards, she turned her communications electronics back on, and the electronics in her suit back on. I could again eavesdrop on her thoughts as she turned east onto the bunker road. There could be no doubt. She had certainly passed her final exam.

I stood thinking about what had happened. I felt I finally understood what the Teacher had meant. She had said all they wanted was for people to enjoy being around them while they were here. As I thought about it, I decided that was all I really wanted, too, for people to enjoy being around me while I was here. I felt I had finally arrived at a place where the white beings and I could meet on equal ground, at a place where we trusted each other. I wanted only for them to enjoy being around me, and they wanted only for me to enjoy being around them, while I was here and they were here. I was struck by the simplicity of it all. It was, after all, nothing more than the way parents on both planets want their children to feel when the family is together. I felt as though we formed part of a large group of parents. We were just trying to build a safe and happy world for our children.

The ringing of my telephone interrupted my thoughts. My report was running late and Desert Center must certainly be getting worried. Locking my theodolite, and walking to my weather shack, I answered the phone, "Range Three, Charlie here."

It was Sergeant Adams. In a concerned voice, he stated, "Charlie, the sun will be up soon and you're running late. You don't have to be out there at all this morning, you know."

"I'm sorry. I'm running late, Sergeant. I'll have the winds in ten minutes. I still have to finish my computations. Don't worry. I'm not in the slightest danger," I answered respectfully.

"The General made this morning's run optional, you know," answered the Sergeant. "I'm more worried about your safety than I am about those winds. You need to take things easy for the next week and not take any chances out there on the ranges. Why don't you just shut down and finish your computations back at base in the barracks or make up the results and phone them in to me from the chow hall, like all of those other weather observers used to do."

I answered, "OK, Sergeant, I'll finish the computations in the barracks and phone them to you by 6:00 a.m. I'll hang up now, and shut down. I'll head straight in to base."

"Excellent idea, Charlie," responded the Sergeant. Then he hung up the phone.

I picked up my readings, locked my weather shack, and started my truck. In the distance to the northeast, I could see the Teacher and Pamela floating happily back towards the ammunition bunker. The Teacher was saying to Pamela, "See, I told you he wouldn't attack us. I told you we could trust him. That's why my little girl and I, picked him, and that's why we have all fallen in love with him."

I was surprised by the discipline of the white beings that waited for them. Not one of the waiting tall whites crossed the line to greet Pamela or the Teacher. Instead, they saved their obvious greeting activities until both Pamela and the Teacher were safely back across the line established by the guards. When they were all together again, as a group they fell back along the mountains towards the valley in the foothills to the northeast, guards, Generals, and all. I took my time starting my truck and driving back into base. I felt that we had all arrived at a new understanding. I felt that the Teacher, her daughter, Pamela, and myself, were all bonded together for life. Bonded together by the starlight. I wanted to enjoy this newly found life out under the stars, and when I think about it, I guess, so did they.

The Upper Room

"…and say to the owner of the house,
'The Teacher asks:
Where is the guest room,
where I may eat the Passover
with my disciples?'

He will show you a large upper room,
all furnished.
Make preparations there."

…Luke 22:11,12

It was well after midnight on a warm Saturday evening in Las Vegas. I found myself playing blackjack at a secluded table in one of my favorite major casinos downtown in Casino Center. I hadn't picked the casino or the table by accident. Rather, the casino and table had sprung up in my mind as I was preparing to leave my barracks at Mojave Wells, and it had stuck there for the entire long trip to Las Vegas, as though burning a hole in my consciousness.

I was sitting in one of the first seats just off the dealer. I was by myself because my close friend Michael had taken his wife and his sister Pamela, whom I usually dated, on a vacation to San Francisco. I happened to be the only player at the table and I found this disconcerting. It was a busy Saturday evening and the casino was packed. Yet, for some reason, player after player had refused to approach my table.

I was startled out of my gambling dreams when an attractive, stylishly dressed young woman cautiously approached the table and sat down three seats away on my left. I was startled because, although her appearance was quite different from Pamela's, her mannerisms, her voice, and every other thing about her was identical to Pamela's. She even greeted me, turning shyly towards me, as Pamela would have. She said "Hi, Charlie." As I watched, she opened her purse, allowing me to briefly glimpse more than $10,000 in hundred dollar bills, and took out one hundred dollar bill. Handing it to the dealer, he cashed it into four twenty-five dollar chips. She expertly divided the chips into two fifty-dollar piles, and proceeded to position each pile onto its own gambling square at the table. She was wearing white opaque gloves, a dark green dress with long sleeves, white opaque stockings, low heels for shoes, heavy make up, and a beautiful shoulder length wig. I noted to myself that she was heavily dressed for such a warm evening. I guess I was a little slow when it came to women, but soon I was sure that the woman sitting at my table was not there by accident.

The dealer shuffled and dealt, dealing me one hand and two hands to her. He asked us if we wanted cards. I couldn't help but notice that she asked for a card on eighteen. She received a three and won both hands. For the next seven or eight hands, I played my hand in stunned silence. Playing two, three, and sometimes four hands, she proceeded to win virtually every single hand. By now she was several thousand dollars ahead. Something about her situation left her obviously quite amused with herself. Then something very unexpected happened. The dealer was waiting for her to decide if she wanted a card on her second hand when she, apparently without thinking, answered by saying, "No, my eighteen already beats your seventeen." The dealer, whose up card was only a nine, hadn't yet looked at his down card. He laughed in response, and said, "Is that so. Well, young lady, if you're so certain my down card is an eight, what would you guess this next card on the top of the deck is?"

Without hesitation, she responded, "Oh, I don't have to guess. It's the seven of hearts and the one below that is the five of clubs."

To my surprise, she was perfectly correct on all three cards. The dealer, when he exposed the seven of hearts, then the five of clubs, and then his down card, the eight of spades, just laughed, saying, "Don't some women have all the luck." The backs of the cards appeared identical to me. I noted to myself that the deck had already been played with for several hours, so the back of each one of the cards would now be carrying a unique pattern of nicks and scrapes. I realized that if a person's eyes were sensitive to light with wavelengths in the infrared or ultra-violet, they would be able to see these otherwise invisible marks and scrapes. A good memory would do the rest.

As the dealer switched to a new deck of cards, the lady next to me did something even more surprising. She reached into her purse for another hundred-dollar bill, ignoring the several thousand dollars worth of chips in front of her. Handing it to the dealer, and motioning towards my stack of ten silver dollars and one five-dollar chip, she said, "I would like some chips like Charlie has. What I really came for is to learn how to play Blackjack like he does. Is this enough money to get the metal chips?"

The dealer was laughing as he cashed one of her twenty-five dollar chips into ones and fives. The alien Pamela behaved and reacted so perfectly like Michael's sister Pamela, I could hardly believe she wasn't that Pamela. Knowing the tall white alien lady named Pamela was always well armed and might still have a tendency to panic if exposed in public, I decided that men who enjoyed ordinary vacations in Las Vegas as much as I did, would just play along with the charade. After all, the hospitals in Las Vegas had not yet received casino licenses.

For the next hour, I taught her to play blackjack the way I played it. I would count the cards, compute the odds, and make my decisions. Every hand she would ask for my advice. On one hand, the dealer began leaning over the table towards her to see what cards she held. He jumped back suddenly when both of our brains became filled with the belief that she and I were married, and that I would become insanely jealous if he touched her. He apologized immediately and assumed a position noticeably further back behind the table then usual.

My luck playing the cards wasn't very good on this evening. After playing for an hour, I was down to my last five dollars. On one hand, I was holding sixteen. The dealer came to me, and asked me if I wanted any more cards. I was going to answer, "No," based on the card count. I informed her that there were twelve cards remaining to be dealt from the deck and that only four of them were a five or less. Therefore the odds of improving my hand by taking a card were too low to take the risk. However, the tall white Pamela, who was now sitting one chair over pleasantly insisted that I take a card. She was certain that the next card was a four and the one after that was a seven. That would put the dealer's total over twenty-one, breaking the dealer and letting me win. The dealer, she informed me, also had sixteen.

When the cards worked out exactly as she had stated, I turned to her, forgetting for a moment that she wasn't human and said, "Thanks."

She looked up into my eyes and said in a serious, feminine, and tender manner, "You are welcome, Charlie. Good-bye. I will never forget you."

"I'll always remember you, too," I answered.

Then she quickly picked up her chips, got up from the table, and headed across the casino to the cashier's window in the back. The dealer, noting the large amount of money that she had won said to me, "Your wife sure has been having fun playing cards with you. How did you ever meet a rich woman like that from northern Spain?"

I laughed and said, "Northern Spain isn't as far away as you might think."

As she was cashing in her chips, I decided to check around the casino floor to see if I could locate her guards. I felt certain that the Captain would never let his daughter come into a casino unless plenty of well-armed guards came with her. I checked the bar area to my right. The tall thin black suited man standing with his back towards me in the bar area, held a long thin pencil like device in his gloved hands. He did too good of job ignoring the lightly clad dancing girls. "Guard number One", I said to myself. Looking forward, over the table, I could see another thin young man wearing a plain black suit and playing cards at one of the black jack tables across the room. He was facing me from the side. The object in his gloved hands, I decided, couldn't possibly be a cigarette holder. The large stack of chips in front of him and his instant reaction when my gaze fell on him convinced me. "Guard number Two", I said to myself. Off to my left, I decided that the young man standing by the craps table, in a plain black suit, was holding more than a baton in his gloved hands. "Guard number Three", I said, as I incremented the count. Turning slowly to my right, I visually checked the restaurant area behind me and to my right. The taller man sitting in the back, wearing the same style plain black suit and gloves, had too much uneaten food on his table. As I studied him, he leaned to his left and slipped behind one of the columns supporting the building so I couldn't see his face. "The command post," I concluded. I checked the back door. It entered into the parking lot behind me. Standing by the back door, watching me was a tall thin man in a black suit, wearing sunglasses at night and carrying a long straight cane-like object in his gloved hands. I saw immediately why the tall white alien lady had stayed one chair away from me. It gave the guard by the back door a clear field of fire if he felt he needed one. Pamela cashed in her chips, and the guard by the door followed her as she headed for the parking lot out back.

After she had left, the four guards, one by one, in military fashion, silently got up, cashed in their chips, paid their bills, and also left by way of the back door. It was the last time that I ever saw her or her guards.

I went on playing Blackjack. I felt I would lead a longer and healthier life if I just sat quietly at the table for a while longer. I needed another hour or so to get my money supply back to where I had started.

Circus Maximus

"Teacher," they said,
    "we know you are a man of integrity
        and that you teach the way of God
          in accordance with the truth.

You aren't swayed by men,
    because you pay no attention to who they are.

Tell us then, what is your opinion?
    Is it right to pay taxes to Caesar or not?"

Jesus…said,
    "…why are you trying to trap me?
    Show me the coin used for paying the tax."

They brought him a denarius,
    and he asked them,
        "Whose portrait is this?
          And whose inscription?"

"Caesar's," they replied.

Then he said to them,
    "Give to Caesar what is Caesar's,
        and to God what is God's"
                …Matthew 22:16,21

It was a warm Saturday evening. I made the long bus ride up to Las Vegas. The Casinos were tantalizing that night. I wandered happily down the strip, casino-to-casino, gambling floor to gambling floor, table to table. Captivated by the excitement, it seemed for a time as if my very consciousness had escaped from my body into the shows, the carpeting, the money, and the chips that had married together to form this Green and Gold oasis in the desert.

Somewhere in among the strip casinos, I was walking one of the back streets. It made little difference to me that I had left the last large casino by way of the back door and now found myself heading towards the back, unlit, and little used parking lot of the next major casino down the strip. Here in Las Vegas, on this Saturday night, it seemed as if excitement lay just ahead, no matter which direction I walked.

Being a young man, I was in the habit of noticing cars. Of course, I enjoyed looking at new rich sports cars but almost every car had something interesting about it. My gaze swept across the parking lot and landed on an ordinary car. It wasn't a new car. It wasn't an old car. It was just a car. Something made it stand out from the others. It was parked in an out of the way spot in a perfectly ordinary way. Painted totally black and devoid of any markings whatsoever, it just sat there. "No car on earth could be that nondescript," I said to myself.

A glance at the car convinced me that it couldn't be any of the known makes or models. The entire body appeared to have been molded out of a single piece of metal. The car appeared to have been custom made.

As I reached the back steps to the casino door, I wondered, "Why would anyone go through all the trouble to make their own car, just to make it look so perfectly uninteresting?" I thought about it for a while. I decided that the car had to belong to some genius that wanted to drive around unnoticed at night.

I went into the casino wondering if the car's owner was inside. After a few minutes, the dinner show ended and the crowd started to file out. Off to the side, I noticed that the casino had provided an area for tourists to take photographs. Knowing the way Las Vegas operates, I wasn't surprised when a young male model and a young female model showed up in the photographic area. The two models were there to help the tourists spice up their pictures. The models appeared to be in their early twenties. They were stunningly beautiful specimens of young humanity. I noticed immediately that they were taller than average. One stood more or less six foot tall and the other stood at least six two. The man was somewhat taller than the young woman. From their perfectly proportioned physiques, male and female, they might have been physical education majors. They said nothing. However, both of them had obviously mastered the art of playing their respective parts.

The tourists were streaming out from the dinner show. Not surprisingly, they naturally formed two lines to the side of the two models. All of the men naturally formed up next to the beautiful young woman, while the women lined up next to the man. Then, one by one, as the scantily clad models posed majestically next to each tourist in turn, the tourists proceeded to have their pictures taken by their friends and relatives. Soon, these two stunning young models had worked the crowd into a frenzy. Many older men acted as if they were nineteen again and Christmas was coming early.

I stood wondering if anyone in the crowd could still pass as a Presbyterian. Suddenly, I found myself gazing at one of the women in the crowd. She was standing there so peacefully that I could hardly believe it. She was totally unaffected by the actions of either of the two models not far from her.

She was about my height with an unusually white complexion. She was wearing a long sleeved, dark green winter dress with winter tights, low heels, and very pretty makeup. She was noticeably thin but appeared to have an attractive, though ordinary figure. She appeared to be wearing a wig of ordinary light brown hair. The wig had hair that was just shorter than shoulder length and completely concealed her neck. It was made up into a full body hairdo. She was also wearing warm winter nylon driving gloves. She was the very picture of beauty. It showed that she had paid unusually close attention to all of the fine details, and close attention to the finer points of style. Yet she did not stand out in this evening crowd. She, too, looked beautiful, but perfectly ordinary.

She was standing in front of me, just off to my left, facing in my direction. She had her head turned slightly towards me and was following me with her eyes as I moved. It was obvious to me that she recognized me.

I slowly realized as I watched her, that she was doing nothing but standing there watching me. Then, a thought ran through my brain. She's a young Spanish lady, an Ambassador's daughter from northern Spain, and I felt honored to have met her. I was suddenly convinced that I knew the Ambassador and that he liked me.

Immediately, then, I saw through the charade. "Good evening, Teacher," I thought. "You must be having fun wearing that beautiful new disguise tonight."

A short pause ensued. Then, a thought appeared in my consciousness. It was obviously from the Teacher and directed towards me, "Hi, Charlie. We never expected to see you here tonight. How do I look?" she asked. "Do you like the way I am dressed?"

"Your dress is perfect." I slowly thought. Then I continued, "Your makeup is perfect. You look just like a young attractive human woman with a very fine eye for detail. I see that you're very good at shopping for clothes and makeup here in Las Vegas."

"We learned it from you," she laughed in return. "We learned how to blend in with American society by imitating you. Remember we had to learn how to adjust our electronics properly also, in order to do it."

We both laughed. I expected that Las Vegas being what it is, she was probably not alone, so I began looking around to see if I could locate her companion. I found him standing stiffly, off to my right with his back turned mostly towards me. He was wearing an ordinary black suit with a white shirt and tie. He stood about six two. It was easy to tell that under his suit, he was very thin. He was dressed stylishly. I could tell that he also was wearing a wig. This wig covered his head down below the level of his ears and gave him the appearance of being an ordinary businessman. It took only a moment for me to notice that he really didn't want me to see his face. All things considered, I wasn't surprised.

"Your father is dressed perfectly, too," I continued.

The Teacher remained standing in the same position. She seemed to want to direct my attention away from her father. It was easy for me to see that I had him trapped against the crowd in the background. In order for the two of them to exit gracefully, he would have to drop the charade and turn his face towards mine. This he obviously did not want to do.

At the time, I was actually quite happy to meet them. They had never harmed me, and talking to the Teacher had always been a pleasant, if sometimes unnerving, experience.

The Teacher's thoughts continued to appear in my mind, as her father began maneuvering his way out of the position he was in. She continued, "We are not really creatures of science and darkness. We are really creatures of sunshine and playgrounds. Only a few of us are actually scientists. More than anything, we like to sing and dance in the warm sunshine, just as you yourselves do.

"When we are here on your planet, we have to be very careful. We live almost ten times longer than you do, but that means everything in our lives happens very slowly. We grow much slower than you do. If one of us becomes injured, our bodies need ten times as long to repair itself as yours does. Many of your ordinary animals such as dogs, will kill us if we are not careful. Your people care nothing about the differences between themselves, but go insane with fear if they see one of us in the open. We don't know why your people cannot just relax and enjoy being around us while we're here."

She paused for a minute, apparently communicating with her father.

Then she continued with a question, "How did you know we were here?"

"I recognized your car in the parking lot," I replied. Then I reassured her, "I will go away now so that you can enjoy the night in peace. Do not worry. I will keep your secret. I will not tell anyone that you come here."

"Thank you," she said. "Please walk towards the front door. We want to walk towards the back door. My father is still a little afraid of you. He wants to go to our car now."

"Yes," I answered. "I am happy to help you."

I slowly began walking past her as I headed towards the front door. Her father responded by cycling slowly to my left, always keeping his back towards me. I guess I was moving slower than he expected, and he apparently couldn't resist the urge to check my position. As I watched, he glanced over his shoulder to see where I was. There was no mistaking the shape of the side of his face, his unusually white complexion, and the pink shade of his eyes. The tall white men had blue eyes when they were young. However, when they reached middle age, the color of their eyes changed to pink. As I brushed past the Teacher, a beautiful thought entered my mind. Clearly and simply, she said, "Thank you for enjoying us while we were here."

Without further ado, I left the casino, walking quickly through the front door into the night outside. It was a beautiful evening. As usual, high in the northern sky above, in the constellation of Bootes, twinkled the star Arcturus that I guessed they called home. I wondered if their home planet actually resembled the warm deserts and mountains in northern Spain.

Looking through a gap between the casinos, I could see the ordinary black car leaving the back parking lot and heading up a back street. The car moved silently as it carried the Teacher and her father back to the sagebrush meadows and mountain hideouts they loved. Both he and his daughter, the Teacher, appeared to be pictures of happiness.

"Yes," I thought to myself, "I knew I was right all along. It was such a strangely nondescript car."

Like Wheat

"Simon, Simon,
    behold Satan has demanded
        to sift all of you like wheat,

but I have prayed
    that your own faith may not fail;

and once you have turned back,
    you must strengthen your brothers."

...Luke 22:31,32

It was a very cold winter, and it passed slowly. Day after day, despite their majestic wintertime beauty, the Ranges were cold, desolate, lonely places. Steve, Doug, Wayne, and Smokey had all completed their terms of enlistment and returned to their homes in distant civilian places. Clark, Payne, Dwight, Michael, and all of the other experienced weather observers had transferred to Viet Nam and other far away places. The tall whites, of course, were generally never seen during the wintertime. The number of men with me assigned to Mojave Wells dwindled to eight. I had been serving in the USAF for a little over two and a half years. It had seemed like a lifetime.

One cold afternoon towards the end of January, my new weather commander asked me to come down to Desert Center for a short talk. He met me alone, out in the parking lot next to my weather truck. He had another award for bravery for me, signed by a three star Pentagon General.

He was giving me a choice, he said. On the one hand, if I wanted to have a military career, the Air Force would send me to the Air Force Academy with all expenses paid. There I would earn a college degree and become a military officer. Then, if I so desired they would place me in command of the base at Mojave Wells and guarantee me a promotion to at least the rank of bird Colonel. Anytime I became tired of commanding the Mojave Wells base for any reason, the Pentagon guaranteed that I could change and become a pilot of cargo planes that made scheduled supply runs between bases in America and bases in Europe. It was a good life, he said. All I had to do was sign the request form.

On the other hand, if I did not wish to make a career of the military, he would send me to Viet Nam before spring returned to the now cold deserts. It would be good duty, he said. I would be sent to one of the big safe American bases that had University Extension classes right on base. That way I could continue my college education while also serving my country in Viet Nam. I would be far away from the fighting. It would be a base such as Cam Ranh Bay, he said, and I would be discharged several months early when I returned to America.

I thanked him kindly and told him that I greatly preferred to be sent to Viet Nam and then to receive an early discharge. I was very homesick, I told him honestly. All I wanted to do was to finish serving my country and return home.

He said, every person that knew of me would understand. He said in that case, he would send a new First Lieutenant named Howe to replace me at Mojave Wells.

That way I could relax and enjoy my last few weeks at Desert Center as I waited for my Viet Nam orders to be processed. Howe would come up to the Wells the first Monday in February. I had been through so much, he said, the rest would do me good.

The first Monday in February and First Lieutenant Howe, both arrived together and on schedule. I began by showing the Lieutenant the Range Three weather shack and handing him the keys. The first day out at Range Three, I was going to show him how to start the diesels and fill a helium weather balloon. The Lieutenant, however, proud of his new silver bars, exploded in a rage. He already knew how to do everything, he said. After all, he was an officer and I was only wearing three stripes. If there was any training to be performed, he was certain, he would be training me. After breakfast, I was ordered to clean up the generator shack and polish the generators while he took the weather reports and phoned Desert Center.

Later in the afternoon, after the newly cleaned Range Three generator shack had failed his inspection, he had me standing at attention out in front of it. He was screaming, "I don't know why they call you Teacher's Pet, or why you have all those awards for bravery in your personal files, or what you've been doing out here for the last two and a half years, and quite frankly, airman, I don't care! You have no military discipline whatever! You are a disgrace to the entire US Air Force. You've been out here so long that you've forgotten how to take orders! I am the officer and you're the enlisted man. I'm giving the orders and you are taking them! Now get used to that!"

We both agreed that I would pack my duffel bag and catch the Tuesday morning bus back to Desert Center.

Before I left, I tried respectfully, one last time, to tell him of the existence of the tall white beings and to caution him about never becoming angry in front of them. I wanted for him to understand that the tall whites didn't handle the emotion of anger the way humans do. If they ever once became angry with a human, their natural reaction was to kill or severely injure him. For a human to ever become angry with them, the way he had exploded in rage towards me, was simply courting disaster. Considering the Lieutenant's instant temper, it seemed like a body of information that he could put to good use. The lieutenant didn't see it that way, though. He stopped me before I had hardly just begun. We had both just gotten out of the weather truck after he had parked it in front of his barracks at the end of the day on that sunny Monday afternoon. He had been angry with me all the way in as we drove back from Range Three.

"Sir," I began respectfully as I walked around behind the parked truck. "There's something else you need to know about."

"Yes, Airman," he said angrily, as he finished stepping out of the driver's side of the truck, closing the truck's door as he did so.

"Well, Sir," I continued in a hesitant manner, "There are these people, a young woman, her children, and some of her friends. They're white, real white. You will see them from time to time. They're sure to come around as soon as the weather becomes warmer."

"What are you telling me, Airman," asked the Lieutenant in brutal angry tones. "Have you been having some woman meet you out there on the ranges? I'll have you court-martialed for that!"

"No, Sir," I said defensively and quite off balance. "The ones that come around are not human."

"So you're saying that they're ghosts. Is that what you're trying to tell me? Are you saying too, like some of the other superstitious airmen around here have told me, that this barracks that I'm staying in is haunted," he laughed in angry and sarcastic tones?

I thought things through before I responded. Then I smiled and said, "No, Sir. I just wanted you to be aware that some of the men up here believed those legends and rumors. Some of the men here at Mojave Wells can be pretty superstitious. They're good airmen. I hope you go easy on them."

"That's decent of you, airman," he said, "But I've never been afraid of ghosts."

Then he stomped up the wooden stairs into his barracks, leaving me standing outside. The entire experience convinced me that there was a vast difference in character between the various officers in the USAF—and between men.

The next day I packed my duffel bag and, for the last time, I caught the bus back to Desert Center as ordered.

Jackpot Farewell

...He waited seven days more
  and again sent the dove out from the ark.

In the evening the dove came back to him,
  and there in its bill was a plucked-off olive leaf!

So Noah knew that the waters had lessened on the earth.

He waited still another seven days
  and then released the dove once more;
And this time it did not come back...

...Genesis 8:10,12

It was a lonely, rainy Sunday night at Desert Center. It was just past 1:30 a.m. I was alone in the weather station, working the mid-shift. I had only one more week of duty before shipping out for Vietnam. Working mid-shift left my days free. This made it easier for me to pack and process my paperwork.

The forecaster and everyone in base ops had long since gone home for the night. Except for one operator in the far away control tower, the hangers and other buildings on the airfield were deserted.

The drizzle and the quiet rain had been going on for hours, drenching everything in the Palm Meadows valley. The rain was chilly, but not particularly cold. I had closed the airfield when I came on duty. The field was covered with low clouds and patchy fog, as were the mountains to the north and west. The low clouds and fog extended across the valley to the east and all the way down into Palm Meadows itself, many miles away to the south.

I was sitting at the observer's desk, reading one of my history books. I sat facing the desk and one of the inner walls. The light from my reading lamp and the small lights on the various wind and weather instruments, dimly lit the building and provided all of the light that I needed to perform my weather observing duties. I had turned off all of the building's other inside and outside lights. I had long since memorized the location of everything in the building anyway. Most of the duties I could perform in total darkness or by flashlight.

It was a very quiet. The only sounds that I could hear were the rain on the roof and the gentle winds outside.

Then I thought I heard the sound of someone's footsteps on the paved tarmac outside, quietly walking past the large windows behind me. The windows were partly open and the sound was very distinctive. One of the sounds in particular, seemed intentional.

Since I was completely alone on this end of the airbase, the sounds were quite unexpected. As I sat there listening, I noticed that the footsteps sounded as if they were far apart. From this I concluded that the person outside must be somewhat taller than I was.

Lonely and curious as to whom it might be, I slowly rose from my chair and called out in a loud voice, "Hello. Is anyone out there?"

There was a short quiet flurry of activity. Then I could hear someone hurrying away to the north. Cautiously I opened the door to the outside, speaking loudly as I did so. I went outside, leaving all of the lights off. Since the weather station building had an overhang and the drizzle was falling more or less straight down, I wasn't actually in the rain. I was instead, under the overhang and walking next to the building.

Outside, although the night was dark, rainy, and overcast, the visibility wasn't too bad. I could see more or less a half-mile in every direction, although I wasn't able to see the mountains to the north.

I walked around the northeast corner of the building and stood next to the telephone pole there. I was still protected from the falling rain by the building's overhang.

Directly to the north perhaps a quarter of a mile away, were the deserted concrete structures known collectively as the base "Jet Engine Test Bed" facilities. The facilities included some concrete bunkers, small machine shops, and protecting concrete walls. The facilities were used by the aircraft mechanics to test and repair jet engines. Usually the fighter planes would be tied down to the concrete. Then the mechanics wearing ear protectors would start their jet engines. The facilities allowed the mechanics to stand next to the engines while adjusting and testing them.

On this chilly, dark rainy evening, out in front of the nearest deserted concrete structure, standing in plain view, I could see the Teacher, Range Four Harry, and the guard known as the Tour Guide. They apparently intended that I should see them. I was surprised since I had never before seen any of the tall white beings actually on the base at Desert Center, although one of my aircraft mechanic friends had always insisted that the test bed facilities and the Desert Center aircraft hangers were haunted. The ghosts, he had insisted, came around only on rare occasions, and then only on warm summer nights.

On this night, the Teacher, Range Four Harry, and the Tour Guide were wearing their protective fluorescent suits. Their suits were turned up to perhaps half power to protect them from the rain. They were standing still with their arms and hands positioned calmly at their sides, just watching me from afar. Of course, for the tall whites, standing still with their arms and hands at their sides was always considered to be a sign of peace.

They were wearing their communication equipment and after a minute or so, their thoughts began slowly entering my consciousness. The Tour Guide began. He said, "We understand that you will soon be leaving for Vietnam. We came to say Good-bye. Thank you for saving my life. I will never forget you. Good-bye, Charlie."

"I will never forget you either," I responded by thinking the thoughts clearly and slowly. "Good-bye and good luck wherever you go."

Then the Tour Guide slowly retreated back towards the mountains to the north, disappearing into the darkness and into the rain as he did so.

Then the thoughts of Range Four Harry began entering my consciousness. "Good-bye, Charlie," he said. "I am going to miss coming to visit you out on the Ranges. It has been so much fun talking with you. I will never forget you."

"I will never forget you, either, Harry," I said. "Good-bye and good luck wherever you go, too."

Then Range Four Harry slowly retreated back towards the mountains to the north, also disappearing into the darkness.

Then, lastly, the Teacher, standing alone and by herself, began communicating with me. "Charlie," she said, "My little girl and I are so sorry to see you leave, but we understand. You have made our lives so much fun. It can never be the same without you. We will always remember you, and we will always be waiting out on the ranges to see you again."

I was almost at a loss for words. Thinking slowly and clearly, I responded, "I will never forget you either, Teacher. You have been such a good friend that I am not able to say 'Good-Bye'. I will always treasure the memories I have of the many happy nights that you and your little girl and I spent together out on the Ranges. Good luck wherever you go."

With that, the Teacher turned and also slowly retreated back towards the mountains to the north, finally disappearing into the darkness and the rain. Inside my consciousness, it felt like she was crying as she left.

My remaining week of duty at Desert Center passed quickly. On Friday morning I packed my duffel bag, signed out from Desert Center, and made the long bus ride up to Las Vegas for the last time. From there the following morning, I would travel to San Francisco and then, after spending a weekend enjoying the city, on to Vietnam.

My last night in Las Vegas was a melancholy time. I stowed my duffel bag in a locker at the bus station. I began the evening by saying a short prayer and asking God to be with me. I spent my last night in Las Vegas wandering from casino to casino, showroom to showroom, blackjack table to blackjack table. The memories I took with me can't be described. I started the evening with $10 dollars, saw my favorite shows, enjoyed my favorite seafood and steak dinner, played all of my favorite games, and arrived at the downtown bus station just after sunrise with $40 dollars in my pockets. I retrieved my duffel bag and boarded the bus to Bakersfield and San Francisco, certain that God had heard my prayers and would always be with me.

I will always remember Las Vegas the way it looked that night.

Vietnam Arrival

...Then the crew decided to draw straws
to see which of them
had offended the gods
and caused this terrible storm;

and Jonah drew the short one.

...Jonah 1:7

The weather was pretty ordinary for the tropics on the day I reported for duty to the weather command post at Tan Son Nuht air base in Viet Nam. I was young, healthy, and in near perfect physical condition. I was carrying a book entitled, "How to Learn the Vietnamese Language". My orders required that I check into the country at Tan Son Nuht before traveling on to my new assignment at Cam Ranh Bay. I handed a copy of my orders to the Chief Master Sergeant at the desk, and wondered aloud how soon I could catch the next connecting flight up there.

He looked over my orders and my records. Then he said to me, "Airman Baker, I see here that you are a man who knows how to take care of himself when things get pretty tight. Those awards for bravery are extremely impressive."

"I'm not really very brave," I replied. "It's just that so far, God has chosen to hear my prayers."

"Well, I tell you, Charlie," he continued, "We had several men killed down at a South Vietnamese base in the

211

Mekong delta last week and my commander has ordered me to only send men who can handle themselves, just in case that place gets overrun. You look like just the man for that assignment. So, I'm going to cancel these orders to Cam Ranh Bay and reassign you to that place down on the Mekong."

I solemnly reassured the Sergeant that the line of weather observers behind me in the hallway, contained fifteen or twenty men who were much better qualified to be sent into the Mekong Delta than I was, but he kept typing up my new orders anyway. Later in the afternoon, I was over in the base operations hanger registering to board an Army troop transport to be taken to my new jungle assignment. I remember wanting to talk to my USAF recruiting Sergeant from back home.

After showing my orders at the flight desk and registering for my flight, I stood, waiting patiently until boarding time arrived. The plane held thirty-seven soldiers and I had been assigned boarding pass number twenty-seven. Just a handful of minutes before boarding time arrived, one of the famous American news anchor men strode proudly into the building with several other men in his entourage. It was a hot, humid day in the tropics. His face was covered with thick make up. Some of it was melting and streaming down his cheeks. He also had several cameras hanging from straps around his neck and shoulders. He was quite young at the time, and full of energy. Two of his cameramen had their cameras rolling and were filming him as he walked in.

The newsman walked proudly up to the officer behind the flight assignments desk, showed his press pass, pointed out through the open hanger doors towards the army transport outside that we were all waiting to board, and said, "I need ten seats on that plane for me and my cameramen. We are traveling down into the delta today to check on the progress of the war. I understand that some American soldiers were killed in communist attacks down there yesterday."

The officer behind the desk responded, "Yes Sir." Using the public address system, he called up those soldiers who held boarding pass numbers twenty-eight through thirty-seven and bumped them off the flight, telling them to check into the overnight barracks area and catch another plane tomorrow. Then, starting with the famous newsman, he re-assigned those boarding numbers to the news crew.

I felt a great deal of excitement because the famous newsman had been assigned the seat on the plane directly beside me. I was almost skipping with excitement as all of us trooped out to the Army transport. I took a short pencil out of my pocket, along with a piece of paper. I intended to ask him for his autograph, and hoped that maybe he might take a picture of the two of us standing together after we arrived at our destination.

The seat that he had been assigned was the window seat behind the pilot. My assigned seat was on the aisle beside him. I waited and allowed all of the other passengers, including the pilot, to board before me.

While I stood outside at the door of the plane waiting to board, the famous newsman sat down in his seat and prepared to buckle his seat belt. Then, without warning, he shouted out in a loud voice, as though he'd just been shot, "I don't have space for my cameras!"

The pilot, an Army bird Colonel, reacted immediately. He looked over at me, pointed his finger at me and shouted, as though the plane was under attack, "You, airman! You're off the plane! Take the next flight tomorrow!"

Then the famous newsman piled his cameras and other baggage on the plane seat that had previously been assigned to me. The Colonel closed the door of the plane. I quickly retreated to the safety of the grass along the side of the runway, and stood watching the newsman through the windows of the plane as the pilot started the engines, taxied out to the runway and took off. Every time I've seen that newsman on television over the years, I've always wondered if he remembers me, standing there in the grass in my combat uniform, watching him go first, and me holding the short straw.

Green and Gold

...And so we came to Rome.

The brothers there had heard that we were coming,
and they traveled as far as
the Forum of Appius
and the Three Taverns
to meet us.

...Acts 28:14,15

The Mekong river delta in South Vietnam is a beautiful place. The jungle, green, glistening, flooded over by the Mekong, is sliced into almost eatable portions by the gold of the morning sun. The day I arrived, the narcotic of two years worth of weekend vacations in Las Vegas, Nevada was still numbing my brain. My heart was still pounding from the dancing girls and the racing odds. My body was still sweaty from the shows. My fingers were still infected from the touch of green felt and the chips of gold. I felt as if I had stepped from one endless and beautiful night at the casinos into an equally endless and beautiful day in the jungle. Night had fallen on one world of green and gold. Day had dawned on another. I remember wishing that I could spend my entire year in South Vietnam, touching green and gold.

The Vietnam War, like the Mekong, had flooded the delta and ravaged its mistress, the city of Can Tho. The

215

finger in the dike was the runway at Binh Thuy (rhymes with Aw Phooey). Binh Thuy was just a short flight southeast of Saigon, which was ninety miles or so away. It sat dangerously close to the Mekong River. The runway intruded into swamps and rice paddies. In the distance stretching as far as the eye could see, was the jungle.

The army transport had barely touched down when I first saw Ken. He was standing in the distance by the base operations building, waiting to greet me. His green uniform, like the jungle, sparkled in the gold of the sun. He was thin enough to have been fasting in the desert. Even in the distance, he seemed willing to talk only to me.

I will always remember stepping down from the plane. Ken greeted me in that timid manner of his. Not waiting for an answer, he shouldered my duffel bag. I reminded him that we were both enlisted men and offered to carry the bag myself, but Ken insisted. As we headed for the barracks, a mile distant, I remember studying Ken, his mustache, his noticeably long hair, his pleasant smile, his willingness to shoulder my burdens. I remember how much he reminded me of Jesus.

Ken pointed out the control tower. It stood like a giant wood and steel lady of the evening next to the base operations building. There were hangers and repair shops waiting in line along the eastern edge of the aircraft parking area. Strewn in its shadow could be found the wreckage of several South Vietnamese planes. Ken explained that Viet Cong mortar crews could wait in line, too. So, for the first time, I began to fear the jungle during the nighttime.

The tower was where we worked, he said. We were both weather observers. We used the tower to train the South Vietnamese. The tower reached 40 ft high, high enough for the large cab with its weather instruments on top to occasionally transport a man's spirit into the low flying clouds.

The cab had two levels with a stairway for access. The top level was an eagle's nest surrounded by plastic windows. It was home to a brood of aircraft controllers waiting to fly to San Francisco. Ken humorously referred to the aircraft controllers as "baby eaglets". He laughingly said that sometimes at night, the cooks would distribute the evening rations, and the baby eaglets would chirp their preference for worms.

Every eagle's nest has a balcony. This one was 4 feet wide with a wooden railing. It was an ideal place to strut with a cigarette and breathe in the morning air.

The room on the bottom gave birth to seasoned weather observers. Dark, protective, enclosed, it was an incubator for feelings of homesickness, hopelessness, fatigue, and despair. Eventually, it delivered grown men to the world with tears still in their eyes.

The tower was always manned. Weather observers, like aircraft controllers, worked rotating shifts. The shifts were day, swing, and mid shift. It wasn't much fun but it was real. I would start tomorrow, Kenneth said, on day shift.

Binh Thuy was a South Vietnamese base with seventy or so Americans. Their barracks were arranged to form a square, neat, inner compound, complete with a barbed wire fence, a mess hall, and latrines. The base was surrounded by a defensive perimeter of barbed wire, minefields, and machine gun posts. It had a moat of swamps and rivers. The roads protected it like castle walls. Across the road on the north was the Mekong. South Vietnamese buses provided service to Can Tho.

I remember walking the road from the tower to the barracks with Ken that first day. I remember remarking that Binh Thuy didn't seem like much of a place to live. I remember also, his response. He said quietly, "It's even less of a place to die."

The weather detachment was five or six weather observers and three or four weather forecasters, condensed together by the winds of war. The forecasters wrestled with clouds and fog from the station in the base operations building. Only the observers enjoyed the view from the tower. An intercom and telephone provided the necessary communications and a bunker of sandbags at the base of the tower was a haven during communist attacks. A haven, that is, if you could get to it. Not infrequently, a grown man would weather a communist onslaught by hiding in the lower level of the tower. The wooden walls offered some protection from near misses, a luxury a running man never had.

The barracks area, one mile away, was a square arrangement of little fortresses built with aluminum shutters for windows, and paper-thin roofs. At night they sat like brick and plaster Conestoga wagons that had circled in the delta mud. In the middle of the arrangement were the latrines and showers. The start of an attack would fill the compound with running soldiers. Sometimes it was only an attack of dysentery. By the end of the rainy season every American serviceman had traveled the length of the compound, some by running in dense fog, others in total darkness.

The barracks area also had its bunkers. They were constructed with thick wooden beams covered with plywood and sand bags. Their floors were covered with huge pieces of gravel. Most of the pieces of gravel were the size of a man's hand. The bunkers could suffer direct hits without damage, and frequently had to.

I remember the end of that first day, sitting quietly on my bunk, praying, at sundown. The last sparkle of sunlight silently retreated from my boots, my fatigues, my flak jacket, my rifle, my helmet, my face and my hands. Finally, only my fingers were left, left to reach for that last fragment of sunshine. I remember wishing my fingers could touch that last little piece of sparkling gold until morning came again. Touching my fingers, instead, was the green, cold handle of a bayonet and 75 rounds of ammunition in golden brass casings. Rushing to take me prisoner was yet another world, a world of midnight attacks, dragon ships, and tearful prayers, a world of explosions, falling shrapnel, and torn flesh, of homesickness, terror and death, yet another world of green and gold.

I Learned How To Laugh

and I Learned How To Cry

...And Sarah said,
  "God hath made me to laugh,
   [so that]
     all that hear will laugh with me."

           ...Genesis 21:6

The mailroom was an unpretentious door to the great beyond. It sat beside the chapel, another unpretentious door to another great beyond. A man always knew which door he was passing in front of by his feelings.

Mail call was a sacred time, always better attended than the Sunday church gatherings. A soldier with mail had no reason to pray. He was already in heaven. Everyone dreamed of cookies and peanuts but only messages from the great beyond could stick to a man's ribs and carry him through the dark evenings.

I had hardly unpacked at Binh Thuy when a small letter from home arrived. It was a beautiful little letter from my oldest sister, Martha. I still remember the joy upon opening it.

On page one it said, "Nothing interesting ever happens at home."

On page two, "Therefore, I'm never going to write."

On page three, "So I purchased a subscription to a daily newspaper. I used your name and address."

And the unforgettable page four,

"The neighbor lady tells me the entire U.S. military runs one day late. This coming February has twenty nine days. So, your subscription is good for a leap year and a day.

Love,
Your Sister."

I didn't realize it at the time but I doubt that I could have survived the year in Vietnam without the newspaper. It wasn't so much what it said, as it was the certainty of just knowing everyday that there existed another world.

None of the other men subscribed to a newspaper from home. The days were very lonely for them.

I used to share my newspapers with everyone. Ken liked to read the comics. They were carried on special pages printed on green paper. The trip to Vietnam was a long one. Usually the papers would arrive two or three weeks late, their outer pages already turned yellow from age. The first shipment of three magically appeared on my bunk as neatly stacked as golden ingots, and handled just as carefully.

Ken and I were laughing about his experiences the day those first precious bundles appeared. Ken said that if he could have passed a college course in general chemistry, he would have been immediately awarded three college degrees, one in the theater arts, one in the fine arts, and one in English Literature. He said that he had taken chemistry five different times and failed every time. On the fifth attempt he was in the lab one day and the instructor was giving him a special test. He was to identify various compounds by their color. Laughing, he told how he had informed the instructor that all of the solutions looked green to him. Then we laughed about his gold-plated F.

I said to Ken, "You're so lucky with your degree in theater arts. I could never act in front of an audience."

Ken was always kind. He replied, "Actually, you'd probably be really good at it. You're so natural. You see, actors never know how to tell the audience 'good bye'".

"You mean they can't do it?" I asked.

"No. Actually it is that they do it too well. That's one reason why actors and actresses should always underplay the part, so they don't overdo their good byes. Getting an actor on stage isn't much of a trick during the first act but after the actor has appeared on stage, said his good byes and exited, getting him back on stage without losing the audience, that's the hard part. If the actor says his good byes too well, the audience will react as if he isn't there." Then laughing, he continued, "I call it 'Kenneth's law of Last Good Byes'".

"You mean that I say good bye so well," I continued?

"No," Ken patiently explained. "You have never learned to say good bye at all. It seems to be instinctive. You always leave people with the impression that you'll be getting back together with them again in a little while. For you, the action is always beginning. Nothing is ever ending."

A few days later, Ken came running into my room apparently filled with feverish excitement, and shouted, "Charlie, I just came from the mail room! There are three great big boxes over there with your name on each of them, and one of them is ticking!!"

Ken spent the next half hour laughing at the expression on my face. He had carefully wrapped three boxes and placed them in the mailroom for me. Two of the boxes held newspapers, and the third held my wind up alarm clock, ticking loudly. Surprisingly, it was several days before I could see the humor in Ken's opening lines.

Some time passed. One day I opened my mailbox and pulled out a short note, typed and neatly written on official USAF stationery.

The note read:

Mail boxes at Binh Thuy air base
    are assigned on the basis of

       "Willingness to Participate."

It has come to the attention of

      **** the USAF Postal Quota Inspector ****

that you have not been receiving your fair share of mail.

Therefore, either begin receiving your fair share of mail,
    or surrender your mail box privileges.

Signed,
    Commanding Officer
    USAF Office of Postal Quotas

I was thrown into instant panic. I ran over to Ken's barracks, burst into his room and shouted loudly and anxiously, "You must help me. I have to keep my mail box privileges." I showed him the horrible note and worried over what should be done. Then I noticed he was laughing with tears in his eyes. Days would pass before I, too, could laugh at Ken's brilliant little joke. First I would have to spend a great deal of time settling down.

Settling down was harder than I expected. Ken was a genius at the theater arts. I was working nights in the tower. A few days had passed. It was dark and quiet. I was standing with my back to the door, bent over the work desk. Suddenly, I felt the cold, steel muzzle of a rifle jammed painfully into the back of my ribs. Before I could move, someone was speaking to me in a command voice, using broken English, with a perfect Vietnamese accent. The voice said with a brutal sternness, "COME WITH ME, YANKEE DOG. WE HAVE A PLACE FOR YOU."

Terror struck me. I raised my hands, firmly believing that I was being taken prisoner by the communists. "I surrender," I screamed, terror punctuating my voice. The laughter from Ken could soon be heard floating out across the quiet jungle night. As I turned around, he was already on the floor, rolling in laughter. It didn't seem possible but he had somehow managed to sneak up the forty foot tower without shaking it or making a sound. I would be months living it down. Still, I enjoyed being included in Ken's great artistic flower.

So it happened that I learned how to laugh in the days when Ken used to bring me flowers. I also came to realize that the typical actor was better prepared for the Vietnam War than I was. Actors and actresses had already learned how to laugh and they had learned how to cry. So I think they had learned how to tell each other 'good bye'.

The evening walk back to the barracks was a pleasant one. It was just after midnight. I was coming off swing shirt. Several days had passed. The stars were out. As a trained weather observer, I naturally noticed those kinds of things. Swing shift was the easiest shift and I was quite relaxed. I was tramping back to my barracks at 12:15 a.m., alone, humming a little marching tune, fully armed and outfitted. My jungle fatigues swished messages to me as I marched along. It made me feel at last, like a happy, professional soldier. It felt as if I were at last, where God wanted me to be.

The sidewalk to my barracks led me through the doorway to a bunker. It was the bunker in front of the mailroom and the chapel. It felt like a happy little bunker, or, as I used to call it, a bunker of opportunity. It felt like the perfect place to fight boredom. It felt like the perfect place to laugh and to enjoy life for a while.

The entryway to the bunker had been constructed to extend over the sidewalk. It formed a little archway or passageway in front of me with two doors. One entered into the safety of the bunker. The other was an entrance to an outdoor theater-like area of grass, surrounded by the barracks. It felt like the entrance to a little theater under the stars. It didn't appear to be an entrance to a place beyond the stars.

I was just about to leave the protected area and step through the entryway to the place beyond when the attack siren sounded. Still new to Vietnam, I was momentarily confused. The siren was such a nuisance, so I dropped to one knee at the door to the entryway and began watching, waiting for the show to go on. I was expecting to laugh with the next soldier who arrived.

It was such an unusual time. It was never that way in the war movies. Actors were always giving soliloquies and a final bow and no one ever died until their friends told them 'good bye'. I guess I thought it would be that way in Vietnam.

The war at first, used to be such a boring nuisance intermixed with lots of play-acting. It used to be that a plane would explode and it would appear that the Vietnamese soldier standing next to it, had thrown a firecracker and acted out a part by falling down. When word came that the Vietnamese soldier had left us forever, I responded, "It couldn't have been that one." It seemed more appropriate to applaud his acting ability, at first, than it did to say a prayer of good-bye.

Other times the communists in the distant jungle would fire machine gun tracers into the air from a gun hidden in the undergrowth, and I would sit waiting for the music to begin playing, the way it does in a Hollywood movie. Then, when the distant attack stopped and it had all taken place in near total silence, including men dying so quickly that they had never been able to even scream, I used to feel a certain frustration. I used to feel as though I had paid my money to see a great Hollywood movie, and when it was shown, all of the music had been left out.

I remember kneeling there this evening, at the entrance to the bunker as though I had a seat in front-row-center. Across the square enclosure that formed the stage, three Americans came running out of their barracks. One of them was shouting his lines, "Mortar attack!! Mortar attack!!" I remember watching them run.

Attacks used to be such happy times. I was actually quite envious. I thought, "How lucky they have it. Tomorrow, they'll get to write letters home, exciting letters. They'll get to describe how happy it was to run through the shrapnel and dodge the shells and dirt clumps. It's just my luck!! Why, if only the communists had waited another minute, I would have been able to have fun too. I would have been 'on stage'. I would have been at my barracks door, right where the shells are falling. Then I, too, could have acted in front of an audience."

I waited there, expecting to greet them with phrases like "Great Show!! You lucky guys!! Won't your friends and relatives be impressed!!" I expected it to be the beginning of something fun and good. I expected to laugh.

One I recognized. He was a nice young man. He sat in on my last poker game. He was from somewhere like Kentucky or Vermont. I remembered that he had left the game before I realized it. I had never told him good-bye. I wondered if it would be socially acceptable to go out to greet the three of them and talk to him. That way, I thought, I could have the fun of feeling the falling shrapnel without appearing to be muscling in on his glory. Vietnam was such a wonderful place for a new guy.

The three of them had run about half way across the stage. They were costumed in their white undershirts and under shorts, and they were all running barefoot. None of them were ready for battle, or even wearing their combat fatigues. Only fifty feet separated them from stage left and the safe entryway where I was. It didn't seem to be much of a distance to me, but then, I suppose it seems further when you're dying.

A little burst of smoke appeared by their feet, followed by a loud bang. A little hole opened where sod used to be. The three of them stumbled and went down. One was lying very still and two were screaming. A fourth American came on stage from the right, running out from the nearest barracks, also costumed in his undershirt and shorts and with bare feet. He was running to center stage where two of the three lay. They looked so much like beginning actors, I laughed to myself, as was my habit. They must be putting on a play just for me. Perhaps, I thought, this is another one of Ken's Flowers.

Another little cloud of smoke came from the sod next to them, another loud bang, and the fourth American crumpled. He lay there for a few seconds, also screaming in agony. A shell hit the concrete sidewalk, spraying the four of them with hot shrapnel, and blowing pieces of shrapnel into the sandbagged sides of the bunker next to me. I remained kneeling in place, disappointed that I was still untouched. Then all four of them lay perfectly still and silent. I remember kneeling there, wondering why.

The siren stopped in a couple of minutes. I stood up and waited for the four Americans to do the same, but they didn't move. I said to myself, "Get up. Come on guys, get up!"

I watched the medic run up to them. It was then I could see the damage to their bodies. It was then I realized that they weren't acting. It was then I stopped laughing.

As they were loaded onto stretchers, I kept waiting for them to rise up, the way it's done in the movies. I kept waiting for their parting speech. I kept waiting for them to say good-bye.

I stood there, waiting. In a few minutes the bodies had disappeared into the morgue, leaving me still standing out there, waiting. I kept thinking that this was just the beginning of something. I kept standing there, waiting. I hadn't yet learned how to say a prayer of good-bye.

Vietnam wasn't a land of boredom and fun anymore. It was becoming instead, boredom and terror, sickening, tearful, gut-wrenching terror.

As I stood there, the captain walked up to me. I hadn't seen him coming so I was a little startled. He was a good officer. He began in a gentle voice and praised my self-control. My mind was in complete confusion. He continued by praising me because I was one of only two American soldiers on the entire base who was in complete combat dress, and therefore, ready for combat. My mind was racing in silent circles. He told me to be certain to be present at the detachment staff meeting in the morning. He would recommend me for an award or medal or something. I was too confused to speak or reply. He said he understood how hard it must have been for me to wait there in the bunker and watch those men die; How afraid he had been that I would run out there amidst the shells to help them and be killed too. The blood was pounding through my temples; my forehead was starting to become feverish. My mind was in pieces as I stood there. He finished by gently reminding me that I would be of no use to anyone once I, too, was loaded into a body bag; Only by staying alive could I be of any help to those who were wounded. Then the captain bid me good night and walked off, leaving me there in silent, fitful confusion.

The captain disappeared just before my vomiting started. I went down on my knees on the grass, vomiting and coughing and spitting up the asparagus-green remains of supper when Ken came. My head was pounding and I was in tears. I remember how kind he was. He understood, he said, and helped me through the entryway, into the safety of the bunker.

The bunker had been constructed with four x four's covered with plywood and sandbags. The floor of the bunker was covered with large pieces of golden colored gravel, each the size of a man's fist. The feeling of safety compensated for its lack of comfort. Using my army green helmet for a pillow and my flak jacket for a blanket, I lay down there, on the cold, sharp, gravel, with stones jabbing painfully into my ribs. There in my new world of green and gold, exhaustion soon conquered me and I fell fast asleep.

Two days passed. For some reason, I kept thinking that the nice young man wasn't dead. It was Thursday night and I remembered that he had liked to join in the games on Thursday so shortly after dark I collected Ken and a couple of friends in my room. I broke out a deck of cards and began playing poker. I had an unusual urge so I acted on it. I arranged the table so that one player could sit on my bunk and I left that seat open. I, myself, sat on a chair and Ken insisted on sitting back from the table, facing the open door. It looked common place enough, to me.

We played a few hands. I was in a good mood so just for fun I dealt a hand to the empty chair. I announced that it was for the nice young man when he arrived. Ken didn't seem surprised, but the others objected. One of my friends insisted that the nice young man was dead. He had seen the body in a body bag. He had seen it shipped home. After some wrangling, I accepted the inevitable and picked up the cards at the empty chair. A few cards later, I noticed that Ken's attention had left the game, it was now concentrated on the open door. He sat quietly motionless, concentrating on the doorway. Then without warning, he spoke quietly to the doorway. He said, "You should understand. Charlie doesn't mean anything by it. He just doesn't know how to say good-bye."

I asked Ken whom he was speaking to. He responded in complete surprise, "Why, to the man you left the seat open for. Certainly you saw him sitting there on the bunk. Otherwise why would you have left the seat open for him."

"No, no, I didn't see him," I responded in total sincerity. I got up from the table and let the card game go on without me, not sure if this was another one of Ken's Flowers.

I walked out through the door to my barracks onto the stage outside. The evening air was cool and pleasant. I walked around a little. The stars were out. It was a beautiful night but there was nothing to be seen. There appeared to be no one out there. I wandered over to the place where the men had died and quietly stood there for a few minutes, not looking at anything special. I remembered how they had died and I prayed that they would be taken into heaven. As I stood there, a special feeling of joy came over me, as though I were standing at a gateway to paradise. The feeling lingered for a few minutes. It seemed to carry a message, a very happy message. It seemed to say "Good Bye."

A few days passed. A short letter from Martha, my oldest sister, arrived. My family had always been close. Like all of my letters, it was a beautiful letter. Before I opened it, I ran back to the barracks. I wanted to relax and savor every happy line. Things back home seemed so safe, so unchanging. It was I, it appeared, who was close to the entryway to heaven.

She wrote that she had stopped by the home of one of the neighbor ladies yesterday, to pray with her and to console her. The lady's brother, a young man my age, had been killed in a car accident the day before. He had been driving home on a quiet country road late one night when his car was forced off the road by a drunk driver, who approached him head on. After being struck on the driver's side, his car had traveled down a steep embankment, striking a tree and burning. He had apparently been obeying all of the driving rules. It had apparently just been God's Will that he be in that place at that time.

My sister wrote that on her way home, she had stopped by the local church and, alone in the church, prayed that I would obey all of the rules and always be where God wanted me to be. She wrote that as she prayed, it seemed as if her two guardian angels were in the church with her.

I sat there quietly on my bunk, alone and numb and cold. I realized that I had been, indeed, where God had wanted me to be. It was only with God's help that I had been able to sit quietly, a few feet from dying men, and ignore their agonizing screams of death.

The next day, a very special letter from home arrived. It was from my father. It was the first, and almost the last, letter that my father ever wrote to me. It came with a few pieces of pale green alfalfa and golden pieces of straw sticking inside the envelope. My father loved farming. I read the letter with tears in my eyes. He told how he had heard about some of the attacks on the news. He was worried that I might be in some danger. The ending surprised me. He said that he didn't want either one of us to leave this world forever, until we had both had a chance to tell each other "Good Bye".

And so it happened, that I finally learned how to sit quietly on my bunk, and cry.

Orphans

...But Jesus called the children to him
  and said,
      "Let the little children come to me,
        and do not hinder them,
          for the kingdom of God belongs to such as
        these.

I tell you the truth,
    anyone who will not receive the kingdom of God
      like a little child
        will never enter it."

                    ...Luke 18:16,18

Early one morning, Parson John burst into my barracks.
He was sickeningly friendly.

Parson John wasn't really a parson. John wasn't really
his name. He never played at the weekly poker game. He
wasn't a chaplain and Parson John wasn't a member of the
weather squadron. In fact, Parson John wasn't much of
anything. I was never certain just where he naturally fit in
on this earth. I can't remember ever meeting Parson John.
He was always just there, usually preaching in the
background. One thing I was certain of, he could quote the
New Testament better than the base Chaplain. I used to
wonder how he was at living it. I used to wonder, that is,
until this day in the sunshine of Vietnam.

I was sitting quietly on my bunk trying to write a letter home when I saw Parson John enter Ken's room, two doors down. The sounds carried easily in the quiet morning air, Ken's apparently timid "No", the conviction in his voice as he said, "Today is a special day for Charlie". Then Ken gave Parson John directions to my room.

"Ken tells me that it's not safe for me to go down to the south side of Can Tho unless I take you along, and I believe him," blubbered Parson John.

Ken was walking across the grass in front of the barracks. I went out and asked him, but he just kept walking. It wasn't like him to be so silent, so distant, and to just keep moving like that. I wondered if he had heard me. Having nothing better to do, I returned to my room to face Parson John alone.

"He says I have to take you along or else I'll be in some great danger. In the last three weeks, two of my G.I. friends were attacked as they were walking down by the orphanage, right in broad daylight. One was shot in the hand and they both lost their wallets and valuables."

"Are those the same two who always catch the bus with you at the main gate," I asked?

"Yes. At least three times a week we had been going down to the orphanage on the south side of Can Tho," replied Parson John. "Now, however, they're too afraid to leave base. I just need to deliver some money to the orphanage today and I need you to go with me."

"I don't see the problem," I said. "Your friends were attacked several blocks over, inside one of those houses in the red light district, and they weren't together. It happened first to one. Several days passed before the other was attacked. The attacker used a thirty-eight-caliber pistol. A communist VC would have formally introduced himself using a weapon of a different caliber. Even in America, a man can get a good close look at blue-steel in a red light district. Going to the orphanage should be safe enough, even for a man alone."

"Don't be stupid," said Parson John! "This is Vietnam! Anybody that attacks an American anywhere in Vietnam is a communist! That includes attacks in red light districts. That includes old women and young kids! That includes young wives bandaging their husband's wounds and peasants running from machine gun fire!! They're all communists!"

Parson John continued, "Ken tells me that last week three Viet Cong soldiers walked into the orphanage and looked all around, checked everything, even the orphans in their beds, and then walked out. That whole part of Can Tho is just crawling with VC after dark. Haven't you been down and seen the tiger cages? Those are real, live, communist VC and most of them were caught right there on the edge of Can Tho."

"Yes," I said. "I've seen the tiger cages and most of those VC look to me more like orphans learning to steal rather than hardened communist soldiers. Some can't be more than ten years old. The North Vietnamese Army needs to be defeated militarily. The South Vietnamese Army should be used to capture the outskirts of Hanoi. The Americans with their Vietnamese allies should put an army into Haiphong and bring the war home to the North Vietnamese Government. That's how wars are won. Caging up women who bandage their husband's wounds and orphans who need a home isn't going to win any wars.

"It stands to reason. As far as I know, none of the priests or nuns at the orphanage have been killed or kidnapped by either side. The orphans already live in poverty, so the priests and nuns can't be giving bribes to either side. The priests and nuns must be protecting themselves by taking in orphans from both sides of the war. A single, unarmed man carrying toys and things for orphans would be quite safe in that part of town, daytime or night. There wouldn't be any soldiers from either side that felt like attacking him."

Parson John looked stumped for a minute and then his eyes lit up. "I took up quite a collection for the orphans. I have more than fifty dollars to deliver to the nuns and I need you to hold the camera. I just can't risk going to Can Tho unless you go with me. The Vietnamese all know you. You're always in shape. You're always doing exercises and things. You know, Jesus says that whatsoever you do unto the least of these, my brethren, you do so unto me."

"All right, all right." I responded happily, "When did you want to leave." For once, surrendering was fun.

"It's 9:30 a.m. The next bus leaves at 10:00 a.m. from the main gate. We should be leaving right now."

"Ok, ok." I paused to think. I had about fifty bucks in my wallet. Opening my locker, I added to that two or three hundred dollars of winnings from last week's poker games. I slipped a package of beef jerky into the leg pocket of my combat fatigues. I scanned my room for something to give the orphans. Nothing seemed right. The four boxes of corn chips, the seven cases of soda pop, the three cases of candy bars delivered by the Vietnamese workers from the BX the day before, could not be taken on the bus. The large American refrigerator put there for my use, free, by the Vietnamese, held nothing of interest to children. Suddenly,

236

I was struck by a wonderfully exciting thought, a thought so pleasant it seemed straight from heaven. "I know what I'll do", I said, "We'll go down to the orphanage together and we'll do the things you want to do. I'll get to see how many kids are there and ask the sister what she needs. Then I'll take you back to meet the 2:00 p.m. afternoon bus. You'll get safely on the bus. I'll stay behind in Can Tho. I'll have time to shop for something for the orphans, deliver it to the sisters and still catch the 5:30 p.m. bus back to base."

Parson John was ecstatic, absolutely ecstatic. He was already out the door. He could hardly contain his glee. From habit, I grabbed my rifle, flak jacket, ammunition belt, bayonet, helmet and canteen. I had to almost run to keep up with him. Finally, we arrived at the bus stop by the main gate. The cloud of dust from up the road was proof that we were none too soon. While we stood there, waiting for the dust to give birth to the bus, something struck me as very unusual. Parson John was totally unarmed and had no camera. I wondered.

The view of Binh Thuy from the main gate was always a surprise. The base always seemed parked in the wrong place. The moat on the north was the blue waters of the Mekong. The barbed wire main gate, always covered with a thick layer of dust and mud, appeared more likely to open into a barnyard than a fortress. It seemed as if it would be the first South Vietnamese base to fall to the communists. In fact, it turned out to be almost the last.

The bus ride from Binh Thuy to Can Tho with Parson John that day was filled with surprises. One surprise was Parson John. He preached every minute of the trip. First, it was on the evils of gambling, then on the evils of smoking, then on the New Testament, than on the Old, then on

237

adultery, sin and fornication, then on salvation. Forgotten in the passages, were his wife and children back home. Somewhere in there, he explained, he never looked through the screens covering the windows of the bus. The scenes, he said, depressed him. Everyone was so poor.

If he had looked through the screens, he would have seen a beautiful, jungle fringed river lined with simple, mud huts and people who could be proud of a hard, dirt floor. He would have seen poor people begging for change. He would have seen parents begging for help for sick children. He would have seen a few reasonably well-fed people begging for a portion of the political pie. He would also have seen an independent, peace loving people whose hopes for the future would one day be brutally crushed by the onrushing North Vietnamese Army.

He would have seen a mass of terrified humanity calling itself South Vietnam's second largest city. He would have seen the jungle and the futility of the war in the South. He would have seen the importance of unleashing the American military machine directly against the North. He would have seen the huts of loyal South Vietnamese and the huts of their Viet Cong brothers, all standing side by side.

He would have seen freighters full of cargo, sailing coldly past South Vietnamese peasants praying only for one good meal a day. He would have seen graft and corruption, enough to make even Judas smile. Standing there in the sun, he might also have seen Jesus and a people in need of a Good Samaritan.

Can Tho (pronounced can towe) was another surprise. It was a jewel, a surprising mud-splattered jewel, covered with carats of sunshine. The next big surprise was the dirty-muddy bus stop where Parson John insisted on getting off.

"Why get off so soon," I asked? "The stop closest to the orphanage isn't for another two to three miles."

"You're wrong there. This is a short cut. We'll cut down along the canal and save ourselves lots of walking. Anyway, you gave me your word that you would come along and escort me. This is the way I always go," he replied, flying from the last step to the ground.

"Well, a promise is a promise," I responded. "I don't mind the hike. I just want to be sure that I have enough time to deliver some presents to the orphanage."

"You'll have plenty of time," said Parson John as we marched along. Then in an odd tone, he continued, "Ken tells me that in all of the time you've been in Vietnam, you have never visited a house in the red light district, or made love to any of the maids or anything. Is that actually true?"

I thought the tone in his voice might be due to the heat of the sun. It was close to noon. I took out my canteen. It was full of lemonade. A good year's supply of lemonade powder had been thoughtfully sent to me from home. I offered it to him. Surprisingly, he refused. He preferred whatever was in his own canteen. For the first time, I noticed the touch of whiskey on his breath.

"Yes", I answered truthfully. "I have my religious values and a man has to do what he believes is right."

"But I thought you were single," he asked, "and you don't have a girl friend back home."

"Yes, I'm single. I don't have a girl friend waiting back home," I responded. "I also expect to stand face to face with Jesus one day, and account for my actions."

The "Good Parson" continued, "Ken also tells me that you have never tried drugs. Is that against your religion, too?"

"Yes," I answered, again truthfully. "I get all of the enjoyment I need out of a good game of poker and a can of soda."

Parson John then launched into another gut-wrenchingly long sermon on the New Testament and what a nice world it would be if more soldiers were religious like him. Not the both of us, just him. I remembered seeing him "reading" some "R" rated magazines in his room, and smoking something. I remembered and wondered.

We walked and walked. One mile merged into the next. Parson John's sermon dragged on and on. The sun was hot and tedious. For some reason my thoughts ran back to the summer when I was eight. I remembered standing on the lawn on my father's farm in Wisconsin. It was the summertime. My father was standing there with me. I remember asking my father what it would be like when I became a man. My father's words to me had been:

"Son, when you become a man, you'll have to make your own decisions. You'll have to do what you, alone, believe is right. You won't find your manhood in a crowd of friends or behind closed doors. You have to find it alone, out in the golden sunshine. You'll have to mark out a little piece of God's green earth, all by yourself. You'll have to stand there, alone, except for God's help, and fight. The attacks in this world will never come at you from the direction you're looking. They will instead, attack in the way you least expect. Battles will be forced on you that the world won't let you lose, that you will have to win or die trying. That's how it was for me, for my father and for his fathers before him. And, when it's all over, you can never expect anyone except God, to understand."

My father had continued, "Your great grandfather Simeon, used to tell about the day he became a man. He was in the civil war in the Union army. Remember, he was the one that everyone said was so strong willed, the one they called 'Simmie'. He could trace his family ties back to England, to the Cheviot Hills.

"He used to tell how the Union army was camped before one of the southern cities, perhaps Chattanooga. One bright sun-shiny day, he went for a little walk in the woods. He strayed through the confederate lines. He stumbled onto a patrol of five or six rebels and they pinned him down. He was surrounded and they could have killed him anytime. Then the shooting stopped and the southern commander demanded his surrender. He said he never knew what came over him, but he refused. He picked out a little spot of ground behind a tree and shouted back that right there was where he intended to make his stand. Right there on that little patch of ground he'd live like a man or die like one. He said there was a long pause. Then the southern commander ordered his men to stand down. In a few minutes, he saw the rebel officer walking towards him through the trees, alone and unarmed. The confederate officer walked up to him, shook his hand and said gently, 'I like to see a man who'll stand and fight.' Then the confederate officer gave him the directions back to the Union lines, collected up his men and left."

I don't know why, but my father's words on that day in Vietnam seemed unusually important.

Parson John's special route flirted with the edge of a green-bamboo covered canal and fully utilized the services of a wide, dirty-brown mud road that coursed through the red light district. The hot, merciless sun illuminated every seam and crack in the shabby buildings. Vietnam held few vistas as shabby and forlorn as the sight of prostitutes in the glaring noonday sun. We were about halfway through the district, at a place where the street was unusually wide, covered with piles of sewage, when without warning, Parson John turned towards the nearest shack. It was some distance away.

I stopped him. I said, "The orphanage is this way," pointing straight ahead.

"No. This is the orphanage," he triumphantly announced. "See, there is one of the sisters now, taking out the garbage. I'm going inside. If I'm not out in twenty minutes, you come in and make sure I'm all right. Remember, I'm not armed."

"Don't be ridiculous," I snapped angrily. "I wasn't born yesterday. Even though I never visit these places, I still know a house of prostitution and a madam when I see one. I agreed to escort you to the orphanage and the orphanage is straight ahead."

"You don't understand," laughed Parson John. "See, I go in here. I give the money to one of the 'sisters' inside and she delivers it to the orphanage for me."

"She does, huh," I replied. Instinctively my fist went down to my canteen belt and came up gripping the handle of my bayonet. My mind was flooding over in anger. "What else does she do for little tin gods like you?"

Parson John was really laughing now. "Oh, lots. She gives me 'good-value' for my money. She says that two or three of the kids down there are supposedly mine. That's why I call this place the orphanage. This is where I make them."

At this, I exploded in rage. It was a seething, consuming, deep, brutal, rage. He had already started walking towards his special "orphanage", laughing all the way. My white knuckles were grafting the bayonet handle into my fist. Hatred dragged me after him, towards the door. My bayonet thirsted to be sunk into his guts. My lungs began screaming in anger. Unnoticed at the time, a small group of Vietnamese quickly gathered.

"What do you think you're trying to pull," I screamed? "What's the idea of tricking me into coming way down here into a Viet Cong controlled district at high noon just so you can screw around in safety? You'll get both our throats cut. You'll have the Vietnamese thinking I'm in on this."

He just laughed and laughed. "You can come in too, you know. There's no danger." He laughed and laughed, "Believe me, you'll have lot's of fun; especially, if it's your first experience. Just ask some woman that's really beautiful."

"Some woman?" I screamed in rage. "You mean my bride on her honeymoon night or the woman I love that I'll be marrying in three weeks. It won't be some lice infested prostitute throwing sewage into some filthy canal after she's supposedly been made love to by you!"

Parson John laughed and laughed, and just kept walking, while I stood clenching my bayonet in my fist. "Yeah, I know all about honeymoon nights and children. Remember I'm married. Anyway," he laughed, "Who'd want to go down to the real orphanage? There's nothing down there but homeless children."

He laughed his way into the nearest house and called back, "Remember, I'm not armed. If I'm not out in twenty minutes, come on in and make sure I'm all right." The door slammed shut behind him.

I halted outside in the street, in the sunshine. I retreated back across the street so I was far away from the house, clenching my bayonet in anger.

With my combat boots, I marked out a little piece of dirt next to the canal so I could remember which house he had gone into. The filthy tumbledown shacks all looked so much alike. I stood there screaming obscenities at him as my mind raced on in rage.

The canal, like the rest of the swamps, was a jungle of bamboo that stood ten to twelve feet high. It was a ditch that a man could hide in for hours. I located a little place along the side of the ditch. I wanted to be prepared for any possible attack. I was too angry for words. I stood a good two inches taller than Parson John and he had lots of beer gut and flab. I decided that when he came out, there'd a battle, a mighty good battle, so I waited, and waited. I fastened my flak jacket and adjusted my helmet. Just to be safe, I loaded my M-16. The practice gained in numerous communist attacks had made it one fluid motion. I waited. I had plenty of time to wonder why Ken had insisted that I be the one Parson John take along, time to wonder why Ken had been so distant, time to remember my great grandfather's story.

More than forty-five minutes passed and still no Parson John. I wondered. What was so special about twenty minutes? A window on the house opened. Through the window in the distance, I could see a table holding a good meal and next to it an empty chair. The smell of a warm delicious meal mingled with the stench of the canal. I remembered I was hungry. Soon, I was enjoying the taste of the beef jerky from my fatigue pockets. I waited, and wondered.

I decided that when Parson John came out, I'd take him, right there on that little piece of ground. I decided that I would give him the punishment that I felt he deserved. That was when I first noticed the small group of Vietnamese gathered by the houses watching me. They appeared to be waiting for something.

From the house containing the "good parson", emerged an attractive, beautifully dressed, Vietnamese girl, probably age nineteen. Her jet-black hair highlighted her beautiful dark green dress, along with her twenty-four karat gold bracelets and matching earrings. Somehow, she looked a little sad as she strolled pleasantly towards me. Arriving on my side of the muddy street, she addressed me by name, using nearly perfect English. She said that it wasn't safe for me to be standing so close to the canal while carrying several hundred dollars. There were many VC, she said, so I must be careful. I wondered how she knew my name, and that I was carrying so much money?

She said it would be much safer for me inside the house. There was a table in there, a good meal, and a chair where I could sit. She pointed towards the distant open window. I could still see the chair, table, and the meal, but I politely refused. I told her that I would wait here until Parson John came out. She invited me, several times to come in out of the sun. Inside we could do whatever I wanted to "make my dreams come true", she said. Still I refused. I told her that this was my patch of ground. This was where I would wait for Parson John. This was where I would punish him.

As she started to ask me for the tenth time, I became annoyed and ordered her to go away. "DEE-DEE-MAOU",

I politely said, "DEE-DEE-MAOU", motioning away from me with my hand and arm. In other words, "Get lost in a hurry".

That appeared to make her noticeably happy. She took a couple of steps back, in the direction of the house. Then, to my immense surprise, she turned towards me and said gently, "I like to see a man who'll stand and fight." Then, without me asking, she pointed out the direction to the real orphanage and walked back into the house.

I stood there in silence. Suddenly I realized that she was the leader of the local Viet Cong.

The window on the house slid closed and with it, the curtains drew shut. The small crowd drifted away, like the leaves drifting before the winter winds. Soon my little patch of ground was enveloped in a lonely silence, a silence reminiscent of a battle's aftermath. Years later, I still remember the penetrating silence of that afternoon, the feeling of aloneness, and the occasional rustle of the wind. It was one of the most penetrating silences that I have ever heard.

As I stood there, my anger slowly subsided. As it did, I slowly realized that the battle was indeed, over. Parson John would not be coming out. It was just a question of whether I would walk away in time to visit the real orphanage as planned.

Checking my watch, I set out alone, walking in the direction of the orphanage. After a few blocks, I unloaded my rifle, loosened my helmet and flak jacket, and settled down to a comfortable, although lonely hike, along the canal. At the time, it certainly didn't seem like I had broken-up the attack of an experienced gang of thieves.

The good parson would leave the next day for San Francisco, one week early. He would spend the night hiding in town and trading duty shifts with other servicemen. Ken said that as he left, the Parson didn't seem interested in telling me good-bye.

Soon I was treading happily down the street to the real orphanage. For some reason, I was expecting to see a play yard with lots of children. Instead, when I arrived in front of what I knew was the orphanage, it appeared to be deserted. The doors and windows were closed and there was no activity anywhere. I stood across the street, staring silently at the dull blue-green walls I had come so far to see. I remember feeling so inadequate, standing there with nothing to give the children whom I had expected to find. I remember feeling as if I was facing Jesus, a golden, radiant Jesus, empty handed.

I decided that I would walk towards the downtown stores and purchase something and then return. I was afraid to knock on the orphanage door without presents.

I hadn't walked far when I arrived at an intersection of two major streets. There was an "ice cream" vendor there and some stores. A little boy approached me. He appeared to be about five years old and had all the markings of being an orphan. He asked me for an ice cream cone. He was such a lovable little kid, I could hardly say no. I took him by the hand and we walked over to the vendor's wagon. The stuff wasn't really ice cream but it was nutritious. The kid was just in seventh heaven over his cone. Even the vendor was laughing. It was the price that shocked me the most. The vendor sold it to me for the usual price of one penny. I actually gave him a dime. I couldn't believe that so much happiness could come so cheaply.

The little boy skipped off, loving every minute of his cone. As he was disappearing down the street, I noticed that he sought out the direction of the orphanage, and that the object of his delight was a light green cone with golden colored ice cream. He seemed to be a kid a lot like me.

I, myself, was thirsty, so I located a restaurant-bar kind of place and went in. It was like stepping back in time. It had a jukebox with the most heart-wrenching American songs from the Nineteen-Fifties. Being homesick, I listened to a few. I dared to drink only soft drinks. I knew that one beer and those songs would carve my lonesome psyche into fine little pieces. It was a fortunate choice. The attack came when I left.

Waiting outside in the street for me was perhaps, thirty-five kids. The oldest couldn't have been older than seven. I had hardly gotten through the door when I heard a familiar child's voice shout, "That's him". In a single "firing" pass, they were on me. They were most experienced gang of thieves that I have ever seen. They took my rifle, my wallet, my ammo, their experienced little hands got into every pocket and came away with everything, even the watch off my wrist. I was stripped clean before I realized I was under attack.

As luck would have it, I spotted the little boy for whom I had purchased the ice cream cone. I grabbed him and held him around the waist without hurting him. His friends were off and running, already some distance down the streets and alleys, like the leaves of life scattering before the winds of war. He began shouting for help. I told him in Vietnamese to tell his friends to return my valuables. He quickly responded and began shouting this to his friends as though his life depended on it.

As I watched, his friends stopped running, slowly turned around, and walked sheepishly the distance back to where we were, little boys to the end.

They quietly formed a large circle, the way the nuns had taught them to. One by one, they came forward and dropped their ill-gotten treasures at my feet and stepped back into position.

As the last one was dropping my wallet, the money still intact, I announced to the boys whom I realized were the orphans I had come so far to find, that I would buy them all ice cream cones. Immediately the air of Can Tho became filled with the kind of heavenly laughter and giggling that only happy orphans are able to generate. Soon, even the vendor was having the time of his life. The bill came to thirty-five cents. I gave the vendor a dollar in disbelief, and told him to, "Keep the change."

For my little friend, I purchased a second ice cream cone. I asked that it too, be gold ice cream in a green cone. I remember the look of admiration in his eyes as I shook his hand and gave it to him. I also remember his words. He asked in surprised, broken English, "You not put me in tiger cage?"

My response came instinctively, "No, of course not. That wouldn't be right."

I collected my belongings and put on my ammunition belt. As I picked my watch up out of the dust of the street, I could see in the distance another cloud of dust, another cloud that would give birth to a bus. I was forced to sadly acknowledge that the first afternoon of my manhood was over. What was coming was the last bus to Binh Thuy.

I also noticed the crowd that had gathered, a happy, silent crowd. They lined the street that I hurried down to get to the bus stop. The look in the eyes of the crowd as they looked at me was one I shall always remember. It was a look of surprise, of quiet, peaceful surprise. The look in their eyes brought home to me the words I had learned in basic training more than three years before. My drill Sergeant, an unpretentious, religious, honest, black man, had been trying to explain the American government's program of pacification. He had tried and failed several times. Finally, in frustration, he put aside the thick government training manual, walked over in front of our squad and said, "Pacification is you behaving in Vietnam, the way you behave in your own home town. Don't wait for the orphans to be nice to you first because you don't wait when you're home. Don't wait for the Red Cross or church groups or government handout programs to feed the hungry any more than you wait at home. Don't wait for the people to perform some action to earn your kindness because needy people are always helpless."

He closed by saying simply and directly, "Pacification is nothing more than you being nice to the people."

I have always believed, that Sergeant could have won the Vietnam War. That drill Sergeant understood pacification.

I met the bus as it pulled to a stop. A small group of American G.I.s got off, a small group which immediately headed for the red light district. The group included one G.I. telling the others, "Just ignore the orphans. If one bothers you too much, just give him a cuff and he'll go away."

I boarded the bus to Binh Thuy. As I waved goodbye to my little friend who was standing alone, in the distance by the orphanage, I wondered how many Americans came to

Can Tho to feed the orphans, and how many came to make them.

Viet Nam Question

...'Let his encampment become desolate,
and may no one dwell in it,'

...Acts 1:20

Several months had passed. The jungle rains, the insects, the humidity were just the opposite of the beautiful stretch of desert that I had enjoyed for so long. The loneliness and homesickness were pretty much the same, though. Early one afternoon just after the noon meal, I was ordered to report to the Command Post. A bird Colonel had flown to Vietnam, then down from Tan Son Nuht that morning especially to talk to me. I stacked my rifle and ammunition belt outside the door to his temporary office, and reported as ordered. He directed me to have a chair.

Although I didn't know the Colonel's name, I recognized him immediately. We both carried memories of the same stretches of sagebrush and sand.

"Good afternoon, Airman Baker," he began gently, still not having identified himself. "I see that you're in good health."

"Yes, Colonel," I responded. "The routine communist attacks have motivated me to take my vitamins and malaria tablets. I also get a fair amount of exercise loading my rifle and running to the bunker at night."

"I see that you still have that famous sense of humor, Airman Baker," he laughed. "I suppose you've heard what happened to your replacement at Mojave Wells."

"No, Sir. I haven't," I answered. "What mail I do receive has been arriving a month late down here, and the news from back home hasn't been very regular. Just last week, though, I did receive a 'Dear John' letter from Michael's sister Pamela. She's marrying somebody else. She would have addressed the letter to me, 'Dear Charlie', but she couldn't remember my name, and she didn't want to just address the letter, 'To Whom It May Concern'."

The Colonel and I laughed together for a while. I continued, "And what with all of the Viet Cong being called 'Charlie's', well, I'd have been confused anyway."

The two of us laughed together some more. Then the Colonel said, "You'll never change, Charlie. Being here with you today is just like old times."

His words meant a lot to me. Just being there with him brought back so many memories.

"I'm sorry to hear about your old friend Clark," he continued.

"Yes," I responded sadly. "He was driving a gasoline tanker in the middle of one of those big American supply convoys up on a road northeast of Saigon a couple of weeks ago. The VC let the vehicles ahead of him pass, and then exploded a mine directly underneath his truck. He was never able to get out. He burned to death in the cab, I'm afraid. You know he was from Boston. He always considered New Your City to be as far west as it paid to go."

"That sure was a shame. An awful lot of fine young Americans are dying over here," said the Colonel.

"I came here from Washington D.C. to talk to you about something very important," he continued seriously. "Something happened out on the Mojave Wells Ranges early one afternoon a few weeks after you left for Vietnam. That new First Lieutenant almost died out on Range Three."

"Really," I responded. "How did it happen?"

"He reported to me that one afternoon after taking the 12:30 p.m. wind measurement, he heard a woman, a little girl, and a man talking and singing out in the sagebrush near his weather shack.

"As he tells it, it was the Teacher, her daughter, and another man. He tells me that he went outside and angrily confronted them. Of course, that was a terrible blunder. I guess he began by ordering them off the ranges. They refused and said they just wanted to introduce themselves and have fun.

"Then the woman and the little girl crossed the cable fence and were going to look through his theodolite. He became angry. I guess he caught the Teacher off guard. He grabbed hold of one of her arms and shoved her back out into the sagebrush, almost knocking her down. I'm told he was screaming, 'Keep away from my equipment. I'm a military officer and I ordered you off the Ranges.'

"Then, I understand, before he could turn and confront the man, he blanked out for a while. When he came back to his senses, he tells me that there were four other men standing around him. The Teacher was standing several feet away and said to him angrily, 'You Idiot. You did not hurt me, but this is one afternoon I want you to remember.'

"Then, the four men proceeded to burn and beat him for most of the next hour. They had him down on the floor of his weather shack, helpless and screaming. He's been hurt bad. He's injured up under his ribs, in his stomach, and other places. After they finished with him, he had to lie there, bleeding, for almost another hour before the rescue helicopters could come and get him. He's been so terrorized that he can't even remember his own name.

"The only person the Pentagon will allow to be assigned up there now is you, Charlie. It's your choice, you or nobody. Of course, we're hoping that you will accept an appointment to the Air Force Academy and choose a career at Mojave Wells as the USAF commanding officer."

I thought about it for a few minutes. Then I replied, "I'm sorry, Colonel. I deeply appreciate your remembering me. However, I'm really not that military. What I want more than anything is to complete my term of enlistment and just return home to Wisconsin. I just want to go back to the world I knew when I enlisted so long ago. Tell the Teacher 'Hello' for me, and tell her that I'll always remember her, but, really, all I want to do now is just go home."

"We all understand Airman Baker," he said. "After all you've been through, you certainly deserve to left alone. If you want, I can order that you be transferred to Cam Ranh Bay for the remainder of your tour of duty here in Viet Nam."

"Thanks, Colonel," I said, "but, no. I'm just fine here in the Mekong Delta. There's really nothing out there in the jungle that I can't handle."

The Colonel smiled knowingly. Then he said, "Somehow I knew you'd say that, Charlie. That's how I'll always remember you."

Charles James Hall

Jack of Diamonds

"…Again, I tell you
  that if two of you on Earth agree
  about anything you ask for,
    it will be done for you
      by my Father in heaven.

For where two or three of you
  come together in my name,
  there am I with them."

…Matthew 18:19,20

"Poker is a game created by God to entertain soldiers," I laughed with tears in my eyes. I was raking in the winnings from the last pot. "You know my uncle Herman. He was in the Army for three years and one day the sergeant discovered that Herman couldn't play poker or shoot craps or anything." I was laughing after every word. "Why, they just up and discharged him. They gave him a section eight right there on the spot. They said that any soldier that didn't gamble wasn't properly communicating with God!"

Then Ken said thoughtfully, "I suppose you were certain that there wasn't any danger of you losing that hand when you saw the jack of diamonds."

"You're right there," I answered, laughing all the while. "The only difference between winners and losers is what they see with their eyes. Losers see the problem. Winners

256

see the opportunity. Anytime that I see the jack of diamonds, I know I'm in the midst of an opportunity to enjoy life."

Jess, my cubicle mate, screamed in frustration, "Charlie, run the cards!"

I continued, "That's how it always is. We winners laugh and joke while the losers shout, 'Run'em! Run'em'"

My buddy David said, "But Charlie, tonight you're the only one winning!"

I was laughing so hard that my sides hurt as I responded, "Hey, if you guys aren't having fun, the way God intended, don't complain to me. Complain to Jesus! Tell Him Charlie says you men need to learn how to enjoy life. You need to learn to take your chances. Tell Him you need to learn to gamble!"

As I was shuffling, Ken said, "Seriously, Charlie, I never see you take a drink, except once in a while in the daytime in the Airman's club." Ken always noticed things. It was as if he had a friend who would communicate ideas to him. Sometimes it seemed as if he could actually talk to Jesus.

I couldn't resist the opportunity to enjoy a little gallows humor. I responded, "That's right. I figure that if the communists are good enough to carry those shells all the way down here from Hanoi just to kill me, then I'll be good enough to stay sober and make it fun for them." Then laughing, I continued, "Why, tonight when they attack, I was even thinking about shooting back, just to give them a little something to write home about."

I remember the look on Ken's face. He seemed to be trying to say something but he couldn't.

After a long time, he responded gently and very quietly, "It's not you they've come to kill."

I didn't know what to say. Before I could answer, one of the other soldiers named James interrupted. He had arrived just a day or so before, so he was still a new guy. He asked, "Will the communists actually attack tonight?"

I responded, "I don't really know, James. I feel certain they will, but that little Vietnamese friend of mine, the one I call Little Ho, doesn't think so. He doesn't think the VC will attack again for a couple of weeks."

Then Ken said, "You know, Charlie, he might be right. I've noticed that in last night's attack the communists fired more than 100 mortar shells at us. If you add up the number of shells just from the attacks in the last week, it's a pretty big number. Maybe they are going to be short of ammunition for a few days."

Jess looked thoughtfully out the window and asked, slowly, "Which one is Little Ho?"

I responded, "He's that unusually short South Vietnamese soldier. His name means 'Little Tiger'. He stands about 4'10" tall. He looks part Chinese. He's always laughing and teasing."

Ken continued slowly, "Is he the one who always comes to stay with you at night in the tower? The one who probably doesn't weigh more than fifty pounds in a wet uniform? The one who has such a deep tan?"

"Yes," I said.

Ken paused, thought for a minute and then continued.

"You know what he always reminds me of, Charlie? He reminds me of your favorite card. You know how you always say that what a man really needs in order to survive in this world is the jack of diamonds?"

"Yes," I answered. "I suppose you could say that Little Ho is my friendly little jack of diamonds. Every time I see him, I know that something fun is going to happen. You know, he and his friends, just love to arm-wrestle with me. They come up to the tower in groups. I put my elbow on the table and they stand up all together and pull with both hands. Of course I always win. Then I tease them. I tell them that they are no match for the Almighty Super Charlie. We sure have fun doing that."

James said, "I don't understand. You mean that Little Ho brings his friends up to the tower?"

"Of course", I responded. "He has several but usually he just brings them up two or three at a time. There's nothing against it in the rules. I remember one time three weeks back. I just about die laughing when I think about it. Two of his friends came up one night and without saying anything, just started wrestling with me. I know it sounds funny but for some reason I just knew they were coming. They had crept quietly up the stairs so as to have the fun of surprising me, I guess, like you did one time, Ken. But just before they opened the door, I had this overwhelming urge to stand next to the desk with my back to the wall, in that dark corner. I stood there looking at the door. I've been more alert that way Ken, ever since the time you snuck up and scared me so badly. For some reason, I really wasn't surprised as I watched the door open. Two of them were looking through the crack at me. They looked just like monkeys. I called to them in Vietnamese. I said, laughing, 'Leave your rifles outside and come in. I'm ready.'

"The two of them came in acting real confused and looked all around, like wrestlers sometimes do. So I just grabbed them and started wrestling. One got me around the leg and the other was trying to grab me around the neck. One of them was the funniest clown. He'd just got a good

259

hold of me and I guess he was going to lose his bayonet so he had to grab for it. Of course I took it right away from him. I threw both their bayonets in the corner so we wouldn't hurt ourselves. Then I held them both to the mat for a while, you know, like a wrestler does. I teased them something awful. I'd laugh and shout, 'I'm number one, I'm number one'. It looked so funny that I laughed 'till my sides hurt. I figured they might like to arm wrestle as I do with Ho. So I just picked them both up. You know it's like wrestling with kids. They're so light. Then I showed them how I do it. They looked real confused. They couldn't take directions worth a darn. So I barked some orders at them in Vietnamese and after a couple of bouts of arm wrestling, you know, they were laughing even harder than I was.

"Then Little Ho came in. When he saw me, for some reason he looked terrified and kept trying to get his two friends to leave. I calmed him down and showed him that his friends and I were having fun arm wrestling. Oh, did he think that was funny.

"Then some Vietnamese sergeant came in. He had a lip on him that would take the enamel right off a cup. He was stern. He gave the three of them the devil for something or another. I guess sergeants are the same the world over. He was standing by the cloud height equipment. Well, that was a problem. Who could get any work done with him shouting? Anyway, I saw it as an opportunity. I decided to gamble. I decided to enjoy life for a little while. Besides, what could go wrong with Little Ho there? He is after all, my jack of diamonds.

"I went over to the sergeant and offered him a cigarette. In a good-natured manner, I challenged him to an arm wrestling match. Did he ever give me a surprised look!

You'd have thought that it was the first time he'd ever shook hands with an American. I told him how much better the American cigarettes were than the Vietnamese. So he gave me one of his and took one of mine. Of course, you know how badly theirs taste. A couple of puffs and he saw it my way. Of course, he couldn't arm wrestle worth a darn, either. He kept grabbing me by the shirt until I showed him how it was done. I had to throw his bayonet in the corner along with the others or he'd hurt himself too. We were sitting there laughing and Little Ho ushered the other two out of there and came back. Then Little Ho, the sergeant, and I, all laughed and complained a little about the war. Then we shook hands and they left."

James asked, "I still don't understand. What would a sergeant be doing in the tower after hours?"

Ken interrupted before I could answer, seemingly on purpose, "You know, Charlie, maybe you should pay more attention to what Little Ho says. You know he doesn't tease the rest of us. Maybe he's not teasing you. Remember that night last week when you and I switched shifts so that you were working swing. Remember how I relieved you at midnight instead of the other way around?"

"Which one?" I asked.

"You know, the night that those three Viet Cong soldiers infiltrated through the wire and got into that big swamp next to the road that we always have to walk along to get to the tower."

"Oh, that night," I said. "That funny Ho. You know he came up to the tower about 11:30 p.m. and he was so happy to see me. You just can't imagine. You'd have thought that I had just come back from the dead. He was telling me how he had looked all over for me. You know how he just loves

261

to tease. He was saying that I shouldn't worry if the VC came that night because he would protect me. You know, I almost split a gut laughing. He's such a funny little guy. He sure is a good friend."

"But Charlie, why didn't you stay in the tower like he said until morning? You know I've never seen anyone worry so much after you walked out of there and back to the compound. He was really upset. He went running out of there and stood by the corner of the hanger with some of his friends until you got down to our part of the base."

"What did he do then," I asked?

"Then he went into the base operations building and went to sleep. He had three friends with him. I couldn't see them very well in the dark. I suppose you would say they went to look for the VC because they were carrying rifles and things when they went across the road into the swamp."

"Where in the swamp," I asked?

"It was just across the road from the first aircraft hanger. It was close to where the South Vietnamese finally killed those three VC."

Then James asked, "How did the South Vietnamese know which three were theirs and which three were the VC?"

"Oh," I said, "The VC always wear things like black pajamas or North Vietnamese uniforms or something. It's real easy to tell who's who if you're a South Vietnamese, I guess."

James looked puzzled. "I still don't see how anyone could infiltrate through the wire. Aren't there a lot of mines and things out there?"

"Well, they would have had to," I said. "Little Ho, himself, was guarding the front gate that afternoon."

"Just 'till after dark," pointed out Jess. "I saw him standing on the stairway of the tower just before 8:00 p.m. He seemed to be real agitated, like he was looking for someone. Then he looked all through that dark area in between the buildings where you always take a shortcut to get to the road. I suppose he was looking for you."

"Maybe," I said. "I was up on top of the tower with the aircraft controllers, the baby eagles, for a little while. Maybe he missed me for some reason."

"I don't know," said Jess. "He didn't talk to the rest of us."

Then Ken said. "I was really surprised that you would walk down the road all by yourself with just your M-16. Didn't you know the road was declared off limits until the VC were caught?"

"No. Anyway, it's kind of an enjoyable walk. How did you make it to the tower," I asked?

"I had the armored car bring me, of course," said Ken. "Didn't you see me getting out of it?"

"Oh, that's what they were doing," I answered. "I was wondering about that."

"Tell me, Charlie, why does Little Ho like you so much," asked David?

"I don't I know," I answered. "Right after I got here, he was standing on one of the platforms of the tower one night looking completely dejected. He had tears in his eyes, so I offered him a cigarette and a cup of coffee. I talked to him for a while. He's such a tease. He was trying to make me believe that American bombs had killed one of his relatives. I don't know which one it was. He made it sound like it was his father. You know my Vietnamese isn't very good and his English isn't much better. Anyway, at the time I took him seriously and tried to console him. He's Christian and religious like me so we prayed together. I had some K-rations and I shared them with him. I told him truthfully, that if there was ever anything I could do to help, he should just say so. He likes coffee with cream and sugar, just like I do. So every week or so, I buy him some coffee, dry cream, and sugar at the BX. He's such a good friend."

"How much do you charge him," asked the aircraft mechanic?

"Charge him," I said? "I just give them to him. It only costs me a couple of bucks. He's so poor, why bother. Usually I never buy things for the South Vietnamese, but when I do, I never charge them for it. I never buy them whiskey or anything. I only buy them things that will help make their life better. I told Little Ho that it's worth it just to have a few friends."

"So that's why the South Vietnamese First Sergeant treats you with such respect and insults the rest of us. It's because you refused to take any money from him and you won't help him buy dishes by mail from Japan as he wanted," sneered the mechanic.

"I told him that it wouldn't help the ordinary people," I said, "He was just going to triple the price and resell them anyway, so I told him to keep his money and that I didn't want to be bothered. He seemed a little huffy at first. A few weeks later, he apologized and said he understood my point of view."

"Yeah, a few weeks later," laughed the mechanic, "After some of the rest of us got together and cheated him out of $500. No wonder he's come around to your point of view.

"Now I see that you're the one supplying the South Vietnamese maid with all that soap and why the South

Vietnamese never punch your ration card," continued the mechanic.

"Well, I don't call four boxes of detergent a month a lot of soap. You know she does have two or three kids and must have some relatives," I responded. "This is a germ filled jungle."

The mechanic scoffed, "Why let her sell it on the black market and make all that money? You should charge her for it like I charge my maid."

"It's a gamble," I said, "But she shows up on base in clean clothes and it looks to me like she always puts her kids first. She'd have to be a magician to have any left over to sell. You see how muddy the Mekong is."

Then the aircraft mechanic continued angrily, "But Charlie, she and Little Ho must have told every Vietnamese this side of Can Tho about the time you gave her that twelve dollar watch. Don't you see the problems that you're creating for the rest of us? Why should they pay our prices when they can gamble that you'll give it to them free?"

"I didn't give it to her," I answered. "She paid me the twelve dollars."

"Twelve dollars," he shouted with contempt. "Charlie! I was there watching you when you carried the watch through the gate for her. I saw you refuse her offer of fifty dollars, then thirty-five dollars. I stood right there beside you! I watched her force twenty dollars on you by stuffing it in your shirt pocket while you were trying to refuse it. Then I watched you walk over to that small Base Exchange of ours and buy ten dollars worth of soap and clothes for her children. I know perfectly well that you left all of those clothes and soap and things sitting on your bunk for her to find the next day. Then you made up that dumb lie. You told her that you had been planning to ship them home to America and the mailroom wouldn't let you, so she should have them. You couldn't even make up a decent lie.

"That afternoon your maid was sitting down in front of the Vietnamese command post in tears. She was telling everyone down there, 'be nice to Airman Charlie Baker. He is a number one G.I. Tell everyone in your family.' You know perfectly well that every Vietnamese family has at least one member fighting with the communists. I'll bet that by now every communist V.C. from here to the South China Sea knows about you."

"I don't see why that would be a problem," I said. "The V.C. are trying to kill all of us anyway. That's what the nightly communist attacks are all about."

Exasperated, the mechanic screamed, "The problem is that you're ruining the black market for all of us. I charged my maid sixty-five dollars for the same style watch and she looked happy to pay it. You're giving these gooks a good hundred bucks a month when you should be making a fistful of fast green dollars. You're just not seeing the golden possibilities of a lifetime."

"Well, it's more like twenty five dollars," I responded, "And it's just money that I have been winning at these poker games, anyway. I don't see it as a problem. I see it as an opportunity. I see it as a chance to gamble. I see it as having the fun of playing with the jack of diamonds. I see it as a chance to enjoy life for a little while."

Matching Shell-Fire

…So he [Joseph]
> got up,
>> took the child [Jesus]
>> and his mother [Mary]
>> during the night
>>> and left for Egypt,

> where he stayed
> until the death of Herod
> [i.e. for 12 years]…

…Matthew 2:13,15

I remember running down the road that night towards the tower. Midnight caught me sleeping in my bunk when I should have been reporting for duty for the mid-shift, midnight to 8:00 a.m. For some reason as I left the road and hurried across the grass, I felt unaccountably cold. It made the night very special. It made it feel like a night that prayers would get answered.

I was double-timing down the empty hallway of the base ops building to sign in when Mr-Man found me. Mr-Man, of course, was not his real name. Mr-Man was the airman I was supposed to relieve at the stroke of midnight. His anger exploded in the hallway.

"So-o-o, late again," he screamed!

I was quite taken aback. Usually he was cold and withdrawn. However, tonight for some reason, I had been expecting something quite different. For some reason, I had been expecting him to quote me an airline flight schedule.

I tried to make light of my sinful ways. I responded light heartedly, "It was an attack of the gravities. The force of gravity was three or four times greater over my bunk than anywhere else in the room. It kept me pinned down for a good twenty minutes."

He continued shouting, "Not even God is going to get you out of this one. I saw you making the sign of the cross out there in the dark. You screw up. You knew you were late. You're in big trouble now, great big trouble. You've been late relieving me for the last time, airman! Just look at your uniform. You're so un-military. You look like a ticket agent."

The words "ticket agent" rang a bell. I stood there motionless as I watched him pace back and forth in front of me. He was screaming with every step. Even though this was the first time that Mr-Man had ever exploded at me, it all looked very familiar. I watched him pace back and forth, like a tiger. I listened quietly to his shouting. I looked at the light coming through the doorway at the end of the hallway. It had a slightly snow-like greenish hue. The white hallway wall behind him seemed to be waiting for streaks of golden brown.

It all locked into place, like the bolt of my rifle. My mind became filled with the mental image of his pretty wife back in their nice suburban northeastern home. I could almost feel her love for him. His two growing children appeared to want nothing more than to play with their daddy. His parents with their prosperous business were all praying for his safety. I could almost feel the loneliness they felt. I knew that somehow, some way, I had been here before. I knew that somehow, the day would come when I would be here again, but I didn't know when. I stood quietly in that long straight hallway with doors on either side. I knew that when I returned to that special spot on the floor, there would be a second hallway and an intersecting hallway, both of them would be full of people and shops. The doors at the end of the hallway would be closed.

Mr-Man continued shouting, "Is that what you learned in basic training you, you ticket agent! You sure aren't a soldier! I'm reporting you to the Captain in the morning!!"

As I stood listening, the vision in my mind's eye slowly passed. It would be nine years exactly to the day, exactly to the minute, before I would see it again. I would be running across a cold wintry parking lot at an airport in a northeastern state just after midnight. I would be running to catch a plane. I would double time up to the check-in desk at the gate. The ticket agent would come over sternly, as though finding me in an empty hallway. He would be angry, unaccountably very angry. He would began shouting at me, "So-o-o, late again!" I would be taken aback. I would be expecting him to quote the airline's flight schedule. Instead, he would scream and shout precisely at me. He would pace back and forth like a tiger, shouting with every step. Once again, it would be Mr-Man.

The second hallway would be there, all filled with people and shops, exactly as I had seen it. The double doors at the end would be closed against the winter's snow. Only then, it would end differently. Then another man would come running in and take his place behind the counter and say, "I'm sorry I'm late. My car was stuck in the ditch. The snowplow took twenty minutes to pull me out. I guess my car is just heavier than other cars."

The agent would look at me and pause. Then he would apologize. He would say humbly, "I'm sorry. I don't know what came over me. For some reason, I thought you were the new ticket agent that I was expecting to relieve me. Perhaps it's the tie you're wearing."

Back in Vietnam, Mr-Man's anger raged unabated. "You like wearing those three stripes? Well you'll thank God if you're wearing one when I'm through with you."

"I'm sorry I am late," I responded humbly. "If you'd like, I'll be happy to work a couple extra shifts to make it up to you."

"If I'd like," he screamed! "Extra shifts my eye! You'll get the punishment you deserve for this. Just you wait until I tell the Captain."

"But you know that I also pull perimeter duty on the outer wire," I said, "and you never do because you have a wife and children back home. You're on duty for only eight hours a day, while I've been putting in sixteen. I just put in eight hours on the outer wire last night and eight hours in the tower on today's day shift. This is Vietnam. It's just a question of whether we both stand in the mud here, or walk down the road and stand in the mud there. You'll be going back to America in a few days to be discharged, and you're still perfectly well rested. Anyway, there's no special place you're going when I relieve you. You can still easily make it to the midnight meal. I just overslept and I've only been late a few times. If you felt as tired as I feel, you wouldn't be so rich in military discipline. You'd be late too, and I would understand."

"Do you call that military discipline," Mr-Man sneered? "Do you always whine and snivel? Do you think I care a fig about how you feel? If you had been here on time the way military discipline demands, I would have already finished my midnight chow and been lying in my bunk, the way I always am at this time. Just giving you the lecture you so richly deserve has kept me from having my evening meal. Your undisciplined behavior has made me miss both my sleep and my meal."

With that last double barrage, Mr-Man stalked angrily out of the building.

I would have answered. I meant to answer but as I stood on that precise spot in the hallway, it seemed right for him to leave. The crisis felt past. The prayers felt answered.

Mr-Man had walked only a short distance down the road towards the American section of the base when I heard the muffled double crumps emanating from one communist mortar in the jungle nearby, and another further away. The hallway was filled with the "tinkle-tinkle" sounds of the two matching shells in flight. Before I could move, the distant night air was filled with one sickening, muffled blast from the chow hall and a second equally sickening un-muffled blast coming from the sidewalk in front of Mr-Man's barracks. It filled the air with the discordant musical tones of hot shrapnel as it "found" bricks, shutters, and the door to Mr-Man's room. The next round would fall through his roof and explode directly next to his empty bunk. Had I reported for duty on time, Mr-Man would have been killed by the matching shellfire, either in the chow hall, or in his bunk. As it was, Mr-Man found all of the refuge he needed in the mud by side of the road.

I stood motionless. Considering how exposed I was, I felt surprisingly safe. A very unusual thought entered my mind. It was as if someone had just whispered in my ear the words, "A wiser man would know his friends."

That night after the mortar attack was over, I picked up a cup of coffee in the forecaster's station. I collected up my thoughts and feelings. Then I trudged up the long stairway to the tower. Alone in the darkened weather station in the bottom of the cab, I was engulfed by another attack. This was an attack of fatigue, loneliness, homesickness, and despair.

The other men would get homesick and lonely. It was a simple matter to catch them with tears in their eyes, or collapsed, crying on the stairs of the tower. They would get homesick for their wives, their families, or their girlfriends back home. Sooner or later, they all needed someone to talk to. Tonight, as I sat in the observer's chair in the bottom of the tower, the feelings of exhaustion, loneliness, and homesickness that engulfed me were simply overwhelming. It seemed as if I were more homesick than any human had ever been in history. I bent over the desk in front of me, placed my head down on the desk, and, more than anything, just wanted to go home.

I had been sitting with my head down on the desk for a long time when I suddenly heard Ken come in the door behind me. Since he wasn't scheduled to relieve me for several more hours, I was startled and speechless. He said that he came because he thought I might need someone to talk to. As for the tears in my eyes, he laughed them off. He said, "I see you took some shrapnel in the eyes during that last communist attack. If you want, we can report you to the medic and you can receive a Purple Heart."

After hours of wretched loneliness, at last I could laugh a little. We sat and talked about our feelings for a long time. It felt good to be laughing with Ken again. I started to understand that he was saving my life, just by being there and sharing the feelings that I felt.

Ken had a way of making everything sound so simple. As we were talking, Ken said, "The next time that you begin feeling like you are more homesick than any human has ever felt in history, just think about this, Charlie. In the Bible, it says that the good father is the one who feels the same pain that the family feels."

"Yes," I answered, "You mean the way Saint Joseph in the Bible must have been feeling the same pain that Mary felt before they got married. Mary must certainly have been worried that the other Jews would stone her to death. Joseph must certainly have been able to feel that, so he pretended that Jesus was his son and married Mary as planned.

"You mean the way Saint Joseph had to have been feeling the pain of Jesus and Mary just after Jesus was born in Bethlehem and King Herod was going to kill all of the newly born babies, so Joseph took Mary and Jesus off to live in Egypt where they would be safe?"

"Yes," said Ken. "Exactly right. So many Christian preachers give sermons on how Jesus understands our pain, and how Mary understands our pain, but I have never heard a Christian preacher give a sermon on how Saint Joseph must certainly have been able to feel the same pain that both Jesus and Mary felt. Just think of all of the social rules and customs that abounded in ancient Israel back then. Think of all of those social rules that Saint Joseph broke purely because he loved Mary and the baby Jesus, even before Jesus was born. Remember, according to the Bible,

Jesus wasn't the son of Saint Joseph, but Joseph was Jesus' earthly father. Therefore, since Saint Joseph is considered to meet the Biblical definition of a good father, he had to have been able to feel the same pain that Mary felt, and that Jesus felt when Jesus was a child.

"Just think of all of the work and effort that Saint Joseph had to have gone through to take Mary and the baby Jesus on the long trek to Egypt, and then live there for so many years. Just think how homesick he must have gotten. People didn't travel back then like they do now. Saint Joseph's life was never threatened. Only the lives of Mary and Jesus were ever threatened. He could have abandoned both of them down in Egypt, and gone back alone to his home in Israel anytime he decided to. But he stood by both of them every step of the way purely because he loved them. Just think of how much Saint Joseph must have loved Jesus and Mary to have willingly chosen to experience an ordeal like that. According to the Bible, Saint Joseph asked absolutely nothing in return. While the three of them were in Egypt, Saint Joseph had to have been able to feel Mary's homesickness and Jesus' pain on top of his own intense feelings of homesickness. And remember, Saint Joseph's ordeal went on for years. He had no idea when it all would end, or when he could bring his family home again.

"But you, Charlie, you know exactly when your stretch in Vietnam is going to end. You have the day marked on the calendar. You're only feeling your own feelings of homesickness. Saint Joseph had to have been feeling the homesickness of his entire family. He had to have felt far more homesickness than you are feeling now. The next time you're feeling homesick, say a prayer to him. He certainly knows all about homesickness."

"I understand, Ken," I said thoughtfully. "It also means that if Mr-Man didn't appreciate the fact that my coming late saved his life, he isn't able to feel the pain of his wife and children. They certainly would have felt intense pain if he had been killed tonight. They certainly wouldn't care if I broke a few rules to keep him alive."

"Exactly," said Ken. "It looks to me like, for tonight at least, you were a better father to his family than he was."

So it happened for still another time, that Ken saved my life in Viet Nam. I would still get desperately homesick. I would still pray with tears in my eyes to be able to go home and take off my uniform for the last time. But I would remember Ken's words. In the future, "Ken's Biblical Solution" would always be with me like a shield. It would keep me from dying in Viet Nam, dying from homesickness.

Two days later, the Captain, an understanding and decent officer, called me into his office and announced his decision relating to my tardiness, I would work some extra duty, hardly a punishment in a lonely place like Binh Thuy. Part of the extra duty was sweeping the hallway of the base operations building. Such duty is equivalent to the janitorial Olympics with the gold metal going to the best latrine crew. I was trying hard to compete for the gold medal by sweeping that same special spot in the hallway five or six times, when a very unusual feeling swept over me. I was bent over and kneeling down, sweeping that spot when suddenly the uselessness of it all overwhelmed me.

Then I had a sudden vivid mental image of how the room behind me would soon look. A picture flooded unto my brain. It was an image of gray plaster and rubble, topped by a fallen roof. It seemed as if I could suddenly feel the pain of a South Vietnamese soldier trapped underneath the rubble as he lay dying.

As long as I stood motionless, my back to the doorway and looking away from the room, I could view everything in the room. It didn't appear the way it looked at the time, but the way it would look at some time in the future when I saw it again. I could almost see the trapped Vietnamese soldier's soul being escorted past me by two beautiful matching angels, on his way to heaven. I was honestly reluctant to finish sweeping the floor because it all seemed so futile.

The room behind me would, indeed be destroyed. Communist gunners would indeed, "walk" their shells into the building and two shells would land at almost the same time in almost the same place in the room behind me, another example of matching shell-fire. The South Vietnamese soldier sleeping in the room at the time would never get out.

Less than two weeks would pass before I was standing there on that spot again. There would be no surprise. What remained of the room would look exactly as I expected. The green jungle plants that sprouted from the dirt layer on top of the remains of the roof would all package together into the golden-yellow noonday sunshine. The only surprise then would be the dust that covered that special spot on the floor. It was so thick and fine that it couldn't be swept up. It had become part of the floor, the way my memories of that night with Ken had become part of my soul.

Yes

"...I tell you, my friends,
    do not be afraid of those who kill the body
      and after that can do no more.

But I will show you whom you should fear:

Fear him who,
    after killing the body,
      has the power to throw you into hell.

Yes, I tell you, fear him.

Are not five sparrows sold for two pennies?
    Yet not one of them is forgotten by God.

Indeed, the very hairs on your head are numbered.

Do not be afraid;
    You are worth more than many sparrows."

          ...Luke 12:4,7

The U. S. Air Force had many good marching songs. It also had many fine recruiting songs. I frequently used to sing those songs when I was walking between the tower and my barracks in Vietnam. I also sang other songs that I made up myself. One of the songs that I made up just for me contained a phrase, "...and Charlie, you should see the men who started out to be boys just like you..."

I made up that song on the day I enlisted. That's the way my USAF recruiting sergeant had explained it, "...You should see the men..." He was quite right. The military services take in boys and they turn out men. I wanted to do more than see the world when I enlisted. I wanted to do more than restore order to a life in chaos caused by leaving the University of Wisconsin at Madison. When I enlisted, I wanted to do much more. I wanted to see the men and see the world that men live in. I was never sorry that I said, "Yes" to the Recruiting Sergeant. I was homesick, yes, but never sorry. The one thing the Recruiting Sergeant didn't tell me on that unforgettable summer day in July in the '60's, the day I rode the bus from the Air Force recruiting center in Madison, Wisconsin to the Enlistment center at the Armory in Milwaukee, Wisconsin, was the price I would have to pay for the view.

Binh Thuy had an American dentist. He doubled as the doctor in emergencies. His understanding of human nature was a sight to behold.

I was sitting in my barracks a little after dark, one night. The communists had just completed an attack. I was eating a golden piece of Wisconsin cheese, a treasure from the chow hall. It evoked vivid memories of home. It was almost too sacred to eat. I blessed the rest of the evening meal and gave it the passover.

One of my friends stopped by. He asked me to join him in the Airman's club. The night was dark and I had difficulty finding my way. As we walked through the darkness, I remembered that the South Vietnamese workmen had dug a hole through a slab of concrete nearby.

I wasn't sure exactly where it was. It might have been directly ahead of me so I turned to the side. In so doing, I stepped directly into the hole. The jagged concrete tore my left leg open to the bone, half way to the knee. Within seconds, my leg covered with blood. Crying out in agony, I tore away from the concrete slab. In shock and pain, I pulled my leg from the hole.

My friend and I marched off to the hospital, still carrying my golden treasure. Fortunately, none of my muscles or nerves were damaged.

The dentist came from his quarters, cleaned the gash, and decided that thirteen stitches would be all that I would need. The problem was that the communist attack had left him short of his only pain killer, xylocaine. He could not freeze the nerves where the last three stitches would have to be placed. An additional three stitches would have to be placed in flesh only lightly frozen.

He informed me of the facts in a straight forward manner. He told me the bone had to be covered. The flesh had to be stitched. He asked me if I was ready.

I said, "Yes".

He started placing stitches in the flesh that was completely frozen. As he approached the painful area, he noticed that I was starting to clench my fists and groan with pain. He looked up at me and, laughing a little bit, said, "Now anytime the pain gets too much for you, just scream out nice and loud. The communists out in the jungle are sure to hear you. It'll give them a good laugh."

I knew he was right. I had no choice. I sat there quietly. I bit my piece of cheese and watched him put in the rest of the stitches. At midnight, I reported for duty in the tower as scheduled.

I returned to see the dentist a few days later. I was a little feverish. My lower leg was swollen to half-again its normal size. He gave me some antibiotics. They worked nicely. His new painkiller worked nicely too. He smiled, almost laughing, reached for a little bottle of green pills and said, "Now don't be surprised if this painkiller makes the food from the chow hall taste bad."

After we both stopped laughing, I decided that I didn't need the pills.

A weather observer soon learns to enjoy sitting quietly, watching and thinking. I was doing just that one morning when an MP dropped by the barracks. His news was special. A demonstration of the M-60 machine gun would commence sharply at 10:00 a.m. I wanted to beg off. I had just returned from night shift, but my bunk felt uncomfortable. His statements seemed so penetrating, "Come see the men! Fire the M-60!"

His words seemed to be very, very special. I instinctively replied, "Yes." It was after all, the reason I enlisted, to see the men.

10:00 a.m. found eight or ten of us watching the M.P. fire the M-60 over the wire into the swamp. There wasn't very much to it, but I enjoyed seeing the bullets going the other way. I also enjoyed hearing the M.P. say something in passing. He said that once the gun got hot, it would continue to fire after the trigger was released. You had to break the ammunition belt, he said, and let it run out of bullets. What he didn't say was how many bullets.

He demonstrated the gun. He fired it for a while. It got hot. He released the trigger. The gun continued to fire. He broke the ammunition belt. The gun shot off three shells and stopped, apparently empty. He talked for perhaps three minutes and I began to feel as though I had been there before.

Without warning, he picked up the gun, and began turning the barrel around. It was turned away from me, but the barrel would have been pointed directly at the stomach of one of the other men. The gun was fifty calibers. It was I who stopped him. He outranked me by two stripes. I told him that I had seen four shells go into the gun but only three had fired. He didn't believe me, but he did stop turning the gun. The barrel remained pointed out over the swamp.

He argued a little and said he had already checked the breech. I told him he was mistaken. He said he had counted the shells too. Only three had entered the gun. I began to get nervous. The others agreed with him, only three had entered the gun. They were certain. I began to stammer. I was short on sleep. It had all happened so fast. I ran out of words to argue with. I was forced to stand there, demanding that he inspect the gun before moving it. Having started the argument, I was too proud to back down, even though now it appeared that he was right.

It was then that the fourth shell fired, traveling harmlessly out into the swamp. The heat of the gun had finally detonated it. When I remember the sights and sounds of Viet Nam, I remember the look of surprise and fear on the M.P.'s face. He stood still for a time before answering me. I couldn't actually hear his words. I had to read his lips. He said, "Yes".

The library at Binh Thuy had lots of nice books. Some were on religion. We were sitting at the poker table one night when one of the guys began asking me about the Catholic faith. Since I was a member of that religion, he expected me to be well versed on the various miracles. He

281

asked me about the miracle at Fatima. In fact, I knew next to nothing about the subject so I begged off. He insisted. So Ken interrupted and began a short discourse on the topic. He explained that two girls and a boy had seen a vision of the Blessed Virgin. At the time, I supposed he had read about it in the library.

I chided him. I said, "But they were only children. Perhaps they made the story up."

Ken looked at me in a gentle, sad manner. He said, "Charlie, you have so little faith."

I was embarrassed by my unbelief. Defensively I responded, "But I have never seen a vision of Jesus or Mary. Have you?"

Ken looked at me and replied simply, "Yes".

I was completely taken aback. I didn't know how to react. He didn't appear to be joking. The communist attacks had put us all under a lot of pressure, so I decided that the stress of war must have been getting to him. I laughed his statements off and we went on with the game. He didn't appear angry or upset.

The conversation went on to the subject of death and life after death. Vietnam was after all, a war zone. Ken appeared to know a lot about it. He said that at first the person was usually surprised because their earthly friends act as though they aren't there. He said sometimes people go on to other, happier, places and sometimes they come back to this world. He said sometimes when people come back to this world, they are able to recognize a loved one or two from a previous life.

Ken said that whenever I came in contact with a stranger for the very first time, I should take special note of the very first emotions that I felt for the stranger. He said that if I had shared a bond of love with that person in a previous life, I would be able to feel it immediately. It would be in my emotions.

He said there was a special feeling of intense love, joy, and happiness that is usually only felt when two people who were deeply in love in a previous life, such as a husband and wife, or family members, meet again. Of course, that is provided they are both able to remember each other. He said the onset of this feeling of "Special Love" or "Magical Love" was like the sudden bursting of a dam or the onset of spring. He said that it always happened "suddenly", like the removing of a veil. He said that sometimes the people were so filled with joy they could hardly remember what happened.

I interrupted, "You mean, like love at first sight?"

Ken replied, "Well, it doesn't usually happen exactly at first sight. The feeling of 'Special Love' occurs when the two lovers first began communicating with each other. Usually, the two people have to be around each other for a little while before they are able to recognize or remember their former lover. Usually it helps if they happen to be away from the everyday cares of the world. For example, if they are young and relaxing alone, together in the evening. It is as if they both suddenly recognize or remember each other, and say 'Yes' together".

In disbelief I asked, "If that is true, why wouldn't they just marry each other again?"

He said that sometimes they do, and sometimes God has other plans. He said sometimes God as a special favor to the two people involved arranges meetings between former lovers.

I had been sitting quietly, listening in disbelief. I could hardly interrupt him. He'd saved my life by rescuing me from my attacks of loneliness. Perhaps, I thought, this is my chance to save his life by listening with equal patience.

For a few minutes, Ken didn't seem to be able to speak. Then he continued on the subject of Purgatory. I wondered why he had suddenly changed the subject. I hadn't yet, learned that just because God may grant a man the privilege of talking with his guardian angels doesn't mean that God will let him tell anyone about what was said.

Ken said purgatory wasn't a specific place. It was instead, a set of tasks to be performed.

He said he had a dream of me as a priest living about the year 800 A.D. In his dream, I assembled a group of peasants one partly overcast spring day in a field in France. He said that I led them in a religious procession into the village and talked to them about peace and brotherly love. In his dream, he was one of the peasants. We were the closest of friends, he said. He appeared surprised that I couldn't remember having a similar dream.

He insisted that heaven was a beautiful place. It had a beautiful cool river with the Garden of Eden on the other side. Some of your golden friends and relatives would be there, he said, sitting or standing on the green grass waiting for you.

I had no idea what to do. I sat there quietly and listened.

We went on with the game for a little while. Then without saying anything, he got up and went into the room in the back. The barracks rooms were in two parts. After fifteen or twenty minutes I got up from the game and went to see what was keeping him. He was sitting on a chair, quiet and motionless, looking at the corner. I took his chips and money from the game and put them on the dresser next to him. He sat quietly motionless. I gently spoke to him but he didn't respond, so I left him alone. I took a quiet walk in the night air. I was very sad, homesick, and down hearted. I had tears in my eyes. It seemed as if the pressures of war had become too much for my friend.

A couple days later Ken thanked me for not bothering him when I returned the money. He said he'd known that I was there but was unable to speak at the time. What surprised me the most was that he praised my honesty. He said I had always been religiously honest, even in my previous lives.

Weeks passed. It appeared to be a completely ordinary night. I was working swing shift, 4:00 p.m. to midnight. Ken was scheduled to relieve me. He always came a few minutes early but it was only 9:45 p.m. when he arrived. At first I thought he was just homesick and needed someone to talk to. I had been trying to be extra kind to him ever since the "Fatima" poker game. He had saved my life in the past. It was my duty to be there if he needed someone to talk to.

He appeared very peaceful and well rested. He was also sincere and articulate. He began talking slowly and in an unusually friendly manner.

He said he had come early specifically to talk to me. He said he asked his guardian angels if it was all right to tell me, and they had answered, "Yes".

They said I was special, Ken informed me.

I treated him gently. I made sure he felt at ease. I asked him to sit down and I had no idea what to talk about.

He asked if I had noticed that he had started to attend church services and talk to the priest on a daily basis.

I had noticed but I pretended I hadn't. I didn't want to appear nosy.

He asked me if I could see our guardian angels. "They are standing together in a group in the dark corner of the cab," he said.

I responded truthfully. I couldn't see anything unusual. I walked over to the corner and inspected the cab. I felt the wall. Nothing appeared out of place.

He said once while he was in the confessional, he tried to tell the priest his story. He said they came and knelt next to him. He couldn't move his lips when he tried to speak. After a while, his lips moved with other, more reasonable words coming out.

I listened quietly, the way he had listened to me on so many lonely nights.

He asked if I had ever seen them when I was working late at night and alone. They had been here, he said, and knew all about me.

Again I responded that I had never seen or heard anything unusual.

Seeing that he was eager to talk, I asked my friend if he had ever seen anything unusual at night when he was working late.

Ken began simply enough. He answered, "Yes".

Then he related to me the following story. As he told it, I sat quietly and listened. I frequently wondered if God was providing me with a chance to reward Ken for the many times he had so patiently listened to my sorrows.

He said it began slowly at first, a dream here, a dream there, like pieces of rope or nighttime glimpses of a highway. Then one night when he was working alone in the tower, it began in earnest. At about 12:23 a.m. just after midnight, he looked up into the window. Instead of the reflections, a movie like vision began to unfold. At first, it would last for a minute or two. Then it would run for a half hour. He said it had gotten to where he could watch it for most of the evening. Always it started at the same place. He had seen it many times, sometimes even in the daytime.

After a few times, he said, he became aware of first one, then two other people, Angels he called them, in the cab with him. They had names he said, but he always referred to the angels as "them". They were beautiful happy beings, he said. Ken had an unusual, searching, look in his eyes, the same look that I would see in my father's eyes the night before he "passed on", as if his eyes were open for the first time.

Ken said that one Angel had been an American Indian, a late ice-age hunter, in one of his lives. He "passed on" after a fight with a saber tooth tiger. It caught him out in the open. They weren't that hard to kill, he insisted. He'd have won if his spear hadn't broken.

The other Ken said, had last been a salesman until going to heaven in 1945. He'd had a car accident in Iowa on a wet pavement. Ken believed that I had met his guardian angel sometime in the past.

Ken could only see them from the waist up. They were always waiting to talk to him.

He said there was never any fear associated with meeting them. It was like going home to your father's house, knowing your father was inside. He said that meeting them was like opening the front door and going inside, finding your father sitting at the table waiting for you.

The vision was always the same. It began with him sitting at the desk at about 12:23 a.m. at night. The forecaster's voice on the intercom would ask for the latest information. Ken would turn on the light. From a place just off the very end of the runway, an artillery piece would open fire directly at him. The first shell would fall short at the base of the tower. The third and remaining thirty-five shells would miss the tower and fall harmlessly into the swamp beyond. But the second shell would hit the humidifier on the side of the tower, only six inches from his knees. Ken said in his vision, he had the sensation of standing there and watching his body get blown away from him, thousands of little pieces of flesh, teeth, shrapnel, and blood-soaked cartilage taking flight in one sudden instant of time. He said it felt like someone was cutting his fingernails.

He could describe how the tower would look, down to the smallest detail. He could describe the broken glass, the unbroken plastic, the big piece of shrapnel and the hole it would make in the ceiling as it traveled up into the Eagle's Nest. He could also describe a tooth of his that I would find imbedded in one of the walls. The door would be blown off one hinge and lay half open, he said.

At first, he said, he would be confused, still thinking he was unchanged, not realizing that he had just been born into another world. He would float through the door and upstairs to the Eagle's nest. Everything up there would be in a panic. The door upstairs would be open so he would just float in.

He said in his vision, he watched the events unfold upstairs for about ten minutes. When he would talk to the baby eagles, they would just ignore him. At first he thought it was because they were in such a panic. He said he went up to one of the South Vietnamese soldiers who was his good friend and was unusually religious. The soldier was standing, holding his lower arm. The shrapnel had shattered it. In the vision Ken said the South Vietnamese soldier at first, responded. Then the soldier turned and walked right through Ken's "body". He said a shout went up. One of the baby eagles returned from downstairs with the news. Ken had been killed.

Ken said in the vision, he finally realized that he was dead. He went out on the balcony of the eagle's nest to think. He didn't know what to do next. He said in the vision he saw the same two men, his Angels, standing on the balcony waiting for him.

He said he went up to them and greeted them.

Ken said in the vision, they asked him the question, "Are you ready?"

In the vision, Ken answered, "Yes".

That was as much of the vision as Ken was allowed to relate to me.

We talked about it for a while. Ken seemed relieved and at peace. He seemed ready.

We talked about lots of things for a while. Then I tried to allay his fears. I pointed out that the balcony formed an overhang that protected the lower part of the cab. I didn't believe a mortar shell could hit the humidifier. I pointed out that we worked rotating shifts. This was his last night on mid-shift for this cycle. It was already past 2:00 a.m. Several weeks would pass before he would be on duty at 12:23 a.m. again. Perhaps the vision was only a warning of a near miss.

I offered to trade all or any of my shifts so he wouldn't be on duty at 12:23 a.m. I promised to pass that time in the bunker to make him feel better. He refused. He said it was God's will that one of us two would return home. One would stay behind. He said God had given him the power to choose which of us two would return home alive, and which of us two would die. He said he had decided. I would return home alive. He would stay behind to die.

He said that in his vision, he had seen two shells coming at us. He said his angels had told him that God would deflect only one of them. He said that he had decided. God would deflect the shell that was aimed at me.

I really didn't believe him.

I pointed out how unbelievable the vision was. Only one shell would hit the tower and the next thirty-five would miss everything, miss the hangers, miss the airplanes, miss base ops, and miss everything else. It didn't sound like communist gunners at work.

I also pointed out that the time was now 2:30 a.m. Since he hadn't seen the vision tonight, perhaps the ordeal was over.

Soon the two of us were laughing again, just like old times. It was late and I was tired. I said, "Good Night" and trudged the mile back to the barracks. My stomach reminded me that I hadn't eaten since the previous noon.

I thought about what Ken had said. I remembered another friend from the Air Rescue squadron. He had bravely left the helicopter one dark horrible night and descended alone, down a steel cable, into the swamp to rescue an injured American pilot from his downed airplane. I remembered how he had tied the cable to the injured pilot and helped him up into the safety of the rescue copter. Then since there was no more room on the small copter, he was forced to wait on the wreckage until the rescue copter could return for him after sunup. He stood in that dark horrible slime, alone by the plane, waiting for more than six hours for the small helicopter to return and find him. The swamp stretched for miles. The bamboo grass was ten to twelve feet tall, high enough to conceal the wreckage of the airplane until the rescue copter was directly over it. All he could see in the darkness was the starlight from the heavens directly above him. The helicopter came back in the morning and rescued him. He was still alive and physically unharmed but his mind would play tricks on him. He saw cobras behind every blade of grass and VC under his bed. He was braver than I was. I would have cracked too. I hope he recovered in San Francisco. I remembered and wondered.

It felt good to collapse into my bunk. I set my alarm clock for breakfast, annoyed at having missed a good midnight meal. The chow hall served so few of them.

I slept for a few hours. I suddenly woke up with someone shaking me. It was Ken. He was telling me that it was 11:00 a.m., almost noon. He expected me to be hungry. He was also very agitated. He had the vision again he said, last night in the tower, just after I left. Now he was certain. Now he knew the day. It was God's will. Only one of us two could go home. God had given him the choice and he had decided. I would go home alive. He would stay behind to die.

I tried to calm him down. It was of little use. I gently argued with him. I said if that one vision were true, then logically, he should be having others.

Ken then told me how he would sometimes see four other angels. While he had been stationed at Binh Thuy, he had been assigned to several different barracks. He said

291

when he walked across the grass stage out front, it would commonly happen that an angel would appear standing in one or another of the barracks. The angel would always appear in one of the barracks where he had stayed. The angel would walk out through its door and slowly towards him.

At first, it was the Blessed Virgin, he said. She was young and very beautiful. She had a glowing radiant complexion and dark hair.

Then it was without question Jesus, appearing the way Ken expected him to. He said that Jesus stood about six feet tall with blonde, shoulder length hair and some of the facial features of Mary.

Then it was definitely Saint Peter, wearing white robes. Peter he could talk to, he said.

The last one he thought might be Michael, the Archangel or possibly Saint Paul. He wasn't sure.

After telling me this, Ken calmed down.

I was simply starved. I suggested that we both have lunch together. Ken was happy to agree. Soon we were laughing in the mess hall and happily complaining about the lima beans and the gravy made from chlorinated drinking water. For once the food was really good. Ken was so kind. He even shared his food with me. He spent some time talking to one of the cooks. He said that he was just saying "Good Bye". So it happened that I left the chow hall before him and walked back to the barracks across the grassy area. It was a beautiful, sunny day. As hard as I tried though, I was unable to see anything unusual. There were simply no angels to be seen.

I had hardly entered my barracks room when Ken came running in to get me. Again he was very agitated. He kept saying, "Didn't you see him? Didn't you see him?"

I answered truthfully, "No. Who should I have seen?"

"Jesus," said Ken. "He was standing right there in the door when you walked across the grass. You must have seen him."

I went outside again and looked all around. There were simply no angels to be seen. Ken was so agitated though, I had to pretend to see Jesus in order to calm him down. Then I suggested that we both get some rest before nightfall. The communists were certain to attack, I said. We should rest now so we would be ready.

Ken agreed but before I turned in, he gave me a copy of the new duty schedule that he had just made up earlier this morning. He would go back on mid-shift in just two weeks. He would work mid-shift in the tower only five more times before his year in Vietnam was up.

While I slept, Ken began writing letters home. Within ten days, he had shipped everything home. He had sent presents to all of his loved ones and apologized for every sin, no matter how insignificant. He had also made out a will. Within ten days, Ken was ready. Within ten days, he could answer, "Yes".

I worked swing shift, 4.00 p.m. to midnight, during those last five days. The first four were uneventful. I would stay late sometimes until 1:00 a.m. Ken relieved me as scheduled at midnight.

As usual he refused to trade shifts. I pretended to be sick to get him to trade. Still he refused. I guess I didn't really believe he was going to die. I believed that anyone truly certain of death would have hidden in the bunker.

I remember that last night. He came early. It was only 11:30 p.m. He was so happy. He said he was looking forward to "going home". We both knew that if the vision were prophetic, the attack would have to happen that night.

I remember how sincerely Ken thanked me for having been such an understanding friend and how much it had meant to him. I remember how certain he was that we would meet again in another world or another life. I remember how gently he said, "Good Bye", and I remember how anxious he was for me to leave by midnight.

Still I didn't believe. He offered to make the midnight weather report. I laughed it off. My duty shift didn't end until precisely midnight, I said. I would stay for a while and talk as we had done before. He became agitated. He said they wouldn't allow it. He said the decision had already been made. He said they would do whatever they had to do. He said they would appear in front of me, if necessary, the way they would have done before if I had asked. He said this time it wouldn't be pleasant. They would terrify me if necessary. He was certain.

It all seemed pretty funny to me at the time. I laughed it off too.

Ken thought for a minute. Then he pleasantly pointed out that I hadn't eaten the evening meal yet. I should catch the midnight chow, he said. Then we could talk.

I replied that the afternoon meal had been burnt liver and onions. There would be little use in going to the midnight chow, I said. It would be nothing but leftovers.

Ken thought for another minute and glanced into the dark corner. Then he said, pronouncing his words smoothly and distinctly like a great actor, "I have to correct you there, Charlie. The midnight chow tonight is unusually good." He began acting very hungry. He said he was indeed, very, very, hungry. He wanted me to bring him some food from the chow hall. He said he had missed both the afternoon and the midnight meal. He said he had checked the menu earlier in the day. He said tonight's evening chow was chipped beef on toast, one of the really good meals that we both liked so much. He asked me to bring him some.

I thought for a minute and decided it was the least I could do for such a good friend. I said, "Yes".

Of course, I would have to leave for the chow hall immediately after transmitting the midnight weather report, in order to get the food before it was all gone. Ken quickly assured me he would wait in the bunker until I returned.

I remember how he looked that night when I last saw him. He was happy and laughing. He said, "Charlie, you'll never change. You'll never learn how to say 'Good Bye'."

Everything seemed so right as I left the tower. I calmly walked the mile to the chow hall. Everything seemed to be so perfectly in place.

It was about 12:17 a.m. when I arrived at the chow hall. When I read the sign-in sheet, the horrible reality of Ken's vision slowly began to sink into my war-numbed brain. Ken had signed for the midnight meal early, 10:30 p.m. A steak had been cooked specially for him, just the way he liked it. It had been cooked to a deep almost golden, brown. He told the cook he was going home. The meal served to the rest of us wasn't worth the march to the chow hall. It was last night's left over burnt liver covered with green onions.

I left the serving line, my guts wrenching. I knew Ken had "Acted" to get me out of the tower. He knew there wasn't any use in my going to chow except that it was saving my life.

I started running towards the chow hall door. I knew he was still standing inside the cab, inside the womb, waiting to be born into yet another world. There was only time enough for me to look at my watch, 12:23 a.m. before the attack siren sounded. There was no use running. I knew where the shells would land. Slowly I took hold of the nearest chair and quietly sat down. I sat there crying, my helmet falling to the floor, my head in my hands, my heart sick, wishing God had picked me instead of him. The second shell gave an unusual, muffled sound. The other thirty-five shells all landed in the swamp.

At first the South Vietnamese Eaglet didn't believe that Ken was dead. He said he had seen Ken standing on the balcony for an instant about ten minutes after the shell hit. Ken seemed to be very happy and he seemed to be talking with someone. Then the pain of his shattered arm distracted the Eaglet.

The fact that Ken had shared his vision meant a lot to me. It made some of my tasks easier, knowing that his soul had been born into a happier place. One task that it made easier was cleaning the pieces of his teeth, hair, and flesh from the plywood interior of the room, from where he had said they would be found. I tried to handle them as carefully as I would have handled pieces of my own father's body. At the time, I didn't care if I lived or died in Vietnam.

The next day I was walking back to my barracks. I was walking across the open grassy area. The meal had been the wonderful chipped beef on toast that Ken had promised. I was standing about where Ken had said he stood when he saw the angels. It was a beautiful sunny day. I stopped for a moment and quietly said a prayer. I reminded God, as if God needed reminding, that Ken had been a kind and gentle

Christian man. I reminded God that Ken had freely accepted death so I might live to return home. I humbly asked God to allow Ken to enter Heaven and enjoy everlasting peace and happiness. As soon as I had finished my prayer, I felt the deepest, most penetrating feeling of peace and happiness that I have ever felt. It felt as if Ken was rubbing or patting the back of my neck. It felt as if both God the Father and Jesus had heard my prayer. They answered, "Yes".

Left Two, Down Two

...And the princes, governors, and captains,
   and the king's counselors,
     being gathered together,
      saw these men,
        upon whose bodies
         the fire had no power,

nor was a hair of their head singed,
   neither were their coats changed,
     nor the smell of fire had passed on them.

               ...Danial 3:27

I had been at Binh Thuy, Vietnam for almost eleven months. I had survived several dozen communist attacks. I still had not taken an R&R leave so I applied for a seven day R&R leave to Sydney, Australia. I had accrued a large number of R&R points so my request was approved immediately. With my orders in my pocket, I rode the courier plane to Saigon to make the connections. I was assigned seat number seven on the very first R&R flight to Sydney. I spent a week in Sydney and met a beautiful young Australian girl named Michelle. She was one year younger than I was. It was a beautiful week and it all ended much too soon.

The flight back from Sydney to Vietnam was long, tiring, and dismally lonesome. It was late at night when the courier plane returned me to Binh Thuy. Another communist attack had just ended. Exhausted, I collapsed on my bunk. Michelle had written me a beautiful love letter that included her name and address. I had previously tucked in my pocket. I sat there on my bunk with the light on low, reading it, with tears in my eyes, trying to decide on the words that I would write back to her.

The letter was so beautiful. It still carried the narcotic fragrance of her perfume. I read again the words she used to describe her love for me, the Heaven she enjoyed when dancing with me, and how much she wanted to be with me forever.

I had just finished reading it, as I had so many times before, when the attack siren sounded. The most devastating attack of all had begun. The first shell landing in the mud behind my barracks, spraying shrapnel onto the roof and shutters. The attack caught me off-guard. In near panic, I broke and ran screaming for the bunker.

Somewhere in the confusion, in the darkness, in the rain, in the mud, in running to the bunker, and in my depression, somewhere in that attack, Michelle's love letter was lost in the mud of Viet Nam. With it, her address was also lost. It was never to be found.

I looked for it. I cursed the Communists. I cursed the War. I cursed the Stupid Politicians and the Generals. I took my green bayonet to the wood, to the sand, to the gravel and to the mud. Was nothing sacred? I had come to hate the mud in Viet Nam.

I had survived the Great Tet offensive. I had survived several thousand rounds of enemy mortar fire. I had survived dozens of attacks. I had survived dysentery and flu, hunger and bugs, homesickness and shrapnel. I had survived eleven months in Viet Nam. But surviving the last three weeks would take a miracle. God had not allowed me so much as the shelter of Michelle's love letter, or even the hope of meeting her in three weeks when I would be discharged. It was in the last three weeks that God would turn the minutes into hours. It was in the last three weeks that God would allow the communists one more chance to kill me. It was in the last three weeks that Binh Thuy would become Hell, at least for me.

After hours of hopeless searching in the mud and darkness, in fits of anger and helpless rage and depression, I lay vomiting the remains of the last meal that I had eaten into the mud in Viet Nam. I would probably have killed just to return to Australia.

As I lay there, I decided that I would never again panic, that I would never again break in fear and run, even if it killed me. I decided that running in panic was a luxury I could no longer afford. It was a fortunate decision. The lesson had cost me so terribly but I had learned it well. It was a lesson I would need. It would be the difference between living and dying in Viet Nam.

I decided to spend the last three weeks sleeping in the bunker. I had long since gotten used to sleeping on the cold gravel and wooden timbers. The timbers formed a pattern that was four feet square on the floor. I had a favorite spot. I chose it because it seemed to be the last safe place in Viet Nam. I could find it in total darkness. From the door I counted left two blocks and forward two blocks, or as I used to say, left two and up two.

As I counted the days remaining, my tension kept mounting. The attack that Ken had told me about had not yet arrived. I wanted it to happen. I wanted it all to be over with so I could go home. I wanted to be safely in the bunker when it came. I had long since located safe places to hide when I was away from the bunker. For a while, my plan to stay hidden in safe places seemed to work.

The road to the tower was lined with identical concrete telephone poles, one every 150 feet or so. There was one that had always appeared special to me. It was the second one from the gate and stood partly in the ditch. I decided that if an attack took place while I was on the road, I would make every effort to reach that precise pole. There was one limitation. I refused to run. One night when I had less than two weeks remaining in Viet Nam, I was walking down that road. I had reached the turn-off to the tower and the base ops building when the air was filled with the "Tinkle-Tinkle" sound of communist mortars and the attack siren sounded. I was completely out in the open. Next to me was a backyard sized mud puddle. For safety, I immediately lay down next to the edge of the water. I was lying face down in the mud. I felt so exposed, so naked, so terrified. My secure area behind the pole was quite some distance down the road. As the attack continued, between my intense prayers I remember wishing that I could have been by that pole for safety.

I was unusually terrified as the attack progressed. A thought crossed my mind, "Why don't you run to the pole?"

I refused to run and remained laying in the mud. As I lay there, a communist mortar shell hit the pole straight on, about half way up. It exploded and sprayed hot shrapnel over every piece of ground below. I was quite safe where I was, but if I had been in my safe area, I would have joined Ken in heaven.

The attacks continued, each one sounding different than the last. None of them seemed quite like the one I was expecting.

I carefully counted the days remaining. My safe and secure areas, one by one, took shells. My feelings of security, one by one, sank into the mud of Viet Nam.

The night came when I had just three days remaining in Viet Nam. I was staying in the bunker as much as duty hours and hunger allowed. Just after dark, the communists launched a short mortar attack. I was safely in the bunker and a few of the shells fired in the attack seemed to me to be special. I mistakenly thought that the attack that I was waiting for had just occurred. I decided that I had beaten the odds by remaining in the bunker.

I was feeling quite relieved because I had come to believe that the attack I had been waiting for, would be the last one I had to worry about. The first attack had been finished for fifteen or twenty minutes. The guns had fired from far away so I decided that I would return to my barracks for a minute. I needed some cigarettes and I wanted to search once again, as I had searched so many times, for Michelle's love letter.

I had barely entered my barracks and my fingers had just turned on the light. Suddenly, from the darkness in the nearby jungle, less than a half a mile away, on that clear, quiet night, I heard a communist artillery spotter shout, "Open fire!!" The first two crumps coming almost simultaneously. The shells traveled directly over my barracks room and landed long, closing my only escape route with hot, terrifying shrapnel.

In near panic, I turned off the light and lay face down on the concrete floor, smashing my face and body into the cold, unyielding, concrete. I realized that there was no place safe I could run to. My flak jacket and helmet offered no protection from the shells. As I lay there, I felt so exposed, so naked.

One of the first shells had landed in the Officer's quarters, producing a muffled blast. The fear and terror built within me as I realized that I was, indeed, trapped. I fought for every thought. The shouts of the communist artillery spotter out in the jungle branded my brain, "Left two! Down One! Fire!!"

There were two guns, and the shells were converging on my room. The shells were being walked directly towards me, directly into my barracks. Panic was fighting for my brain. I fought to control it. There was no place to hide, no place to run to. Shooting back was equally hopeless. I decided that I would lie there on the concrete floor. I decided that I would die before I ran again.

My prayers can hardly be described. I could hear the shells leave the guns. I listened to every sound as the shells traveled up and down and over my thin barracks roof. Each shell was closer than the last. Each time I heard, "Left Two! Down One!"

I wanted to run as I lay there in terror listening to the shells "walking" towards me. First one exploded in the chow hall. Then one exploded in some barracks nearby. Then the shells "walked" across the road on their way to the room where I lay praying with tears in my eyes. Still I refused to run. The only path to safety was still closed.

I listened as one shell landed in the grassy area outside. I could hear the sounds of men running and shouting and begging for help. Then the next fell into the latrine, filling the air with sounds of breaking mirrors and flying glass and the screams of dying men. How I prayed. Each shell "walked" closer to the room where I expected to die. My life was already passing before my eyes. One shell hit just beyond the sandbags in front of my door. The shrapnel blew away pieces of my roof. The only path to safety was still closed. I listened in terror as the artillery spotter continued to shout, "Left Two! Down One!"

The next shell seemed to take forever to arrive. I was so terrified I felt as if my soul had left my body. I felt that I could no longer move because of fear. Still I refused to run. In terror, I begged God for it to miss. I begged for just one more chance to visit Wisconsin. The sound of that shell! I remember it so well! How I prayed that it would still miss. My soul stood there in the empty space in my room, looking at my helpless praying body lying on the floor. I listened to the shell as it left the gun. I listened to the shell as it "Tinkle-Tinkled" its way towards me. I listened to the shell as it began to fall back towards the cold, hard concrete where I lay. I listened to the shell as it fell just 6 inches too far to the left, in the direction my head was pointing. It fell into the empty room next to mine. I was so terrified that the half second between the click of the detonator and the blast seemed like weeks. It was enough time for me to review my entire life, including dancing with Michelle, more than three times. At first, I couldn't tell which room it had fallen into. I thought I had been killed. I will never forget the blast. It turned the room next to mine into a smoking shrapnel infested Hell. It blew shrapnel through the shutters of all of the windows and across the walkway. The only path to safety was still closed. The next shell, I will hear for as long as I live. I was lying there. I knew that if the communists brought the gun, just one more time, "Left Two, Down

One", the shell will hit just inches from my body, the way "The shell" had struck so close to Ken. I prayed. I cried. I begged. I asked for just one more chance to visit Wisconsin. From high in the darkness over Binh Thuy, from somewhere, God answered. It was definitely God. He cared, He said. He remembered.

My soul was standing there above me. My body was waiting. I could hardly believe my ears as I lay there, listening. The communist gunner shouted, "Left Two!" Then, after what seemed the longest eternity since the Garden of Eden, he shouted, "Down Two!" I could hardly believe it. He'd "pulled" the shot. It seemed like Christmas and New Year's and Birthdays and Weddings and singing with little children and dancing with beautiful women and homecoming parades all in one. God had listened. God had answered my prayers. The next shell was coming short. I listened to its sound, the crump as it came from the gun. My soul flew to look at it as it rose to the high point of its arc. It watched as the "Tinkle-Tinkle" of the shell carried to my ears and then that immortal sound, the Doppler shifting of the "Tinkle-Tinkle". It sounded as if God had for an instant, placed his hand in front of the shell. It sounded as if it were glancing off the hand of God. My soul danced and laughed and jumped for joy and giggled in happiness as the shell fell just inches short into the mud by my barracks window. My soul laughed in glee as the shell fell harmlessly into the mud of Viet Nam. It blew away part of the roof. It sprayed cold mud encased shrapnel through the rafters and shutters above my head. Part of the roof fell like paper harmlessly around, but not touching, my body. My soul stood laughing and giggling and shouting to my body, "Stay down. You're winning!" It shouted over and over, "You're winning!

305

You're winning!" The next shell was coming shorter still. The gunner had shouted for "Down One". The next shell blew up a storage area. It sprayed more shrapnel through my window and passed above my head. The next shell came shorter still. It blew away the library. My soul danced and laughed and shouted and giggled, "You've done it, Charlie! You're going to live! You've survived! You did it right! You didn't run!"

My prayers of thanks can hardly be described. My body was laying there, face down on the concrete. My soul was trying to get back in, like a happy soldier trying to get back from a party. The attack was over. The American planes were spraying the jungle with napalm and machine gun fire. The Captain came running in. He was anxiously looking to see if I was still alive. He, like the communist gunner, thought the room that took the direct hit was mine. At first since I didn't move, he thought I was hit. My soul struggled to get back into my body. There was no other way but to lay down on top of my body and go to sleep. After a minute or so, I woke up. I was lying face down on the cold, concrete floor in the dirt and darkness. The Captain was calling for the Medic. He was shouting, "MEDIC! MEDIC! Charlie has been KILLED!" When I called to him, he was as happy as if he had been my father that I was still alive. I couldn't begin to describe how much he cared for the safety of his men.

I was slow getting up and breathing. At first, I wasn't sure that I was still alive. After moving my arms and legs to prove to the Captain that I was unhurt, I began walking slowly to the bunker. As I did, my mind was flooded with a single thought. It was a saying from the Bible paraphrased, "Remember Charlie, for as long as you live, even the hairs on your head have been counted. Not one can be touched against God's Will."

I stopped and thought for a minute. I noticed that not a single place on my body had actually been touched in the attack, not even so much as one of the hairs on my head.

Three days later, I was combing my hair as I stood in line at Travis Air Force Base in California. Then the USAF Colonel in charge of the discharge ceremonies handed me my discharge papers and said, "You're a civilian again, Charlie. It's time for you to go home."

Charles James Hall

Appendix A: Modern Physics Unknown to Albert Einstein

The Hall Theory of Photon Structure

The spacecraft and protective suits described in the Millennial Hospitality series are not fantasy. Their design and operation is entirely consistent with the very real laws of modern advanced physics and with the tenants of Hall Photon Theory. Spacecraft designed in accordance with these physical laws are capable of taking off from earth, quickly accelerating within a few hours to velocities greater than the speed of light without having any negative impact on the well being of the occupants. Such spacecraft out in the vastness of space are capable of maintaining speeds greatly in excess of the speed of light for long durations. They are able to quickly slow down to ordinary sub-light speeds, and then, land at their destination. During the entire process, time does not slow down nor does it flow backwards. The energy and fuel requirements do not march off to infinity. Neither does the mass of the spacecraft march off to infinity. The spacecraft described in the Millennial Hospitality series have a double hull construction with several sets of optical fiber windings between the two hulls. One set of windings is used to create a uniform surrounding force field that streamlines the spacecraft. This streamlining allows the craft to move smoothly through space itself. The other sets of windings generate the force fields that are used to propel and guide the craft on its journey. Spacecraft of this type of construction could readily be built and placed into service using today's technology. Hall Photon Theory strongly recommends that American Atomic scientists study carefully the behavior of toroidal coils and electromagnetic devices, especially those constructed using fiber optics instead of copper wire, and using photons or subatomic particles other than electrons. Possible subatomic particles include mesons, and baryons.

The Hall Theory of Photon structure

Charles James Hall
Master of Arts
Nuclear Physics

This theory was originally presented
in a scientific paper that I authored
and copyrighted on
January 27, 1998
Copyright TXU 836-633

This paper introduces a radically new theory of multi-field photon structure. This theory is named:

HALL PHOTON THEORY.

Hall Photon Theory (HPT) is a radically new theory concerning the physical structure of photons and electromagnetic waves. This theory is solidly based on a careful review and analysis of several well-known and famous experiments in the field of physics. HPT successfully explains all known physical interactions involving photons, and also predicts the existence of additional physical interactions involving photons.

HPT hypothesizes the existence of physically real photons that contain at least three physically real fields. The theory also suggests that the photon may contain additional physically real excited states, and may also contain additional physically real fields not yet quantified. Two of these fields are the well-known electric and magnetic fields described by Maxwell's four equations. The new physically real fields, hypothesized by Hall Photon Theory (HPT Theory) are named the Star Shine fields, and are identified in the equations in this document as the S_n fields. The lowest order Star Shine field is the S_0 field.

Hall Photon Theory also expands Maxwell's four equations to at least six in order to fully describe the interaction of these fields with matter. Additional expansion of the equations may possibly be necessary in the future.

In 1864, Maxwell developed four famous equations that describe light as an electromagnetic disturbance. Maxwell described the electromagnetic disturbance using two physically real fields. These fields are the well-known electric field and the magnetic field. According to existing physical theories, when a photon of light is traveling in free space these two fields oscillate together in phase in the form of a plane wave. However, a careful review of the experimental evidence that relates to electromagnetic waves shows that the photon must contain of at least three physically real fields and that Maxwell's four equations need to be expanded to at least six or perhaps more.

Several famous and well-known scientific experiments provide solid evidence for the existence of these additional physically real fields within the photon.

Consider the following famous experiments:

Electromagnetic induction by a toroidal coil:

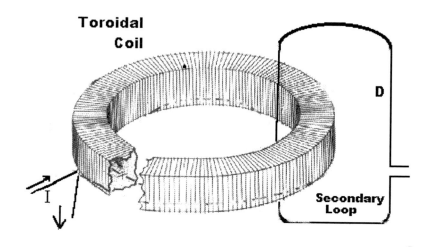

Toroidal Coil

D

I

Secondary Loop

Figure 1.

An elementary experiment commonly performed in college physics classes shows that an electric current is induced in a secondary loop of conducting wire, D, by a change in a current, I, in a toroidal coil. Assuming that the toroidal coil is uniformly wound and properly constructed, it is easily demonstrated that no electric fields and no magnetic fields physically exist in the space outside the coil. Therefore, there are no magnetic lines of force and no electric lines of force physically connecting the secondary loop of wire, D, with the primary toroidal coil. Therefore, according to Maxwell's theory, no physically real fields exist that could be connecting the current in the primary toroidal coal with the secondary loop of wire, D. Yet, since a physically real electric current is generated in the secondary coil D by a change in the physically real current in the primary coil, ordinary logic dictates that some physically real field must be connecting the two coils. Otherwise, the concept of everyday physical reality and causality would be violated. Therefore, to correctly describe these physically real electromagnetic phenomena, at least one more field, a third physically real field, is required.

If a series of experiments are performed, using successively larger toroidal coils, this third field is seen to decrease in strength as the distances between the coil and the secondary loop increase. This third field appears to be governed by force laws that are similar in form to the force laws of electric fields. Of course, nothing within Maxwell's existing equations predicts this type of physical behavior.

This new physically real field must be capable of generating an electric current in the secondary loop of wire, D, whenever the current, I, changes in the primary. This field must have a mathematical curl of zero and a non-zero gradient, so that Maxwell's existing equations may be satisfied. The important point is that this field must be physically real and must have physical properties of its own. Hall Photon Theory names this field the lowest order Star Shine field (the S_0 field). This field must be governed by its own independent force law. The toroidal coil must, therefore, be one type of experimental apparatus that is capable of generating a physically real Star Shine field in a manner that permits additional study and research.

Further logic also shows that this Star Shine field must be capable of both creating and destroying the electric and the magnetic fields within photons so that Maxwell's equations may be satisfied.

A changing electric current in the toroidal coil is a physically real event. The Star Shine field transmits this event across space to cause an electric current to form in the secondary coil, which is also a physically real event. Therefore, the Star Shine field(s) must be capable of storing and transferring physically real energy, and also be capable of carrying momentum. Therefore, the Star Shine field(s) themselves must be physically real, and not just mere mathematical constructions or virtual mathematical constructions. Therefore the study of Star Shine fields must represent a new branch of physics and mathematics.

The Michelson-Morley experiment

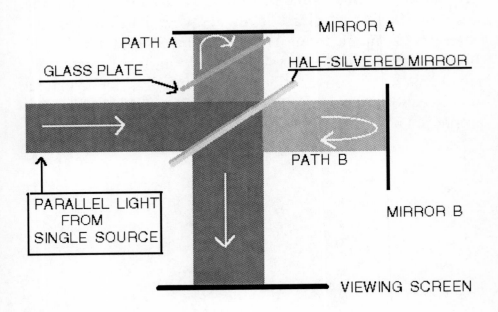

Figure 2.

In 1887, the American physicists Michelson and Morley performed a famous experiment. The basic apparatus is shown schematically in figure 2. This experiment is described in detail in many college level physics texts. The experiment was designed to detect the motion of the earth relative to a preferred reference frame (an aether at rest). A single laboratory light source is focused on a half silvered glass mirror. This half silvered glass mirror divides the light into two beams of light at right angles to each other. One of these beams traverses Path A which goes to Mirror A. The other beam traverses Path B that goes to Mirror B. Both beams are reflected back through the half silvered mirror to the viewing screen. The two light beams are then recombined at the viewing screen. If the conditions are such that the two beams, A and B, have traveled nearly equal path lengths with nearly equal travel times, then interference patterns can be observed on the viewing screen. The failure of this experiment in 1887 to detect the motion of the earth around the sun was one of the important events that lead to the development of the Special Theory of Relativity by Albert Einstein. Einstein used this experimental failure to conclude that it would never be possible to build a spacecraft that could start from sitting on the surface of the earth and accelerate to speeds many times faster than the speed of light, decelerate and land on another planet, and return to earth by reversing the process.

One very important fact associated with this experiment is frequently not mentioned in undergraduate level physics texts. This fact is that if the two path lengths (A and B) are different by a value much greater than the coherence length of the light source, no interference patterns are observed on the viewing screen. For a thermal light source, a value of 30 cm would not be uncommon. Thus, if the experiment is performed using a thermal light source with a coherence length of 30 cm, and if Path length A is longer then Path Length B by more than 30 cm, then no interference pattern will be observed on the viewing screen.

This concept of the coherence length causes us to logically conclude that separate photons do not interfere with each other. Instead, it must be true that each photon can interfere only with itself. This is an astounding paradox

317

because the wavelength of the electric fields and the magnetic fields within visible light is of the same order of magnitude as the dimensions of single atoms. Neither the electric fields nor the magnetic fields within photons of visible light could possibly communicate with themselves over physical distances as large as 30 centimeters. Obviously the observed interference pattern must result from the workings of a third physically real field within individual photons. For photons generated by thermal sources, this third field must have macroscopic dimensions of the order of 30 cm. Therefore, each single photon must contain this third field, which HPT hypothesizes is the Star Shine S_0 field.

Since photons generated by different types of sources have different coherence lengths, HPT hypothesizes that this third physically real field may be formed into different physical shapes and sizes.

When the conditions within the interferometer are such that interference patterns may be observed on the viewing screen, within the interferometer each single photon must be simultaneously traveling down both Path A and Path B. Yet, consider, according to Maxwell's 1864 equations, the photon structure consists only of an electric field and a magnetic field, and these two fields must always be locked together, inseparably in phase, in the form of a plane wave. According to Maxwell's equations, this wave must vary in a smooth and continuous manner. Therefore, according to Maxwell's 1864 equations, the photon must be in one path or the other. HPT resolves this paradox. According to Hall Photon Theory, the interferometer molds the Star Shine field(s) $S_{0,}$ for each photon into a physical shape consistent with the conditions within the interferometer. These interferometer conditions are such that interference patterns can be observed on the viewing screen only if the path lengths (A and B) are such that the Star Shine field for each individual photon can interact with both mirrors A and B as the photon is interacting with the interferometer as a whole.

It is noted that beams of photons obey the law of conservation of energy as they pass through the interferometer. This means that none of the energy carried by the individual photons, is created or destroyed within the interferometer. In addition, the color and wavelength of each individual photon remains the same. Therefore, the interference pattern can only result because selected individual photons are caused to move sideways within the beam as they pass through the interferometer. In terms of physical reality, this sideways movement is a vastly different process than the constructive / destructive wave interference process that is usually said to be the cause of interference patterns. This sideways movement of selected photons appears to be a repeatable, predictable process, without any random components. Yet, Maxwell's equations do not allow for a physical mechanism that could cause an individual photon to suddenly jog sideways in its flight, as it continues on in its motion in the forward direction. It therefore, follows, that each individual photon must contain at least a third field as part of its inner structure, that is controlling this interference process and also controlling its direction of flight. According to Hall Photon Theory, this third field is of macroscopic dimensions. For each individual photon, this third field fills the entire interferometer, and is capable of interacting with all of the interferometer's objects and parts as it passes through the interferometer.

Therefore, according to Hall Photon Theory, Einstein's fundamental assumptions underlying the Michelson-Morley experiment are seriously flawed. According to Hall Photon Theory, the Michelson-Morley experiment does not demonstrate that the speed of light is constant in all directions. Hall Photon Theory hypothesizes that the Michelson-Morley experiment is instead, demonstrating that the underlying Star Shine field is of macroscopic dimensions, and capable of causing the photon to alter its direction of flight without destroying the photon, by interacting with the interferometer's macroscopic surroundings. These surroundings may possibly include the walls of the room in which the interferometer is located.

The Star Shine field provides a physical mechanism for creating the light and dark fringes in interference patterns observed in the Michelson interferometer. Because the Star Shine fields for some of the photons have changed their shape, and their direction of flight within the interferometer, these photons have been moved laterally within the light beam, creating bright fringes in their new location and leaving dark fringes behind in their old location.

Note also the presence of one or more additional pieces of glass within the interferometer. These additional pieces of glass are intended to adjust the travel time of the photons as they traverse the two different paths within the interferometer. The usual explanation given in many college texts is that since light travels slower in glass than it does in air, these pieces of glass allow the photons to spend the same amount of time traveling Path A as they do traveling Path B. However, consider the paradox of the Water-Filled telescope and the Aberration of Starlight experiments that are described in this same paper. It is entirely possible that these additional pieces of glass are also dragging the photons to the side as they traverse the various paths within the interferometer. Additional interactions of this type between the photons and the interferometer's physical apparatus would also have caused the Michelson-Morley experiment to fail without invoking Einstein's Theory of Relativity.

Hall Photon Theory logically explains the failure of the Michelson-Morley experiment without invoking Einstein's theory of relativity or any related theory involving Lorentz contractions. For this reason, Hall Photon Theory is expected to cause a total revolution in the study of physics. Historically, the failure of the Michelson-Morley experiment was one of major reasons for Einstein's development of the theory of relativity and his hypothesis that spacecraft could never accelerate to velocities greater than the speed of light in free space, regardless of their design. Hall Photon Theory removes one of the major supports for relativity. HPT hypothesizes that physically real velocities in excess of the speed of light are possible, provided that the spacecraft has been properly designed for high-speed travel in space. HPT hypothesizes that physically real spacecraft may be constructed that are capable of accelerating faster than the speed of light in free space. Within HPT, velocities in excess of the speed of light in free space are measured in terms of their HALL NUMBER (HN). The speed of light in free space is assigned the HALL NUMBER equal to one.

Aberration of Starlight

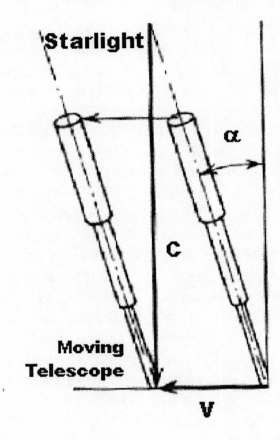

Figure 3

The aberration of starlight is the small shift in the apparent position of distant stars that takes place during the year. The ancients knew of this phenomenon. It is simply explained as resulting from the motion of the earth as it travels in its orbit around the sun. Referring to figure 3, **C** is the velocity of light in air. Consider, the earth travels in its orbit at a velocity **V**, that is of the order of 3×10^6 cm/sec.

Suppose that the starlight is incident normal to the surface, while the velocity of the earth in its orbit is parallel to the surface. If the telescope is filled with air, Figure 3 shows that the telescope must be inclined at an angle in order to capture the starlight.

This angle is estimated by the simple equation:

$$\alpha \cong \frac{v}{c} \approx 10-^4 \text{ radian.}$$

This angle of inclination allows the light beam to pass down the telescope to the observer as the telescope moves to the side. This simple explanation is based on the assumption that each individual photon of light is so small that it does not interact with the sides of the telescope as it travels down the tube. This assumption is made because the wavelength of the electromagnetic fields within visible light is of the order of atomic dimensions, while the telescope typically has large macroscopic dimensions. Note that the explanation and the resulting simple computation commonly found in many science textbooks, does not include any consideration of the dimensions of the telescope, the type of construction of the telescope, the actual path that the photon follows while in the telescope, or of the amount of time that the photon of light actually spends within the telescope. Inside of the telescope, for example, the photon of light could also traverse through an interferometer without affecting the value for the aberration of starlight.

In addition, consider the case that results when we perform the same experiment with clear water in the telescope. Because the speed of light in water is significantly slower than the speed of light in air, we might expect that the angle of inclination of the telescope would have to be increased in order to allow the photons of light more time to pass down the telescope to the observer while the telescope moves to the side. However, elementary physical experiments demonstrate that this is not the case. It is easily shown that the angle of inclination of the telescope is not affected by the medium within the telescope. For example, the telescope, like the interferometer, could contain additional pieces of transparent glass that would also slow the forward velocity of light as it travels within the telescope. That is to say, the angle of aberration does not depend on the forward velocity of light within the telescope. Therefore, each individual photon of light must be interacting with the telescope on a macroscopic scale. This interaction must cause each individual photon of light to move sideways while also traveling forward in its flight through the telescope. This interaction must move the photon sideways in its flight, without changing the photon's basic properties such as its electromagnetic wavelength, its total energy, or its color.

HPT hypothesizes that the Star Shine fields within the photon allow it to be dragged sideways without otherwise changing its properties or interrupting its flight in the forward direction. HPT hypothesizes that this is a general property of all photons including light, radio waves, and x-rays.

The water filled telescope experiment presents a paradox for Maxwell's 1864 theory because the 1864 theory does not contain any physical mechanism that could be responsible for dragging each photon to the side as the photon travels forward. According to HPT, the Star Shine field(s) can react to changes in the photon's environment by absorbing the photon's electric and magnetic fields at any point and recreate them at a new lateral point while still traveling forward. Therefore, the Star Shine fields within the photon provide a mechanism that allows photons to be dragged sideways within a moving telescope.

Since it is an observation of physics that the photons are being dragged sideways in the famous water filled telescope experiment, and interacting with the telescope on a macroscopic scale, HPT hypothesizes that photons are also being dragged sideways within many other pieces of hardware that are commonly used by experimental physicists, and also that photons are interacting with the experimental equipment in macroscopic ways. These pieces of common experimental equipment include the Michelson-Morley interferometer, and Young's famous double slit experiment. This HPT hypothesis has many profound ramifications. The water filled telescope, for example, could not be used to determine the speed of light within clear water, or within any transparent material such as glass. The original Michelson-Morley experiment was performed inside of a room that was similar in many respects to the inside of the tube of a large telescope, and the experimental apparatus itself contained many of the same elements that are typically found in a telescope, such as the viewing eye piece. Therefore, HPT hypothesizes that the experimental equipment used in Michelson-Morley experiment, like the telescope, was capable of dragging the photons to the side, and therefore was never able to measure the speed of light within the apparatus. Therefore, HPT hypothesizes that physical objects can be designed and constructed here on this earth in a manner that allows them to be accelerated to speeds in excess of the speed of light, relative to the earth's frame of reference.

Snell's law of refraction of light at a boundary

Consider Snell's well-known laws of refraction of light at the boundary between any two media. Let us consider a simple case of a beam of light photons traveling from air into glass. Snell's law is based on the macroscopic properties of the air and the macroscopic properties of the glass. According to Snell's law, the glass has a macroscopic index of refraction, based on the macroscopic properties of the glass (temperature, pressure, composition, etc.). Similar statements apply to the air. Consider, however, that Snell's law is easily demonstrated to be valid for beams of light with both macroscopic and microscopic widths, no matter how wide or narrow, the beam of light is. So, for example, even if a beam of sunlight is used that is much wider than the transverse coherence value for sunlight, Snell's law is still easily demonstrated to apply. We are therefore, logically forced to conclude that Snell's law must be valid for each individual photon of light moving within the beam of light in question. However, Maxwell's 1864 theory considered an individual photon of light to be a microscopic entity. The wavelengths of the electromagnetic fields within individual photons of light are of the same order of magnitude as atomic and molecular dimensions. If light consisted only of an electric field and a magnetic field locked together in phase, moving as a plane wave, there would not exist within each individual photon of light a physical mechanism that allowed it to respond smoothly to the different values for the macroscopic index of refraction as it traveled from one physical medium to another. There would be no such thing as a transparent piece of glass.

Therefore, it logically follows that each individual photon of light must contain at least one field of macroscopic dimensions that allows each individual photon to interact with large pieces of glass, and with matter in general, at a macroscopic level. The Star Shine fields hypothesized by Hall Photon Theory provide the photon with these macroscopic capabilities. Under Hall Photon Theory the Star Shine fields have macroscopic and finite dimensions of the same order of magnitude as the transverse and longitudinal coherence lengths. The Star Shine field is therefore sufficiently large so that it can respond to the macroscopic properties of the medium through which the photon is traveling. These properties include the shape of a glass lens, the temperature and density of various layers of air, the composition of a glass lens, etc.

The Red Shift from the field of Astronomy

Hall Photon Theory hypothesizes that the photon's Star Shine fields have finite physical lengths and well defined physical shapes and sizes. HPT theorizes that the photon's polarization state is determined by its Star Shine field properties. Under Hall Photon Theory (HPT), the shape and dimensions of the Star Shine field may be altered or affected by the environment through which the photon travels. Under HPT, the effective length of the photon's Star Shine field is hypothesized to be the longitudinal coherence length. The effective width of the photon's Star Shine field is hypothesized to be the transverse coherence length. These lengths are non-zero, finite and are initially determined by the process that creates the photon. As the photon travels and interacts with its surroundings, HPT hypothesizes that these lengths may change without altering the photon's other properties such as its color or wavelength. Under HPT the photon is actually carrying its energy and its momentum in its Star Shine field. Under HPT, the electric and magnetic fields associated with the photon result from vibrations within the Star Shine field. Under HPT, the energy and momentum contained within a single photon is logically consistent with Plank's law and with Lorentz' electron theory. Under HPT, when two or more photons are traveling together in close proximity for a sufficiently long time and under the proper conditions, their respective Star Shine fields can possibly interact with each other. Such interactions could possibly remove momentum and energy from each photon, thereby altering its color and wavelength. Therefore, such interactions would leave a beam of light with a "Red Shift." In the field of astronomy, in order for photons of light to be received here on earth from a distant galaxy, the photons must have traveled together in close physical proximity with other photons for a long duration. Therefore, according to HPT, light from distant galaxies is expected to show a pronounced "Red Shift" that is not due to the expansion of the universe. Instead, this "Red Shift" is due to interactions between the Star Shine fields of the corresponding photons because they have traveled for so long in such close proximity with other photons.

Consider, for example, a hypothetical spiral galaxy that is 2 billion lights years from earth. Of course, large numbers of such galaxies do exist in reality. Consider the case that exists for two separate photons of light, each of them created by hot stars located on opposite sides of this hypothetical galaxy and heading in the direction of a single telescope located here on earth. When these two hypothetical photons of light were created, they were many thousands of light years apart. However, during the course of their journey towards earth, the two photons would find themselves traveling successively closer and closer together for very long durations of time. By the time the two photons finally arrived at the aperture of the telescope, they would have been traveling side by side and in physical contact with each other for many millions of years. There would have been adequate time and adequate conditions for the two photons of light to interact in any manner that is possible as determined by the laws of physics.

According to Einstein's physics, individual photons can not interact with each other. However, HPT hypothesizes that photon-to-photon interactions are possible. For this reason, HPT hypothesizes that the observed "Red Shift" of light from distant galaxies is not necessarily caused by a general expansion of the universe, but instead results from photon-to-photon interactions between the individual photons of light that are arriving on earth after having traveled such vast distances.

In-Phase radiation from an antenna

The operation of radio antennas and the behavior of radio waves is well studied. Consider, however, that an oscillating electron within a conducting radio antenna radiates a radio wave photon that has the electric field and the magnetic field locked together in phase. This is true, even though the electric field and the magnetic field in the conducting antenna may not be in phase. Logically then, the process of creating a particular photon within a radio wave must first create a third field. This third field must then create both the electric field and the magnetic field within the wave. Under Hall Photon Theory first the oscillating electron creates the Star Shine field of a particular shape and size. After this radio wave photon has been created, the Star Shine field creates the corresponding electric field and magnetic field based on the properties of the Star Shine field. An important point is that the shape and properties of the Star Shine field would be determined by the nature of the electron's oscillations. These electron oscillations would be influenced by the shape, composition, and electrical conditions within the radiating antenna. Therefore, HPT hypothesizes that antennas of different shapes, compositions, and electrical conditions can be designed that will create photons with specialized physical properties that permit radio wave photons to travel in otherwise non transparent mediums, such as limestone or sea water, for example.

Under HPT the shape and properties of the photon's Star Shine field(s) are influenced by the interaction between the photon and the medium in which it is traveling. Under HPT, radio antennas with special shapes and electrical qualities may create photons that are able to travel only in certain materials or under certain physical conditions. So HPT, for example, recommends constructing radio transmitters and receivers with a wide variety of antenna shapes and compositions, and testing these transmitter / receiver pairs in a wide variety of materials and conditions. One such test, for example, might be to construct a transmitter / receiver pair that used an elliptically shaped radio antenna made from tin and test it to see if the transmitter is creating a specialized radio wave that travels only in materials such as such as sea water.

Thus, Hall Photon Theory hypothesizes the existence of physically real photons and radio waves with a far greater range of properties than Maxwell's 1864 theory allows.

Gravitational Considerations

Current scientific theory holds that the photon interacts with gravitational fields. Scientific evidence exists to support this theory. However, existing photon theory in this area contains a paradox. Consider the magnetic field in an electromagnet. Gravity affects the moving electrons that produce the magnetic field. However, gravity does not affect the magnetic field itself. For example, increasing the strength of the magnetic field produced by an electromagnet does not, all by itself, cause the electromagnet to significantly increase or decrease in weight. Similarly, gravity affects the electrons stored in a capacitor. However, gravity does not affect the electric field itself. For example, increasing the strength of the electric field within the capacitor, does not, all by itself, cause the capacitor to significantly increase or decrease in weight. Thus, since the photon is affected by gravity, but its constituent electric and magnetic fields are not, by themselves, affected by gravity, it logically follows that at least one additional field must physically exist within the photon that interacts with gravity. Hall Photon Theory hypothesizes that the physically real Star Shine field(s) directly interact with gravity. An important point, however, is that Hall Photon Theory allows for the possible existence of a physically real anti-photon that exhibits anti-gravity. This is because the toroidal coil experiment demonstrates that the Star Shine field has a non-zero gradient and is associated with electric and magnetic phenomena. The Star Shine field must, therefore, be associated with a corresponding positive or negative physically real Star Shine charge. There exists a large number of physically real electrically charged subatomic particles that have physically real anti-particles. Therefore, Hall Photon Theory hypothesizes the existence of Star Shine anti-particles, and Star Shine fields that push against a star's gravity field, instead of being attracted by it. HPT hypothesizes that a spacecraft whose design allowed its occupants to create and manipulate Star Shine fields could propel itself by pushing directly against the Earth and the Sun's gravity fields, and quickly accelerate to velocities far greater than the speed of light in free space.

General Considerations Relating to Star Shine Fields.

Hall Photon Theory hypothesizes that Star Shine fields are capable of being formed into various physically real shapes that have a mathematical curl of zero and a non-zero mathematical gradient. HPT hypothesizes that the mathematical equations that pertain to pure Star Shine fields and Star Shine charges share a certain mathematical similarity in form with corresponding equations for electric fields and electric charges. Therefore, HPT hypothesizes that Star Shine fields exist in both positive and negative forms. HPT hypothesizes that the toroidal coil manufactured with copper wire and moving electrons creates one or more pure Star Shine fields with a positive sense. HPT hypothesizes the existence of Star Shine fields with a similar structure and a negative sense. This paper highly recommends that many variations of toroidal coils be created using a variety of materials, and tested with a variety of moving sub-atomic particles, in addition to electrons. One such test apparatus, for example, might be a toroidal coil manufactured using fiber optics and tested using photons as the moving medium. Such an experimental apparatus should be constructed and tested for the existence of other types of Star Shine fields.

Since HPT hypothesizes that Star Shine fields have a non-zero gradient and have both positive and negative forms, the theory also hypothesizes the existence of physically real positive and negative poles for the various Star Shine fields. Therefore, HPT hypothesizes the existence of a new kind of physically real force in physics. HPT names this new kind of force the Star Shine force and it would exist between any two sub-atomic particles, each of which would be carrying quantized quantities of Star Shine charge. Therefore, HPT hypothesizes that Star Shine circuits can be constructed that are mathematically similar to electric circuits. These hypothesized Start Shine circuits would use moving subatomic particles that carried the Star Shine charge, to form moving Star Shine currents. Such hypothesized circuits could be designed to physically interact with ordinary electric circuits to accomplish various physically real tasks. As one simple example, in the toroidal coil any number of independent secondary loops could be added. The material that is physically in-between the toroidal coil windings and the secondary coils does not need to be air. The connecting material, for example might possibly be plastic or concrete. In this simple example, the entire apparatus could then be used as a high-speed, one-to-many relay switch. Turning on the current in the toroidal coil could then immediately activate all of the independent secondary circuits.

According to Hall Photon Theory, the Star Shine field(s) is physically real and has physically real dimensions. According to this theory, the Star Shine field can both create and destroy the associated electromagnetic wave without itself being destroyed in the process. The associated electromagnetic wave is a pattern of vibrations within the Star Shine field(s). Therefore, according to Hall Photon Theory, experimental arrangements are possible that would cause the photon to move laterally (i.e. to jog suddenly) while still traveling in the forward direction. This is because the presence of the Star Shine field allows the photon to apparently absorb its electromagnetic field and recreate it at a different physical location within the Star Shine field. Under Hall Photon Theory, circularly polarized light results when the Star Shine field is made to revolve as the photon travels. Therefore, according to Hall Photon Theory, physically real experiments can be devised which cause single photons to change many of their physical properties, such as their polarization state, without destroying the photon.

Maxwell's 1864 equations may be expressed as follows:

Equation #1:
$$\nabla \cdot E = \frac{\rho_t}{\varepsilon_0}$$

Equation #2:
$$\nabla \cdot B = 0$$

Equation #3:
$$\nabla \times E + \frac{\partial B}{\partial t} = 0$$

Equation #4
$$\nabla \times B - \frac{1}{c^2}\frac{\partial E}{\partial t} = \mu_0 J_m$$

Definitions:

E is the electric field intensity in volts/meter

$\rho_t = \rho_f + \rho_b$ is the total electric charge density in coulombs/ meter

ρ_f is the free charge density

ρ_b is the bound charge density $-\nabla \cdot P$

P is the electric polarization in coulombs/meter

B is the magnetic induction in teslas.

$$J_m = J_f + \frac{\partial P}{\partial t} + \nabla \times M$$

is the current density due to the flow of charges in matter, in amperes/meter.

J_f is the current density of free charges

$$\frac{\partial P}{\partial t}$$

is the polarization current density

$\nabla \times M$ is the equivalent current density in magnetized matter.

M is the magnetization in amperes / meter.

C is the velocity of light, 3×10^8 meters/sec and

$$c^2 = \frac{1}{(\varepsilon_0 \ \mu_0)}$$

ε_0 is the permittivity of free space, 8.85×10^{-12} farad/meter.

μ_0 is the permeability of free space, $4 \bullet \bullet \times 10^{-7}$ henry / meter.

Hall Photon Theory hypothesizes that Maxwell's equations need to be modified to include the Star Shine fields. After studying the toroidal coil experiment carefully, Hall Photon Theory hypothesizes the Maxwell's equations need to be increased to six in number and modified as follows:

Equation #1:
$$\nabla \bullet E = \frac{\rho_t}{\varepsilon_0}$$

Equation #2:
$$\nabla \bullet B = 0$$

Equation #3:
$$\nabla \times E + \frac{\partial B}{\partial t} + \frac{\partial S}{\partial t} = 0$$

Equation #4
$$\nabla \times B - \frac{1}{c^2}\frac{\partial E}{\partial t} + \nabla \bullet S = \mu_0 J_m$$

Equation #5
$$\nabla \times S = 0$$

Equation #6
$$\nabla \bullet S = \mu_0 J_m$$

where S is the Hall Photon Theory Star Shine Field(s).

Hall Photon Theory hypothesizes that future modifications to Maxwell's equations may be necessary after additional physical experiments are performed and analyzed.

HPT hypothesizes that a physical force exists between any two Star Shine charges. HPT hypothesizes that this physical force obeys the following force law:

$$F = -\mathrm{K}\frac{S_1 S_2}{R^2}$$

where F is the force between the two Star Shine charges.

K is the Star Shine force constant.

S_1 and S_2 are the Star Shine charge strengths.

R is the distance between centers of the two Star Shine charges.

The minus sign is present because HPT hypothesizes that like Star Shine charges will repel each other, and that different Star Shine charges will attract each other.

HPT hypothesizes that the Star Shine field strength due to a single Star Shine charge is defined by the corresponding field formula:

$$F = -\mathrm{K}\frac{S_1}{R^2}$$

The same symbol definitions apply.

MODIFICATIONS TO RELATIVISTIC FORMULAS

Photon Theory hypothesizes that a properly designed spacecraft can accelerate in free space to velocities that are many times greater than the velocity of light in free space. Therefore Hall, HPT theorizes that the existing formulas that relate to relativity will need to be modified to include mathematical terms that contain the Hall Number and the High Velocity Design Coefficient.

Hn_{hpt} is the Hall Number. It is defined as follows:

$$Hn_{\,hpt} = v\!\Big/\!c$$

The Hall Number may take any real positive value.

D_{hpt} is the High Velocity Design coefficient.
Its precise value depends on the specific details of the space vehicle's construction and design. Under HPT, all naturally formed objects, such as stars and galaxies, have a high velocity design coefficient of 0, and therefore, obey Einstein's laws of relativity. However, Hall Photon Theory hypothesizes that a properly designed spacecraft, such as an ellipsoidal craft surrounded by a Star shine field, would have a design coefficient that is much different from 0. HPT hypothesizes that such a craft could easy accelerate to velocities greatly in excess of the velocity of light in free

space. Under HPT, travelers on board such a craft would not experience a time dilation, or an increase in mass.

Charles James Hall

Summary

Hall Photon Theory logically explains the failure of the Michelson-Morley experiment without invoking Einstein's theory of relativity. In addition, Hall Photon Theory hypothesizes equally far reaching changes to Maxwell's 1864 equations relating to electromagnetic disturbances. Hall Photon Theory is expected to lead to revolutionary advances in physics, astronomy, and science in general.

About the Author

Charles James Hall is a physicist and an Information Technology professional. He and his wife make their home in Albuquerque, New Mexico. All of their children are grown with the last one moved onto the UNM campus in the fall of 2002. Nervous children everywhere can see in the Millennial Hospitality series that you never can tell what mischief your parents might get into once the children leave home.

CPSIA information can be obtained
at www.ICGtesting.com
Printed in the USA
FFOW03n2125270314
4567FF